Welcome to Eudora

**Center Point
Large Print**

**This Large Print Book carries the
Seal of Approval of N.A.V.H.**

Eudora Novel #1

Welcome to Eudora

MIMI THEBO

CENTER POINT PUBLISHING
THORNDIKE, MAINE

This Center Point Large Print edition
is published in the year 2009 by arrangement with
The Random House Publishing Group,
a division of Random House, Inc.

The text of this Large Print edition is unabridged.
In other aspects, this book may vary
from the original edition.
Printed in the United States of America.
Set in 16-point Times New Roman type.

ISBN: 978-1-60285-396-6

Library of Congress Cataloging-in-Publication Data

Thebo, Mimi.
  Welcome to Eudora / Mimi Thebo.
    p. cm.
  ISBN 978-1-60285-396-6 (library binding : alk. paper)
  1. City and town life--Fiction. 2. Large type books. I. Title.

PS3620.H43W45 2009
813'.6--dc22

2008045701

To Andy and Libby Jo,
with all my love

Jim Flory is preparing to open the movie house. You can tell by the way he walks around the front, pulling up bits of grass that have grown between the paving slabs of the sidewalk. You can tell because he's parked his cleaning cart outside the front door, with the bottle of Windex twinkling blue in the thin autumnal sunlight. And you can tell because he is wearing a button-up shirt and a bow tie.

No one has said anything about it, not yet, but there is a certain syncopation in the slightly brisker footsteps of the businesspeople in town, a kind of muted tapping in the daily dance of unlocking doors and opening window blinds. The staff of the bank notice that even Clement McAllister pulls his golden keychain from his trouser pocket a trifle less ponderously than usual.

Ben Nichols and Odie Marsh, sitting in their sheriff's patrol car and waiting, think Margery Lupin snaps up the bakery blinds with unusual energy and panache. They notice and then they look to see if each other has noticed, but neither Ben nor Odie speak about Margery's panache or Jim's bow tie and Windex. Some things are too good to let go of too quickly.

Eudora is a small town, in the middle of wheat, oil, and cattle. It was once only one of many small towns, a family of brother and sister towns grouped loosely around the great parent city in the east. But all its siblings have died. It is the only one left of its generation. Wal-Mart has come and gone and it has survived. In this part of the world, there is no greater resilience than that.

The hospital and the funeral parlor both remain. Only two windows downtown are boarded up, and by their unswerving loyalty the citizens even managed to retain their fabric shop and stationery store. If you are a patient person, and this virtue is highly regarded in Eudora, there is no reason to go to the city at all.

Lottie Dougal is not a patient person. In fact, she has none of the other qualities Eudorans value. She is not reticent, she is not calm, she does not consider sufficiently before she acts, she is a spendthrift and inclined to dress flashy. In a town such as Eudora, where everyone knows you from birth to death, it takes a brave woman to color her hair. Lottie did, great flashes of brassy red that made her curls glow like the neon sign at Chuck's Beer and Bowl.

Strange birds like Lottie are occasionally fledged in Eudora, but they more or less immediately migrate to find their own kind, returning only for the major holidays. Lottie did this herself, flying off to college and even to study abroad, but then unaccountably coming back. It was Lottie who ran the stationery store upon her father's death, when everybody had been pretty sure her sister, Pattie, would make Becky Lane manager of the fabric shop and come to run it herself. Lottie said she wasn't going anywhere. She said she loved Eudora. Eudora was still considering whether it loved her in return, but it was inclined to doubt they had enough in common for the long run.

Lottie Dougal openly dances down the sidewalk when she sees Jim Flory preparing to open the movie house. She skips. She waves gaily at people who nod soberly in return. She even gives a little twirl before putting her key in the door, and smiles when the burglar alarm goes off, quickstepping behind the counter and punching in her code with rhythm.

Ben and Odie, watching all this from the bakery opposite, regard each other gravely. This is too much, they seem to feel. This effusion of spirits is dangerous. But then, there is no law against it, she is no kin to either of them, and they are both married men. It is nothing to do with them. Margery, in the process of wiping down the glass case before displaying her night's work, glances across at Lottie's actions and sucks her teeth audibly. She is a good woman and says a Hail Mary for Lottie's soul as she moves the bear claws into position.

For a moment, they all reflect upon the doctor.

Now, in a place like Eudora, doctors come and go. The hospital is small and run by nursing staff.

There are two doctors for accidents and emergencies, and two paramedics on the ambulance. They're all kept pretty busy. Farming and the oil business are good for quite a few fingers and hands through a year. Then you have the quarry and the schools. There's one obstetrician, and one nurse is a trained midwife. But for anything complicated, they send the helicopter out from the city. Some of the nurses are local girls and live in town, but the others and the doctors tend to live out there by the hospital, where the municipal golf course was also handily located. No one really knows about staff turnover out there.

No, it is the GP's office in the center of town that concerns Eudorans. P. J. O'Connell had been Eudora's doctor for sixty-five years. During that time, he had trained battalions of other young men, who served under his autocratic rule with greater or lesser degrees of patience and escaped to their own practices far, far away as soon as possible. Now P.J. is finally dead, has been dead for nearly ten years. And in those ten years Eudorans have suffered three new doctors. The last came only sixteen months ago.

This is an unsatisfactory state of affairs. No one wants to explain everything constantly to their doctor. New doctors do uncomfortable things that are sometimes seen as stupid, like the time one diagnosed Betty Jones's diabetes and gave her lessons on how to inject herself, then wondered why

Betty was unable to do so and kept crying silently whenever she was pressured to try. Everyone knows that Betty's eldest, Diane, died of a heroin overdose after Betty had tried everything to cure her. Betty was in the hospital before someone thought of one of the expensive new machines where you don't see the needle. A doctor who knew you would have started with that in the first place.

The new doctor is a single man. This is seen as a bit of an advantage, after the last doctor's wife and the wife before that. Neither had fitted into Eudora with any grace. They had come, with their painted wooden geese and their ideas of country life gotten out of magazines and novels. But they had not been staying kinds of people, and when they discovered that country life did not conform to their cozily stenciled interiors, they grew dissatisfied. A man does not tend to stay in a place where his wife is dissatisfied.

But if a single doctor came in and married a local girl, that doctor would stay. The local girl would fill him in on the way things were. And then Eudorans could relax about that aspect of things again and no longer feel a faint anxiety every time they sneezed.

Now, the reason Margery, Ben, and Odie are reflecting upon the doctor is that Lottie seems in an unusually cheerful mood. Because of all the good girls in Eudora, girls who win best pie against their elders, girls who quilt, paint, line-dance, golf under par, or bowl 300, Dr. Emery had, some time ago, fallen for Lottie Dougal.

It was not a safe pair of hands. No one knew what that girl would do next. And so Eudorans (who generally prefer not to think about anyone's sex life, including their own) are watching the courting behavior of the pair much as a zookeeper would watch the courting behavior of giant pandas. To Eudorans, this courting behavior is just as foreign and alien as the pandas' would be.

Consider the facts. The whole world knows they met at last year's Maple Leaf Festival.

The Maple Leaf Festival is an enormous two-day event to which half the state seems to travel. The festivities are numerous and varied, from the first pancake flipped at the five A.M. Saturday Breakfast on the Prairie to the last bow sawed in the Gospel Fiddling Contest (which one memorable year had stretched nearly to the ten o'clock news on Sunday night).

Lottie Dougal loves the Maple Leaf Festival, simply loves it. She loves the parade, during which she tends to sit on the sidewalk with her feet in the gutter, like one of the poorer children in town, instead of in a folding chair placed the night before and covered with plastic against the dew, like a lady. She hoots with laughter at the extremely intricate formations of the miniature fire trucks, Cadillacs, Mustangs, and Formula One racers the Shriners construct so ingeniously from riding lawn mowers. The year before she met the doctor, when Representative Dale Winslow threw a handful of candy at her feet, she threw it back with enough force to hit him in between the eyes with a Hershey's Kiss. It really made him jump, but it wasn't the kind of thing you wanted to do, even though he *had* just voted for a bill that threw the state park open to oil exploration.

But after the parade, Lottie proved she had Eudoran blood in her veins after all by forgoing the rest of the heady delights and rejoicing in the true meaning of the festival, which is reversing the flow of money from Eudora to the city by any means possible. Therefore she did not appear in the audience at the Battle of Black Jack reenactment but had, on her sidewalk table, a set of buff notecards on which the main highlights of the reenactment appeared in woodcut form thanks to the artistic ability of young Priss Lane. She found five minutes, while the boy she'd taken on ran the table, to go around the quilting exhibition, so that she knew who was using a machine and who was still piecing by hand (a touchstone of female conversation for the remainder of the year), but the bulk of her knowledge about current patterns and designs came from the attractive four-color poster that she had caused to be produced and the profits of which the stationery shop shared with the Eudora Art Center. She had a Breakfast on the

Prairie recipe booklet. She had a coloring book of The History Of The Maple Festival. And, like everyone else in town, she had a small red metal cash box from which she dealt out change and into which she put, with every evidence of the delight all Eudorans feel at such moments, the large bills of the city folk who had come to rejoice in their roots.

The doctor also got into the swing of things. He had an extensive collection of videos and DVDs that he was selling in front of his office, and 50 percent of the proceeds were to go to the American Cancer Society, a fact that was prominently displayed on his handwritten sign. Not displayed was the fact that the remainder would go to Amazon.com to replenish the collection with new movies. The Eudorans on either side of him, when setting out their tables during the parade that morning, had glanced over the titles and recognized nothing. Still, none of it looked pornographic, just foreign and different. So they had smiled, talked about how little leisure they had available for television, and left him to it, shaking their heads over what a waste of time it was, as no one was going to want to buy that sort of thing.

But they had been wrong. Business was booming and the little card table had city folk some three deep. The doctor had gotten so carried away that he had replaced his stock twice and was now selling things he had intended to keep for the rest of his natural days. And then the big man had come, and he only had hundred-dollar bills. Neither of the doctor's neighboring merchants had that kind of money in their red strongboxes, so the doctor picked a direction and started off down the street, the hundred-dollar bill clutched in his hand.

Now, anybody thinking would have gone down to the bank, where McAllister had his coin collection, but the doctor, in his commercial frenzy, turned the other way and got nothing for his pains but shaken heads until he got to the bakery, where a weary Margery Lupin waved him away in a direction that seemed to the doctor to be across the street. And so he had fought his way through the throngs of people interested in commemorative Maple Leaf Festival stationery and got his first good look at Lottie Dougal.

Lottie Dougal and Pattie Walker got sick like anybody else did, but they seldom visited any doctor. They weren't Christian Scientists, but good Catholics like half the town. Their medical aversion wasn't religious but hereditary, dating from an unneeded hysterectomy performed on their grandmother before they were born. Once the unnecessary nature of the operation was made clear to Grandmother Imogene Branch, none of the Branch kin (and of course their mother, Lisa Dougal, was born Lisa Branch, just as Pattie Walker was born Patricia Dougal) gave a penny to anyone who paid dues to the American Medical Association unless they could help it.

From Imogene they had inherited a book, which by now had stretched to a library, of natural cures and herbal remedies that took care of most everything a body could get. You add that to the keen interest most Eudoran ladies take in nutrition and the combination was a powerful defense against the dark arts of the medical establishment. You could see the Dougal girls at certain key times of the year out at the state park collecting all kinds of seed heads and roots, and they frequently ordered in supplements and essential oils from Park Davis, the pharmacist who'd taken over the Maple Leaf Pharmacy from his uncle Hal Davis. Park and Hal said there was no real harm in any of it, though there was no way of telling if it was their cures or the Branch constitution that was responsible for the family's legendarily quick recovery from disease, the plants probably weren't hurting them any.

So as Lottie hadn't been to see the doctor professionally and he had spent most of his spare time in the luxurious apartment above his office, watching, as everyone in town now knew, entirely too many movies, they had only seen each other at a distance. But as Lottie counted her quarters to see if she should make up a roll, a hand rested on the edge of her white tablecloth clutching a hundred-dollar bill between its long, white,

16

sensitive fingers. It was a hand she did not know, placed familiarly on the Eudoran side of the table, not reached, as the city folks would reach, across the merchandise from the sidewalk.

Can a person fall in love with just a hand? The doctor could tell you that when her burnished head tilted back and he was at last allowed a long look at her lovely face, the large green eyes were already burning with strong emotion. The impact was such that it nearly made him step back a pace from where he was leaning in, close enough to be heard over the general hustle and bustle and the horn section of a neighboring hamlet's Fighting Tigers Memorial Marching Band's medley of Steven Sondheim's greatest hits.

She said, "Can I help you?" and her lips curved into a smile that was as clear an invitation to sexual intercourse as the doctor had ever been privileged to witness.

He stammered. Of course, our hero should not stammer, and he didn't usually all that much, but it would have taken a very strong man not to stammer at that moment, to be able to say, "Oh, my God, you're so lovely, why haven't I seen you before?" and not what he did say, which was, "H-Have you got change for this? He hasn't got any-thing sm-smaller."

Lottie smiled again, and when she bent down over the contents of the red box, one long red curl that had been tucked behind her right ear fell for-

17

ward, against the pale marble of her forehead, and the doctor suddenly felt an almost vicious desire to take out his pocket knife and cut that curl away to have, to touch, to smell, perhaps even to eat.

So when Lottie said, "Coins, too, or will just bills do you?" the doctor gulped and stammered again.

"N-No," he said, and then left his mouth foolishly hanging open while he realized that this wasn't enough of an answer and then closed it and managed to say, "No coins."

He was recovering a little, enough to be asking himself that all-important question—Who Is This Woman? He glanced around wildly, at the sign behind him on the glass window, at the small stack of business cards at Lottie's elbow. He saw "Dougal's Stationery Supplies" on the window and read the name Charlotte upside down in the fine, clear, raised print of the cards. That was all he needed to know for now. It was all he could know, all he could take in.

That was because most of the doctor's brain was busy noticing things—the freckles sprinkled across Lottie's aquiline nose, the adorable cleft in Lottie's forthright chin, the swell of Lottie's small round breasts, and the slender bones of the ankle displayed beneath the hem of her long batik skirt. Not that the doctor knew the skirt was batik at the time, though Lottie later told him this fact in a conversation that took in many facets of textile production previously unknown to the doctor. But he knew it was blue and it was soft and looked very nice and very comfortable.

The doctor managed to say thank you and back away into the crowd, off into the middle of the street with the money unregarded in his hand, buffeted by the flutes and piccolos of the Fighting Tigers Memorial Band, a glazed expression on his face that made several people think he might have a touch of sun.

He was called to himself by the big man, who, looking for the change from his hundred bucks, plucked him out of the winds back to the other side of Main Street and relieved him of his boxed set of *Twin Peaks* episodes.

Meanwhile, Lottie Dougal gave an absent answer to a prosperous-looking lady who asked if she'd produced the quilting poster, and left it to her new young assistant to explain the breadth and ability of Dougal Stationery Supplies. Lottie, who, whatever else you might think about her, could not be seen as a recalcitrant businesswoman, was staring off into the street after a thin, nervous man in worn chinos and a superfine broadcloth shirt carrying a hundred dollars in small bills in his elegant fingers, and failed to ask the nature of the woman's inquiry altogether.

Luckily, no one noticed. No one had much time to notice much on Maple Leaf Festival weekend.

Of course, after the weekend, it was different.

The doctor had a habit of leaving his blinds pretty much closed. Previous tenants of the luxurious apartment above the doctor's office had been seen flitting from room to room, dusting or running the vacuum cleaner. The doctor before last's wife had even put their dining table in the bow window so they could look out over Main Street during lunch and dinner and Main Street could look in and notice it was meatloaf again and that to wash it down had taken the doctor three glasses of cabernet sauvignon.

No one knew what this doctor, Dr. Emery, had put in the bow window because the blinds were never open at more than a slight angle to let in a little bit of light.

The Monday morning after the Maple Leaf Festival, this changed. The blinds were not only open but drawn completely to the side, exposing to view a big La-Z-Boy recliner, a standard lamp, and a small wooden table with a piecrust top. And more, Doc Emery himself was sitting in the La-Z-Boy, swiveled so that he could see the bank and beyond.

From where he sat, if he had known the signs, he could tell that Jim Flory was preparing to open the movie house. Just as it was nearly a year and a half later, so it was then. The Windex, the bow tie, the sidewalk, the works. But the doctor didn't know the signs. So when he saw Lottie Dougal nearly dancing down the street, swinging her satchel and calling gay hellos and good mornings to her neighbors, he thought she was so happy because she had fallen just as deeply and irresistibly in love with him as he had with her.

It was this that emboldened him to elicit information from Zadie Gross.

Zadie Gross was a permanent fixture at the doctor's office. Doctors, wives, dining tables, and painted wooden geese had come and gone, but Zadie Gross remained. She had only eighteen months before she retired after suffering many weary years of P. J. O'Connell and several just as weary ones without him. Nothing was going to shift Zadie Gross.

Zadie had felt sorry for the young doctor when he arrived and had tried to hint a bit of background information about his patients in hopes he might avoid some of the more unfortunate embarrassments of his predecessors. Unfortunately, Dr. Emery had seen this hinting as an opportunity to give a kind but stern lecture entitled "Why Gossip Is the Enemy of Patient Confidentiality." As a result, Zadie had retreated back into her most icy professional demeanor, a trifle more (if that were possible) bitter than she'd been before.

So when Doc Emery came down a few minutes earlier than usual and asked Zadie if she knew anything about one Charlotte Dougal, Zadie only gave a meaningful sniff. The doctor then recollected his previous lecture and began stammering that he wasn't intending to gossip or use the information in any inappropriate way, upon which Zadie sniffed meaningfully once again.

Later, reporting this conversation faithfully at the Eastern Douglas County chapter of Businesswomen of the Midwest (of which she was secretary), Zadie found it impossible to conceal her triumph, and it was so in the office at the time as well. Dr. Emery knew himself to be beaten and also that he had deserved the beating. He asked Zadie's pardon and for a cup of coffee, and retreated to his office to await the day's patients.

Now, Lottie Dougal and Pattie Walker were not members of Businesswomen of the Midwest because they were members of the Chamber of Commerce. Funnily enough, no female business owners were members of the Businesswomen of the Midwest because the Chamber of Commerce had welcomed women into its organization some thirty years previous to the time of this story and the women didn't feel the need to meet each other privately as well. The BOTM was thus composed of women who worked more or less unhappily for other people, and therefore stories of minor triumph such as Zadie Gross's were always listened to with considerable interest. Becky Lane, whose managerial aspirations had been blighted by Lottie Dougal's return, was a member of BOTM, and she formed an avid part of Zadie's audience at the Tuesday night meeting.

Becky told Pattie the next morning, and Pattie spent her lunch hour going down to tell Lottie, but Lottie only said, "Hmmm," and then talked about something else. That drove Pattie right up the wall, as she told her husband Wednesday night over his supper until he said he couldn't take any more of that stupid kind of talk and was going out for a beer. Phil Walker had three beers and then repeated what he'd heard while sitting at the bar of Chuck's Beer and Bowl on league night. So by Thursday morning the entire population of Eudora knew about the passion Dr. Emery had conceived for Lottie Dougal. It's worth noting that even at that early date, no one felt optimistic.

Least of all the doctor himself.

Now, July is not the best time to arrive in Eudora, unless you arrive in time for the Fourth celebrations. Dr. Emery arrived just as the annual drought and heat wave combination kicked in, and was immediately enveloped in the lethargy that accompanied the weather conditions. *The temperature,* he wrote back to his family in Seattle, *has been above 115 degrees Fahrenheit for the past two weeks.* He read it on his computer screen and felt it didn't accurately convey the misery he was undergoing. He continued, *The humidity is 98 percent.* But again, the numbers just lay there; they didn't say anything. They didn't elicit the kind of sympathy he felt he deserved.

He felt he should perhaps mention all the cases

of heatstroke the hospital was dealing with, including the roofer who had nearly died, but he hadn't treated any of them and so it sounded like he was grabbing someone else's glory. He tried to tell the story of the men he'd seen going out to start their wives' cars and run the air-conditioning before the delicate flowers had to travel, but it read like babbling on the screen. Someone had fried an egg on the sidewalk outside the barber shop, but just as the doctor started to write this down, he remembered Zadie sneering that they did that every year, and the worthiness of the anecdote slipped away from him.

He ended up writing, *You can't imagine how hot it is.* And left it at that. Because they couldn't imagine and he couldn't tell them.

And then the rain had come and the cool crisp nights and he'd had his first bronchial cough come through the door. By then his habits, his driving into the city on weekends to see his cousins, his stocking up on TV dinners and rotisserie chicken at Food Barn, his solitary six-pack on Friday night, were already set. He had not mixed, and he had grown used to not mixing.

But with his interest in Lottie, the doctor became friendly.

Now, friendliness as such is not completely disparaged by Eudorans. It is useful for some people to be friendly, while it is compulsory for others. You could not have, for example, a farm machinery salesman who did not slap his brethren on the back. You could not have insurance agents who did not hop up with a smile whenever you walked into their office. You would not wish a priest or a preacher to keep to themselves. But a doctor could go either way. And it was felt that once you had established yourself as a not-friendly doctor, it was not quite right to then become a friendly one.

Especially with motives as transparent as the doctor's. He, for example, went down to Margery's one morning for a cup of coffee, as if everyone in town didn't know he had installed an espresso machine in the office kitchen and taught Zadie how to use it. He'd then started talking to Margery about all the different kinds of donuts and breads she and her assistant made and then laboriously worked the conversation around to how many people in the town Margery might see every day and finally asked if the businesspeople across the street ate a lot of her donuts.

Now, if he'd bought a dozen glazed and taken them back for the waiting room, Margery might have been more inclined to give her opinion of the Branch family's aversion to sugar and fried goods. That might have given the doctor a bit of an insight into Lottie's character, which could have saved him a great deal of trouble in the long run, and it certainly would have been worth the $6.27

it would have cost him. But because he just had a cup of coffee and because he wasn't even really drinking it and just standing there wasting her time with an itch in his pants, Margery knew an unchristian impulse not to tell him a damn thing. And though she confessed it later to Father Gaskin, she gave in to her impulse. The doctor left his first social encounter with a Eudoran as completely ignorant about Lottie as when he'd arrived.

Now, certainly Father Gaskin never said a word (and wouldn't have even known about it until Saturday anyway), but somehow the knowledge of this unprofitable interview came to be known in Eudora. And in that unhealthy way the intimacy of a small town can sometimes take, the residents closed ranks against the doctor's inquiries. No friendliness to local businesspeople, no beer bought for the drinkers at Chuck's, no interest shown in the latest models at the Ford/Isuzu dealership availed Doc Emery one little bit. Indeed, he found the woman at the fabric shop downright hostile when he brought up the subject. For the rest of the town, as far as he could tell, Charlotte Dougal did not exist.

So it was a mystery how the doctor discovered that she was Catholic.

Eudorans took the freedom to worship as one chose to mean making a clear choice between churches and then sticking to it. When someone new moved into the neighborhood, their movements the first Sunday were closely observed and felt to constitute a commitment. Some people did not go to church at all. Chuck, for example, though he kept his doors closed on Sunday, watched football or went fishing, depending on the season. But these were rare exceptions.

The doctor had been one of them and this had not occasioned any censure in the minds of Eudorans. If it was difficult for the business community to render up to both Caesar and Jesus, it was felt that to also worship at the altar of science might be asking too much of any man. Besides, he might be in one of the newer religions for which Eudora did not cater. When the geological survey was in town, the superintendent was thought to be a profane man until it was discovered (through Don and Albert Simpson, who were putting a new kitchen into the house he'd bought for the year and developed at a tidy profit) that he was a Buddhist. He had his own little altar and prayer mat and was at it twice a day on the quiet, Don said, enough to shame a preacher.

But though it had been impossible to discover what might have been happening behind the shut blinds of the luxurious apartment on Main Street, the doctor did not seem to be that type. Of course, he was often out of town on Sunday mornings, having spent the night in the city with his cousins. But one week at eleven o'clock in the morning on the Sabbath, the doctor had tried to buy a six-pack of beer out at Food Barn. Of course the law prevented this outrage. Still, it was generally assumed this was not the work of a devout man.

So when Sunday morning rolled around and bang on the dot of ten-fifteen the doctor emerged from his front door and joined the faithful at St. Anthony of Padua, eyebrows were raised. He was wearing a navy blazer and a thin green and white striped tie, which may have had a significance lost on his fellow men and women. Other than that, it was the same basic wardrobe of chinos and cotton shirt that had proved so serviceable in the past months. A sharp eye would have noticed that these had been subjected to rather more rigorous ironing than they had previously enjoyed. And there were lots of sharp eyes that morning.

Pattie and Lottie were sitting together, Phil having been to the early Mass with two-year-old Ben, leaving Pattie only five-year-old Daniel and eight-year-old Patrick to manage. She did this by putting one on either side of her, leaving Lottie on the aisle to guard against any escape attempts. The doctor sat on the other side of the aisle two rows back. His approach was minutely observed, and we can here report that he took holy water at the door, looking around for the basin before he saw it, took a bulletin, service book, and hymnal all in order, genuflected in the aisle, looked apologetically at the pew's current occupants as they shuffled over, and dropped to his knees to pray for a few minutes before sitting back. By which we can all clearly see that the doctor was a Catholic, either by birth or by some other sort of means. The curious and imitative never manage it all correctly.

This knowledge gave the faithful of St. Anthony of Padua what leisure their devotions allowed to observe the doctor's eyes straying across the aisle and two pews up while they waited to see what he did about communion. Now, communion is always a great test of character for your fallen-away Catholics. When the odd birds come back to Eudora from their far-flung flocks, at Thanksgiving, say, or Christmas, and attend Sunday Mass with their families, attention is paid to how they conduct themselves at this crucial point in the service.

If they boldly walk up the aisle and take the Eucharist, they are clearly damned, as it is nearly impossible for anyone to believe that they are living in a state of grace. If they remain in their pews, sitting, and don't sing the communion hymn, they are very nearly damned as well, since their indifference must be killing their parents. If, however, they do not take communion but pray on their knees the entire time it takes the congregation to do so, singing, they are commended for their honesty as well as their respect and potential repentance. Of course, the most favored should be

29

those who make a point of going to confession the night before, so their state of grace is obvious and unquestionable, and then line up for the host. But this is seen as cheating and those who do it as smug and untrustworthy.

Everyone knew the doctor had not been to confession. And everyone also knew the doctor had not been to Mass the previous twelve weeks and could not, therefore, be in a state of grace. So.

The litany came and went with the doctor giving his responses without cause to refer to the service book, right up until the creed, which he did read, but then almost everyone does. He put five dollars in the basket, which was thought generous but not too showy. He shook hands at the sign of peace with everyone he could easily reach, but he didn't lean and start glad-handing. So far so good.

Communion began, and the doctor slid back in his seat to allow his neighbors out of the pew. And then he sat on his butt for a few moments, kind of staring blankly ahead, like he'd forgotten where he was. The hymn started, and his hand automatically shot out to his hymnal and found the page. And then he did it—he slid back down onto his knees and covered his eyes with his hand, the hymnal drooping over into the next pew.

And everyone in the congregation who noticed, by which I mean everyone, felt a deep sense of satisfaction. Here was humility, they felt, here was potential. Even Margery Lupin began to feel that the doctor and Lottie might not be such a bad match.

For Pattie Walker, coming back down the far side of the church, her first glimpse of the doctor was in this revealing attitude. She was so struck by the difference between this and the blustering friendliness he had displayed in his visit to the fabric store (ostensibly for shirt buttons) that she suddenly stopped walking and caused a three-person pileup behind her, which was embarrassing and made her concentrate on her own business of apologizing and finding her place and kneeling down with a hot, red face. But when these duties had been accomplished, she could not help glancing behind her. The doctor was still on his knees, singing lustily in a light baritone of restricted range.

Pattie Walker had trouble concentrating on the remainder of the service. The prayers for the departed and the dismissal went by in a blur, and she only really registered the recessional because the bulk of Father Gaskin cut off her view.

Her sister, however, seemed completely oblivious to the doctor's presence.

So added to Pattie's responsibilities of ensuring Daniel and Patrick did not immediately commit some heinous outrage that would endanger the safety of their newly blessed souls was the task of steering her sister into the doctor. She was an organized woman, accustomed to multitasking,

31

and managed this so neatly that in any other place of habitation it would have gone completely unnoticed.

But even when the two were walking side by side down the sidewalk, Lottie remained resolutely unaware of the doctor. He had to speak. And so he said, "Oh, hello. It's Miss Dougal, isn't it?"

And again, Lottie looked up and smiled that smile. It wasn't fair of her to do it, and it rocked the doctor back a step, almost into the walking frame of old Mrs. Bumgartner. But he was a brave and determined man and he recovered, catching back up with the party to say, "I'm the new doctor, James Emery."

A charitable woman would have stopped walking then, would have put out her hand to be shaken, smiled properly, and perhaps even asked the doctor how he liked Eudora. But Lottie kept her eyes on the sidewalk and said nothing to this information, only nodding her burnished head.

Pattie, a boy on either hand, could do nothing but watch and curse her sister's perversity, which she did internally with great energy.

The doctor hung in there. He said, "I wanted to thank you for the change last week. He ended up spending forty-five dollars."

And Lottie finally spoke. She said, "So you didn't need the change after all." And then she twisted her lips into a little grin and from under her hair shot the doctor a look so naughty, it made the poor man's eyes water.

He said, "I think I needed *that* change."

And Lottie came to a stop. Pattie dragged the boys half a block farther, but Patrick shouted, "Aunt Lottie, come on! I'm starving," before his loving mother could slap her hand over his mouth.

Lottie smiled. She said, "I have to go."

He said, "What is there to do around here? Besides Chuck's, I mean."

She started walking again, and he followed her. She said, "Well, it looks like we're going to have a movie soon."

They were passing the Eudora Empire Cinema at the time, and the doctor looked at the empty white of the Coming Attractions. "Oh," Lottie said, "Jim won't put that up until the last minute."

"When do you think it will open?"

Lottie shrugged. "Sometimes he gets the can on Monday. But usually it's Tuesday or Wednesday."

"Would you come with me? On Monday or Tuesday or Wednesday?"

They had reached the turn-off to the Walker house. Pattie and the boys had gone down the street, the boys running ahead, Pattie walking slower at an oblique angle, which allowed her to view the proceedings.

The doctor stopped walking and waited for an answer. He pushed his fine brown hair out of his fine brown eyes with one of his fine white hands.

Lottie had walked a pace ahead but turned back. She smiled that smile again. She said, "I'd like that."

He said, "Do you live above the shop?"

And she said, "Lord, no." She said, "Give me a call." And then, as the doctor showed no sign of doing anything in the interim but standing and staring into her face, she said, "Look, I've got to go. I'm in charge of the gravy." Which made no sense whatsoever to the doctor until he was invited to Sunday lunch some three months later, but allowed Lottie to walk after her sister and nephews.

The doctor stood there for a few moments longer, watching her step onto the porch and into the house. She did not turn and wave. He then watched the door where she had disappeared for another few moments. Then he slapped his hands together and, smiling, turned to walk back to his luxurious Main Street apartment.

Now, courtships in Eudora follow a well-prescribed pattern. The couple generally begins in a group of four or six, chatting decorously throughout the evening. Then they go bowling or to the movies (the only restaurants in town accounting for the boarded-up windows downtown). This might be repeated several times before the next step, which is Sunday lunch with the family or dinner with the family, which should ideally happen two weeks in a row with both sides of the family. After this, the couple has more or less license to court, and if they stay out all night together in the city after six months or a year, no one is at all surprised. Of course, an engagement announcement is expected to follow fairly hard upon the heels of this outing, should all have proved satisfactory, though there have been cases where the ceremony of marriage is skipped altogether and they simply set up house.

Divorce in Eudora usually takes the form of emigration, so the cause is often confused with the effect. Chuck's last wife, for instance, is said to have "gone to Boston," which is true, but not before smashing her entire wedding service to bits on the driveway of their shared home while screaming details of Chuck's varied incompetences to the outwardly uninterested ears of the neighbors. Chuck, indeed, with his three marriages, has been a major source of loss to the local electoral roll.

Such are the customs of the town, which were nearly immediately flouted by the doctor and Lottie Dougal.

They attended the movie alone together, when they could have easily asked Phil and Pattie to come along. It was a film called *Meet the Parents,* which bemused the cinema audience in the beginning. It was a comedy, but at first had seemed like a drama, a tense drama about the horrors of modern life. The main character was traveling and had problems doing this, with which all right-thinking people could only identify. As Phil Walker put it later in the week, when he and Pattie did attend a screening, "You had to feel for the guy."

Whether Lottie and the doctor felt for the guy is a secret only their Maker can see in the fastness of their hearts. But that they began to laugh at the guy's predicaments straightaway was known to the whole of the community. While everyone else was gripped by empathy and tension, those two were . . . well, they were sniggering. There's no nice way to put it. They were sniggering and they were snorting. The one just as bad as the other. By the time the really funny parts came on, the things that everyone could see were *meant* to be funny, they'd already just about laughed themselves sick.

Well.

You could see that the doctor and Lottie Dougal were two of a kind, but two of a kind does not necessarily make for a comfortable courtship or a happy marriage. Take Clarissa Engel (who was Clarissa Barford and thus a Branch and cousin to Lottie and Pattie) and Artie Walker (Phil's brother), for instance. They went out in high school and were so suited to each other with the way they loved books and all that kind of thing that their mothers were pretty sure it was going to be a match.

But then they went to different colleges, and although at Thanksgiving they were still to be found walking hand in hand down Eudora's streets, by Christmas something had changed. They attended the Knights of Columbus Snow Ball Dinner and Dance, which takes place in the church hall. Other denominations are welcome, as it's a fund-raiser, and pretty much the whole town turns out to eat fried chicken and dance to the sounds of Big Irving Townsend's Magical Melodies. So though both Clarissa and Artie are Catholics, not only their families but the entire town was there to witness the destruction of the relationship.

You could not say that there was no passion in the way they danced that night. Artie was always a demon on the dance floor (all the Walkers could boogie down, and Artie was something special even by their standards), but that night he seemed a man possessed. He whirled Clarissa around in a breathless waltz. He flung her out and pulled her back in a frantic jitterbug. But it was during one of the slow, smoochy numbers that he went too far, holding her, kissing her neck while she pushed him away and started to cry.

And there, while Irving Townsend kept beating time with his back to the scene and the band kept playing softer and softer so as not to obscure a word of Artie's speech, that Artie accused her of having another man at Bowling Green State and

Clarissa tearfully admitted that she loved another and would never be Artie's again.

They still had three years to go at college and met only infrequently after that. In her junior year Clarissa got married at St. Anthony of Padua amidst an extravagance of flowers unmatched in her generation. Artie's marriage, in his senior year, took place close to Christmas at lovely little Danforth Chapel on the campus of the University of Kansas. The photographs showed an austere service but the bride was prettier by far than Clarissa, whose nice boy with a bit of money was rather homely.

They started their careers away, Clarissa teaching near Bowling Green and Artie doing a master's degree in Iowa near his wife's people.

And then they both came home, applying successfully for jobs unbeknownst to each other. Clarissa became the new English teacher at Eudora High and Artie the new town librarian, a combination that forced them to spend no little time together professionally. Breaths were bated, but between them had flared only a friendship, which included their partners. The four of them participated in many local activities as a unit, and their babies were born only two months apart. It was noted, however, that Clarissa and Artie never danced together, which everyone could only see as sensible considering that the depth of emotion displayed at that Snow Ball could never be completely expunged.

With this example obvious in the minds of Eudorans, the laughter of Lottie and the doctor was not seen as a precursor to happiness.

And so the whirlwind courtship that followed was viewed with misgiving.

The movie had screened on Tuesday night. On Wednesday night, the doctor came to dinner in the small house Lottie inherited from her father and stayed until no one could drag their dog another time around the block to see his departure. On Thursday they bowled atrociously, taking a whole evening to complete a single game and consuming only one pitcher of beer between them. Friday the doctor bought two lobsters from the tank of their doleful fellows at Food Barn along with large potatoes, bags of salad, and packets of those leafy herb things. Lottie went home early from work and knocked on the doctor's door in a flowered print dress that had belonged to her mother. Saturday and Sunday they were in the city together, having traveled in the doctor's car. Even allowing for the fact that the doctor had kin there whom they might be visiting, this was thought to be fast work.

And so it went on, week by week, until bad weather forced them to stay in town one weekend, to go to Mass holding hands and visit Pattie and Phil's for Sunday lunch. Pattie reported later that the doctor, instead of watching football afterward, insisted on doing all the dishes by himself, cleaning off the table and getting them glasses of iced tea so Pattie and Lottie could sit down and talk. Pattie didn't know what she thought of it, whether it was the nicest thing or whether it was deeply suspicious. Becky Lane thought it inclined toward the latter; as no one could actually be that good, he must be obscuring his true nature for some evil purpose.

Now, Lottie had been a regular at confession before this romance and had continued (when in town) right through it. So when she walked home with the doctor that Sunday night, went up the stairs to the luxurious apartment with its king-sized bed and Jacuzzi in the bathroom, and did not emerge until past five o'clock on Monday morning, and then the following Saturday went to confession and the following Sunday took communion, no one could tell if she had committed a fresh, new, interesting sin or had simply been owning up to her regular imperfections. But though Eudora could not tell for certain, Eudora had a pretty good idea.

As the months went by, the censure with which the citizens regarded such behavior was slowly replaced by a communal feeling of concern. However much regular doctoring was required and however well Doc Emery had done so far, Lottie was one of their own and had (admittedly through her own loose morals and general heedlessness) placed herself in an extremely vulnerable position. Her safety now lay entirely in the hands of the doctor, who did not seem to be alive to the urgency of declaring some kind of public commitment.

The communal concern was tinged with alternating feelings of impatience and admiration. For Lottie was one of life's risk-takers, and risk-takers can end up doing quite well for themselves. You need look no further than how she had expanded her father's business, going aggressively after contracts he would never have aspired to get, to see that fortune favored the brave. Lottie was also blessed with the natural resilience of the entrepreneur. Doors closed in her face seldom worried her; she only thought about ways to make them open. If Clement McAllister talked about such things, which he most assuredly does not, he would say that Lottie's investment portfolio showed an adventurous and optimistic spirit.

Though the town may not have known this, it felt it. And so the light words that another woman would have had dropped into her ear did not get dropped in Lottie's. No one was absolutely certain she did not know what she was doing.

In short, though Lottie Dougal was playing with fire, Eudora didn't know if she was unaware of the danger posed by the flames or was protected by asbestos gloves.

Well, Pattie Walker knew her sister as well as

anyone could, and Pattie, though giving the impression to the rest of the world that Lottie knew what she was doing, privately believed that she most probably did not. So Pattie took it upon herself to bake a few too many pumpkin pielets and take some over to Lottie's one night when the doctor was out of town.

But though anyone else would think it foolish to ignore the advice of a woman who had managed to ensnare the dashing Phil Walker into a lifelong partnership he'd had every intention of avoiding, Lottie refused to talk about it. As a result, there was a sisterly argument, during which Pattie was driven to use the well-worn dairy parable of a man who would not buy a cow when he was getting the milk for free. When Lottie asked Pattie why she'd brought the dairy business into a discussion of her private life, blinking those green eyes as though she didn't understand exactly what Pattie was saying, Pattie had to leave before there was murder done. She ended up walking around her own block seven times before she could cool down enough to tell Phil what had happened without swearing, but it didn't seem to bother Lottie at all.

And so it went on until Christmas.

Now, it's very hard to tell when you've gotten through to a woman like Lottie. She is adept at ignoring things she doesn't want to hear, and she is equally facile at fielding questions with smiles and pretenses of misunderstanding. Moreover, she has been like that since the day she was born, so her true character remained a mystery, even in her own hometown. Pattie Walker had a good idea of what her sister was really like, but she had an equally good idea that no one would believe her if she told them. So Pattie did not live this period in complete despair, but hoped her words had planted a seed of thought that might grow into a tree of wisdom in the intricate gardens of Lottie Dougal's brain.

Christmas starts early in Eudora, where the Advent calendar is taken as seriously as the public's responsibility to enlighten and entertain. There are pageants and shows. There is a parade and a Victorian Evening. There is the Living Nativity (the holy family that year being Clarissa and John Engel and Artie and Julie Walker with baby Branch and baby May respectively, taken in shifts, while the animals and barn were provided by Jeb Taylor, as usual), which is well attended by people from neighboring towns and even city folk. And then there is the Snow Ball.

Sure enough, the doctor saw a poster for the Snow Ball and asked Lottie to go. She did not tell him about it or offer him a seat at the family table. It was all him from the get-go. He even told her that he had something to give her. Everyone knew this, just as everyone knew he was going back to Seattle for Christmas and that he had been seen carrying the deep purple shopping bag of a well-known city jeweler in from his car on a Saturday afternoon in the third week of December.

While rolling out Christmas cookies with Lottie in the Walker home, Pattie casually mentioned these facts. She did not mention how many people had come into the fabric store ostensibly for the odds and ends so necessary to Christmas decoration but actually to drop these facts into the conversation in hopes that Pattie would then inform her sister.

The fact was, Eudora was getting hopeful that Lottie had played her cards just right; that her casual, optimistic, and undemanding ways, so generously displayed, had spoken to the depths of the doctor's better nature. When I say this, what I mean is that Eudora was already planning the wedding and wondering if they'd send the kids to board at schools in the city.

Lottie's dress that night was the standard by which all frocks were measured for a considerable space of time. It was a simple sheath of dark green velvet with a foaming collar of cream-backed devore displaying leaf motifs shaved out of green velvet and trimmed at the neck with gold. The sleeves were also the same devore, which matched Lottie's sheer cream stockings. Against all this Lottie's hair glowed like a rocket and her eyes shone like distant stars.

The doctor could not dance, but he was game to

try, and though Lottie's lightfooted skills were better displayed as she spun around the floor with her brother-in-law, there was chemistry alight in the way she and the doctor shuffled around the floor that night. Small tables at the Snow Ball were generally in use by unpopular or unknown couples, relegated to the outer edges of the festivities and therefore unobserved, but the doctor's table might as well have been in the front row, with all the attention it garnered that night.

They ate fried chicken, but no seconds. They drank champagne. They sat at the Walkers' table for a while. They danced. They drank a little more champagne. They sat and talked.

And then the doctor drew forth a little square box from his pocket. If it was a little larger than anticipated, most folks put that down to playfulness. Lottie would open it and then the smaller box would be inside.

But when Lottie opened it, there was no smaller box inside. Instead, there was a small silver-plated model of a Cadillac.

Lottie is a hard woman to get to know. But there was a minute, when she drew the thing out and rested it on the palm of her left hand, when her disappointment was very clear on her face. The doctor began talking fast, explaining (we later learned) that it was in honor of the Shriners' riding lawn mower versions and bought to remind her of their meeting at the Maple Leaf Festival. Lottie smiled and nodded and her face became its normal, impassive self once again. They even danced a little bit more before they went home.

The next day the doctor flew off to Seattle. And when he got back, something had changed.

Lottie had acquired a cat.

Three days before Christmas and in full possession of their bonus allowances, which allowed heretofore unthought-of generosity to blossom, Lottie's nephews had asked what she wanted from Santa Claus. And Lottie, minding them on the Sunday afternoon to allow their parents a trip to the big mall in the city, thought about it. Her face, so guarded of late around their parents, dropped into its natural lines of worry and grief, and she closed her eyes and leaned her head back, looking, Patrick thought, suddenly older than Momma. Finally she said, "I'd like a kitten."

This announcement was greeted with enthusiasm, as nobody charged you anything to take away a kitten—kittens were free. And if they could get Aunt Lottie's present for free, there was that much more money left to buy Daddy something really good. Of course, as Daddy had to drive them fifteen miles out of town to pick up the free kitten and then also had to purchase the supplies that enabled the kitten to survive until Christmas morning, the trade-up to the large size of Old Spice talc might not have seemed a good bargain. But the main thing was that it allowed the boys to associate giving with a deep sense of personal satisfaction.

The doctor did not associate the gift with personal satisfaction; in fact, it was quite the opposite. His first night back, he dropped by Lottie's but was asked to go home early, as she was trying to get the kitten into a routine.

The next night, Lottie went over to his luxury apartment but left after a few hours because it wasn't fair to leave the kitten on its own.

She didn't want to go into the city for the night because of the kitten.

She'd love to go away for a three-day ski trip, but she didn't want to leave the cat.

Some two months separated the penultimate excuse and the last. And the doctor got the idea. Lottie had closed shop. There was no more milk from that particular cow.

Yes, he tried to talk to her about it, of course he did. And was baffled by her enigmatic smiles and non sequiturs. He even asked Pattie Walker to go for a walk with him one lunchtime and approached the subject obliquely, mentioning that the cat seemed to constrict Lottie's movements quite a bit and wondering if it had been a good idea. Pattie approached the subject equally obliquely, mentioning that unmarried women who were thereby denied the feminine right to children

47

were inclined to overemphasize relationships to their pets.

Whereupon the doctor grew less oblique and said that he did not intend to marry so young. Whereupon Pattie also grew less oblique and said if he didn't intend to marry, he shouldn't go around with nice girls. The rest of their walk was conducted in silence.

After this conversation, the doctor began to see less of Lottie Dougal. They would still take in all of Jim Flory's films; there were nights when they attempted to bowl, and meals were still prepared and eaten together. But these grew less and less frequent. One night, the doctor was seen to watch Lottie walk down the street from his bow window and not tap the glass. Instead, he reached to the blind cord and shuttered the sight of her away.

When it got to the point where weeks went by without him, Lottie began to pine.

Her hair grew out of its color and was not touched up, the drab brown suddenly seeming less natural than the red fire had been. She ate less and went from thin to skinny in a matter of weeks. That might be why her boots seemed to make her shuffle, and why she wore those drab-colored cardigans over her winter skirts. They were horrible shapeless things with deep pockets kept full of the wadded Kleenex Lottie used on her perpetually runny nose. Lottie's new assistant went to more and more sales meetings while Lottie stayed behind the counter and stared down Main Street toward the doctor's office, unable to face opening the boxes of valentines intended for display.

In the first week of February, Pattie had had enough. One morning, she dragged her sister back to the Walker house and got out various volumes of the Branch library of remedies and pharmaceuticals. At first Lottie simply flipped the pages listlessly, but then something caught her eye and she sat up with a snap. While Pattie got Park Davis on the phone and ordered a large quantity of Saint-John's-wort, Lottie read and read and read. And then she went into the garage, where they kept their collection, and began to measure.

Pattie was pleased that something had managed to interest her sister, even though Lottie's good-byes and promises to take the Saint-John's-wort regularly seemed perfunctory. A large square shape was imperfectly concealed under Lottie's coat, and by this Pattie knew one of the books was being borrowed, a thing that was, under Branch law, forbidden (though the holder of the library could be asked to turn out of bed for research purposes, the tragic loss of Auntie Nona Branch's handwritten recipe for mustard plaster had promoted strict usage guidelines). But again, Pattie's pleasure at Lottie's interest caused her to look the other way.

Later that evening, when she at last had a moment to put the books away, Pattie noticed with misgiving that the volume in question was *Herbal Lore for Cures and Curses,* a useful but dangerous compendium that had to be kept from teenage Branches. After an agonizing hour, she laid the problem in front of Phil, who for a change was a font of good sense, saying, "All's fair in love and war." He then went on to talk about fairness in love, much to the detriment of the doctor's character and the admiration of his loving wife.

The fact was that after the miniature Cadillac made its appearance on Lottie's palm at the Snow Ball, the town's attitude toward its new doctor cooled as quickly as the weather. This last was, by the way, extraordinarily cold and snowy, even by Eudoran standards. But the increase in patients for which the doctor had accordingly prepared simply did not come. In fact, though the wind chill dipped below minus sixty and the wind speed went up to twenty and moved snow across the prairie like a giant plow, though a wet blizzard raged for four days so hard that you couldn't see across Main Street and then froze the earth into a solid sheet of ice that defeated the snow plow of Stanley "Buck" Owens, and though wherever the doctor went he heard wet, claggy coughs, the citizens of Eudora were not seeking much medical advice.

Instead of visiting the doctor with their bronchial coughs, they were letting them get better or worse on their own. If they got worse, they went out to the hospital, where their lungs could be looked at by X-ray and pneumonia diagnosed and treated. If they got better, they felt pleased about not spending the $69.50 on antibiotics and not giving the doctor one penny from their pockets.

For a man can not act as the doctor had acted in a town like Eudora and get away with it. You could do that sort of thing in the city, and in Seattle, well . . . Who knew what kind of licentious behavior was condoned in a place like that? It was all microbreweries and punk rock music as far as you could tell from here. A young man raised there might think trifling with young ladies and breaking their hearts was just a way to pass the time of day. But it wasn't like that here, and it would be just as well for the doctor to know that.

And the doctor did. He wasn't an overly sensitive man and not much given to paranoia. But gradually it was borne in on him that the whispers he was overhearing and the oblique comments he was receiving and the dark looks he was intercepting were not all in his mind. Moreover, being a bright person, fully capable of adding two and two together, he realized that the fall in his income was not unrelated to same. But the doctor was not to be bullied in this fashion. All through February, while it grew colder and colder outside, inside the luxury apartment on Main Street, the doctor was steaming mad.

And so finally he did what he should have done

a long time ago. He talked to his mother and father about Lottie. He chose to do this during office hours, after his last patient of a very slim day. Thus we have his side of the conversation verbatim thanks to the excellent hearing of Zadie Gross.

No one knows why, in these days of cable and fiber optics, you should still sometimes get a bad line, but the doctor had, if not a bad line, bad enough to hang up and try again, a bad-ish line, which caused him to have to raise his voice a trifle. And so, without leaving her desk, Zadie could hear everything.

At first he talked a lot about the weather, she said, whining about the cold and the wind like a girl. And then he talked about snow tires and ice. Then they must have asked him about the practice, because there were a few moments during which she could hear only murmuring, and then, after he apologized for the bad line, he said louder, "I think the town is mad at me."

The parents must have asked why. The doctor briefly and succinctly explained that there had been "this girl" who was "really funny and sharp and pretty" and that he'd been "pretty much bowled over by her." And then the parents, or more likely the mother, asked if he was still seeing her. He said, "No, that's the problem." He talked about how everyone in town seemed to think if you dated someone and slept together a few times you had to marry them. He said *"marry* them" in this very scornful way.

And then he listened for quite some time, saying nothing but, "Yes. Well. I thought . . . but . . . well, yes . . . oh, very much . . . yeah, I guess," and similar. By which it can be clearly seen that the parents were making a distinction between behavior expected of a student doctor in a large conurbation and behavior expected from a small town's only general practitioner. At one point he exclaimed, "I never wanted to *hurt* her! I care for her, Mom, I really do." After which he listened a long time again, saying, "No . . . yes . . ." and "I see" at intervals.

After he replaced the phone in its cradle, the doctor sat and drummed his fingers on the table, which habit Zadie had already learned meant he was thinking. When he came out, his face was pale and set. He said, "I think you might as well go home, Zadie. I don't think anyone else will come."

And Zadie went home and used her phone until it was hot.

Meanwhile, Lottie Dougal's sniff seemed to have disappeared. When she took off her jaunty tam o'shanter that morning, it revealed a newly reddened head. She had found a natty green and black tweed jacket to replace her cardigan, and she looked with interest at the sales calendar, interviewing her assistant with remarkable energy about his successes and failures of the previous weeks and giving him a raise in pay and many thanks for keeping things going so well while she had been ill. She then pointed out a few new targeted clients and announced she would be back after lunch, as she had some errands to run.

Now, no one is certain exactly what all Lottie collected over the following three days. But it included some rather arcane items. From the Branch family collection she had removed some ylang-ylang, sandalwood, and yarrow. She bought three dozen red roses from the astonished florist out at Food Barn. She ordered some jasmine essence from Park Davis and asked him to ask the essential oil company to overnight it. And then she went to where that new restaurant was opening up to see if they had any idea where she could lay her hands on some habanero chiles.

The new restaurant was opening up where the old restaurant had been, but they were taking their time about it. Something was happening, but it was happening slow and often at night. The windows had newspaper over the bottom half, but if you stood on your tiptoes you could see a big machine working in the back, with a couple of women running it. In the front it looked like a construction site. Every once in a while a heap of wood on the floor would suddenly become recognizable as a booth or a table, but progress wasn't rapid.

It took Eudorans quite a while to realize that there were people coming to the back door of the restaurant and going away with something in their bags. But since the people weren't anyone that anyone knew, there was no way of finding out just what was going on.

This state of affairs could not continue.

Margery Lupin was unable to get the few hours of sleep she allowed herself, thinking about the back door of the old restaurant. Zadie Gross let the phone ring nearly fifteen times and the doctor finally had to answer it, so absorbed was she in contemplation of the back door of the old restaurant. Pattie Walker suspected her sister Lottie knew all about it, but could not find a way to ask, which (as usual) drove her right up the wall.

Every time a Eudoran passed the restaurant, he or she would glance over the newspaper, accidentally rising just a little to kind of see. But Lottie Dougal simply walked down the alley and stood in line at the back door with the Mexican women gathered there. And though Lottie went home with something in her bag, it was not the habaneros, though, as her assistant subsequently learned, she went back later that night and was given two for free.

The doctor drummed his desk all that long day. And then, informing Zadie he had his cell phone with him if she needed him, he flung himself out the door and down Main Street to Dougal's

Stationery Supplies. Lottie's assistant was in the back room, and so he came straight to the point. He said, "Lottie, I miss you."

Lottie had been adding up a row of figures. She continued doing this as though she had not heard until she got to the end, noted the number in her notebook, and then looked up. She said, "Good afternoon, Doc."

He said, "Did you hear me? I miss you. I really miss you."

She smiled. She said, "I miss you, too, Jim."

He said, "We've let other people get in the way of something beautiful."

She let a sad look steal upon her face and nodded.

He said, "Come over tonight. We can talk."

She said, "I'll come over next week."

He said, "Next week?"

She said, "Yes, I should be ready Tuesday, or maybe even Monday."

The doctor was a medical man and so leaped to a physical explanation involving menses at this point, blushed, and said, "If that's what you want, fine."

She said, "That's what I want. I'll call you."

The doctor left the shop, closing the door behind him and wondering what had just happened.

Well, Pattie Walker had heard of the doctor's telephone conversation with his parents and also of the visit to the stationery shop, and was torn.

She felt that if Lottie knew about the telephone conversation with his parents, she might feel better. But she also felt that too much had perhaps been made of this conversation and that it was better not to get Lottie's hopes up. Lottie was still, she felt, dangerously depressed. Another blow could seriously injure her.

She was still torn on Sunday when, after they had done the post-lunch dishes, Lottie brought a little calico parcel out of her coat pocket and asked if she could see Pattie's wedding ring for a moment.

Now, between sisters there should be no clinging to personal possessions, but Pattie felt more than a bit uneasy about this request.

"My wedding ring!" she exclaimed. "What do you want with my wedding ring?"

"I just need to see it for a minute," Lottie said. "I won't hurt it or anything, I promise. You can stand right here and watch me."

Pattie knew better than to sleep in her rings and so it came off quite easily. Still, she held it tight in her fist for a moment.

"I promise," said Lottie. "It's nothing, really."

Lottie sat down at the table and unrolled the calico parcel. There were two little bottles inside, one with the familiar label of the essential oil manufacturer Park Davis favored and one a small pink glass ball with a cork stopper. Lottie held the wedding band over the neck of the pink glass ball and, with such great concentration that the tip of her tongue protruded between her lips, carefully poured three drops of essence of jasmine over the wedding ring and allowed it to drip into the ball. She then quickly replaced the stopper and wiped the ring with a bit of paper towel before returning it to her sister.

Pattie opened her mouth to ask questions, but just then Phil bellowed from the living room, "Hey, Pats, bring me a beer, would ya?" and Pattie rolled her eyes at her sister.

But Lottie said, "He loves you, Pattie. You know he does. That is a true-love ring."

To which Pattie answered, "Yeah, right," but she thought about it later.

So many little things had to come together to make what happened next happen. Pattie not telling her sister about the doctor's phone call to his parents was one of them and Pattie not noticing that the *Herbal Lore for Cures and Curses* had returned to her shelf was another. For a long time afterward, Pattie blamed herself for not looking through it to discover what Lottie was doing. It was months before she took the time to do so, before she worked through the various love potions to the one that promised "to turn a man's thoughts from passion to marriage" and used fresh red rose petals and oil of jasmine dropped over a true-love ring. But then, who would have thought a family with Yucatecan roots would open a restaurant just at that time, and that the doctor would invite Lottie that day? When so many things like that come together, it's hard not to believe in either destiny or predestination.

You see, as Pattie was eventually to learn, the love potion required administration at the full moon to ensure that after the man had then made love to the woman he would be irresistibly drawn to commitment. The method of distillation and combination was fairly straightforward. But Lottie was late to the shop on Monday morning and looked like she hadn't slept much. Which many people later took to infer that she had worked with the ingredients in the pink glass ball in more intensive ways than the book actually advised.

So.

Tuesday night, Lottie Dougal went to the doctor's luxurious apartment on Main Street, and there they began the kind of evening they usually had, the doctor having got hold of some sea bass on his weekend trip to the city.

The doctor had also got hold of something else that weekend. He might have thought that by leaving it in his car until midnight and then running out in sweats and slippers under his overcoat, no one would be able to see the small purple bag from a well-known city jeweler entering his luxurious apartment on Main Street. And in a way, the way Eudora was at the time, no one did. Only the four-to-midnight security man from the quarry was witness to the doctor's jog to the car. He was coming to help his sister and brother-in-law set up their new restaurant by putting in a couple of hours of carpentry before he hit the hay. For now, he was nobody, so nobody knew. But they knew later.

If only things had been like they were later, Oscar Burgos would have told his sister, and his sister would have told Lottie, and Lottie would not have administered the potion. But as things were, he told his sister, and his sister, Maria Lopez, sucked her teeth and wondered about it, having heard from Mark Ramirez, Lottie's new assistant, how things were between Lottie and the doctor. Lottie had been kindness itself when she had come to ask for the habaneros and had, on her second visit, praised the tenderness of Maria's tortillas, but still, Maria did not know if Lottie had actually seen her.

For a strange thing about Eudora was, up until about this time, it did not see its large Latino population. For example, on the day that concerns us, the day when Jim Flory is about to open his movie house once again, one of the people standing by the bank, waiting for Clement McAllister to open it with his personal key on his golden keychain, is Hector Rodriguez, who had risen through the ranks of junior and senior cashier to become senior managing vice president of the First State Bank of Eudora and could have opened it easier and quicker with his own key but refrained out of respect and admiration for his boss.

There are other examples, but they are too numerous to list here. Perhaps the most glaring evidence that Eudorans were hard put later to figure out how they had overlooked was that more than half of St. Anthony of Padua was, on any given Sunday, and not to put too fine a point on it, brown. You try to book the church hall for a Friday or Saturday night and you'll find that a whole host of Martinezes and Sanchezes have gotten there before you, and the music coming out of these *quincea-ñeras*, golden wedding anniversary parties, or wedding receptions is not Big Irving Townsend's Magical Melodies but something so infectiously rhythmic you will be dancing down the sidewalk like a fool. But somehow the pale blue eye and the translucent white ear of Eudora had not heretofore registered this elemental fact.

Once they thought about it, Eudorans realized that they knew the quarry was the major employer of the town and that quarry workers had always been, by and large, Mexican and then Mexican American. But for a long while, they simply had not known they knew.

Until, as said, about this time, though not quite early enough to save Lottie Dougal and the doctor from their bizarre fate. For on that night, just as they had finished the crème brûlée and coffee and Lottie had taken off her shoes and her sweater and they were curled up on the sofa, kissing desultorily and then less desultorily, Lottie had said, "Open your mouth and taste this." She brought out the round pink glass bottle and had just removed the cork stopper and tilted it up so that its contents, distilled down to one potent, powerful drop, fell onto the center of the doctor's obedient tongue, when the telephone rang four times and the answering machine broadcast the doctor's father's voice. He said, "Jimmy, pick up, your mom's had a heart attack."

The doctor was on a plane in less than two hours, including the fifty-five-minute-drive to the airport.

And Lottie had to wait.

It was during these suspenseful two weeks that the entire Latino community of Eudora suddenly became visible. It happened this way:

The first profits of the back-door tortilleria enabled Maria (born Burgos) and Bill (born Guillermo) Lopez to buy the flooring and hire the electrician. The county health inspector then inspected, and the certificate was issued. A sign appeared over the window, and when the protective plastic was removed by Bill and his brother Frank (born Francis, Martina Lopez having been a bit of a Sinatra fan), who were working on two planks suspended above the sidewalk on two ladders and fixing the sign with cordless hand drills, it read "Mayan Memories" and displayed palm trees and a wave of blue-green water that represented the sea.

Now, at the end of February in this particular part of the world, any representation of the tropics will draw any individual's eye. Intellectually, the individual may know spring is coming, that the grass, when revealed, will soon turn green, that the bare branches of the trees will bud, that the lifeless prairie will once again echo with birdsong and bounce with what wildlife their poisons and traps have not been able to eliminate. But emotionally, looking around in the gray light at the unmarked expanses of white, the glassy drifts plowed either side of muddy roads, the slick black shine of frozen bark, it's hard to believe. And so any pattern of hibiscus flower, palm tree, or golden sand will rivet one's attention as much as a televised fish will fascinate a hungry cat.

Frank and Bill folded their ladders and withdrew at ten A.M. All of Main Street had read the posted menu by eleven. The menu was a super idea, as it not only allowed you to read what the restaurant was going to offer but also allowed you to look past it, into the window that for so long had been available only in snatched glances while walking on tiptoe.

What Eudora saw was favorable. Red leatherette booths lined the walls, with two long tables down the center of the room. The kitchen was at the back and was clearly visible—you could see what they were doing to your food. From here, Maria and her assistant, Linda Bustamonte, in their flowered dresses and long aprons with scarves over their hair, were thought to move like they knew what they were doing, and though no one could tell from that kind of distance it was also thought to look clean.

The big machine at the back was still working, and part of the conveyor belt came into the kitchen. But the rest had been partitioned off, the two women Maria had trained to work it hidden, the line of people going away with something in their bags concealed. Now, if any of the Main Street inquisitive had thought of going around to the alley behind the restaurant (which was also behind the doctor's, the bakery, and every other business on that side of the street), they would have seen that the tortilleria now had a hygienic counter and a little waiting area with a simple bench around the walls.

It was not unlike the small white porch at the back of the bakery, where Margery's assistant, Betty Requena, sold maranitos, campechanas, and fruit empanadas over a little counter built on top of the bottom half of the back door. Part of the reason the Latino population was invisible was this habitual trading at the back of such establish-ments. This may have been due to modesty on the part of the Latinos or prejudice on the part of the Europeans at some earlier period but was now largely due to habit and a reluctance to pay the twenty cents required to park on Main Street. Even the great Hector Rodriguez (of whom we shall later hear so much) had, the previous November, collected the calendars produced by Dougal's Stationery as gifts for the more favored of the bank's clientele from the back door of the shop and from the hands of Mark Ramirez.

Nor was this habitual trading at the back door with a Latino member of staff a question of lan-guage, since at that meeting, for example, both Hector and Mark conversed in English. The fact was, the Mexican community had grown used to being invisible, and it felt a little unsettling to sud-denly pop into sight. The back doors were far more comfortable.

But then there was the question of Mayan Memories. The day it opened, Clement McAllister and Hector Rodriguez walked down Main Street and entered its doors for lunch together. Now, this is both less and more remarkable than it seems. Less, because Clement had always made a point of personally supporting any bank client, and it was a small loan raised against the security of Maria and Bill's home that had allowed the lease to be signed and the tortilla-making equipment to be imported. Less also, because Maria had thoughtfully presented her menu so that the left-hand side was headed "Traditional American Recipes" and had steaks and baked potatoes and corn chowder and pork chops. But more, because though Hector and Clement had worked together for some eleven years and enjoyed each other's company, they had never before socialized.

Now, as might have been gathered from the previous narrative, the Eudoran character is inquisitive but not foolhardy. Quite a few people noticed that the restaurant was serving lunch, and quite a few people noticed that Hector and Clement ate at one of the red leatherette booths. But nobody else actually came in.

Sitting in a quiet restaurant with just two people at a table can be a constraining experience. But Hector and Clement did not find it so. Just after they ordered, before their Cokes even arrived, Hector told Clement something that had happened at the bank counter concerning their most junior member of staff that had Clement in tears of laughter. Clement then told Hector how he had done something similar while working his way up in the bank under his father, and Hector confessed a ten-year-old secret involving his own early trials in the banking business. Their food seemed to arrive with remarkable rapidity.

Clement's was an appetizing plate of pork chops

and mashed potatoes, with peas and carrots and a small dish of applesauce on the side, along with some light brown gravy. But as nice as it was, it was simply eclipsed by Hector's meal. This consisted of a large white plate on which gaily colored rice, glossy refried beans, and crisp salad rested with a white bowl full of a black substance so fragrant it steamed Clement's glasses from across the table. Clement, whose fork had been moving at its normal mealtime piston pace, actually *stopped eating* to watch Hector cut a mouthful of something like chicken that emerged from this delicious miasma and place it into his mouth. And Hector, who had been so intent on entertaining his boss that he had ordered almost unconsciously, now neglected Clement entirely, closing his eyes and moaning in appreciation.

Any Eudoran would have asked what Clement asked next: "What *is* that stuff?"

Hector took his time, swallowed, wiped tears from his eyes with his napkin, and said, "Pollo mole." And then said, "Sorry, boss, it's chicken in a chocolate chile sauce. One of my aunts used to make it, but not like this."

Any Eudoran would have said what Clement said next: "Can I try a little?"

Hector looked doubtful. He said, "Do you like spicy food?"

Now, this is something that showed Hector had never before socialized with his boss. A bottle of

Tabasco was permanently at Clement's elbow during breakfasts at home, to enliven his hash browns, his eggs, and once, as a memorable experiment, his toast. Clement's was also one of the regular entries in the annual Rotary Club chili cook-off, for which book was made and bets were laid.

Clement said, "Hell, yes."

Hector then gave Clement a generous portion of his pollo mole. If Clement had not been his boss, it would not have been so generous; in fact, it might not have been given at all. It was one of the finest things Hector had ever eaten. While Clement got up his courage, Hector took the opportunity to taste the frijoles refritos and the arroz. Delicious. Everything was utterly delicious. He had heard Maria Lopez was something special in the kitchen, but this was over and above his expectations.

Clement raised his fork. This is an important moment. In a way, it is the moment when the entire Latino population of Eudora suddenly sprung into view. Because though Clement finished his pork chops and mashed potatoes and though he pronounced it good, he said he was going to call his wife on the phone and tell her not to cook that night and he was going to come back and have some more of that Moley Chicken, by jingo, that's what he was going to do.

And that's just what he did. Of course, by then

he had spoken to about half the town about what he had done, and in his telling of the anecdote, he figured largely as a brave, experimental figure who also numbered Hector Rodriguez, a Mexican American, among his closest friends and colleagues. "I figured that if old Hector thought it was so good, I'd better get my choppers around it" was one of the phrases he repeated several times that day.

From which Blake Bumgartner realized that a Rotary Club invitation was long overdue to one Hector Rodriguez. This invitation, once issued, was the start of the remarkable election of the following year. Clement's anecdote also inspired a good portion of Main Street to eat their supper at Mayan Memories that evening. Some went away contented, and those who had ordered from the right-hand portion of the menu went away lyrical.

One of the lyrical was Lottie Dougal, who attended that first night's seating along with her sister, Pattie, and her brother-in-law, Phil.

Now, one other thing Eudora had preferred not to notice was the increase in consultations of the Branch family library due to the unofficial boycott of the doctor's services. All the Branch cousins had been seen over the past few weeks, needing herbal remedies for tickly and productive coughs, for kidney pain and cystitis, to take down bruising of a sprained foot, and so on. On these occasions, they went to see Pattie, though it was really Lottie they wanted, as she was thought to have inherited more of the family skill in such things. And as February had worn on and the false spring Eudorans got nearly every year (and looked forward to as a bit of a break in which to get the car washed and the windows cleaned) failed to appear, friends, workmates, and fellow members of the PTA began approaching Branch cousins with small medical troubles of their own. Some nights, Lottie was doling out advice and remedies in the Walkers' kitchen until the ten o'clock headlines and was conscious that (a) this was all her fault and the people concerned would be going to the doctor if they weren't busy being supportive and (b) Phil and Pattie might feel invaded.

So, in order to say thank you for this and for Pattie's concern over her health as well as for the couple's caring ways in general, Lottie had offered to send them to Mayan Memories on her nickel and stay home and babysit the boys.

But this had not suited Phil and Pattie, who thought, with the doctor absent and leaving so suddenly the way he had and only one phone call since he'd arrived in Seattle, that Lottie should share the treat. They also thought that this was an excellent reason to ask Artie and Rosemary Walker to babysit, something they had been meaning to do for quite some time. Since the birth of the Walkers' angelic baby daughter, May, nine months previously, both Artie and Rosemary (though Artie was the worst) had been quite vocal about child-rearing techniques, putting May's saintly nature down to superior parenting. Phil and Pattie had been eagerly awaiting an occasion to allow them to take care of Ben, Daniel, and Patrick for an evening, ostensibly to demonstrate these practices for their and their offspring's edification, but actually to shut Artie and Rosemary's smart mouths. So they loaded up the kids with sugar, hid the evidence, and put on their coats as Artie and Rosemary were taking off theirs, making certain to leave their cell phones behind.

If it was a lively evening at the Walker house, it was also a lively evening at Mayan Memories. Linda and Maria were busy, and Gabe Burgos, Oscar's eldest, who had inherited Maria's grandfather's interest in food and helped out after school, was washing plates and fetching things from the big cooler, big plastic buckets of sauces and trays of cut lettuce and tomatoes. It was exciting watching everything get put together, and Maria came and examined every plate to make certain—no, a little more cilantro here—that it was perfect before it left the counter and was carried to your table. She seemed to be everywhere. Out of everything that happened that night, the least important seemed to be that Lottie Dougal reached into her bag and pulled out a glass jar with an eyedropper top to give to Clarissa Engel, explaining that she should not try to put the eyedropper in young Branch Engel's mouth but drop the solution on her finger and rub the gum where the tooth was emerging.

Maria, feeling bolder in her relationship to Lottie Dougal than she had the previous week, said, with surprise and a little good-natured ribbing, "You some kind of *curandera?*"

Lottie, handing over the bottle to Clarissa, turned to her assistant, Mark Ramirez, who was dining at the middle table with his cousin Vince, and asked, "Mark, what's a *curandera?*"

And Mark, who had been discussing the relative merits of Kylie Requena and Donna Bustamante and had not heard Maria's question, said, "Oh, it's a witch doctor," and turned back to Vince. If he had heard Maria's question, he might have put it differently. But that's what he said.

Lottie then turned to answer Maria Lopez but Maria had gone off to another table. "Did you hear that?" she said to Clarissa. "Maria thinks I'm a witch doctor!"

They had a good laugh about it, as did Phil when Lottie repeated the story back at their table while they were waiting for their pumpkin ice cream. Perhaps Pattie was too distracted to laugh, wondering how Artie and Rosemary were coping with the boys, or maybe there was some other reason, but she didn't even smile at Lottie's anecdote and in fact looked thoughtful for the remainder of the evening.

The doctor arrived back in town at eleven o'clock on a Tuesday evening, nearly exactly fourteen days after he'd left it. Lottie did not pick him up at the airport, since he had put his car in long-term parking and so could drive home himself. Indeed, Lottie did not know of his imminent arrival, though she was very eager to see him, find out how his mom was doing, and continue their evening and her herbal experimentation where they had left off.

But though Lottie Dougal was not with the doctor, and his mother (even given a remarkable recovery and the best of modern medicine) would surely be unfit to travel by air, when the doctor drove back into town there was a woman in his car.

No one ever knew much about Angela Requena. The Requenas of Eudora, who tried to take her to their bosom as a cousin, although the connection, if there was one, was of a remote and historical nature, found her difficult, and the rest of the town was not predisposed to be warmly welcoming to the doctor's new wife. Angela was extremely beautiful, and if discerning residents thought she had Lottie's enigmatic calmness without Lottie's effervescent emotion, less discerning residents thought she was the same type. Seeing Angela, you could see what made the doctor fall for Lottie. Knowing Lottie, you could see why the doctor had gone for Angela.

Of course, why the doctor had gone for Angela was a complicated thing. He had been without the comfort of a close physical relationship with a woman for some months, and this was unusual for the doctor. It is also important to remember that Angela was a beautiful woman, unhappy in her current situation as a nurse's aide, but (at least in the doctor's presence) kind to his mother despite her unhappiness. The doctor was host to an emotional cocktail of worry, relief, resentment (of both Eudora in general and Lottie personally), love, and financial strain. Added to this, the good Lord only knows the effect of that triple-distilled drop Lottie had placed on his tongue.

Some months later, we learned from his mother that the doctor shook Angela's hand in thanks and she smiled shyly at the doctor with her large brown eyes. The doctor pressed her hand and she pressed back. The doctor then excused himself from his mother's bedside and was not seen again until the next morning, when he announced he had found the woman of his dreams and that they were to marry on Friday. Angela did not return to work, and when Mrs. Emery next saw her, she was wearing the engagement ring the doctor had bought for Lottie Dougal.

A week later, the doctor scooped her from the car, carried her through the doorway of the luxurious apartment on Main Street, and kicked the door shut with his foot.

It was Hector's brother, Manuel Rodriguez, who saw the doctor carry Angela from his car. Manuel worked the twelve-to-eight security shift at the quarry, and though he saw Oscar Burgos as he clocked in and they exchanged a few words about the weather and the state of security that currently existed at the quarry in general and the unreliability of the number seven camera in particular, he did not think to mention the doctor and the car and the carrying of a woman. By which you can see that Manuel was not a true Eudoran, and his subsequent leaving of town for a job in the city surprised no one. He only mentioned seeing that crucial moment at the big family celebration of Hector's election the following year, by which time, of course, no one could do anything.

So Lottie heard about it all from Zadie Gross.

You see, the following morning was a Wednesday. Zadie had been just as punctual in the doctor's absence as she had been in his presence, taking telephone calls, lining up what appointments there were for the following week, maintaining stocks of supplies, and updating the inventory of all the fixtures and fittings. Say what you like about Zadie, but she ran a tight ship. Grass did not grow under her feet.

On Wednesday morning at about eight-fifty, Zadie let herself in, sat down to take off her fur-lined boots and put on her work shoes, hung up her coat, put her lunch in the refrigerator, and girded her loins to deal with the doctor's fancy coffee machine. The doctor came clattering down the stairs, which didn't actually surprise her, as she'd been expecting him one of these mornings, but she acted like it did, holding her hand to her throat and gasping, just to let him know he should have thought about calling the office every once in a while and letting her fill him in on what was happening.

The doctor completely ignored this, telling Zadie good morning and when she'd got her coffee would she mind bringing it into his office?

He looked different, Zadie noticed right away. Older. Harder. She put this down to worry and hoped they hadn't had to bury his mother.

It was the first thing she asked about when she came through the office door, but the doctor announced his mother's recovery brusquely. He said, "You only have a year to go before retirement, don't you, Zadie?" That's when Zadie noticed her personnel file open on the desk along with the practice's checkbook, which was usually kept in *her* desk. She said later she knew what was coming and only wondered about the amount.

Whether this last is true or not, the doctor spoke at some length about how efficient and useful Zadie had been and what a boon it was to a new doctor to have someone like Zadie running the practice, a safe pair of hands. But then he said he was planning to make quite a few changes to the way things were done and thought it would be more comfortable for all concerned if Zadie retired a year early. He then produced a check for Zadie's entire salary for the coming year, handed it to her with a small gift box that turned out to hold a silk scarf in becoming lilac tones, shook her hand, and pushed her out the door.

Zadie's hands were shaking, positively shaking, as she got her lunch out of the refrigerator, took off her work shoes and put on her fur-lined boots, and got her coat off the hook. It was this that might have made her a little slow. Because before she turned to go out the front door, Angela came down the stairs. Zadie was struck to stone. She couldn't have moved if she wanted to. She stared at Angela, and Angela stared coolly back with an odd little smile and then called, "Jim, darling?" through the office with a charming Castilian lilt.

When the doctor appeared, Angela put her head to one side and, still looking at Zadie, said, "Won't you introduce us, Jim?"

The doctor smiled, his hand on Angela's slim shoulder, and said, "This is my wife, Angela Emery, Zadie. Darling, this is Zadie Gross."

Angela had placed one hand over the doctor's hand on her shoulder. She gave the other to Zadie, who took it, she said, just like a robot.

"We were married just last week. In a way, I guess you could call her your replacement." The doctor and Angela laughed gaily, showing their strong white teeth. It reminded Zadie of wolves.

Zadie said she had to go, and stumbled out the door. She stood for a moment on Main Street, her lunch still clutched in her hands, her bag hanging unregarded from the crook of her elbow, banging against her haunch in the brisk wind of early March. Which is when Lottie Dougal, on her way back from a successful breakfast meeting with Clement McAllister and Hector Rodriguez at the bank, stopped and asked her what was wrong.

Zadie was unable to speak, so Lottie dragged her across the street and into the fabric shop, clear through the bolts and pattern files, to sit her down in the back room and get her a glass of water. Pattie Walker and Becky Lane, who had not actually opened yet and weren't due to for another half an hour, having come in early to change over some stock for the new season, both looked at Zadie with concern.

Lottie rubbed Zadie's back.

Now, the more Lottie did for Zadie, the worse Zadie got. Every time she tried to speak, she spluttered, and yet she was puffing up, almost like an inflatable mattress, puffing up and puffing up until Pattie, Lottie, and Becky were pretty sure she was going to burst. And then she did, into tears, and her lunch slid from her fingers and was caught by Becky Lane just in time, which was good because the smell of tuna casserole would not have left the fabric shop in a hurry.

Through her sobs, the women gathered that the doctor had let her go. But Zadie also waved the check at them, and, looking at the figure inscribed neatly on the face, no one could understand Zadie's grief.

Once she touched the check, Lottie stopped rubbing Zadie's back and giving Zadie helpful advice about breath control. Indeed, Lottie stood stock still, her face showing deep shock and foreshadowing the grief that was to lie on it for nearly the whole of the coming year.

So when Zadie did take a deep breath and closed her eyes to deliver the news, Lottie's face did not change much at all. It was as if, simply by touching the doctor's signature, she already knew.

Though Pattie tried to stop her, Lottie left the fabric shop and walked to Dougal's Stationery Supplies. Several people tried to greet her on her way, but she didn't register them. She walked, Jim Evans said later, as if she'd been hurt in the head. As Jim was a farmer and had seen quite a few head injuries in his time, it was considered an extremely apt description.

She walked into Dougal's Stationery Supplies and sat down on the tall stool behind the counter. Mark Ramirez, who had been stocking the Easter cards into a display, asked her how the meeting at the bank went. Even from his position on his knees and somewhat to the rear of Lottie, he could tell something was wrong. He went to his employer only to find she was sitting in her coat, still holding on to her briefcase, and trembling.

He got her a glass of water and Lottie thanked him mechanically, putting it onto the glass counter without using the coaster. Now Mark was really worried. He said, "Have a drink of water, Miss Lottie," but she only thanked him again in that dead voice. He asked her if she was all right and she said nothing at all.

Mark was a young man like any other young man, and so knew himself immediately to be in a situation beyond his capabilities. Women were either all right or not all right, and Lottie was clearly not in the least all right no matter what she was saying. He left by the back door and went down the alley, knocking on the back door of the fabric shop. But when Pattie distractedly opened the door and he beheld Zadie Gross sitting in tears, sobbing about wolves, he shut the door again and stood there making rapid eye movements. Pattie had already been requisitioned.

And so he went to Maria Lopez, who was in the middle of lunch preparations. He said, "I don't know what's happening, Miz Lopez, the whole town has gone loco. Something is the matter with Miss Lottie, and her sister is . . . that fat woman who works for the doctor is with her sister."

Maria was a sharp woman and realized immediately that Zadie Gross had learned something about the doctor that had shocked Lottie Dougal.

Christian charity and natural curiosity dragged her from her pots and across the street, where she found Lottie in the same state as Mark had left her. Maria wiped her hands on her apron and put the glass of water to Lottie's lips. "Drink this," she commanded.

Lottie obeyed and a second later blinked. She saw Maria bending over her and tried to smile. "What happened?" Maria asked.

Lottie was as malleable right then as a child, and with a child's innocence she said, "He slept with her in Seattle. He must have slept with her and because of my potion he *married* her."

Maria and Mark exchanged glances. "Who slept with whom?" Maria asked.

"What potion?" Mark asked.

But then Lottie blinked again. Her face, while still set in the lines of grief, seemed to gather itself. She said, "Thank you. I feel better now."

She stood up and took off her coat. She put her briefcase on the floor. She smiled at Maria and said, "It was so nice of you to come."

By which both Mark and Maria knew they would not get any more information from Lottie that morning. Maria returned to her bubbling pots, exchanging another glance with Mark, to which he replied, "I'll come over for lunch," in a whisper.

Now, the coffee machine at the fabric store had been acting funny for some weeks, and Phil

Walker had promised to have a look at it but of course had not done so. So in this moment of crisis, when everyone needed a good cup of coffee with maybe more cream and sugar in it than they usually allowed, the thing shot craps. Which meant Becky Lane had to put on her coat and go down to the bakery, and thought she might as well get some donuts while she was there. Which meant Margery Lupin was told the entire story at nine-ten and the whole of Main Street was in possession of the salient facts by nine-thirty.

Ben Nichols and Odie Marsh came by about ten-fifteen, having started their day at the county courthouse and being somewhat late on their rounds, and so the news was spread to the outlying areas of the town by lunchtime. Jim Evans, hearing it from the mailman, informed his wife that he'd known something like that must have happened from the expression on the poor Dougal woman's face, and then he uttered the apt description of being hurt in the head, which Mrs. Evans repeated at that night's quilting bee and which henceforth became definitive.

Thursday was a Rotary Club lunch, and this one was held as usual in the grand boardroom of the First State Bank of Eudora but catered for a change by Maria Lopez, who along with sandwiches and a crudité platter had also provided tamales and chicken flautas and had placed salsa and chips around the large mahogany table at generous intervals, all innovations that met with much approval, as did the suggestion that Hector Rodriguez should join their ranks.

And it was after the meeting, at which the fund-raising events for the summer had been planned, including the new musical element to the Fourth of July fireworks display suggested by Tony Bumgartner, when the unofficial boycott of the doctor's services became official. This happened when Clement McAllister, speaking about the imminent opening of the municipal golf course to several interested parties, said, "You know, my bursitis has been acting up again, but I'll be danged if I'll go see that man about it. I might just ask Lottie Dougal for one of her recipes." By which he meant he would ask his wife, who served on the Chamber of Commerce tourism committee with Pattie Walker, to ask Pattie to ask Lottie, which everyone knew, but still, the senti-ment was there and so neatly expressed that men found themselves repeating it in their minds and wanting to say it themselves.

"My throat feels a little sore, but I'll be danged if I'll go see that man about it."

"I grazed my knee with the chain saw, but I'll be danged if I'll go see that man about it."

"I've been having trouble with my regularity, but I'll be danged if I'll go see that man about it."

And the men's wives, who constituted the privi-leged auditors of these forthright statements, thus understood and approved. For the doctor had gone too far, and as far as Eudora was concerned, this was now war.

But it was only as far as half, or a little less than half, of Eudora was concerned. For the doctor and his new wife, acting on advice from the doctor's uncle and father, had been making changes to the practice.

Paint had been bought, as had a new runner carpet. Activity around the back of the doctor's office had been constant and effective, removing trash cans and the back gate to provide a new, commodious entrance to which Don Simpson added a rubber-covered ramp and a solid handrail. And then the mysterious advertisement appeared in Sunday's parish bulletin.

The St. Anthony of Padua's Sunday bulletin had accepted decorous advertisements from local Catholic businesses for some years, and for all those years, Nancy McAllister (Clement's widowed sister-in-law) had been, as the parish secretary, in charge of layout and insertion. Nancy was therefore well placed to know of any upcoming sales or special events, and her intimates never bought, say, a handful of big quarters from Pattie Walker's calico bin the week before they were due to be discounted. But even Nancy was unable to reveal much about the doctor's advertisement because it was written in Spanish.

After that advertisement appeared, the racial

equality that had flourished so briefly in the town that forms the setting of our tale came under grievous threat. For though Eudora agreed on many things, it did not agree on whether or not the doctor's marriage constituted grounds for an official boycott, especially since he had married a Spanish-speaking wife and offered such reasonable rates for complete checkups along with free parking at the rear.

So the ten-thirty Mass at which the bulletin containing the divisive advertisement was distributed was the last time for a considerable stretch that all Eudora was thinking the same thing. It was obvious. For although 49 percent of Eudora felt the doctor was a scoundrel and 51 percent of Eudora thought the doctor had done the right thing marrying a good girl of Spanish descent instead of a *gringa* of loose personal morals, they were all united in a reprehensible desire to be present when the two women first met. And so that morning, there was much shoe-tying and acquaintance-greeting around the entrance to St. Anthony of Padua. There were several parties intent on examining the newly emerged crocuses. There were scores lining up to make a quick obeisance at the grotto of Our Lady of Guadalupe on the west wall.

And none of this activity was in vain. For just as Pattie and Phil Walker arrived with their three boys and Lottie Dougal in tow, and stopped to exchange greetings with Rosemary and Artie Walker, the doctor and his wife stepped off the sidewalk and into the front yard of the church.

The doctor was wearing a sharp navy suit no one had known he possessed, with shiny black shoes and a shirt so white it hurt your eyes to look at it. His tie was a colorful melange of navy, red, and yellow in a small paisley. And Angela was a vision in a black sheath dress, black stockings, heels, and a beige cashmere jacket with a gorgeous black lace mantilla over her glossy black hair. She carried a well-worn missal in one leather-gloved hand and a rosary in the other.

Lottie, in her black slacks and boots topped by a big oatmeal-colored sweater, seemed young and soft by comparison. Younger and softer perhaps, but also, clearly, no competition to the polished radiance of Mrs. Doctor Emery.

The doctor smiled nervously. He said, "Lottie, I'd like to present my wife, Angela."

Lottie smiled tightly. She said, "Congratulations. I hope you're both very happy."

Angela put the hand with the rosary through the crook of the doctor's arm. "Oh, we are," she said, smiling broadly. And then, moving the doctor, who seemed rather rooted, away, said, "How nice it is to meet you," over her shoulder.

The youngest Walker boy then asked to be picked up, which Lottie did, and then she walked into the church with her family, who all, including

Artie and Rosemary with baby May on her hip, sat in one pew, sandwiching Lottie in the middle as if they were expecting physical attack.

Such was the first encounter, and if you think it looks dull written down like this, I can tell you that not a single Eudoran would have missed it for the world and that every one of the town's Methodists, Baptists, Lutherans, and Latter-Day Saints found some reason to call upon their Catholic neighbors soon after eleven-thirty that day for a full report. Which was not the same thing, but couldn't be helped.

Lottie looked the same before, during, and after this meeting, as if, a few unperceptive souls said, it had meant nearly nothing to her. But the perceptive among the congregation thought it was as if she could know no greater grief than she already had.

Now, whether Lottie coveted her neighbor's husband, wanted to kill her neighbor's wife, or had something even weightier on her conscience we do not know. But Lottie did not take communion that day.

Angela did, with such piety that it either confirmed one's view of her as the savior of the doctor's soul or made you sick to your stomach, depending on your ethnic background. The doctor remained in his pew, his face impossible to read. However, it was noted that he did not kneel and pray and he did not sing a note.

• • •

One of the things that made the doctor's success with the Spanish-speaking community of Eudora so smooth that spring was the retirement and repatriation of Fernando Burgos. Fernando was Maria Lopez's grandfather and had fulfilled the same role in the Mexican community as Lottie Dougal was currently doing out of Pattie Walker's kitchen. Fernando *was* a *curandero,* of a long line of same. And part of the scorn in Maria Lopez's voice when she saw Lottie doling out the teething remedy to Clarissa Engel on the opening night of the restaurant was due to Maria's inability to believe that anyone not of pure Mayan blood could fulfill such a role.

Fernando had been much consulted and well respected. For anything he could not do, there were doctors in the city. In such a way had the medical needs of 51 percent of Eudora been met in the years prior to our story.

But Fernando had gone back to the holy places of his youth, where the *cenote* ran red with Christ's blood every Easter and the heart stones were given up by the grateful earth. He had sold his house and taken his bank card back to Piste, leaving a gap into which the doctor and Angela neatly stepped.

If you were older and found Spanish more comfortable, it was a relief to call the doctor's office and be greeted bilingually by Angela, as you could outline your complaint in a clear and concise manner rather than have your tongue stumble over the stops and starts of English. If you spoke English in the main but for some words fell back on the Spanish equivalent, you still had a feeling of satisfaction knowing that such slips would not render you incomprehensible or, what was more likely, despised. Fifty-one percent of Eudora flocked to the doctor for his remarkably reasonable checkups.

The doctor came down every morning and bought donuts from Margery Lupin and buñuelos from Betty Requena to ornament his waiting room. Each time he wore one of what appeared to be three Italian suits, his shoes shined so highly you could shave in them. Once a week for those two and a half weeks, he sauntered smugly to Phil Turner's barber shop and got his hair trimmed and his neck shaved, and though the majority of the other patrons did not speak to him, Phil still took his money and did a good job.

The fact was, it was not like seeing the man she loved when Lottie Dougal caught glimpses of the doctor during that time, the longest seventeen days anyone could remember. It was like seeing someone else.

And then something changed. The moon waxed to fullness and Lottie spent her evening, as she did every evening those days, working in Pattie's kitchen, making a poultice for Clement

McAllister's bursitis and suggesting a few basic yoga asanas to help Margery Lupin's lower back as well as mixing up more teething serum, this time for May Walker, who had finally learned to cry and fuss. When Lottie left, stretching her own back, and saw the moon, her mouth set in a thin line and she sank down onto the Walkers' top step. It had grown much warmer, but it still wasn't porch-sitting weather, so this reaction was well noted.

As was the doctor's the following day. We have no way of knowing how the doctor greeted his wife that morning, but from his subsequent testimony, it could not have been in a loving manner. For to the doctor, it was as if he'd been asleep not just one night but an entire cycle of the moon. He said later it was astonishing just how wrong things can go if you let them.

You see, the interesting thing about herbal remedies and lore is that they work with the balance of the earth's energies (this is a direct quote from Lottie Dougal), and every so-called spell has a hidden reaction inside it, just as every shot to the backboard has a rebound inside it. The rebound in the case of spell 159, "To Turn a Man's Thoughts from Passion to Commitment," is that the effects last for only one cycle of the moon. Most couples not being as quick off the mark as the doctor and Angela Requena, this allowed for most of the weddings that resulted from its use to be genuine, free commitments on the part of the men, on whom the effects of the potion had worn off by the time the organ struck up Mendelssohn. However, you got the odd one who didn't wait. The doctor was one of the odd ones.

He certainly looked odd that morning. He wandered down Main Street to Margery Lupin's with his hair sticking up and his collar rumpled under the jacket of a suit it looked like he'd put on in the dark. He kept rubbing his face with his hand and had to be told three times to take his change before he scooped up the bills and coins in his fist and thrust them into his trouser pocket. Not only were his shoes clouded but one lace was undone and he kept nearly tripping over it.

And then there was the way he looked at Lottie Dougal.

Lottie had grown used to seeing the doctor since his marriage and had perfected a method of not really seeing him. So she swept past on the other side of the street and the doctor stared after her, holding his donuts in a way that was going to cause sliding and icing damage inside the big white box. His mouth hung open. Then he collected himself and resumed his shuffle back to his office, every nuance of his posture proclaiming to the world that he was a broken man.

It was, considering the circumstances, perhaps unwise for the Dramatic Society of the Celtic Club to enact *Othello* that year as their annual St.

Patrick's Day play. But seeing as the other choice was *A Midsummer Night's Dream,* which would (had they known all the facts at the time) have been much more wounding, it could have been worse. Count was lost of the number of looks sneaked at Lottie, the doctor, and Angela during the performance, but the reaction of the three to certain lines of the play was thoroughly witnessed. Lottie seemed unknowable as usual, her chin held high and her face fixed in the normal attitude of enjoyment that Eudorans adopt at these kind of cultural events. Angela was sitting with her hand on the doctor's thigh, ignoring the efforts of the Society, instead staring back at whoever glanced her way. She had a way of looking at you that made you think she could see the safety pin on your bra strap, as Rosemary Walker later said to Pattie, and most Eudorans, caught in the glare from her implacable eye, were forced to look quickly away again. The doctor seemed wholly absorbed in the production, or else had worked out a way to sleep with his eyes open.

For the doctor was wooden at the play, just as he had been wooden for the previous week. He was wooden and he was absent. He answered when spoken to, and he gave his hand when greeted, but through it all, he never seemed actually present. Eudorans noticed this, and noted the way the doctor stared fixedly at the stage (as usual, this event was held in the Eudora Empire Cinema, Jim

Flory writing off potential profits lost on his taxes) as if he wasn't seeing a thing. Then they noticed the way Angela would squeeze the doctor's knee with her strong fingers and how the doctor would then turn to her and smile, a horrible dead smile. And then they would notice that Angela had noticed them looking and had turned her basilisk stare their way. Upon which they again simulated interest in the machinations of Iago.

Now, it was about this time that Pattie got down *Herbal Lore for Cures and Curses* and began to realize what her sister had done. And though she did not mention this even to Phil, somehow news of Lottie's herbal experimentation leaked into the town and notes began to be compared of red roses, habanero chiles, and jasmine oil. It was also about this time that Phil Walker declared it would be nice to have a kitchen and someday he was going to build one onto the back of his house.

In his youth, Phil had not been a patient man, but time and Pattie's cooking had mellowed him. Still, as month after month went by and he could not strip down to his boxers and relax in his own home because of the steady stream of cure seekers, he began to grow querulous. The decision to move the Branch library was not made quickly. But perhaps it was easier because of Phil's discomfort and Pattie's dark discovery. She did not like making the boys' food with *Herbal Lore for*

Cures and Curses in the same room. And so, one Sunday after lunch, Phil used his truck to help Lottie move the library to the small house her father had built, where she was living. They shifted all the stock of oils, roots, dried flower heads, and so on into the garage out back, putting her Subaru out in the weather. There were no hard feelings either way, as both parties felt it was better to have it like this.

Lottie's heart might be irrevocably broken and her conscience permanently smirched, but at least she was keeping busy. What with the increasing expansion of Dougal's Stationery Supplies and her medical duties, she hadn't had a whole lot of time to feel her feelings. But at the end of March, the medical duties suddenly slackened, and Lottie had more time for consideration of personal matters.

The slackening was due to a number of factors.

First of all, it must be said that to a person used to Western medicine, the slow and participatory nature of natural remedies can pall. Take Clement McAllister's bursitis, for instance. He had received a not unpleasant-smelling waxy substance that he had to rub into the skin (or get Lucy to do it for him because he couldn't reach all the way around to the shoulder blade) twice a day. It left marks on his shirt because there was no way to rub it in enough, and if you toweled off the excess prior to dressing then the stuff didn't work.

So when Clement was in a meeting and it got hot in the room and everyone else took off their jackets and loosened their ties, Clement wondered if he could. Then old Clement was also told to reduce his alcohol consumption and sleep on his back. Well. He had done his best, but Lucy had to move into the spare room because of the snoring. When Lucy consulted Lottie about the snoring, Lottie said the best cure for snoring was to cut out alcohol altogether, which is when Clement started to feel that natural medicine required a bit more participation than the average patient might want to provide.

It was about that time that news of Lottie's possible potion began to leak into the general consciousness of Eudora.

Now, prone as Eudora is to believe in rumor, this time it took a bit of convincing. Eudora does not have a fixed opinion on the supernatural. Things like that might happen, it feels, or they might not, though they certainly don't happen around here. But the behavior of the doctor and the sheer awfulness of Angela Requena Emery lent a weight of credence to the speculation of dark forces it otherwise would not have enjoyed. In fact, the more grief-stricken the doctor seemed, and the more Eudora got to know Angela, the more they were convinced of unnatural interference, especially when Maria and Mark repeated what Lottie had said after her first sip of water the morning she had learned about the doctor's marriage from Zadie Gross.

Given that Eudora was more or less convinced that Lottie had been dabbling in realms best left alone, it was interesting to note that the reaction to this bit of information was again split largely along ethnic lines.

Clement McAllister can represent 49 percent of Eudora, while we will use Oscar Burgos to represent the other 51 percent. Clement, fed up to the back teeth with that damn smelly wax, was heard to say (at the Knights of Columbus Lady Day Steering Committee meeting, held at Chuck's Beer and Bowl) that he *would* have a beer, damn it, and he didn't know that he wouldn't have two. And then he followed this by saying, "If you have to choose between a witch and a doctor, I'm going to go for the doctor every time, even if he is a sorry sumbitch." Which statement, though not repeated to wives, was considered to reflect the feelings of all those present.

If those used to modern medicine found natural remedies inconvenient and slow, the part of the population that had been used to natural remedies found the doctor's new medicines to be brutal and horrifically expensive, the quarry never having provided much in the way of benefits such as health insurance. That the medicines were effective could not be gainsaid, but that they didn't necessarily improve your health and well-being was also obvious. As Oscar Burgos remarked during the golden wedding anniversary celebration of Carlos and Carmen Bustamente, "You have a problem, and so you take this medicine for the problem. So that goes away, but then you get another problem because of the medicine, and he gives you another medicine for the problem with the first medicine, and what you got is now maybe three, four problems when you only went in with one." Which wisdom caused many heads to nod in agreement in the quiet corner of the church hall devoted to the enjoyment of tequila.

Oscar, encouraged by the agreement, then went on to say, "And you've got to get past that bitch on the phone." At which the heads nodded even more vigorously.

For of all the doctor's experiments, the Spanish-speaking wife was the least successful. At first, oh, at first it was very comfortable. But that was before they got to know Angela, the little sniff she gave that meant she could not be bothered with the trivialities of your complaint. The way she repeated some of your words and gave them what she considered the proper Castilian pronunciation. The way she pretended not to be able to understand your Spanish if you maybe grew up speaking English, too, and didn't know all the grammar so good.

And she was prejudiced. If you had light skin and spoke Spanish good, she would sit behind her desk and work away, maybe even chat with you a little. But if you had dark skin and maybe a strong Yucatecan accent, she would take out her nail file and start doing her nails or make a cup of coffee and not even ask you if you wanted one. Once she came into the room when such a patient was waiting and muttered *"indios"* under her breath. Such things had become well known and could not be tolerated, especially considering the way she treated the Requena family when they, in the goodness of their hearts, came to claim kinship with her.

Now Betty Requena had worked at the bakery for some seven years but was rather restricted as to what she could produce under Margery Lupin's guidance. At home it was a different matter, and to be invited to Betty and Don's house for a cup of coffee was pretty much an invitation to pastry heaven and as such was considered a particular honor in the community. This honor was extended to the doctor and his wife.

The doctor, even in the state he was in, wolfed down about half a pound of various delicacies, but Angela sat there looking around Betty's colonial-style living room like, as Betty said later, "she smelled something bad," and waved away every one of Betty's offerings without even looking at them, just with her hand, like she was shooing away flies. She sat perched on the edge of the sofa and barely spoke a word, like she was doing them

98

some kind of favor to come, Don said. Don also said that if Betty didn't mind, they wouldn't be seeing too much of her new cousin no more.

This was not too much of a problem, since Angela refused every other invitation from the Requena family, even to Kylie's quinceanera. She didn't even send a gift or a card with a check in response to the invitation, she with her sheer stockings and pearl necklaces, who could clearly afford to be a little generous to a cousin just starting on adult life.

Given all this, it should not be surprising that to 51 percent of Eudora, the possibility that Lottie had produced a powerful potion (even one that did not work as originally intended) was not proof that she was unfit to dispense medical advice, but, on the contrary, showed evidence of remarkable knowledge and power that it would be a good idea to consult.

But how to consult it? Access to the Branch family wisdom had always been through the Branch family, and though this access had been greatly increased over the last months, the same methods remained: the introduction through a cousin, the patient ostensibly just dropping by with the cousin for coffee or to get a knitting pattern or some such thing, and then conversation kind of working around to the clicking sound in the patient's knee in an organic and circuitous way.

None of this was available to the 51 percent of Eudora now inclined to consult Lottie Dougal. And since Mark Ramirez, Lottie's assistant, flatly refused to have anything to do with broaching the subject, saying his relationship to his employer was purely professional and he intended to keep it that way, the 51 percent had no clear idea how to proceed. So, in the long weeks before Oscar Burgos came across Lottie crying on her back porch, there came a slack period in our heroine's medical duties, which left her time to reflect.

Now, entrepreneurial spirits such as Lottie Dougal are not inclined to mope. Lottie had been regularly taking her Saint-John's-wort and had been attending confession and communion, even going to a few six o'clock Masses. She had taken an interest in others, until her family begged her to take an interest in herself a little more. They didn't want any more babysitting or soup. She had even helped Zadie Gross pick out her around-the-world cruise, going so far as helping her to choose clothing and pack and then driving Zadie to the airport. She arranged flowers out at the nursing home and put such new energy into her business that two large printing concerns in the city were beginning to have unkind thoughts about Dougal's Stationery Supplies. Still, there came times when Lottie had to sit and think about her romantic situation and what she could do to make it better.

And the answer came again and again that she could do nothing.

Now that the doctor was more like himself, Lottie was able to look at him. She had not been able to look at him during the lunar cycle of the potion, because the man she thought of as the doctor had not been there. It was as though the potion had made him into someone else and she could not look at the thing she had made out of what the doctor had been. Now that Angela had to call, in her soft, lilting voice, which barely concealed the needles of steel inside it, "Jim, darling, don't go out in your shirtsleeves, my love, wear your suit jacket," and "It will go on better if you roll down your sleeves and do your cuffs up properly," and "Just let me rub over your shoes with this magic sponge. Look! They shine so nicely then and it's so easy to do if you only remember," now that the doctor slumped down the street in his old way, wearing his natty Italian suits with the jacket flapping and absentmindedly pulling his tie loose and unbuttoning his top button, Lottie could look at him again.

And it was better and worse. Better, because the man she loved had not been eliminated by her mad work of the dark February nights. And worse, because he could never be hers again.

Just about this time, little Stevie Wiseman (a small but muscled Lutheran boy going prematurely bald at eighteen, who had both unnaturally accurate hand-eye coordination and the ability to jump like a flea and was thus the mainstay of the Eudora Cyclones basketball team) hurt his ankle three weeks away from the state championships. His mother and his coach were unimpressed with Lottie's poultice and her advice to let it rest and give it time to heal.

They hustled Stevie to the doctor's office so quickly they nearly made scorch marks on the sidewalk, and the doctor did what he could with elastic bandages and anti-inflammatories, ensuring that the team made it through to the semifinals, where they lost to an inner-city academy in a spectacular fashion, with many nails bitten to the quick in overtime.

This was just one week after Clement McAllister's announcement at the Lady Day Steering Committee meeting, and the official boycott of the doctor's services was henceforth officially over.

Time was hanging so heavily on Lottie Dougal's hands that she began to try to teach her cat tricks, which meant the cat started to spend its evenings away, going out through the flap at sundown and coming home only when Lottie was asleep.

Lottie's house gleamed and the freezer was full of soup and bread. The ground was too hard to garden, and neither television, the Internet, nor her library books provided enough active stimulation to remove her heartache from the forefront of her mind. The Walker clan, including her sister, feeling guilty about pushing her away, dropped by occasionally and found her restlessly prowling the living room, "distracted," Pattie said, "and touchy."

Once or twice a week Lottie got into the car and drove, nobody knew where, but she was gone a long time. Sometimes, several walkers-of-dogs reported, she moved furniture around late at night or cried. One night Chuck dropped by after work, having seen the light on and wondering if she needed anything. From her reaction, it was clear that if she did need anything, she didn't need it from Chuck.

Lottie Dougal grieved.

Also during this time Father Gaskin preached a homily called "Witchcraft: Let He Among Us Who Is Innocent Cast the First Stone." It was an interesting argument, which basically said that anytime you try to influence another person to do or be what you want them to do or be for your own convenience and earthly ends, you are practicing witchcraft. He also said that anytime you do this, you are guaranteed to come to grief because the only way to be happy in our relationships is to follow the Golden Rule Jesus gave to us. He also said that we are all only human and that when we fail to follow the Golden Rule, our fellow men and women should forgive us as we hope God forgives us for all of our sins. The word *manipulation* came into it quite a bit.

When Father Gaskin announced his topic, many glances toward Lottie Dougal's lovely, stricken face were stolen. The doctor and Angela were spending the weekend with his cousins in the city, so she had no competition for attention. But as the sermon wore on, and wives and girlfriends began to examine their consciences, this attention fell away. Men, too, thought about how they'd worked overtime to get out of mowing the lawn, and boys thought of all the various ploys they had used to persuade their girlfriends in the backs of cars and the balcony of the Eudora Empire Cinema.

That week, Lottie Dougal was overwhelmed with invitations to dinner and to excursions to the multiplex. Men offered to come over and rototill her garden. Whole families asked if she'd like to go to the mall, to the city cathedral, to the Wild West theme park. She proved to be an untroublesome guest, silent except around the children, still as powerful and energetic as ever, but quieter, less bouncy, less there.

It was unsettling, like having the ghost of Lottie Dougal at your family outing. Less work than the actual thing had been, but oddly unsatisfying. So after this flurry of guilty inclusion, Lottie Dougal was once more left to her grieving.

Now, as we have seen, Angela Emery was having more luck training the doctor than Lottie'd had training the cat. Doc Emery was made to run errands—fetch donuts every morning, collect parcels, even buy his wife's sanitary supplies from the Maple Leaf Pharmacy. He always had to wear a suit and those black shoes that looked like they hurt him and he was forced to go get his hair cut at ridiculous intervals just, Eudora started to think, because she wanted to see if she could make him.

And she could. She could make him do just about anything. Which she proved one morning when Lucy McAllister, his last patient before lunch (she'd come for something to help her sleep), was writing out her check. Angela looked up from her desk, Lucy reported, and said, smiling sweetly, "You know, darling, we're just about out of window envelopes. Would you please go to Dougal's and buy a box for me?"

Lucy said the doctor looked like he'd been slapped with a wet fish (something Lucy wanted to do at the time, for he'd refused to prescribe any sleeping pills and only gave her advice about over-the-counter remedies, which later Lucy appreciated but at the time didn't because she was simply driven to distraction by Clement's snoring). He said, "Dougal's?" as if he'd never heard of it.

And Angela said, smiling once again, "You know, that funny little stationer's. I *think* they'll have window envelopes, but they might have never even heard of them!"

The doctor said, "Don't you think we'll get a better price if we get them this weekend when we're in the city?" as he nervously twisted his tie.

But Angela said, with a pout, "Oh, if you can't do it, then I'll have to. I'll just leave the phones and . . ."

And so the doctor left with Lucy McAllister, holding the door open for her, so she walked under his arm and heard him muttering to himself something about "insensitive."

Mark had already gone on his lunch break but had come back because he'd left his wallet in his jacket, so he was in the back room when the doctor walked in. There was such a pause between the tinkle of the bell above the door and anyone saying anything that he peered out to see who it was.

The doctor was just standing there and Lottie was just sitting there. They were looking at each other. Then the doctor said, "I need some of those envelopes with windows in them."

And Lottie said, "Sure."

Mark put his wallet back in his jacket pocket so that he could get it out again when Lottie came through, but it was a waste of time, he said; he could have had a purple elephant in his hand and Lottie wouldn't have noticed. She went right to the shelf where the envelopes were, picked up a box, and walked out again, and didn't even seem to register Mark was there.

She put the envelopes on the counter and said, "I'll put it on your account."

And the doctor said, "All right. Thank you."

She said, "You're welcome," and then blushed, and then the doctor blushed and kind of stumbled, turning around. It took him a couple of goes at the doorknob to get out.

You should have seen the way Mark did the expressions over at Mayan Memories to really appreciate the pathos of the scene. It was heartrending.

When Mark came back from lunch, Lottie was still sitting in the same exact position she'd been in when he left, and when Mark reminded her that it was her turn to go to lunch while he looked after the shop (their sales appointments being some-what thin on the ground that day), she just kind of mumbled she wasn't hungry.

This was the last week of Lent; in fact, it was the Wednesday before Holy Thursday. Most of the Easter cards had already been sold and there were big gaps in the display, so Mark had decided to move them together a bit tighter and spread out birthdays a bit more even if Lottie didn't want the Mother's Day cards to go out before Easter Monday. So again, he was right on the spot when the action happened.

About an hour and a half after the doctor had left, Angela Emery came into the shop, her heels tapping the pavement so briskly you could have heard them a mile away. The bell jangled fiercely as she thrust open the door and slammed the envelopes onto the counter. She said to Lottie, "My stupid husband, he got the wrong size. We need the ones you just fold the paper once."

Lottie's face, so white the past weeks, grew two pink spots high on her cheeks. Without saying a word, she took the box and disappeared into the storeroom, coming back with the others, which she slid across to the doctor's wife. Angela smiled sweetly. She said, "Sometimes he gets it wrong at first, but you know he always gets the right thing in the end."

Lottie's eyes narrowed. She said, "I wouldn't call the doctor stupid . . . despite recent evidence."

Angela tossed her glossy black hair and laughed, showing her strong white teeth. She said, "Of course you wouldn't, Miss Dougal. He's not *your* husband, after all." She then laughed gaily and left the shop, leaving Lottie's chest heaving and her face glowing with rage.

Lottie looked at Mark, and Mark looked at Lottie. He said, "She's a real bitch, that one."

And Lottie said, "Language, Mark." But her voice didn't sound like she was scolding him. Their eyes met for a moment and no further words were necessary.

For the record, Lottie Dougal did not at any time during the following events consult *Herbal Lore for Cures and Curses*. We know this because

Pattie Walker had placed one of her niece May's fine baby hairs, so light blond as to be nearly invisible, in such a way that if it had been opened, Pattie would have known. Pattie later checked and would swear on her mother's grave that no monkey business had occurred, and (except for a few disgruntled souls who always believed the worst of anybody) Eudora believed her, putting the subsequent events down to Lottie's inherent personal power and the will of God.

For if Angela Requena Emery was like a wolf, with her strong white teeth and implacable eye, she was also like a wolf in that she could smell weakness. She might not know exactly what had happened between the doctor and Lottie, but she had more than an inkling of the general outline. After all, a man does not usually come to a woman's bedroom for the first time, having met her only hours before, with an engagement ring in his coat pocket. And in her general program of establishing dominion in her home, the doctor's practice, and Eudora in general, she began dropping into the stationery shop quite frequently.

If Angela was a wolf, the doctor was a dog. More and more those days, he seemed like a dog that had been beaten. If he'd had a tail, it would have been between his legs. He even flinched at loud noises, and had developed a nervous habit of running one hand over his face, just like a nervous dog licks its paw.

Lottie was a dog, too. But Lottie was not a beaten dog. She had been a sleeping dog, and Angela should have let her lie.

They tell us that all tragedy contains inevitable consequences of a character's actions, and that the character finds it too hard to choose to do things differently—they are compelled to act through a defect of their personality. We call this their fatal flaw. Angela's fatal flaw was that she didn't leave things the way they were. She had to be top dog.

Who knows what went on in that woman's mind? She had a mother and two brothers—that much we later learned when the tragic events had all played themselves out and she was taken away just as suddenly as she came. But Eudora never really saw them to speak to. The doctor later confessed he hardly knew her, and if he didn't, no one else could. The woman hardly left her house, except to shop in the city.

She didn't cook—the doctor did. She didn't sew—she even bought ready-made curtains. She could drive but seldom did. She read novels sometimes but didn't get them from the library. After dinner she would smoke one thin, black cigar with a glass of sherry. She was sent the cigars and the sherry by mail. She looked at movies with the doctor but, he said later, never really seemed to see them. She was lost in private thoughts of her own. He said that if she had turned out to be a bank robber on the run, or an alien from outer space, it wouldn't have really surprised him. Every day he wondered why she was there, and every night he wondered why she wanted him so much.

For, from hints dropped here and there, we have learned that the woman was insatiable. At first the doctor had thanked his lucky stars for this but then, as the weeks and months of it wore on, had grown exhausted and reluctant. This knowledge was built on a few things the doctor had said not long after the whole thing ended, a few things his mother had said on what was to be a long visit, and a few things Pattie Walker had said one night to Clarissa Engel. None of these minor indiscretions would have been terribly informative on their own, but taken as a whole, they painted a powerful and accurate picture of the doctor's home life with Angela Requena.

So Angela's fatal flaw was not knowing when to quit.

If she had been content with the doctor's submission and Lottie's grief, this account would be so thin as to be unpublishable. But, unluckily for her, she was far from contented with how the doctor looked at Lottie and how Lottie looked at the doctor, and this discontent spawned the actions that led to the subsequent tragedy.

If Angela Requena had not come into Dougal's Stationery Supplies on Wednesday of Holy Week, Lottie Dougal would not have gone to too much trouble with her Easter ensemble. A jolly little suit and a pillbox hat would have done to show she was in the spirit of the occasion, and, in fact, just such an outfit had already been mentally selected. But this is not what Lottie wore.

Angela wore the same polished heels, sheer stockings, black dress, and mantilla as usual, but with a lilac jacket in light wool instead of the cashmere that had become her trademark. Lottie wore a yellow shirtwaist dress with a full skirt, the bottom of the skirt imprinted some six inches deep with a muted pattern of jonquils. The bodice was fitted, the collar sharp, and the skirt wide. The dress was accessorized by a cream patent-leather belt that emphasized Lottie's slender waist and went perfectly with her shoes. A filmy confection of cream straw and yellow chiffon adorned her upswept curls. The collar on the shirtwaist was up in the back, and a little cashmere cardigan in the same green as the jonquil pattern covered Lottie's shoulders and arms.

Lottie looked so fresh and sweet, it was like eating ice cream to see her. Her skin glowed with the ferocity of a hundred Branch family facial recipes. Her hair radiated health and henna from beneath her demure hat. She looked young and sweet and rural, and in contrast Angela seemed older, much older, and her polish so mechanical and contrived as to be sinister. When the doctor saw Lottie Dougal, he nearly fell over backward.

When Angela saw her, she narrowed her eyes. For Angela, in common with the rest of the congregation, recognized the demure dress for what it was.

It was a declaration of war.

From Easter Sunday all the way to the third Saturday in May (which was Art in the Park and its associated Sidewalk Sale) the doctor's predicament was clear to everyone who saw him. Mark Ramirez, whose public profile rose considerably during this period, as he was the source of much on-the-spot reportage, put it extremely well when he said, "Miss Dougal has the doctor's heart, but Angela has him by the *cojones*." It is interesting to note that a certain amount of Spanish had become acceptable by this time, and this word in particular was a euphemism useful to the English-speakers of the town. Mark's sentence was repeated frequently but the word was never translated.

On Easter Monday Oscar Burgos was on his way home from the quarry. He was walking the long way, through the neighborhoods on the west side of Main Street, just for a change, because the weather was nice. He was humming a little to himself and in a cheerful mood, even though he had been working compulsory overtime. When you worked for the quarry, you either got resolutely cheerful or bitter, and Oscar had chosen the former. It was the first really nice night, and the banks of daffodils that adorned the lawns of the town's oldest residential area were nodding in the gentle spring breeze. The moon was high and round. And someone was crying.

Crying, not like you do when you do so habitually, not a sob and a sniff here and there, but crying like you do when something has happened. And Oscar, being Oscar, walked toward the sound of the crying instead of away from it to find Lottie Dougal sitting on her back porch, wrapped up in a quilt over a white cotton nightgown and sobbing as if she'd just heard bad news.

Oscar had eight aunts, three sisters, four daughters, and a wife of twenty-three years. He walked up onto the porch, sat down by Lottie, and put his arm around her shoulders. Lottie turned her keening face into his arm and sobbed even harder. He said, "Miz Dougal, do you want to talk about it?"

Lottie wailed, "I can't," which actually sounded more like, "I caaaaaaaaaaaaaaaaaaaaaaaaaan't."

And then she cried a little harder. Oscar put his lunch box down on the porch and used his free hand to pat her back. He said, "Is it the doctor?"

Lottie nodded into the arm. And then she sat up and wiped her face. She said, "It's not just that. If I had something to do . . . something to take my mind off it. But I just sit here, night after night. I can't just sit here night after night, Oscar. I'll go out of my mind."

Which is when Oscar, hesitantly at first, out-lined the medical needs of the Mexican American community and Lottie, hesitantly at first, agreed to minister to their needs if they wanted to give her a try.

Angela became incensed about ten days later. This was just at the same time she became con-vinced of the reason her Spanish-language skills were not in as great demand on the telephone as they had been previously. That they were not in as great demand she had noticed some four days before, when the doctor himself said something to her about it and about the pale complexions of his patients. This was after Stevie Wiseman's remark-able recovery, ensuring the Cyclones' subsequent respectable showing at the state basketball tourna-ment. The doctor was enjoying a great deal of sup-port from the part of the Eudoran community that had previously participated in the official boycott. He didn't see the paleness of the practice as a problem; he just noticed it. And because he noticed it, he noticed that he could probably deal with any phone calls and Angela herself could go fetch the donuts.

And it was this, this unprecedented rebellion on the part of the doctor, that had made Angela certain that Lottie Dougal was at the bottom of it somehow. One night Angela slipped from the mar-ital bed in the luxurious Main Street apartment (doubtless leaving the doctor spent and exhausted), showered, dressed herself in sweat clothes no one suspected she possessed, and went to look at the small house Lottie Dougal had inherited from her father. What she saw confirmed her worst suspicions. The front room had two forms visible against the curtains, and one of the forms was taking the other's pulse. The back porch had acquired additional seating and every one of the wicker chairs and swings was full of what Angela clearly thought of as *her* patients, one with Lottie Dougal's obnoxious tomcat on his lap.

We are indebted to the reporting of Mark Ramirez for the following account of what happened when Angela came into the stationery shop the next day.

"I need to order another box of invoices."

Lottie made a note in her notebook. "Fine," she said. "Continuing the numbering?"

"Yes, of course."

"I should get them by Friday, Tuesday at the latest. Will you be all right until then?"

You need to see Mark doing this to get the drama, the way he narrows his eyes to do Angela and widens them innocently to do Lottie. And the accents. He's really good at the accents.

"Oh, we should be, though business is good," Angela replied. A pause and then, "Though not as good as it could be."

"Oh?" Lottie blushed up to her hairline in one telling whoosh of color.

Angela leaned forward, a wolf smelling blood. "Yes," Angela said, "it seems some of our patients are going elsewhere. You don't know of any other licensed physician in the area, do you?" From Mark's rendition, the word *licensed* was heavily emphasized.

Lottie seemed unable to speak and only shook her head.

"Hmmm," Angela growled. "I just wondered." She made as if to go but then turned back.

Lottie, who had collapsed onto the stool, drew herself back up.

"You know," Angela said, "a person could get into a lot of trouble practicing medicine without a license. If"—and here Mark's rendition of her smile is truly chilling—"anyone were to tell the authorities."

The bell tinkled and finally Angela was gone.

Lottie looked at Mark and Mark looked at Lottie. They didn't say anything.

The bell jingled again. It was old Mrs. Requena. She had cancer bad but was still driving herself around, one of those iron-willed ladies you don't get so much of anymore. She was engaged in a battle with chemotherapy at the moment and wasn't enjoying her food. Lottie had made a soothing syrup for her stomach. She had the bottle under the counter and automatically drew it out when Mrs. Requena came in. But then she looked at it, Mark said, just for a second, just looked at it and seemed to think about it and then looked at Mrs. Requena again. Once she did that, Mark said, she didn't seem to think about it anymore. She just gave the bottle to Mrs. Requena and told her she hoped it worked. And then she told Mark she had to do something in the city, so she was going to leave early that night. Could he close up?

Now, when Lottie and Oscar had their talk, Lottie had said that she could see people any nights but Tuesday and Sunday, and Oscar had wondered about Tuesday but understood about Sunday, or at least thought he did. He just wondered a little, you know, and then it went out of his mind.

Maria Lopez, however, was consumed with curiosity about the Tuesdays, and in hopes of finding more information mentioned something of this casually to Pattie Walker, who had come in for an early lunch.

Now Pattie had, the night before, brought over a tray of Bonnie Butter Sunshine Cupcakes for Lottie's delectation and had been aghast upon seeing a large group of Chicanos on her sister's back porch. Pattie had tried to confront her sister about why so many people (and it just so happened that on this night men made up the chief gender component of Lottie's patient base) were sitting outside her bedroom door, but had got just exactly nowhere in this confrontation, leaving as ignorantly as she had arrived.

This drove her right up the wall. So Pattie had come on purpose to talk to Maria Lopez and try to get the sense out of her she couldn't get out of her sister. Maria's casual mentioning of Lottie being busy every Tuesday night unleashed a veritable storm of confidences both ways.

Pattie was flabbergasted to learn that Lottie's new patient base walked right through her bedroom to consult in her living room and that she'd mixed up healing herbal baths for two patients in her own bathtub. "But they're . . . ," she gasped. And then she paused. Now, this is an important pause. You might say that a large proportion of the current racial harmony that Eudora enjoys depended largely on this pause. The great friendship that was to ensue between Pattie Walker and Maria Lopez certainly did.

"They're . . . ," Pattie Walker said, and the future held its breath. The moment stretched, and everything became noticeable: the narrowing of Maria's eyes, the increasing rigidity of Linda Bustamonte's listening back. "They're *strangers,*" Pattie finished, wailing the last word in anguish that had as much to do with her own internal sense of ethical pressure as the deeply upsetting situation of her sister.

Maria and Linda relaxed, and Maria told Pattie everything she knew, which was a considerable amount.

The worst of this was that a few young men who

had grown enamored of Miss Dougal had decided to come and complain of things that would require Lottie to touch their naked chests. Lottie had done so and only laughed at them, though Mark Ramirez had subsequently spoken quietly and firmly to the young men in question and it would not happen again. Still, the knowledge that it had happened at all made Pattie Walker nearly swoon in horror.

Maria found it intriguing to know that Lottie was driving into the city for night classes on Tuesdays, that she had been doing so for eight weeks, and that Pattie had not been able to determine what the class was, though it must not be Spanish, Quilting, or Fun with Watercolors because Lottie could have done any of those in town at the Arts Center.

Pattie and Maria talked about what a lovely person Lottie was and how nice it was to have a sister you really liked. And then they talked about how difficult Lottie was to get to know really well and how even if you liked her, even if you loved her, you were always at arm's length. And then they talked about how, in a situation like that, you needed all the help you could get to make sure your sister wasn't doing anything stupid. A compact was thus made and sealed. This compact resulted in greater community coherence of information about Lottie Dougal's actions and a life-long friendship between Pattie Walker and Maria

Lopez (Pattie and Phil became godparents to the first Lopez boy, some three years later). This relationship proved vital in the mayoral elections, which, though they could not know it at the time, loomed before them like a black cloud of controversy.

Many women and quite a few men would droop under Lottie Dougal's workload. But she seemed to thrive on it. The more she cured at night, the more confident she was during the day. One of the large printing concerns in the city sent a newly minted vice president out to meet with her. She took him to lunch at Mayan Memories, and he was so enchanted by her hair and eyes and grasp of the importance of watching your margins in bidding for large printing projects that he nearly propositioned her over the coffee.

It was a warm spring and he appeared the following Saturday afternoon to play tennis with Lottie on the municipal courts by the library. His name was Dennis, and he was blond and muscled and tanned from skiing. He made Lottie laugh. While they were using the water fountain in the library, Artie Walker heard him ask Lottie if she'd come out for a drink after her class on Tuesday and she said yes. Pattie, who learned about this when Artie stopped by ostensibly to borrow a tool from Phil but actually to impart this information, was hopeful about this turn of events, as was Maria Lopez, who had closely supervised the initial lunch and felt there was something there.

For all of her friends felt that Lottie should just get on with life and forget about the doctor. He was married, for better or worse (as they got to know Angela, they realized it was probably for worse), and there was nothing to be done about it. If it had been a sin to administer the potion, if the whole marriage was the result of sin, it did not mean that divorce was any more of an option or would be any less messy. It was the doctor you had to feel sorry for, but then, Eudora felt, that's what you get when you don't do as you should. If he'd pulled a ring out of his pocket at the Snow Ball, none of it would have happened.

A week or so later, Dennis had once again called upon Lottie in his official capacity to begin a tentative outline of business-to-business cooperation methods and then had taken her to lunch again to outline a little less tentatively methods for personal cooperation. The doctor had walked in to get some lunch to go for himself and Angela and had seen Lottie laughing at something Dennis had said and had also seen how broad Dennis's shoulders were and how he was leaning forward in the booth and flexing his chiseled jaw with confidence and a kind of predatory intent. The doctor had gone kind of white and stopped talking in the middle of the ordering and just stared as if he'd forgotten what he was doing. Then he had walked out again only to have to walk back in and try to order even though he was clearly terribly upset, and you had to feel for the guy. And if you noticed, as Maria did, that Lottie stopped laughing and looked rather thoughtful all of a sudden and said, "Oh, nothing," when Dennis asked her what was wrong, her eyes dull and fixed on the salt shaker, the whole thing seemed a shame.

Then there was the moment that Maria missed but Linda caught and told her about when they were sitting down on their break, when the doctor's eyes met Lottie's for a moment as he pulled the door closed behind him, the takeout boxes in his other hand, the way they looked through the glass at each other just for a second . . . Linda couldn't explain it but pressed her hands to her heart and sighed.

Maria sighed, and Pattie sighed when she heard about it on the telephone. She said, "This Dennis is a real catch and she's going to let him slip through her fingers, mooning over Doc Emery."

Maria clucked her tongue, which Pattie already, in the infancy of their friendship, understood to mean that Maria hoped not but feared so. That was because they were *simpatico,* Maria said on Sunday night when she was drinking white wine with Pattie in the Walker kitchen. They then grieved that Maria had been invisible when Pattie underwent her high school years. How this had been so, Pattie was unable to determine, as when they opened Pattie's high school yearbook, there was Maria's lovely face, beaming out on the same page, a small class having the *B*'s and *D*'s in fairly close proximity. What was even more tragic was that Maria had also failed to notice Pattie, even though Pattie's organizational abilities had made her class secretary. Thus both had endured the trials of Eudora High without the comfort of a best friend, which in retrospect, and with two bottles of chardonnay, was a tragedy as well as a mystery. And why Phil was unable to take this seriously and insisted on driving Maria home was another mystery until the following day, when pounding headaches and dry mouths made the latter clear.

Now Lottie had been absent both Tuesday and Wednesday night the week before Ben Nichols and Odie Marsh came to arrest her. Nobody knew where she was, but she had put a small notice on her back porch Wednesday to say she could not see anyone until the following day, and the Subaru was gone from in front of the garage, which served as her *farmacia.*

She was out on business appointments for much of Thursday morning and, because she was in meetings, had her cell phone switched off. Mark Ramirez had been trying to call. Ben and Odie had already been once to the stationery shop, looking for Lottie, and then lingering over their coffee and donuts at the bakery's sole table an unusual length of time, causing the other regulars no little inconvenience. Mark observed it all from the front windows of the shop and made the decision to warn his employer. As he had been present when Angela made her threat, and also knew that many members of that portion of Eudora who were currently disenchanted with the doctor's services were still consulting Lottie Dougal, he had no trouble understanding the motives behind Ben and Odie's inordinate lingering and, after a brief struggle with his conscience, decided to interfere in the workings of the law by calling Lottie's cell, but it had been in vain.

Lottie came breezing down the street just like she always did, and Ben and Odie finally stood up and bused their table, Ben using an extra napkin to get some Bavarian cream out of his mustache, which Odie had just noticed and warned him about. It all seemed to happen in slow motion to Mark, who felt kind of helpless at that point, kind of trapped behind the counter there just watching it all happen like it was a movie or a bad dream.

Lottie was hanging up her coat when the bell tinkled. Mark was trying to warn her, but just like in a bad dream, the words weren't coming out of his mouth, and then she turned around and Ben and Odie were walking into the shop.

She said, "Hi, guys. I've been wondering when you'd show up." Then she reached down and got her briefcase off the floor and put it on the counter and clicked the locks.

Ben's hand flickered to his gun. He said, "Lottie Dougal, we have received a complaint. Have you been giving medical advice to people unrelated to you?"

Lottie laughed. She said, "You know I have, Ben. I gave Molly that raspberry leaf tea to drink before she had your Tommy. How is Tommy? Does he like it at Candy Cane Day Care? It's hard to get in there. I heard Molly got on the list when she saw the first ultrasound."

At this point, Odie Marsh took over. "Lottie, there's been an official complaint that you've been practicing medicine without a license. I'm afraid we're going to have to ask you to come down to the courthouse with us so we can book you."

Lottie started to open the briefcase. Ben said, "Now, Lottie, don't do anything wild."

Odie said, "Step away from the briefcase, Miss Dougal." His gun had appeared in his hand.

Mark thought it was all going horribly wrong and that someone was bound to get hurt. He was still frozen behind the cash register, so close to Lottie that he would be covered in her blood if Odie pulled the trigger. He said, "Calm down! Everybody just calm down!" in such an agitated squeak that he was ashamed of it later.

Lottie just laughed. She said, "Okay, Odie, you take it out of the briefcase. I'll put my hands in the air." Which she then did. Odie put his gun down on the counter and peered into the case. There were files, notebooks, calculators, and samples stuffed inside. He peered at it all doubtfully. Lottie said, "It's that cardboard envelope, the white one."

Ben said, "This one?" and pulled it out of the pile. Odie put his gun back in its holster but left the strap undone. Mark said the tension got a little lighter then but that he still felt like he needed to go to the bathroom.

Lottie said, "If you go ahead and open that, Ben, you'll save us all a long drive."

Ben looked at Odie, and Odie nodded. He pulled the envelope open and slid out a large, rectangular piece of thick paper, embossed with several seals and signatures and bearing a deep border of a rainbow-tinted interlocking bird pattern. "Charlottte Dougal, Herbal Practitioner," he read slowly, sounding out the last two words. Then, Mark said, he read out a lot of letters.

"That's the licensing organization," Lottie said. "Well respected."

Ben and Odie stared at the document a little longer, and then Lottie asked, "Can I put my hands down now?"

"Yeah," Odie said distractedly.

Lottie came around the counter and looked at the license with Ben and Odie. "Pretty, isn't it?" she said. "I'll make you a color photocopy so you can show the lieutenant, but you're still going to miss a lot of the detail on the pattern."

Over the sound of the Konica, she said, "I was going to night classes in the city, but I knew more than the instructor. She's a great gal, though, and got me to take the test to become licensed. It took her four years to get that for herself."

She brought the copy back and gave it to Odie, saying to Mark, "Give him some kind of folder to carry that in, will you, please?"

And then she put her certificate back in the white cardboard envelope, saying, "Usually they mail them, but I had a feeling you guys might come by one of these days, so I drove in last night and picked it up myself."

Odie opened the folder and looked at the color photocopy again.

Lottie said, "Now, that doesn't let me prescribe drugs or do any surgery or anything like that." Odie nodded thoughtfully. "It just lets me do what I've always done, but kind of protects me, in case someone was to get nasty."

The name Angela was in everybody's mind, Mark said, as clear as if it had been written in the air above their heads.

"And it lets me in on the group malpractice insurance plan."

Odie sniffed. He said, "Well, that seems to be in order, Lottie. We'll let you know if we need anything else."

And Lottie said, "You do that, guys. You know where I am."

And Ben said, "Yeah, Tommy likes it a lot over at Candy Cane. They sure teach them a lot of stuff real early. He's smart as a whip."

Lottie said, "Takes after his daddy," and Ben blushed.

Odie said, "Come on, Ben, let's go do some real work," more gruffly than he usually did, no doubt because he was embarrassed about pulling his gun out of the holster. And Ben grinned at Lottie and Mark and followed Odie to the car.

From the window of the stationery shop, Mark and Lottie could see Angela Requena Emery lingering in front of the bakery door by where the sheriff's patrol car was parked and metered. Angela looked sharply at Odie and Ben when she saw that Lottie had not accompanied them across the street. From the window, it was impossible to tell exactly what she said to Odie, but from the way Odie kind of stiffened up it seemed pretty likely she was questioning him about how he performed his duties.

Odie didn't say much to her, but as she stared at the car while Odie backed it expertly out of its spot, Ben's mischievousness caused him to open the folder and press the copy of the certificate to the car window. If Odie paused a fraction longer than he usually did before commencing forward locomotion in order to allow Angela plenty of time to read the unfamiliar wording before reprimanding Ben for this indiscretion, no one could blame him, especially Mark Ramirez, who nearly wet his pants laughing at the expression on Angela's face.

When Mark emerged from the bathroom to congratulate his employer, Lottie shook her head. She said, "I think I've made an enemy."

Mark said, "You didn't make no enemy. She made an enemy out of herself. She's like that."

But Lottie didn't listen. She said, "Love thy enemy as thyself," and sat down, putting her elbow on her knee and resting her chin in her hand. "Really, Mark, what would it be like to come into this town without any friends or family?"

Mark began to outline the way Angela had treated the Requenas, but Lottie held up a hand. "I don't want to hear that kind of talk, Mark. We're lucky, you and me, we were born here. We have our place, our work. Angela doesn't have any of that. No wonder she's so edgy."

They were silent for a moment, Mark because he really thought, he said, that his employer was kidding, that she was going to bust out laughing.

But she seemed serious. She said, "I know. I'll invite her to go to the movies with me and Pattie. What she needs is some friends."

Which just shows you something, Mark said on his lunch break to Maria Lopez (who had taken to giving him a considerable discount ostensibly for loyalty but actually for the news he brought so regularly), but what it was, neither of them could determine. Did it show that Lottie Dougal was a kind and generous soul? Or only that she had the capacity to lay schemes more subtle and far-sighted than anyone else could imagine?

Tactfully, Maria, when reporting to Pattie Walker, put this question to the one person who should know. She said, "You know, sometimes you just don't know what's going on in a person's head. If your sister's really that nice, she should be a saint or something." There followed a long pause.

Finally Pattie sighed down the phone line. She said, "Yeah, well. I don't know. Sometimes I think . . . ," and left it at that.

The fact is, nobody knew why Lottie Dougal invited Angela Emery to the movies with herself and her sister. And nobody knew why Angela came. But come she did, wearing jeans and penny loafers and with a lemon-colored cashmere sweater tied around the neck of one of the doctor's white oxford-cloth shirts. Pattie said that she thought it was going to be uncomfortable, but Angela had been very chatty and had seemed to have a good time and ate popcorn like anybody else would.

For two weeks, Angela and Lottie did quite a lot together, Lottie's various duties allowing. They went in Lottie's Subaru for a long drive and came back with shopping bags from the outlet mall.

They played two sets of tennis, finding themselves evenly matched. Angela finally won the last point, by which time they were both drenched in sweat and utterly exhausted. Hector Rodriguez, who was waiting for the court, said it was better than Wimbledon.

They had lunch together twice at Mayan Memories and seemed to really enjoy it, laughing and talking like they were old friends. And then they had dinner, Angela and the doctor and Lottie and Dennis.

Pattie and Maria had been speculating mightily during the entire time of this acquaintanceship, and when Linda took the reservation, Maria called Pattie before the ink had even dried in the book. Maria said it made her feel nervous. Pattie said something about playing with fire, but it obviously made her feel nervous, too, because she dropped a whole box of seam rippers onto Becky Lane's foot, and one came out of its protective sheath and embedded itself in the carpet, missing Becky's big toe by a quarter of an inch and really making her jump. Pattie's apology contained an explanation for her clumsiness that included information gleaned from Maria's phone call. And so by the end of the day, every table at Mayan Memories was completely booked for Friday night and fourteen people had been turned down.

There is little that went on that evening that we do not know.

Lottie and Dennis arrived first, and Dennis opened the door for Lottie and helped her off with her jacket, taking it to the coat rack while Lottie slid into the booth. When he slid in after her, he didn't slide in too far and squish her, but he slid in close enough to put his arm along the back of the seat and touch her hair with his hand. She didn't lean into his hand, but she didn't pull away, either, and she smiled at something he said.

Regrettably, the Lane family vehicle had been suffering from starter motor problems, and Becky and Janey arrived a bit later than they had planned, for their reserved table adjacent to Lottie and Dennis, so the record does not show exactly what Dennis said or what Lottie's smile might have meant. In fact, the Lanes ended up walking, nearly jogging, to the restaurant, and once Becky finally did arrive, she was red in the face and panting with the unfamiliar exertion and couldn't even concentrate on the greetings exchanged when the doctor and Angela arrived. These, however, seemed conventional enough from less privileged vantage points.

Becky had recovered by the time they began to study their menus.

Now, the law did not allow Mayan Memories to serve alcohol, but that did not mean alcohol could not be consumed on the premises. Clement McAllister had taken, when he and Lucy came for their Tuesday night dinners, to bringing a small swing-top cooler with a bottle or two of his favorite beverage in long-neck bottles. Those sitting by the door that night had seen the doctor bring in a shopping bag from an unfamiliar city store and had noted that it clinked. When the contents were revealed on the table, there were two bottles of wine, one white and one red, and Lottie, Dennis, and the doctor discussed them for what Becky Lane thought an inordinate amount of time.

There was a moment of silence while they all looked at the menu and then, Becky said, they all started to discuss the food. Angela didn't like anything spicy and stuck with the left-hand side of the menu, ordering a steak and a baked potato with a salad, just as if she was in Sizzler or something. And Lottie said that if she kept eating the pollo mole she was going to start clucking, but every time she came in she just couldn't resist it, it was so good. She'd been meaning to try some other things, but she was just stuck on the mole.

The doctor said the same thing had happened to him and he reckoned, counting lunches and dinners, he'd had it ten times in the last month. He then read out something else and wondered what it was.

Angela started to translate it for him, but then Dennis chipped in and told him all about that particular dish, how it's made and everything. And Lottie asked him how he knew all this and he said he spends a week or so every year in the Yucatán, diving in Cancún.

For the record, it should be noted that Becky Lane felt little sympathy for Dennis from this point on, and when the facts about him were later revealed she was one of the few in town not to be surprised. She said there was just something about the way he talked that made her feel sick, all la-di-da, *I go diving, aren't I special.* And though events were to prove her feelings justified, as the only record of the subsequent conversation (the other neighboring booth, in an uncharacteristic over-sight by Maria Lopez, had been given to Manuel Ramirez, who devoted his entire attention to his meal, only noticing vaguely that the restaurant seemed rather crowded), her prejudice should be declared.

The doctor started talking about travel and saying he wished he'd done more before he started medical school. He talked about how Angela had seen so much of the world and he'd seen so little.

They ordered.

Then Dennis asked Lottie if she'd ever been able to travel much, and Lottie talked about when she was a student in London and used to go to the airport and get ridiculously cheap last-minute deals but never knew where she'd be going. She said she wasn't much good at geography and that once she'd bought four days in St. Moritz thinking it was in the Bahamas, only to find herself in a ski resort with a suitcase full of bikinis.

The men laughed. Angela said she used to ski in St. Moritz quite a lot, and asked Lottie did she know this certain hotel. The way she said the name of it, Becky said, you could tell it was the best in town. Lottie laughed and said she'd gone in there to meet some people for a drink and couldn't even afford a mineral water. That the price of a martini was the same as she was paying per night for her room. The men laughed again.

Becky said she looked over the booth at this point. She could see only Angela's and the doctor's faces. The doctor was smiling at Lottie, and Angela was just kind of watching him. The other three were leaning forward on their elbows, kind of chatting and laughing, but Angela was sitting back. She was smiling, too, but it wasn't like a "aren't we having a good time" smile, Becky said.

The doctor said that pretty soon he might be able to take a couple of weeks off, get someone to cover and go somewhere. By next year, he thought. He asked Dennis what he thought was the best place to start. Dennis said of all the places he'd ever been, he'd most like to go back to Botswana. He said people always thought of Kenya when they thought safari, but Botswana had it all and was so beautiful. And the people were so nice, really nice manners and everything.

Then the doctor said, "What about you, Lottie?"

Lottie took so long to answer, Becky looked over at the booth again, but this time Angela noticed and stared at her so hard that Becky kept her observations on the aural plane for the rest of the meal.

Finally Lottie said, "There was this little town in Cornwall. That's in England, in kind of the far southwest corner, a little sticky-outy bit. It was called Porthleven and had a little harbor for fishing boats. It wasn't much of a town, more of a village, really, and the beach wasn't all that great, it was closed half the time—there's a really wicked undertow—but there was something about it. I think about it all the time."

"Isn't it funny?" the doctor said. "How you can be someplace just for a little while and it kind of stays with you? My uncle took me north of Vancouver once, camping, this lake. I can remember everything about that place—the color of the canoe, the sound the birds made at sunset, the smell of the fire, everything."

Dennis said, "It sounds like a special place. What was the name of it?"

The doctor said, "I can't remember!" and everyone laughed.

They were opening the wine when the doctor said, "Where would you like to go on our first vacation, Angela?"

She said, "I was wondering *when* you might ask

137

me, darling. I think we should go to Barcelona and visit my family."

The doctor said, "Of course . . . hmm . . . Spain."

"Barcelona is a beautiful city," Lottie said.

"Gorgeous," Dennis said.

"You mean I'm the only one at this table who hasn't been to Barcelona?" the doctor said. "Well that settles it. We'll have to go."

"Where does your family live, Angela?"

There followed some discussion about the layout of Barcelona. Becky couldn't really follow as various items of the table setting were used to represent landmarks. Finally, Lottie said, "Isn't that a pretty grand part of town?"

And Dennis said, "That's a really old neighborhood."

Angela didn't say anything, and Becky could hear things being moved back to their rightful places.

"How did you meet?" Dennis asked. "Seeing as the good doctor has done nothing but work for the last ten years."

Lottie hurried to answer. "Angela was a nurse."

"What got you into nursing?" Dennis asked.

Angela said, "Well . . ."

And Dennis said, "I mean, if you're from that part of Barcelona and used to go skiing in St. Moritz . . . it's a bit of a different lifestyle, isn't it?"

But then the food arrived, and everyone but

Becky seemed to forget that Angela hadn't answered.

Becky's own food arrived not too much after this, and she was shortly called upon to assist Janey with spot removal due to an unfortunate collision between the full sleeve of Janey's best silk blouse and a towering pile of guacamole on the summit of Janey's ensalada pescador. Also, Becky had, for the first time, ordered from the right-hand side of the menu, in some kind of daze, she said, not really concentrating on her own meal at all, and had ordered the pollo mole probably because Lottie and the doctor had been talking about it so much. Becky was not, as a rule, given to spicy food, but, distracted from trying to reconcile her duties as mother and diner with her interest in the events at the table behind her, she took a couple of big bites before she really knew what she'd done.

Some four glasses of water later, with a side dish of sour cream provided by Maria to mix in and take the heat off, Becky was once again able to witness the events of that pivotal night.

Well, even though Becky couldn't see her and Angela wasn't saying much, Becky could tell Angela had not appreciated Dennis's uncomfortable questioning. The doctor might not have asked Angela, or even himself, why a girl from a good family was working as a nurse's aide in Seattle General before, but now that Dennis had brought it up, he no doubt would. Becky later said that Dennis had opened up a can of worms that Angela would have rather let lie in the closet. While this was an unfortunate way of phrasing it, everyone understood exactly what she meant.

They were ordering dessert when Dennis said, "Oh, goodness, gang, I'm going to have to scoot. You'll just have to tell me how good the dessert is."

"Are you leaving?" Angela asked, and Becky said the way she asked it made it clear she was delighted to hear the news.

" 'Fraid so. Got an early morning meeting, so I'd better get back to town." Others saw him stand up and give two twenties to Lottie. Becky heard him say, "This ought to cover it, and I'll come back and get my change next week, so don't blow it on bubble gum." He kissed Lottie's cheek and Angela's hand and shook with the doctor. Then he grabbed his jacket and went out the door, whistling.

"What time will he make it back to the city, Jim?" Angela asked.

"Oh, nine, nine-thirty."

Angela chuckled, and Becky said it was an unpleasant sound. "Must be a very early Saturday morning meeting," she said.

"Oh, it is," Lottie said. "And he's got some preparation to do, too."

"Nice guy," the doctor said.

"Yeah, I think he is." Lottie stood up, saying, "Look, I'm going to leave you guys to your dessert, if that's all right." Later, Becky learned that she was blushing.

"Sure," Angela said. "I'll call you about that handbag sale. I think we should go."

"This ought to cover our part of the check."

"It's too much," Angela said. "I'll bring you your change."

Becky said it was like Lottie was trying to get away and Angela was holding her. Lottie said, "Well, it's been great."

And Angela said, "Yes, we'll do it again next time Dennis is in town. Do you know when that will be?"

"I—I'm not sure."

"Well, I'll call you about the sale, anyway."

"Okay." Lottie finally got away to find her jacket and leave the restaurant. She was not whistling.

"What do you think, Jim? Do you want the pie or the ice cream?"

"I'm not hungry."

"Shall we just go home, then, and get to bed early?"

"You know, on second thought, that pie does look good."

At this point, the four glasses of water Becky had consumed pressured her bladder so acutely that she was forced to abandon her observation post and visit the sanitary facilities of Mayan Memories (which, by the way, are very clean and decorated with colorful posters of the many Yucatecan places of interest, thoughtfully laminated so that they can be wiped down periodically with an antibacterial cleaning solution). When Becky came back, the Emerys were gone.

Pattie, getting the lowdown from her and Maria the next day, grew more hopeful that Lottie was putting the doctor behind her and giving Dennis a real go. Maria said there were no secret glances full of longing or anything like that going on that she could see. And as for the blush when Lottie got up to go, well, it's awkward, isn't it, being a fifth wheel?

Pattie put Becky Lane's feelings about Dennis down to jealousy, since Becky had never been farther than Branson, Missouri. Becky did not have the vocabulary to impress upon her boss just how chilling Angela's chuckle had been and how the atmosphere at the table had changed after it. She could not articulate how Angela had seemed to toy with Lottie, keeping her standing in front of the doctor, blushing and awkward. Becky Lane felt it was typical of Pattie not to listen to her, not to try to understand what she was getting at, and she retreated into a bitter silence born not just of this little disappointment but of many remembered and nurtured small grievances. Later she was to remember this and wish she had tried harder.

N ow, Mark Ramirez did not trust Angela Requena Emery one little bit and thought his employer was being entirely too generous by attempting to befriend her. Whenever Angela came into the shop, Mark made it his business to be present at all exchanges, as if he felt that at some point he would be needed to protect Lottie from physical harm. And so we know that Monday morning, Angela came into the shop with Dennis's change, calling playfully, as the bell tinkled, "It's only me!" in a way that, Mark said, made the hair on the back of his neck stand up.

Lottie thanked her as Angela gave her the receipt, some bills, and a few coins. Then Angela said, "You don't want to go to the Mulberry sale, do you?"

And Lottie said, "Well, I really don't need any new bags or anything like that."

Angela patted Lottie's hand and said, "I didn't think you did. I'm going to go with Rachel Emery, Jim's cousin."

Lottie smiled at her and said, "Oh, Rachel's the perfect person to go with. Give her my love."

"Oh, you know Rachel?" Angela asked.

Lottie's smile seemed to fall right off her face, Mark said. She kind of stammered, "Well, Um, I . . . I mean, yes, I know Rachel."

Angela said, "Well, I have to run," and opened the door. Mark could feel Lottie's relief, he said;

you could almost smell how glad Lottie was to see her go. But then Angela turned back. She said, "What's Dennis's last name? I don't know if I heard it."

And Lottie said, "Wheatley. From Wheatley and Brewer." And then she said, "Why?"

But Angela was gone.

Over the next week or so, Pattie Walker had reason to congratulate herself on the way Lottie was behaving. The new courtship was moving along at a pace that was consistent with the kind of thoughtfulness and deliberation a sister liked to see in such matters. In fact, everyone who had taken an interest in Lottie's affairs, by which I mean nearly the whole of the population of Eudora, looked upon the burgeoning relationship between Dennis Wheatley and Lottie Dougal with a sense of proprietary satisfaction. For if Lottie Dougal had flouted local convention before, and suffered for it, she clearly had learned from the experience and now toed the line with a scrupulousness that was pleasant to observe.

Flowers were delivered on Saturday morning to the shop, a nice bouquet in tones of pink and cream. On Tuesday, Lottie's Subaru came back from the city precisely two hours later than usual, which was thought to indicate that she and Dennis had perhaps shared a drink, but nothing more indecorous. Thursday night, Phil and Pattie Walker accompanied Lottie Dougal and Dennis

Wheatley to Chuck's Beer and Bowl, where all but Lottie gave a good account of themselves and Dennis was shown to have true skill in picking up spares.

In short, everything was proceeding nicely.

On Saturday, however, Angela Requena Emery spent time in the library. This event did not go completely unnoticed but wasn't accorded the importance it perhaps should have been by Artie Walker, who didn't even mention it to Phil and Pattie when he, Rosemary, and May came for Sunday lunch. This might be because Angela did in the library something so typically Angela-like that Artie had not thought it threw any new light on what was known of the woman. If she'd, say, checked out an armful of the Lake Poets or made copious notes from the library's fifteen volumes on flower arranging, her visit would have seemed more momentous. But as all she did was read over old accounts of the city paper's society pages, Artie had assumed she was extending her considerable social ambitions, which could not be considered news by anyone who knew Angela Requena Emery. He hadn't even looked at the few prints she made, but had collected her forty cents and put it in the cash drawer on autopilot, while thinking about something else entirely.

So as Artie washed and Lottie put away, forty-five minutes that could have made the subsequent events less painful for Lottie and thus perhaps have tempered her emotional reaction were spent singing hits of the seventies. Often, after the fateful day, Artie reflected that a human life had been lost, and that he could have helped to prevent the loss and instead . . . well, the words "Jeremiah was a bullfrog" ever afterward made him feel sick to his stomach.

Monday was a busy day at the doctor's office. The All-State Marching Band, to which Eudora contributed a bass drum, two trombones, and one tuba, had successfully raised funds (through aggressive sales of chocolate) to travel to Belgium, and the insurers of this cavalcade insisted on a medical examination before the trip. A cornet player, two flutists, and a baton twirler who came from neighboring hamlets also required the doctor's services in this respect. On top of that, there was an outbreak of a nonspecific viral infection at the Candy Cane Day Care and the waiting room was full of harassed parents and unhappy babies as well as anxious musicians. This was all added to the usual Monday morning complement of colds and tummy bugs that had not gotten better over the weekend, and Angela was up to her eyeballs in work.

She walked by Lottie Dougal's house that night, but the back porch was full of the same tummy bugs and colds, only browner. Lottie herself had come back to call in the next patient and later remembered waving and asking Angela if she needed anything, to which Angela had replied with a tight smile that it could wait.

It is important that we get the following story scrupulously correct. Afterward there was much speculation, and even on the day that concerns us, thirteen months later, opinion is divided as to exactly what happened on that fateful Tuesday. What follows is the facts as they are known.

Tuesday at just after eleven-thirty, Angela Emery came into the stationery shop carrying a manila envelope. She asked for Lottie. Mark told her Lottie was at a meeting but would be back at three, and Angela seemed, Mark thought, more disappointed than you would expect. Angela was rude to Mark, asking if he thought he could remember to tell Lottie that Angela would be coming by. Mark had to bite his tongue not to be rude in return and said he would pass on her message. When Maria brought over his lunch, he told her that he thought Angela was up to no good and that Lottie's trying to make a friend out of her was stupid—she'd be better off making friends with a snake. To which Maria replied that whatever Lottie Dougal was, she wasn't stupid.

Much has been made of the atmosphere at the stationer's that afternoon. Some local businesspeople (who had dropped by to ask for reprints of various items) later said that Lottie was in a strange, eldritch mood, that the shop seemed to vibrate with an arcane power. But the fact is, Lottie was running a bit late and didn't get into the shop until three-fifteen, long after the actual time of these visits. She was humming and wore a pink rose in the lapel of her navy suit, greeting Mark with the news that they'd finally landed an order from the pet food factory in Oskaloosa and showing every evidence of the simple joy a girl feels when making a packet of money for the family business.

Mark said that they should celebrate and he'd go over to Margery's for cake if she wouldn't mind putting the coffee on. Lottie said she had to use the bathroom but would get right on it after that. This does not indicate an eldritch atmosphere reeking of strange powers.

Angela came in just as Mark got back from the bakery. He was in the storeroom, washing the mugs and putting the small paper plates with the cake slices on the little plastic tray, when he heard the bell tinkle and Angela's grating call, "It's only me!" He went to the crack in the door and observed their greetings, later remembering noticing and being pleased by the fact that they didn't touch, did not shake hands or embrace or pat each other's arms.

Angela then announced that she had some news. "I've got two things I have to tell you," she said. "One is good and one is bad. Which do you want first?"

Lottie said, "You have bad news? And you want to tell me about it?"

And Angela said, "I think you should know."

There was a pause, Mark recounted, and then Lottie said, "You'd better tell me, then."

Angela took the manila envelope from underneath her arm and slid out two pieces of paper. "This," she said, "is Dennis Wheatley on his wedding day, four years ago." She put this down on the counter and then lined up the other one next to it. "This is Dennis and his wife and their two kids, planting a tree for last year's Earth Day. The baby's dress must have been ruined."

And then, Mark said, Angela smiled, a horrible, satisfied, very happy smile. Lottie's head lifted from the paper and she looked at Angela. She said, "You seem very pleased with yourself, Angela."

And Angela said, "Well, that's probably because of the good news, Lottie, I'm pregnant. I'm going to have the doctor's baby. And we will be together, a little family, forever and ever." Angela leaned forward until her face was nearly up against Lottie's. "I've been so looking forward to telling you," she said. And then she laughed.

Mark could not see his employer's face, but her back grew rigid. She said, "I think you'd better leave, Angela."

Angela laughed again. "Oh," she said, putting on a little frowning face, "what's the matter, Lottie dear? Aren't we *friends* anymore?"

And then she laughed again. Later, Mark considered it was this third laugh that had pushed

Lottie over the edge. He was still holding the mugs and the dish towel and he dropped them, just dropped them onto the linoleum of the storeroom and went to go to Lottie's side, because he felt something was going to happen, felt it so strongly that he didn't even remember he was holding anything in his hands. As it happened, neither of the mugs sustained damage, but it shows that the moment contained explosive emotion, enough to be observed, enough to maybe even be communicated to onlookers.

He walked into the room, but it was too late. Angela had already opened the door and Lottie was already speaking. He was moving, he said, as if he was in one of those terrible dreams where the monster is coming to get you and you just can't seem to connect your brain to your feet. He tried, but he just couldn't get to his employer's side in time.

Still, what really mattered in the end was that he was there to witness exactly what Lottie said and did. There was no colored powder involved, no potion hurled to explode above Angela's head. All these were later inventions. Lucy McAllister and her sister-in-law Nancy heard the last part of Lottie's speech, and Mark heard it all.

It must be said that Lottie delivered the words in a deep alto, vibrating with rage, that carried a good way. She had been doing, she said some months later at a Knights of Columbus barbecue after minding the margarita stand for more hours than was good for a person, deep yogic breaths in an effort to calm herself down, and she delivered the fateful words with full lungs and plenty of power behind them.

Also, at some point in the conversation, Lottie had started crying, and mascara had leached into her right eyeball, causing it to sting and Lottie to close it, using only her left.

And it must be said that Lottie did point the index finger of her left hand, the right being used to support herself by clutching the glass top of the sales counter, something, Mark said, that showed just how out of control she was, because normally Lottie could be in the shop all day and need no recourse to the Windex bottle at closing.

The words were exactly as follows.

"You, pregnant? I don't believe it. The thought of you bearing children is absurd." At this point Angela turned to face her, and Mark said she looked both amused and surprised. "Your womb would explode and you would die from the shock of having to give something to another human being."

Angela left, the bell tinkled, the door shut, and Lottie sat down on the stool and burst into tears. Mark got a box of tissues and, not bothering to wash the mugs again, made them both a cup of coffee.

He didn't know what to say. Lottie stopped

crying, swept the photocopies into the trash can, and finally said, "And just look at the countertop. It's disgusting," reaching for the Windex bottle and a package of Handi Wipes.

Mark said, "I don't even feel like no cake now."

And Lottie said, "That's the worst thing about folks like that. They take so much away from life."

And then Mark asked her where she wanted the Fourth of July decorations display and Lucy and Nancy (who had waited a decent interval to allow Lottie to recover and also to discuss what they had overheard) decided to walk on in. Life in the stationer's went on as normal for the rest of the day.

Which just shows something, Mark said when the full import of the incident was revealed, but he found it hard to put what it showed into words. It was Bill Lopez, who later, having been in receipt of Mark's entire account via his wife, Maria, for some days, said that nobody who thought they'd just killed somebody goes and drinks coffee and plays around with rolls of streamers.

Most of Angela's story was told in the helicopter, where she grew strangely communicative to the doctor. He was distraught and the helicopter was very noisy and he never spoke about it, except to his mother who, being a genial soul, passed on the information later in the Walker house kitchen to Pattie Walker and Maria Lopez over a tray of brownies and coffee laced with

Bailey's Irish Cream. This is hardly the most reliable account in this chronicle, but it is the only one available for this crucial point of our tale.

From what we can gather, Angela started feeling uncomfortable that very night. But as she was never much of a cook at the best of times, and they'd had a dinner that consisted of microwaved Szechuan chicken with microwaved wild rice and oven-warmed spring rolls, she put the feeling of pressure in her lower abdomen down to gas. The doctor was extraordinarily solicitous, and she was being looked after in a way she had not been since they were first married, during that magical moon cycle before the potion wore off. Since she had announced her pregnancy, and the doctor had overcome his initial revulsion, he was behaving with a kindness and thoughtfulness that had previously been missing from their marriage.

The next morning the pain was worse, and Angela said that she knew then there was something dramatically wrong. But she was enjoying the doctor's attentiveness so much, she thought she would just give it another day before mentioning something might be wrong.

She gave it another four. By now, many of the doctor's patients and even the checkout ladies out at Food Barn were treating her with a frosty reserve, and so she knew that word of her exchange with Lottie Dougal had gotten around. She was dreading church on Sunday, dreading it so much that she didn't know if she had meant the doctor to hear her cry of pain from the bathroom or if the pain had actually become so great that she couldn't bear it silently any longer. On the daily event of passing a motion, the feeling of pressure in her abdomen became intense, and that morning it seemed intolerable.

He asked what was wrong, calling through the bathroom door. She replied, "Oh, it's nothing, Jim. Don't worry."

But then she had to face it. The bathroom mirror revealed a red patch on the left-hand side of her abdomen. When Angela put her hand there, it was hot. The small mosaic tiles in the luxury bathroom above Main Street swam together before her eyes. She saw her face, drawn and pale, and tried to apply makeup, but leaning over the sink hurt so much she had to stop. Suddenly, she was over-whelmingly thirsty, and yet she could not bend enough to drink from her hands. She went into the kitchen for a glass, grunting with every step.

Jim Emery was waiting for her. He put a hand on her forehead and pulled down the lower eyelid of one eye. He felt for her pulse. She begged for water. And then he wrenched her robe apart and felt the hot red spot. He said, "Oh, my God, ectopic." And then, "How long have you known?"

Angela saved herself from answering this question by swooning. The doctor carried her to the sofa and then used his telephone. The helicopter was waiting for them at the hospital. The local OB/GYN met the car and briefly examined Angela on the gurney while they ran. "I don't know if she'll last the flight," he said to Jim, thinking Angela wouldn't hear, but she did.

"Have you ever done one before?" Jim asked.

The OB/GYN shook his head. The gurney stopped. "I haven't even observed," Jim said. "We don't have a choice. We fly."

The OB/GYN nodded. "Let's go," he said. Right through the hospital they ran, down the corridors to the back and the helipad. The air ambulance crew was waiting with a saline IV and cool packs.

When the paramedics were done, Jim sat close and took her hand. He bent to hear her say, "I'm dying," she said. "When I'm dead, call my family. The numbers are in the back of my diary."

He said, "Don't be silly. You're going to be fine."

She said, "No. That thing you were all hoping wouldn't happen has happened. I felt it. It feels better somehow, but much worse, too."

Jim lifted the cool pack and saw that the red spot had lightened but grown. Angela watched him. She said, "I've known for a few days it wasn't right." And then she told him why she hadn't told him.

Jim started to cry. He said, "I'm sorry I haven't . . ."

"You don't love me," she said. "It's okay. I don't love you. In my family, we know what makes a good marriage, and it is not love."

And then she gave a little laugh and said something the doctor couldn't catch. He thought at the time it was the noise of the copter that took her words away, even though his ear was an inch from her lips.

She said, "My family's motto is 'We hold on to what is ours.'"

Then she smiled, a ghastly expression that told of the ugliness at the root of her twisted soul. It was at that moment, when all pretense was dropped and he truly saw her, that the doctor began to care for his wife. Pity blew through him like a wind, even harder than the anger and revulsion had blown before.

He took her hand. "You're tough, Angela, and you still stand a chance."

She smiled at him then and said, "Oh, Jim, I know. But only if I wanted to live. And I'm very tired of living."

She closed her eyes and her face slackened. Jim shouted for the ambulance crew, who swarmed between Jim and his wife. They never spoke again.

Jim told his mother that was the closest he'd ever felt to her. And then she was gone.

The whispers began on Monday. Already, rumors (greatly exaggerated) as to what Lottie had said and what was wrong with Angela were spreading. By Tuesday, when the doctor called Marling's Maple Hill Funeral Home to make arrangements, the embellishments were getting out of hand. During the Tuesday lunch service, Mark Ramirez told a crowd of interested parties at Mayan Memories exactly what had been said that fateful afternoon. Lucy McAllister was there for lunch with Nancy and they corroborated his testimony, as they, too, had witnessed the second half of what was already being referred to as "Lottie's curse."

But they might have all saved their breath.

For Eudora, normally so level-headed and making up its collective mind based on sound facts and reasoning, had let itself be carried away by the drama of the situation, and the wilder the tales of arcane powers, the better. In the bright safety of the June sunshine, Eudora dabbled in the gothic.

The affair was constantly discussed. Voices would be lowered and the most horrible things suggested in strange undertones with elongated vowels. Hand gestures, usually rather restrained in the town we chronicle, became expansive. Some people even swayed back and forth from the waist as they discussed Lottie's curse.

Only two things stopped this orgy of the occult: the presence of the doctor and the presence of Lottie Dougal. Though often, and without meaning to, the speakers went on for too long, and were overheard by one or the other. This had the effect of making the newly gothic deeply and horribly ashamed of themselves, but though for some the cure was permanent, some were back to screeching and hand waving in minutes.

Lottie seemed overwhelmed. There's no other way to put it. She couldn't know if Angela's death was a coincidence or if she herself truly had some kind of supernatural powers tragically misused, but either way she was simply horrified at the news. It was what she said to Mark when she asked him to cancel her appointments on Wednesday and mind the store.

He said, "Miss Dougal, how are you?"

And she said, "I'm horrified, simply horrified."

It was what she said, over and over, when Pattie and Phil came by that night with a tub of ice cream and a bottle of bourbon. Phil said not to worry too much about what people said; pretty soon something else would happen and they'd forget about it.

Lottie snapped, "Don't be silly, Phil. People are still bringing up when I wet my pants in the first grade. They're hardly going to forget that I killed . . ."

And she started crying again.

Pattie said, "Now, honey, you didn't kill anyone. With your healing skills, you probably just saw it coming, that's all, and in a moment of anger—"

"I cursed the poor woman."

"Oh, horseshit," Phil said. "I don't believe in any of that crap."

Lottie said, "I'm just horrified. Horrified."

Pattie turned to him while she held her crying sister. "Do you think she ought to leave town?"

"Why should she? She hasn't done anything wrong."

Phil Walker was a powerful man. He didn't say all that much, but when he did say something, he expected folks to listen. He said, "You haven't done anything wrong, Lottie. This whole curse thing is horseshit and you know it. And if you don't know it, well, you should."

Lottie lifted her head from her sister's shoulder and looked at him.

He said, "You are going to hold your head up high. You're going to do your work and worship your Maker and if anybody, and I mean *anybody,* gives you any trouble, they're going to have me to deal with. Okay?"

Lottie nodded meekly.

"Now drink your highball and get some sleep."

Phil walked Lottie to work on Thursday morning, which is why he saw the Mercedes hearse outside Marling's Maple Hill Funeral Home.

Not normally inquisitive by Eudoran standards, he joined a group of some four people, including Jim Evans. Jim and two of the other three observers had taken off their hats and were holding them respectfully somewhere in the region of their solar plexi. For a moment, Phil was

159

so absorbed in this rare sighting of Jim Evans's hair (for the record, salt and pepper with a neat little forelock at the front and a side part that seemed burned into his scalp) that it took a minute for it to sink in just what it was they were witnessing.

When the coffin came out, he realized quickly enough. It may have been the deep-colored cherry wood of a range heretofore considered excessive by local inhabitants that let Phil know whose mortal remains it contained, but the company carrying it told their own tale.

It was the doctor who helped lift it from its rolling frame on the sidewalk and place it into the back of the Mercedes. He was aided in this by Ed Marling and his cousin Jeff Marling as well as two strangers in dark suits of impeccable cut and line. Though they were wearing dark glasses and had not spoken, there was something about them that told Phil immediately that they were Angela's relations.

In this he was correct.

A variety of floral displays now emerged from Maple Hill, the like of which had never before been seen in Eudora. Phil could not say what flowers they contained, for he was the kind of man, as Pattie rediscovered on the odd Valentine's Day, who could not tell carnations from roses. But he said they looked expensive and that there seemed to be a lot of them. In some fashion he

160

was unable to see from his vantage point, the flowers were fastened onto the coffin so they wouldn't slip around. Then there were the letters, ferried out by Ed, Jeff, and Marcia Marling, all done in flowers on little wire frames. These were positioned along the windows of the hearse, spelling out "Angela."

The doctor was standing with his hands on his hips, rumpling his suit and staring at the boxed remains. The contrast between how the doctor looked in his clothes and how Angela's brothers looked in theirs was so acute that even Phil noticed it and cut Angela some posthumous slack for trying to get the one to match up to the memory of the other. No woman on earth, he thought at the time, with brothers who looked like that would not set standards high for her mate's appearance.

At last, Ed closed the back door with that firm but quiet sound only those associated with the funeral industries ever get just right. The doctor looked at the brothers. The brothers looked at the doctor. One said, "We must go now."

The doctor said, "It seems weird, just letting her go like this. Are you sure you don't want to—"

Shaking his head, the brother who had spoken before interrupted the doctor by putting his hand on the doctor's shoulder. "She belongs with us," he said.

The other brother said something in Spanish,

which made Mark Ramirez, one of the other four people, Phil now registered, draw in his breath sharply.

The brother who spoke smiled sadly, revealing perfect white teeth. "Our family motto," he said with an air of apology. "We hold on to what is ours." He patted the doctor's shoulder. Then the brothers got into the car with a grace that left Phil feeling clumsy. They soberly accelerated right up to the speed limit. Phil watched them all the way out to the Food Barn. From what Phil could see, they never looked back once.

There was something about the way the doctor stood in the middle of the street, looking after the car, that made Phil feel sorry for the guy. Finally, the doctor looked up and seemed to register that there were people there. He said, "Well."

Everyone who had taken their hat off put their hat back on, Jim Evans looking a lot more like himself once his gimme cap was firmly settled on his eyebrows. It was Jim who was the first to walk up and take the doctor's hand. He said, "You have our sympathy, Doc."

To which the doctor replied, "Thank you."

One by one, the onlookers stepped off the curb and shook the doctor's hand, muttering the platitudes that are so necessary and yet so inadequate at these times. Phil was the last. He said, "It's a tragedy."

The doctor said, "Yes."

Phil started to walk away, but the doctor didn't look right, Phil said. He was just standing there, Phil said, in the middle of Main Street, and he had that lost look somebody has when they've been hit a few times or maybe had too much to drink. Phil couldn't just leave him like that.

He put a hand under the doctor's elbow and guided him to the curb, which the doctor stumbled over getting back up to the sidewalk.

"They took her clothes and her jewelry," he said. "She kept all her makeup and stuff in her toiletries case, and I took that to the hospital on Sunday night, when I still thought . . ." The doctor stopped and rubbed his face. "I mean, there's nothing left in the apartment. She's even out of cigars and sherry. I guess she hadn't ordered any more because . . ."

Phil didn't know what to say. He patted the doctor on the back. Finally he said, "It must be strange."

"Strange? Hell, yes, it's strange. It's like she was never there, you know what I mean?"

Phil nodded, though he couldn't imagine it himself. Pattie had left an impression on the Walker house that would take subsequent owners generations of concentrated labor to erase.

"Do you want to get a cup of coffee?" he asked the doctor, but the doctor kept talking, alarming Phil by appearing to be just short of bursting into tears.

163

"How can life be like this? Just last week I had a wife and was about to start a family. I was looking at houses out by the golf course. I didn't want to move. . . . I didn't really *like* any of it, but it was there, you know? Even if I was miserable. It was *my* misery. And now it's just gone." The doctor waved his hand. "Poof. Magic."

At the mention of magic, Jim Emery realized he was talking to Lottie's brother-in-law, and his face colored. "I mean . . . I didn't mean . . . ," he began. "I mean, no offense, man."

"It's cool," Phil said. There was a moment's discomfort.

"Coffee sounds good," the doctor said, "but I got patients this morning. I'm kind of backed up."

"Yeah, of course," Phil said. "I gotta go myself. I'm late."

"Yeah."

"But you know," Phil said, "if you need anything . . . Really. You know where I am."

There just aren't any other words, as Phil said later that night to Pattie. You hear yourself saying them and you know how useless they are and that nobody could believe you mean it. But just what the hell was he supposed to say to the poor guy?

Pattie said that she felt just terrible about the whole thing, like she could have done something to stop it all and didn't.

And Phil said that the best thing they could have done was just leave Lottie and the doctor alone, and he reckoned that's what they had to do from now on. Pattie cried, and Phil held her.

But the doctor, later, said that Phil was a good person to talk to when you really needed someone to listen. Of course, he didn't say it that night, because he had no one to say it to. He had a stack of microwavable meals in the fridge and had cable, this we know. And so it is suspected that the doctor ate a meal in front of a movie and drank a couple of beers. Dr. Jim Emery, who had lamented the loss of his bachelor lifestyle so thoroughly, now had it back again. And if the sound of the ice maker in the empty luxury apartment above Main Street startled him into a two foot sitting high jump, there was no one to laugh at him about it. There was nobody to notice him at all.

Now, if Phil Walker had been incorrect in stating that the people of Eudora would forget about the strange circumstances surrounding the death of Angela Requena Emery, he had been absolutely correct in the imperfectly expressed underlying assumption that said circumstances would not remain the hottest topic of conversation for long. What they needed (he said to Pattie on Friday night, after an uncomfortable meal with Artie and Rosemary at Mayan Memories, where the other diners frequently lowered their voices, shooting glances across the room to their booth) was somebody to do something interesting. Then, he said, they could all get back to normal.

And indeed three things did happen within twenty-four hours, the first of which occurred on Monday morning. As all of these things prove pivotal to the circumstances that prevail on the day with which we are here concerned, we, like the rest of Eudora, must turn our attention away from Lottie Dougal and the doctor, no matter how unwillingly, while we consider them.

Well, the first thing was that Zadie Gross came home, sunburned and laden with packages, some five months before her dream journey was due to conclude. She had jumped ship in Adelaide, fed up to the back teeth. She was bored, bored senseless on board the ship, and going ashore for her had been one long baffling experience of strange languages and accents and funny toilets.

And the food! She couldn't stand it.

For on that fifty-two-week around-the-world cruise, Zadie Gross, who had never felt she owned a talent, had developed a deep and abiding appreciation of her own plain cooking. She had been nursing visions: a plate of green bean casserole with some fried potatoes nestling beside two pork chops, biscuits and cream gravy with plenty of black pepper, chili and corn bread, macaroni and cheese, meatloaf, and even tuna surprise (this last a dish she had previously considered more of a staple than a delight but found she missed sorely when it was withdrawn) had all played vital roles in her fantasy life.

And the more Zadie had concentrated on these visions, the less she was able to concentrate on the food put in front of her, with such nauseating regularity, on the cruise liner. The fruits de mer, the coquilles St. Jacques, and the chateaubriand had left her cold. And if she never saw another raspberry coulis, homemade pasta, or Parmesan shaving for the remainder of her allotted days on God's green earth, she would consider it a great blessing.

So it was a lean Zadie Gross who emerged from the airport shuttle and received her four suitcases, three zip-up hold-alls, and fifteen shopping bags from the driver, passing back a five-dollar bill in return for his courteous assistance. She had noticed at Caracas that her muumuus were not as filled out as they had been previously. By Sydney her swimsuits had begun to bag badly in areas of the body where bagging meant indecency, and she'd had to buy two more in Perth. While everyone else on board seemed to be blowing up like balloons, Zadie had been deflating.

Zadie burned with more than a little too much UV exposure as she stood in the driveway of her small ranch house, surrounded by her luggage. She burned with a mission. Or rather two. First of all, being a thorough Eudoran, she couldn't wait to find out what had been happening in town. And second, she had plans. For both of these missions, she needed to speak to Becky Lane. And so before she even made herself an iced tea or opened the mail Priss Lane (who had undertaken minding Zadie's house as one of her three after-school and weekend jobs) had thoughtfully stacked on the kitchen table, she reached for her telephone.

The second event was less pleasant.

The quarry was located on the northeast side of town, near the interstate (which was uncomfortably close to Eudora, although without an exit for thirty-two miles and therefore providing no economic benefit to offset the noise and fumes). It was just about as far to the center of town as the golf course on the southwest side was, and socially as well the two places stood in complete opposition.

At one time, the quarry had been locally owned and Eudorans of pioneer descent had provided the labor it required. Barker had been the family name, which some in town still remembered, although the Barkers sold out right after World War Two and went to live someplace else with the enormous profits they had made during it. Now nobody could remember why limestone had been so important to the war effort, but everyone could see that this had been the peak of the quarry's productivity and community interest. Henceforth, it had declined.

Whoever the Barkers sold to sold it on again. And again and again and again and again. By the 1960s, when wheat was high and jobs plentiful, the absentee ownership and lackadaisical management (the latter marked by a profound disinterest in benefits and on-the-job safety) failed to attract new workers. The management company solved this problem by contracting with an unscrupulous person who provided illegal immigrants.

For some twenty-five years, a steady flow of Mexican nationals came to work in the quarry. They lost fingers and hands, and sometimes more, but since they were not officially there at all, they could not sue. Equipment became more and more outdated and the jobs were more and more dangerous. But in 1970s Mexico, especially the more rural expanses far from the capital, which suffered from the problems national politics brought to farming during those years, they seemed attractive enough.

By the time the workers hesitantly embraced naturalization in the early 1990s, the quarry was in a bad state indeed. But now OSHA could be called in and was. The current owners, whoever they were, were forced to invest a great deal of money in updated equipment and facilities, which they did, immediately recovering their investment by selling the quarry to a new arm of a different multinational corporation.

This had happened twice more before the time

with which our narrative is currently concerned.

Each time the quarry changed hands, someone from the multinational would come and speak to the management team and the workforce in general and tell them all about their plans for the operation and how changes were going to be made and they would start seeing some improvements pretty soon. And then the someone would go away and life at the quarry would continue as usual. The someone was never seen again.

But on the particular Monday morning Zadie Gross arrived back early from her around-the-world cruise, the latest someone returned. A rented dark blue sedan arrived in town just after ten-thirty and someone got out and had a cup of coffee and a maple long john at Margery's. And then, consulting a file in his briefcase, he drove, without asking directions, right to the quarry. Stopping at the security hut at the gate, he flashed his pass and was admitted.

He was with the management team for less than two hours before a general meeting was called. Even Pablo Sanchez was ordered out of the security hut and told to lock the gate and come on in, an unheard-of dereliction of duty.

What it boiled down to, said Oscar Burgos later that day (both he and Manuel had been called into the meeting), was that the current owners wanted a tax write-off. So they'd set those unrealistic targets and made it look like the quarry couldn't perform and was losing money and then they could shut it down and write the whole shebang off on their taxes. They were probably doing it all over the world, Oscar said, taking little businesses and making them look bad so they could save a few bucks here and there on their tax bill. And then he called the owners a name. His sister gave him a sharp look and he apologized.

Maria said, "Do you want some more pie?"

"No," Oscar said, "I want a job."

It was two-thirty and there was no one else in Mayan Memories except for Linda, who was making a red sauce. Oscar and Maria sat opposite each other in one of the red leatherette booths Oscar had helped to construct.

Maria didn't know what to say. "It's just awful," was all she could think of.

"Two months," he said. "And then another month's salary for notice. How are we going to make our house payments? Where can we find work? I mean, I can get a job in the city and commute, but some of those guys, rocks is all they know, you know?"

In the quiet of the restaurant, you could hear the tortilla machine whirring in the back. Oscar looked in that direction. He said, "How much do you need the tortilla business?"

Maria sighed. "I need it a lot," she said. "We're still paying for all the machines and stuff."

"The whole town is going to fall right down the

shitter," Oscar said. And then he apologized to his sister for swearing again, even though she hadn't seemed to notice.

The third thing happened on Tuesday at a Chamber of Commerce luncheon held in the big meeting room upstairs at the bank. Lottie did not attend, but Pattie was there, and, as Maria was thinking about joining, had brought her along as her guest. The sandwiches were provided by Margery Lupin and the guest speaker was an expert on foot-traffic patterns from the city, which got quite a lot of folks thinking about their positions on Main Street and how to maximize them.

But as illuminating as the official agenda was, the real news came with the coffee when Clement McAllister said, "I'm not going to run as mayor again this year. Lucy wants me to give it up, and I think she's got a point. Twenty years is enough for any man."

Now, the post of mayor of Eudora is largely ceremonial. It dates from a time when Eudora had ambitions to grow into a township, to incorporate, to levy or to have taxes levied on its behalf. This growth never occurred, and the modest budget the state and county allocate for such things as streetlights and road surfaces, trash collection, the library, and so on are paid directly to the providers of the service. Artie Walker's paycheck comes from the state. Odie

Marsh and Ben Nichols get theirs from the county.

The mayor makes the phone calls. For example, if a pothole develops, the mayor picks up the phone and calls the appropriate department. When the Christmas lights on Main Street became worn out and tacky-looking, it was the mayor who took himself to the county hall armed with photographs and got the matching funds, to which the local merchants contributed their share.

The rewards for this service are not pecuniary ones. First of all, there is the seat in the lead car that opens the Maple Leaf Festival parade. Then there is the best seat at all civic performances and celebrations, including the Snow Ball. And then there is the statewide conference, for which the governor's office foots the bill.

We have only Clement's word for the sumptuousness of this annual junket. It takes place in the middle of August and though in years of austerity is confined geographically to luxury hotels within the state, it has been known to take place in Branson, Orlando, and one memorable year (with the excuse of some outrigger-based team-building exercises) on the island of Maui. Clement says the food is "aaaah." He says there's enough to drink to be truly dangerous to any man. He hints of such things as discotheques and floor shows and talks eloquently of more Lucy-friendly outings to art galleries and museums.

In fact, by and large, the annual conference is the only reason to become mayor of Eudora. And this is the problem.

You see, mayoral candidates should be men of good standing in the community, business owners or experienced managers with healthy family lives and strong religious practice. And anyone like that has a wife. The wives of Eudora do not look upon the annual state mayors' conference with a tolerant eye. Not only have all the hints about discotheques and floor shows been repeated and inflated and repeated again, but it's the timing of the thing. The middle of August.

Something you need to know about Eudora is that gardening here is a competitive sport that lasts way beyond the growing season. Most women would die of shame if an acquaintance saw them buying a can of tomatoes in January, as any self-respecting Eudoran woman would still have row upon row of glass jars in her pantry or cellar, glowing like rubies. She has a freezer full of her own green beans, zucchini, eggplant, and so on, and jar upon jar of pickles and preserves, both sweet and sour.

Every evening in the growing season, after supper, Eudora women are out in their backyards for an hour or two of weeding, watering, and pest inspection. When they sit down with their iced tea to watch television, it is with an inner glow of righteousness that continues to warm the cockles of their hearts until the last jar of tomatoes is made into pizza sauce sometime in early June.

The labor in preserving all of this produce is immense, and every member of the household has a job to do. Even a two-year-old child can be taught to snap string beans or husk corn for blanching. And the height of the growing season, when production is most frenzied and preserving becomes a Sisyphean task, making strong women weep from exhaustion and frustration, occurs in the middle of August.

And this is why, when various men arrived home that Tuesday and musingly noted Clement was about to retire as mayor and wondered idly who would be good to take up that role, naming requisite qualities that they themselves possessed, cold looks were passed across dinner tables and dessert portions were extremely small if they were given at all. By Wednesday, the men of Eudora eligible for such an office had all confessed that they didn't feel they had the time to take on such a role, by which everyone knew they meant that their wives didn't feel they had the time to take on such a role.

By Thursday, Clement knew that retiring was not going to be easy. "Whipped," he said to Hector Rodriguez. "That's what they all are. Under the little woman's thumb. Why, my Lucy has put up with it for twenty years, bless her. A man's got to be a man, after all."

Hector nodded thoughtfully.

"I don't know who we're going to get to do it," Clement said. "We need somebody younger but in a responsible position. He'd have to be a Rotarian, a good churchgoer . . . you know, stable." Clement sighed.

Hector stopped nodding and his eyes widened with a thought he was not yet ready to share.

"I don't know," Clement said. "These things work themselves out. I'm sure the guy is right under my nose and I don't even know it."

"Yes," Hector said musingly. "That's true."

And then Hector changed the subject.

When Zadie Gross left her cruise early, she did not leave empty-handed. She had kept a scrupulous diary of all the shortcomings of the luxury cruise liner and the shore excursions and was able to negotiate a substantial refund along with her return airfare. In fact, she made herself so unpleasant that they were only too glad to give her a check and send her on her way, and if the other passengers had been approached to provide a portion of the funds, hands would not have been slow to enter pockets.

When Zadie deposited this check in the First State Bank of Eudora, she earmarked it for her checking account. The teller, Linda Lane (Becky's eldest), was as conscientious as all the Lane women and asked, "And you don't want this to go into your high-interest savings account, Miz Gross?"

To which Zadie had replied, "No, Linda, just like it says on the slip."

Zadie's car was running just fine when she took it out of the garage and it still had half a tank of gas. And so she was free to go to Eudora's local real estate agent.

The fact was, Eudora's local real estate agent was located in the county seat. They had once opened a branch in Eudora, since the town was the right size and had a wealthy enough demographic to warrant it. But then they had found that Eudorans did not move all that much. The agent spent a great deal of time talking to people and handing out leaflets and assessing needs and desires. One day he went to a meeting at the head office and came back only to clean out his desk.

So it was a sad fact that if you wanted to buy a house from your neighbor, you had to drive twenty-five miles to get the brochure and set up the appointment to view.

That same afternoon, Zadie returned, followed by the agent's car, and they both parked on Main Street. Then they got out of their vehicles and looked at the remaining boarded-up window downtown for a few moments before the agent used his key and they entered the building to look around.

• • •

W hen Hector changed the subject, it was to bring Clement some horrifying news.

Word about the quarry closure had been slow to spread through town. The meeting had been on Monday, but the Latino community had folded itself back into its mantle of silence and invisibility. On Wednesday Pattie asked Maria what was wrong, and Maria had smiled and said, "Oh, it's nothing," even though Pattie knew it was not nothing. Mark Ramirez sighed during a meeting to plan strategy for the Maple Leaf Festival with his employer, and when Lottie asked what was the matter, he (who could have replied that he was wondering if he'd be the only Mexican American in town by that time) said it wasn't anything important.

Later, Maria said it was like she was ashamed, like it was all her fault or something.

But whatever the underlying psychological motivation, the fact was that word had been slow to spread. By Thursday, Hector realized that he had better break the news to Clement.

It was late on Thursday night and the last of Lucy's basket of chicken had been consumed when Clement and Hector felt able to face the worst. Their liability was considerable. Mark Ramirez may have worried about the family home going to the bank, but the fact was, the bank did not need or desire to get into the real estate business, which, as has been previously stated, was slow and due to get considerably slower when the quarry closed. And the number of homes in which the bank had an interest was very high.

Then there were the contingent businesses that had an account with the bank, many of which had outstanding loans and the business owner's mortgage and car loan. Every time they thought they had a total for their worst-case scenario, one of them would think of yet another area of exposure and the worst case would get even worse.

Clement had been active on Thursday afternoon, going to see the quarry manager and coming back with a sheaf of documentation. He'd read through it quickly and gotten somebody from the relevant arm of the multinational on the phone and talked to that person a bit about the situation.

They weren't quite as inhuman as Oscar feared, Hector learned from Clement. They would be willing to sell the quarry. But with the current production figures, there were no buyers. Even if they discounted it and sold it at a loss, no one would be willing to take it on.

It was two in the morning before the light in Clement's office winked out.

Hector had shared a six-pack with his boss as they looked at the figures, but he was cold sober. The streetlights combined with the large full moon to diffuse a pale whiteness through the dark streets of town. Shadows were defined, edged, and the soft features of gardens and trees were stark in black and white. Even the leaves of the maples seemed as jagged and pointed as knives in a scary movie.

It was dying, Hector realized. Eudora was dying. Just as he could truly call it home, just as all his wildest ambitions could be pursued and perhaps even realized, the town was going to pass away.

For if the quarry went and the homes went and the businesses went, then the bank would also go. And so would all the people. Hector was not an emotional man. But as he walked by his sleeping fellow citizens that night, tears came to his eyes, hot smarting tears that had to do with injustice and needless destruction.

For the quarry could make money. He knew it. It sold a good product that was always in demand at a good price because the workers' needs were few—if he was honest, they were too few, he thought. If somebody decent took it over, they could pay for an HMO, at least. Everything was there for it to succeed. The manager did a good job, the workers did a good job, and the supply of limestone was seemingly endless. Why didn't anybody decent ever take it over? Hector wondered.

He crept into the family home and to his room, stopping only to put the plate his mother had left out for him into the refrigerator. He had his own bathroom, for which, he remembered guiltily, they had remortgaged the house. But he had contributed to the payments, and they had done the kitchen and the roof at the same time. He looked at himself in the mirror as he dried his face. He seemed suddenly older.

He lay down, knowing he would never sleep.

Zadie Gross was also awake, but she was not containing an entire community's death inside her throbbing head. No, she was awake with delight, having just signed a lease on the empty store behind the boarded-up windows on Main Street. It had once been a diner, so long ago that only people like Zadie and Clement remembered it, remembered the lines of pickup trucks belonging to farmers who were used to coming in at ten to get the paper and have a gossip and a cup of coffee and maybe, what the heck, a bacon breakfast or a stack of pancakes while they exchanged grim forecasts concerning weather and weeds. And it was going to be a diner again.

Zadie Gross chuckled to herself, wriggling her toes underneath her percale sheets and thermal blanket. She would only open for breakfast and lunch. She'd start after Margery opened, sometime around eight o'clock. And she'd close shortly after Maria Lopez opened, sometime around two. Allow an hour or so for prep and an hour for cleaning and she and Becky would be working eight-hour days. She'd keep her prices and her overhead low, get *USA Today* to put a box outside, and play cheerful music at a low volume.

There would be checked curtains at the windows and brightly colored plastic bottles of ketchup and mustard on the tables. She and Becky would wear cotton dresses, cut comfortable, with little aprons and white nurse's shoes. If they got busy, she'd hire some waitresses to help.

Little baskets with jelly, jam, and honey in individual servings. White, whole-wheat, and rye toast available. There would be a blue-plate special for lunch every day.

Zadie yawned and turned on her side, dreaming of offering coffee to a restaurant full of the very people, who, on the other side of town at the very same moment, Hector Rodriguez was picturing driving away in big U-Haul trucks.

Phil had predicted that as soon as something else had happened, life would return to normal for Lottie and the doctor. This was both true and untrue. From Wednesday, they were seldom subjected to the kind of sudden silence their appearance had previously provoked, and both had their patients return. But they were both conscious of a certain hesitancy in other people's greetings, and a tendency for fellow citizens to say as little as possible to them directly.

They had run into each other only twice, and

both times each had been so excruciatingly conscious of the other person's feelings that they hadn't even managed to make eye contact. *Normal* was hardly the word for either of their behaviors, or of the way their lives were currently in general.

The doctor in particular was feeling the strain. He had been dealing with a casual employment agency in the city and had received from them a succession of receptionists, each a little less competent than the last, until Wednesday, when the agency confessed that they couldn't get anyone else to make the drive for the money. On Thursday, the doctor rang Zadie Gross and asked her if she'd like to come in for a few days, and Zadie had said she was sorry and she *would* but was very busy and couldn't.

The doctor had been reduced to using the answering machine to take his calls and then spent the whole of Thursday night calling people back to arrange appointments. We later discovered that when he had finished this work, he was at his lowest point ever. He sat in the big La-Z-Boy, unable to move, unable even to think about anything. He was hungry, but the effort of feeding himself seemed immense. He was tired, but he didn't feel like he could get through the whole routine of brushing his teeth, washing his face, and taking off his clothes to go to bed.

When his doorbell rang, he groaned as if he'd

been shot and clattered down the stairs and through the office foyer, intent on giving whoever had disturbed him a large piece of his mind. He flung open the door.

And saw his mother standing there.

He blinked for a moment and then fell into her lean arms with a sob. She drew him to her and kicked her suitcase through the doorway before she pushed the door shut with her free hand. "There, there," she said. "Now, don't you worry about it anymore, Jimmy. Mama's here now and everything is going to be all right."

And the doctor wordlessly let go of all he had been holding inside him.

In the morning, he said to her, "I don't understand why you're here. How did you decide to come?"

And she said, "How did you decide to come for my heart surgery? I'm sorry I took so long, but trying to get my cardiologist on the phone to okay the flight was a real pain. Now you'd better show me all about the telephone and the book before we open for business."

The troublesome question of whether Lottie Dougal had or had not inadvertently cursed Angela Requena Emery to her death obviously bothered Lottie herself. It bothered her sister, and Maria Lopez, and a few of her younger patients. But it did not bother the elder portion of the Latin

American community of Eudora, which formed the bulk of Lottie's practice. As old Mr. Sanchez said to his assembled brood on Sunday afternoon, while sitting in his backyard watching his great-grandchild trying to crawl, "Good doctors are always witches."

And as Pablo Sanchez said in the same conversation, "That kind of thing was always going to happen to Angela."

And, further, as Louis Sanchez said later that same day, after thinking about it a while, "Only a fool would go messing with a witch. That wasn't murder, it was suicide."

So, every evening, Lottie changed her clothes, made herself a hasty meal, and then went into her garden, knowing that she would soon be hailed from her own back porch to open her examination room. Now, you would think that this meant Lottie's garden was going to wrack and ruin, but actually it was flourishing in a way it never had before. And the reason was that if patients wished to consult Lottie early in the evening, they brought with them a gardener.

Old Mr. Sanchez, for instance, had brought Pablo.

Pablo himself, who later had strained his back trying to get the number seven security camera down, clean the lens, and put it back up on his own, brought his eldest son, Jason.

Each had weeded and watered and was competent with the hoe. But Pablo knew a great deal about tomatoes and improved Lottie's staking arrangements. Jason had done a science project about using marigolds in pest control and, with Lottie's permission, moved some of these from the flower bed to surround the more vulnerable species of vegetables in the garden.

When Oscar Burgos consulted Lottie on his day off because he couldn't sleep, he brought Bill Lopez, who knew a great deal about mulch. When Bill stopped sleeping as well, he brought Oscar, who was expert at herb cultivation due to long hours spent helping his father. He immediately noticed the lungwort did not have enough root space to do its best and that the pennyroyal was going to run riot if not confined.

Late Friday night, Lottie was sitting on her back porch, regarding this community handiwork, when Oscar came by, once again taking the long walk home. She hailed him and offered him a cup of warm milk to go with the valerian root mixture she had previously prescribed.

It was during the making and drinking of this that Oscar learned the full vulnerability of the town to the quarry's closure.

He, like most of the men and women directly affected, had been thinking of it as a private problem. But as Lottie enumerated the number of businesses that would be subsequently impoverished, Oscar began to realize something. This was not the old story of people with brown skin losing out. This was a different story, a story about city people, who had no idea of the value of community, tearing a town up by its roots and crushing it.

He said later, sitting there looking at Lottie's flourishing garden, that he imagined the town to be just like that garden and the quarry owners were like a big rototiller just coming through and chewing everything up until there wasn't nothing left but a bit of green slime on the dirt.

And though the hot milk began to work on his exhaustion directly after this epiphany, and Oscar stumbled home to his bed without giving it another thought, this conversation was to prove pivotal in the days that followed.

Asked by his sister the next day how Lottie was, however, all he could say was, "Quiet."

Lottie *was* quiet. She was quiet at home, and quiet at work. The remoteness, the absence of her characteristic bounce that had been so marked before Easter, returned redoubled. If at that time she had been merely a ghost of herself, now she wasn't even a ghost, more of a presence.

It was thought by all the partners in Dougal's Stationery Supplies that for the time being Mark should handle most of the customer care. Mark felt, when he came into the shop, that things had been done, but not that there was anyone truly there doing them. Lottie spoke to him quietly, congratulated or commiserated with him quietly, but afterward he couldn't remember a single word she'd said. "It's a bit spooky, to tell you the truth," he had said to Maria at lunch on Friday. And he repeated it on Saturday at Chuck's Beer and Bowl when he and Kylie Requena were enjoying a night out.

Jim Evans, coming into town for herbicide and a ream of letter-sized paper, said Lottie looked like she'd just hit a deer. There is a large whitetail population along the river bottoms of the county and out at the state park, and none of Jim's listeners had failed, on some misty night or another, to either hit a deer, come close to hitting a deer, or see someone else hit a deer. They were all aware that smacking your car into nine hundred pounds of suddenly appearing Bambi does tend to leave a person stunned, and all thus felt the description to be extremely apt.

It was particularly apt because Eudora had undergone one of its strange reversals of public opinion and now could not decide if Lottie had any true culpability in Angela's death. After all, sometimes when you hit a deer it's your fault, and sometimes it's the deer's fault, and sometimes it's simply both of you being in the wrong place at the wrong time and can only be put down to fate, the will of God, or coincidence, depending on your worldview. And this largely is now how Eudora saw the strange circumstances surrounding Angela's death.

If you don't know Eudora, it might seem odd that one week members of the community would be gleefully spreading and embroidering rumors of strange occult happenings that they then would sternly debunk the second week. But if you know Eudora, this phenomenon is not only possible but predictable.

For Eudora had gone too far. It had gotten carried away. It had been silly and it had been drunk on the juice of gossip. There was something about the black hearse and the smartly dressed men who accompanied it that had helped to sober the town up, and the doctor's mother, an energetic and down-to-earth woman, finished the job. No one who saw her at Margery's getting the donuts for the waiting room, at the post office with all the doctor's neglected paperwork, or out at Food Barn with her cart piled high with fresh fruit and vegetables (some of which, cut up, also found their way into the waiting room as an alternative to the donuts) failed to feel a little uneasy about the wild things they had said the week before.

The change was swift and total. One person would be talking to another and mention Lottie Dougal's curse, and the other person would frown and say, "I don't really like that kind of talk. That was just a coincidence, after all."

And if the first person said, "You were the one who was saying blue fire flew out of her fingertips and that you'd seen the little house on Elm Street lit up from inside with blue light," the second person would frown deeper and say, "I think I got a little carried away."

Upon which the first person would immediately recognize the superiority of this stance and adopt it forthwith, positively looking for someone he or she could impress with it. Tolerance and skepticism spread like a virus through town. By Monday morning, the family business partners (having met with Mark Ramirez briefly outside church on Sunday) felt that Lottie should exploit the burgeoning feeling of guilt associated with the new stance by attending sales appointments once again.

They did, however, all agree that Mark was the man to approach a certain well-known Mexican restaurant in the city with a view to providing their stationery needs, including the printing of menus.

And so it was that when the doctor's mother came into Dougal's Stationery Supplies to replenish the medical office's stock of essentials, Lottie was behind the counter.

Now, though the doctor was not a terribly communicative man, his mother was a determined woman. It had not taken long for her to extract the name of the "smart, funny, and pretty" woman with whom so much had gone horribly wrong. And so when Mrs. Emery came through the tinkling door, she was prepared.

But not for Lottie.

For though Lottie had perked up considerably at the town's change of attitude, she was still very ghostlike. She was given to sitting silently, to avoiding eye contact during conversations, to elliptical remarks and non sequiturs, and further, when minding the store, she made a lot of excuses to go into the back room.

The doctor's mother wanted to make sure she had the right person, for though undeniably lovely, this was not a woman to whom the adjectives *smart* and *funny* could currently be applied.

"Miss Dougal?" she asked. She was horrified at Lottie's emotional state, she said later to Maria Lopez and Pattie Walker at that meeting over brownies and Bailey's-laced coffee to which this chronicle has already referred, the state that seemed to leak out of Lottie like a cloud of steam will leak out of a kettle. This horror must have been communicated to Lottie somehow, for she looked up with a movement much more alert than any she had made in days.

"Do you know who I am, child?"

Lottie shook her head, but her eyes had already filled with tears, simply, it is assumed, at the sympathetic tone.

"I'm Jim's mother."

Lottie nodded, the tears spilling over and splashing down her cheeks.

"Oh, you poor dear thing."

Mrs. Emery went right around the counter and put her arms around Lottie Dougal. Lottie, who had not been able to cry on her own, or with her sister, was able to cry with the doctor's mother.

When Lottie was at last able to speak, the first thing she said was, "I didn't mean to . . ."

And Mrs. Emery said, "Well, of course you didn't. Anybody with half a brain knows that. And it was her own fault. If she'd have told Jim earlier what was happening, she'd still be alive today."

Lottie sniffed. "She wouldn't have been Angela if she'd told him."

The doctor's mother was struck by how much affection for her late daughter-in-law was in Lottie's voice. But all she said was, "No, you're probably right."

Lottie sniffed again. "None of it was her fault," she said. "She was just caught up in it all. It was all my fault."

"Oh," the doctor's mother said with a maternal sigh, "I think Jim had a great deal to do with it."

Lottie blew her nose at this point, asking, after she had disposed of the tissue, "How is he?"

"A little shell-shocked."

Lottie nodded and then, it seemed to Mrs. Emery, she gathered a mantle of impenetrability around her shoulders. If there were such things as auras, earlier Lottie's had been larger than normal. If her emotions had been like a cloud, it was a cloud considerably larger than her body and larger than a person's presence or aura should be. But suddenly, Lottie seemed to shrink it, to rein it in some way, until it was smaller than a normal person's, until it was hidden behind her smart navy pantsuit of impeccable, though clearly 1970s, cut.

The doctor's mother later said that it was as if a curtain had come down, to which Pattie Walker had then replied, "Oh, yeah, I know that damn curtain."

With all her other qualities, the doctor's mother was also a tactful woman. She patted Lottie's back one more time and then retreated to the other side of the counter.

The rest of their conversation was restricted to stationery supplies.

Over dinner that night, the doctor's mother attempted to broach the subject. "I met Lottie Dougal today," she said.

The doctor, who was in the act of serving himself some mashed potatoes, hesitated slightly with the spoon but did not otherwise acknowledge his mother's remark.

Undaunted, his mother continued. "She's all cut up about what happened to Angela."

The doctor made a sound that seemed to be a stifled exclamation. It was not promising, but his mother persevered.

"Jim, you don't honestly believe that Miss Dougal is a witch, do you? I mean, you can't think that Lottie cursed Angela and *gave* her the ectopic. It happened at implantation, *weeks* before Lottie and Angela had their run-in. Scientifically, it's just not possible."

The doctor continued eating throughout his mother's speech.

She thought she should probably leave it at that, but then the memory of Lottie's haunted face swam before her. And, as she broke the narrative at this point to confess at length to Pattie and Maria later, she had never liked Angela anyway. She then told an involved story about how in the hospital she thought at one point Angela had been looking at the watch in the doctor's mother's drawer while the doctor's mother was still groggy from pain medication.

There was something about Lottie the doctor's mother liked right away. Any woman, she said later, who could hurt like a cloud could also love like a cloud. Imagine her children, growing up in a cloud of their mother's love.

So though the doctor's mother's natural inclination was to leave the conversation at this point, she went further. She said, "Isn't that right, Jimmy?"

Utilizing ancient male avoidance techniques, he said, "Isn't what right, Mom?"

"Isn't that right that it's not possible that Lottie Dougal cursed Angela?"

The doctor pushed his half-full plate away.

"Mom, nothing is impossible where that woman is concerned," he said, adding, "I'm going to take a shower and hit the hay, I'm bushed," leaving his mother to do the dishes and watch a movie on her own, though she also was bushed *and* had cooked dinner, which wasn't (she said later) like him at all.

In fact, later she said that she decided right then not to interfere, as she could tell she was doing more harm than good. Pattie said, "Right on."

Maria only nodded wisely, but hers were eloquent nods and both the doctor's mother and Pattie understood that Maria applauded this mutual resolution and supported this course of inaction, though she was aware of how much it cost them both to simply observe and hope.

They nodded back at her and at each other. And then the Bailey's was poured directly into coffee cups, without the tiresome intervention of actual coffee to slow its absorption.

Well before this conversation, but about the same time the doctor's mother attempted to broach the subject of Lottie Dougal on the first and final occasion, several things happened: Jim Flory fell down and broke his arm, Zadie Gross and Maria Lopez had an argument, and Hector Rodriguez had an idea. Although all three of these will prove of immense importance to the remainder of this story, Hector's idea is clearly the most essential to the events that followed, and so we will consider it first.

Though it is distasteful to observe a man when he is down, we must at this point observe Clement McAllister, the broken man. Clement had not attended an important committee meeting of the Knights of Columbus and was thinking about pulling out of the annual county Beer and Bass fishing tournament, held out at the state park, where he had once, as he never failed to tell anyone who used the word *fish* in his presence, hooked (though sadly failed to land) Old Sneaky, a large-mouth of legendary age and cunning.

He had worn the same suspenders three days in a row and had taken to using the arms of his chair to heave himself out of it, instead of relying on his quadriceps. These were all bad signs, and Hector had noted them all and had related them directly to the lack of his boss's optimism about the bank's resilience in the coming crisis.

So when Hector had his idea, he did not go to Clement, as he ordinarily would have done.

Instead he crept into Clement's office when his boss was having his after-lunch nap and withdrew the file relating to the quarry, using the photocopier and replacing the file before Clement woke up. He then used the telephone extensively.

By four o'clock on Monday afternoon, he was both more and less frightened about his future than he had been for a week. Less, because he had found out that the arm of the giant multinational corporation that owned the quarry was indeed willing to sell at a loss. And more, because the lowest price he had been able to negotiate was still a very big number indeed.

At five past four, he told Clement his idea and showed him the number. Clement chewed the underside of his lip.

"Now, I know the bank has some reserves," Hector said. "And I know it has some liquid investments. This would be a good investment, we both know it would. And if you consider the liability angle . . ."

Clement said, "I'm not stupid, Hector, you don't have to convince me."

He sprang out of his chair to pace back and forth in front of his desk. "The problem is, I can't just use the cash reserves. There's laws about things like that."

"What about the investments?"

Clement sat back down and stripped off his tie, flicking on his computer screen. "Get the manager of that place. What's his name?"

"Deacon. Royle Deacon."

Clement stopped typing momentarily. "You don't say. What is he? Methodist? Baptist?"

"I don't think he's anything, sir," Hector said. "He golfs on Sundays."

"Lives out there, does he?"

"Yes, sir."

"That's a hell of a name."

"Yes, sir."

"But we can talk. Both of us got quite a mouthful."

Hector remained silent, with his hand poised over the telephone.

"Well, call the bastard," Clement said. "Let's see who we're dealing with here."

By five o'clock, Royle Deacon had arrived. He proved to be a lean, tanned man of indeterminate age, though younger than Clement and older than Hector. He had on expensive but well-worn outdoor wear and good work boots. He didn't say much, but seemed to know a hell of a lot, Clement reported later, about anything to do with either quarrying limestone, wild birds of the prairie, or golf. The first one impressed Clement with a desire to keep the man working for the Eudora quarry and the latter two impressed him as sound reasons the man would want to keep working for the Eudora quarry.

For Royle Deacon spoke of his routines and his interests with a glowing sense of contentment and satisfaction that gave Clement great confidence. Any man who reserves his tee times annually, Clement said to Hector later, is not going to up and walk away from his job. There was a pause of a few moments and then Clement asked, "He's not married, is he?"

To which Hector replied, "No."

And Clement sighed. "No," he said. "You

198

don't get that kind of happy from being married."

Which Hector did not then understand, but would at a time not covered by this particular narrative.

On Tuesday, Hector asked permission to address the quarry workers. Once again Oscar and Manuel were called into the meeting, and once again Pablo locked the gate and deserted his post.

Hector was a young man who dreamed of glory. He spoke to the workers about his idea, that they should form their own company and continue working the quarry. That everyone knew it had made money in the past and could make good money again. And then he used the charts behind him. How much the arm of the giant multinational required. How much the bank could contribute. How much they themselves had to raise. How that would mean that the workers would also be owners and could vote and elect representatives to sit on the board and decide things for themselves.

He said later that he expected them to cheer, to throw their hats in the air or something.

But nobody even smiled.

They had listened politely enough, but there was no enthusiasm in the room whatsoever. And when Hector asked if there were any questions, nobody raised a hand or said a word out loud, though there was, at this juncture, quite a bit of muttering.

An experienced man would have asked what the problem was, or perhaps called a few men by name and asked them what they thought. But Hector was not experienced and these men were, by and large, the elders of his family. His own father was in the crowd and would not meet his eye.

Suddenly, Hector felt foolish, standing there with his charts and his highly polished shoes.

He had walked into the room seeing the world a certain way, a way in which he was a good and important man living in a community that depended upon his wisdom for its very survival. But now he saw another possible reality, that he was a spoiled young man who knew little of life, who had been made ornamental and useless by the indulgence of his family, and of whom the community in which he lived had been tolerant but would in the future be tolerant no more. He stood forlornly on the little dais as the men filed out again, and noticed that his father and his uncles did not even look back.

At the same time as Hector Rodriguez was giving his speech to the quarry workers, Jim Flory fell down and broke his arm.

We have not seen much of Jim Flory in this account. He has occasionally appeared, nattily attired and accompanied by cleaning supplies, to open the small theater in which he shows movies. This is the way Eudorans see Jim, the way they prefer to see him, when he is fit to be noticed. They do not want to see him negotiating his way carefully down the sidewalk, unshaven and badly dressed, perhaps still wearing his pajamas under his overcoat, perhaps clutching a bottle-shaped brown paper bag. Jim would prefer not to be noticed at these times, and so Eudora, which is fond of him, obliges.

Jim is the last of the Florys. He lives all alone in the big Victorian house on the edge of Main Street. At times, years ago, some young men would come frequently from the city and visit him, some one or another of them staying longer than weekends, one for years. But the young men were all gone now, and Jim seldom made it into the city anymore. He was forty-six and his hair was thinning. He had also acquired a permanently petulant expression.

The house takes up a great deal of his time. It is a monster. Six bedrooms plus maids' quarters and an attic. A living room and a parlor as well as a dining room downstairs. A kitchen bigger than Lottie Dougal's entire house. All surrounded by wooden siding and ornamented by carved designs locals called gingerbread, the whole surmounted by a green tile roof. And then there is the yard, which is laid out in the Italian style with a sculpture of a lady with no clothes on, though adequately clothed in her hair, standing in the middle of it behind the bushes and the wrought-iron fence.

There is always something to do when you own a house of this nature and have an income that is too limited to employ workmen unnecessarily.

Jim Flory's small income had been a feature of discussion on the doctor and Lottie Dougal's first date. The doctor had wondered why Jim did not show films more regularly, and Lottie explained that Jim was not always his bow tie self, that sometimes he was his pajama self and that it was only the bow tie Jim who felt able to deal with the effort of showing films, popping popcorn, and pouring Cokes. The doctor, suspecting bipolar disorder, asked if Jim went on spending sprees when he was his bow tie self, and Lottie said no, he just did home maintenance and gardened.

The doctor had not asked any further questions but he had remained interested in Jim. When the doctor had observed Jim in his alcoholic state, he had made another, more accurate diagnosis. And it was this he broached when Jim, who had fallen and broken his arm, came to the doctor's office for a refill of his pain medication.

Jim Flory was, at that point, edging toward pajama territory, though he had made a bit of an effort for the appointment. He had showered, if not shaved, and he had washed his hair, though he had not bothered to dry it.

The doctor took his pulse and looked down his throat. He did the knee-jerk thing with a little hammer. He asked questions about sleeping and eating.

Jim Flory drew himself up in his chair and said, "I fail to see the relevance of this line of questioning, young man. This is a routine refill, after all."

And the doctor said, "If you think I'm going to refill your prescription of Vicodin with your history of alcohol abuse, Mr. Flory, you are sadly mistaken."

Jim inflated on the chair. "Well!" he said. "I have never been so insulted in my entire life." He struggled to get his jacket back around his shoulders—he was still wearing a sling.

The doctor sat down on the edge of his desk and smiled. "I'm not trying to insult you, Mr. Flory. In fact, I think I can help you."

Jim stopped struggling and looked sharply at the doctor. "What do you mean, help me?"

"I think you might be suffering from depression. I think you may have been suffering for years. I had a look at your notes, and at your family's notes . . . your mother and your brother."

Jim said, "How dare you!" but it was, he said later, like it was out of habit. He already felt like the doctor was on to something.

"Your mother clearly had severe postpartum depression after your birth and that of your brother. And I believe that your brother was misdiagnosed as schizophrenic."

"Frank was as sane as anybody," Jim said. "I always said that."

"And I believe you were right."

Jim said later he was just staggered at this point. His bones turned to jelly with the sheer relief of somebody at last agreeing with him.

"We didn't understand depression like we do now," the doctor continued. "Now, I think you've been trying to self-medicate with alcohol for years. It's not an appropriate medicine for the problem, but it was all you could get. Now you've been prescribed this Vicodin and you want more of that. I can't let you have it, but I can give you something that might work better."

"Are we talking about Prozac?" Jim asked. "I've heard it turns you into somebody different."

"Don't you want to be different?" the doctor asked, laying his hand on Jim's shoulder.

When Jim stopped crying, he took the prescription. It wasn't Prozac; it was something he'd never even heard of. And then he went out and asked the doctor's mother to make him an appointment for the following week. When he turned to go, she said, "Wait a minute," and gave him a red and white striped carnation from the bunch on her desk.

"Let me trim the stem," she said, using the desk scissors. "A suit that nice deserves something in the buttonhole."

And though Jim Flory's recovery was to be a

long and rather winding road, that was the first step on it he took. And it felt, he said later, simply marvelous.

Although Zadie Gross had heard about the quarry closure and felt for the families involved, she had not realized how it impinged on her own dream of owning and running a successful diner. For the majority of her sixty-two years, the quarry and those who worked for it had been something to resolutely ignore, and this habit, sadly, was persistent in Zadie's case. So when we say Zadie felt for the families affected, we mean she felt for them as she would victims of a flood in Bangladesh or an earthquake in Turkey. The quarry, to Zadie, was a discrete location, separate from her own life.

If Zadie had required a bank loan to open her diner, Clement McAllister would have been quick to shatter this illusion. But, sadly for Zadie, no such funds were required. She was happily spending the rest of her severance pay and then a great deal of her savings account. Her retirement plan was still in place, but she was aware that it, too, could be called upon in a pinch, though with great penalties.

This awareness may have caused her to be a little less cautious with money than was her usual wont. The store was still full of 1970s tables and chairs and still had the long U-shaped counter and the little round revolving stools screwed into the floor. They all required refurbishing in some way: the metal chair tubes needed to be redipped in chrome, the fat cushions of the round stools reupholstered, the lurid orange countertop replaced with a tasteful dark green Formica. But the bones were in place. The black linoleum tiles looked as if they'd been laid yesterday once Zadie's industrious mop got ahold of them, and the walls were in good shape, thanks to a strong roof. A lick of paint took care of them, with a few happy chicken-shaped stencils to cheer them up.

No, Zadie's downfall was in the kitchen equipment. Oh, she bought used, of course. But there was something about the gleaming stainless steel and the name Hobart that caused her pulse to race. The day the salamander was delivered and installed, she trembled with excitement. And the big revolving bowl of the mixer, with its cathedral-shaped steel paddle, was a marvel to her. In those heady weeks Zadie and Becky Lane, during Becky's lunch breaks from the fabric store, often just stood there and watched it spin, imagining the gallons of pancake batter it would effortlessly turn out.

Now, even in such a crisis as that of the quarry closure, these things did not go unnoticed in Eudora. A white van does not pull up on Main Street and disgorge shining steel kitchen equipment without raising some talk. But as Zadie never said a word, no one said a word to Zadie.

Margery Lupin was more than a bit miffed. She and Zadie had known each other since kindergarten and you would think, Margery said, that if Zadie was thinking of taking such a step, she would consult somebody, maybe even ask for a little advice. But then Zadie was bullheaded and had been bullheaded all her life, Margery said, and so what can you expect? The words of warning that Margery could have given her lifelong neighbor were thus not given.

Margery's lead was largely followed in this matter. In her long years helping to service the medical needs of Eudora, Eudora had enjoyed extensive opportunity to observe Zadie's character and had come to much the same conclusion as Margery Lupin. As Jim Evans put it, "Trying to tell that woman anything is like trying to give a pill to a cat."

So, though tongues were clucked and heads shaken over every new evidence of expenditure, no one felt able to confront Zadie Gross about the insecurity of her investment.

Except for Maria Lopez.

If Maria had known how desperate Eudora and its environs were for a restaurant, she said one night to Bill, who was massaging her shoulders while she used the foot spa, she would have either opened one a lot earlier or not done it at all. There was that old diner, she said; why didn't anyone reopen that? She was doing so much to-go food at lunchtime she thought her head was going to explode, and though the good Lord knew that they could use the money, the fact was that they were working over capacity and something had to give.

And now somebody *had* thought to reopen the old diner, just at the worst time anyone could imagine. And Maria felt guilty, because it was just like she had prayed for it and got it.

So on Thursday of that week, at just about eleven o'clock, Maria took off her apron and walked to the next block, tapping on the thoroughly newspapered door and then, as it was slightly ajar, just pushing it open.

No one knows exactly what happened next. The scanty reports both Maria and Zadie gave in confidence (to Bill Lopez and Mark Ramirez on Maria's part and to Becky Lane on Zadie's) were garbled and emotional. But it was clear from what was pieced together later that the argument started almost straightaway and was fueled by a variety of misunderstandings and suspicions on both sides. Maria left thinking that Zadie Gross was a racist and a bully who, flaunting her cash savings, had every intention of putting Mayan Memories out of business. And Zadie was left thinking that Maria was a liar trying to scare *her* out of business.

But after considerable brooding and airing of her wrongs to Becky that afternoon, as they scraped and painted the pantry, Zadie's confidence began to flag. She asked Becky if she'd heard anything about the quarry closing.

Becky, who'd known better than to utter anything more than two words during the preceding three-hour diatribe, said, "Hmmm. Come to think of it, I did hear something." Whereupon Zadie Gross flung down her rubber gloves and ran down the street to the First State Bank of Eudora, where she insisted on seeing Clement McAllister, even though he was busy with his customary postprandial nap.

Clement said later that it was an emotional moment and that his heart went out to her. He said she turned gray in the face and he thought she might have a heart attack. He buzzed for some water and then actually went and got it himself. He said he would have done anything for her right then, it was so obvious her world was falling down around her ears, but there was nothing he could do, as it was all her own money. At this point in his narrative, he sucked his teeth and shook his head, as if to emphasize the folly of setting up any business with your savings instead of with a good, solid low-interest loan from your community bank.

Zadie went back to the diner. She looked at the empty shelves in the pantry, just waiting for industrial-sized buckets of dry goods. She opened the walk-in refrigerator and looked at the empty wire shelves. And then she sat down at the resurfaced Formica counter and put her head on her arms. She cried so long that Becky Lane had to just leave her to it and go home. Becky said later she fully expected Zadie to still be there, still crying, the next morning.

The doctor's mother had to go home. Everyone knew this, just felt it was time for her visit to be drawing to a close. It is remarkable how such things are measured in a community like Eudora, communally and without discussion. A widowed woman may have been admired from afar by another man for years. On a given Tuesday, it will still be too soon for her to accept an invitation to go bowling with this man. But on the Wednesday, everyone will agree it is time she started dating again.

And so it was with the doctor's mother's visit. Everyone knew, and she knew, that it was time for her to leave.

And yet there were many loose ends to be tied up before she felt comfortable going away again. She fretted about it all one morning, even making a list in her mind. She needed to find someone to be the receptionist for the practice. This would be difficult but not impossible. She needed to find someone who would reliably guide her son and Lottie back together. This clearly *was* impossible. And she needed to sew some new curtains for the bathroom of the luxury apartment above Main Street. She seized upon this task first as something that would be easily achievable, and took herself during the lunch hour to Pattie Walker's fabric store.

Of course she had seen Pattie before at church and various other places and knew her enough to nod to. But it was the first time they had spoken. Now, before they even worked through the florals, an understanding grew between them.

Pattie said, "I expect you'll be off back to Seattle pretty soon, Mrs. Emery."

And the doctor's mother said, "Yes, though part of me hates to go." The doctor's mother at this point was referring specifically to item two on her mental list. More, by saying this, she was testing Pattie's comprehension and tact.

So when Pattie said, "Yes, I suppose you'd like to see the doctor more settled," thereby passing this test with flying colors, the doctor's mother stopped fingering a bold navy and white ticking stripe and looked Pattie right in the eye.

She said, "Yes, I surely would."

Between them passed a meaningful exchange of glances.

Just then Becky Lane came in from the back, saying, "I'm real worried about Zadie, Pattie, she's still mad as a wet hen and with her blood pressure—" She broke off, apologizing, as soon as she saw the doctor's mother. Pattie introduced the two women, and then said, "Come to think of it, Mrs. Emery, Becky might have part of the solution to your problem."

The super-efficient and hardworking Janey Lane had gone into banking, like her sister before her. But Janey had found a large institution in the city and had been commuting from Eudora with the idea of setting up house with her second paycheck and two friends from adjoining hamlets who were similarly employed. But as young country girls often do in the big city, these two had started to run wild, and Janey was dismayed and no longer confident about sharing an apartment with them. She also found the long commute wearing and missed her mama and her sisters.

Pattie said little of this to the doctor's mother but did indicate that Janey Lane was a catch-and-a-half for any employer and would very much welcome a local career. Becky was very grateful and enthusiastic and gave the doctor's mother three telephone numbers at which Janey could be reached.

After which the doctor's mother found a nice navy fabric with a nautical motif picked out in white and pale blue, and Pattie measured and cut it.

Later, Pattie said that she just kind of felt it was important that she and the doctor's mother had some time to talk. And so she said impulsively, "Hey, Mrs. Emery, Maria Lopez and I are baking brownies this afternoon for the Feast of the Ascension bake sale. Why don't you come over after dinner and help us eat the funny ones?"

The doctor's mother accepted this invitation with alacrity, and reflected, while making sandwiches for herself and her son to consume at their respective desks, that she was in a good way to tick all three items off her list without having had to try all that hard.

Earlier in this chronicle we have discussed the momentous and, eventually, fairly bibulous events of that evening around the Walker family table. There is therefore no reason to go into it again, and indeed, considering that the three women polished off an entire bottle of Bailey's Irish Cream and made a small dent in some brandy Phil had been saving, there is perhaps reason enough to draw a veil over the proceedings. The only salient information that needs to be conveyed at this point is that Pattie and the doctor's mother solemnly swore not to meddle in Lottie and the doctor's affairs and that the next morning, after hiring Janey Lane sight unseen over the telephone (and after discovering, to Janey's extreme delight, that the big bank could release her from its training program that very day if she was unwilling to continue), the doctor's mother booked herself on Tuesday's first flight to Seattle and broke the news to her son.

Now, when Becky Lane described Zadie Gross as being as mad as a wet hen, she did not err. Zadie was going through the stages of grief in the opposite direction. She was incandescent with rage and just itching to find out whom she could possibly blame for the horrible state of the town's economic well-being. To do this, she had to elicit information, and to do *this* Zadie did what nothing else had ever made her do before—she swallowed her pride.

At eleven o'clock on Saturday morning, she took herself down to Mayan Memories and knocked with the hand that was not clutching one of Food Barn's $22.50 floral bouquets. Linda peeped through the glass and opened the door.

Maria Lopez herself turned around from the stove and regarded Zadie with what Zadie took to be hostility but was actually the pain of a hang-over the likes of which Maria had not felt since she was a teenager. Linda melted away to the tor-tilleria, leaving them to it.

Again, the information as to exactly what passed between them is slight. Maria confided the general outline to Mark Ramirez as Zadie did to Becky, but there is not enough known to recon-struct the initial dialogue.

All we know is that things got friendly pretty much right away. And we know this because not five minutes after Zadie arrived, Zadie left, she and Maria having hatched the beginning of their famous campaign. They were to meet again at three o'clock, they decided, and instructed each other to gather as many like-minded souls as possible.

Now, the meeting that took place at Mayan Memories on that Saturday afternoon is a bit like Woodstock. If all the people who claim that they were there had actually been there, folks would have had to sit on each other's laps. For the record, the following people were at what was thenceforth referred to as the Three o'Clock Meeting. They are as follows:

> Maria and Bill Lopez
> Oscar Burgos
> Zadie Gross
> Becky Lane
> Mark Ramirez
> Lottie Dougal
> Hector Rodriguez
> Pattie Walker
> Jim Evans

Both Dougal's Stationery Supplies and A Stitch in Time put little signs on their locked doors saying they'd be back in ten minutes. This turned out to be a falsehood. The sign also said in case of emergencies to try Mayan Memories, which is how Jim Evans ended up at the meeting, as he needed some new grommets for a tarp and came to rustle up Pattie or Becky. As it was, he ended up staying, with the momentous results of which we are now so conscious.

Now, as Maria said, the community that was to be immediately affected by the quarry closure felt extremely reticent to discuss its troubles with the general population. As Hector said later, on an occasion that need not now be named, "We assumed nobody would care and so we assumed a mantle of shame." And so it was that Jim, who was ordinarily not to be thought of as out of the loop, had not heard. He came in asking for his grommets and accepted a cup of coffee and sat down and found himself confounded by the long faces.

Though Jim Evans has a gift for the turn of the perfect phrase, he is not a chatty man. Jim is one of nature's observers. In fact, were it not for Mrs. Evans, we would probably never hear of Jim's apt descriptions and the world would be that much poorer a place.

So, though he accepted the cup of coffee and sat down on the fringes of the group, he didn't understand why Zadie Gross was holding forth with a red face and jabbing her finger at a red check on one of Maria's plastic wipe-clean tablecloths. She was saying, "We gotta get involved. It's no good sitting back and wishing and hoping. We gotta *do* something."

At which point Hector, who had been exhibiting such signs of extreme depression as leaving a thumbprint on one of his highly polished black brogues for two and half days, shrugged his hunched shoulders and said, "I don't know what else it is we can do, Miz Gross. If the workers don't want to buy themselves out . . ."

"It ain't that we don't want to," Bill Lopez said. "But none of us is exactly rich. I put most of our money and nearly all our equity in this place. All I got left is a little bit of rainy-day money."

"Rainy-day money?" Zadie snorted. "Well, what do you think, Bill? You're about to lose your job and your restaurant and prob'ly your house as well, because when the bank goes under with defaults some big outfit will take over the mortgages and you just know they'll foreclose as soon as you miss a couple payments."

At this point everyone looked at Hector, whose head drooped even lower over his coffee. He nodded sadly.

Zadie continued, "And that means this whole town is going right down the drain. So if you've got rainy-day money, I gotta ask myself just how much wet you're waiting for."

Bill Lopez set his mouth in a thin line and stared out of the circle as if he could see something important through the opposite wall. There was a moment of silence.

"It might be wet," Oscar said, "but you know, you got a little something and it's all you got, you don't want to just throw good money after bad."

Now Pattie spoke up. "Bill, if you don't mind me asking, do you think the quarry is a bad investment?"

"Hell, no, it ain't a bad investment!" Bill exploded. He got a look from all the ladies present at that point and double from his wife. "Sorry," he said briefly, "but it really gets me going when people talk that way. I ain't dumb, you know. I read them company reports. I know how much money goes outta that place and how much money comes in." He calmed down enough to have a sip of coffee.

"Listen. That's a good quarry," he went on. "Our men know what they're doing. We get good product, top quality. Blocks, chips, or rubble, we can do it. We do big slabs for all kinds of things—altars, people doing carvings, fancy kitchens. You know last year there were six crosses carved outta that limestone? It's a good big deposit, too."

Now it was Zadie's turn to explode. "Well, then, how on earth can you just sit on your behind and watch it die, holding on to your rainy-day money?"

Bill got to his feet. He said, "I don't got to put up with this. I mean, what the hell has it got to do with you?"

Zadie stood up, too. "You know damn well what it's got to do with me, Bill Lopez. I put near about everything I got in that diner and I ain't even opened it and might not get to."

They stood glaring at each other like they'd both like to take a swing. Jim reckoned if they'd been equal age, gender, and weight, they'd have been at it like a shot. You could tell they were both itching for a fight.

"Oh, sit down, both of you," Maria said. "You're acting like kids."

Very slowly, their eyes never leaving each other's faces, Zadie and Bill sat down.

Jim Evans cleared his throat. He said, "You know, this reminds me of something I was thinking about last Sunday." Mrs. Evans was a staunch member of the Baptist community, and since his marriage Jim had regularly attended services, even though everyone could tell his heart really wasn't in it. "I was at assembly," he said, "and the text was the loaves and fishes."

Here Jim took a long drink of his coffee. It is a tribute to his standing in the community and to Eudoran courtesy and patience that all of his listeners at that heated moment sat and watched him do this and waited for him to continue his thoughts.

"That's nice coffee, Maria," he then said, forcing them to wait just that little bit longer. Zadie breathed out in a way that might have meant she'd prefer him to get on with it, but might have just been her calming down—Becky wasn't sure.

"Well, I got to thinking about it. You know I don't go out of the house in the morning without a bit of something to eat packed, a thermos and some sandwiches or a little fried chicken and a couple apples or *something*. Because even though I got the new phone and all and Mary is real good about always cooking a decent lunch, I might just be right in the middle of something or out some-wheres she'd find it hard to get to and I might not always make it. Or maybe I'll get hungry early or run into somebody who hasn't had a bite in a while."

Everyone nodded, Oscar especially vigorously as, during his childhood fishing days, he had more than once run into Jim and his capacious lunch box and been gratefully refreshed.

Jim made sure everyone was with him before going on to his next point. "I reckon most country folks are like that," he said. "I don't know of any-body in an agricultural line who sets off in the morning with nothing. And the further back you go, the more it's true. My granddaddy had a big basket full of walnuts and a cracker he kept in his truck. He had apples in there and Lord knows what else."

Oscar said, "Fernando never sets off anywhere without a bite to eat on him. Does he, Maria?"

And Maria said, "No. It used to drive me crazy when I was in a hurry."

Jim nodded. "That's just what I was thinking," he said. "So I figured, back in Bible times, everyone would have been just the same, because they was all country folks, weren't they, shepherds and fishermen and such."

He took another long drink of his coffee. You could have heard a pin drop in the place. Everyone felt like what he was going to say was important. Maria got up and got the coffeepot and went around with it. Everybody thanked her in an undertone and she sat back down.

"So," Jim continued, "all them people had food on 'em already. That's what I reckon. Five thousand people, all having themselves a bite of this or that hidden under their cloaks or whatever they wore back then. Whatever you call them, it was flowing, you know? You could have half a turkey strapped under your arm and nobody would be the wiser."

Again, the assembled nodded. Pattie and Becky especially agreed, being experts in such matters.

"But they all of them didn't want to share," Jim continued. "My granddaddy was the same. If he caught you with your hand in his walnut basket, you were gonna have sore knuckles for a week. He'd rap you with that dang cracker. Boy, it'd sting." Jim rubbed his hand just thinking about it. "I mean, they were probably all thinking, 'I got just enough for me,' you know what I mean?"

Now that folks could see where it was going, they nodded more vigorously. "And I reckon our Lord, who can see into all our hearts, knew this about folks. I reckon he understood exactly what was going on. So he got that big basket and took what little that disciple had brought along to eat and his own and he made a big deal about sharing it and passed the basket. And it shamed 'em all, yeah, but it also made them stop being such scaredy cats. Which is a real miracle, to my way of thinking, and much more important than some silly magic trick that doesn't teach anybody anything."

This is the most anyone (except Mrs. Evans, in the privacy of their moments alone together) had ever heard Jim Evans say. He refreshed his throat with some more coffee and then finished by saying, "And I figure that's what you got to do. You got to find the disciple with his bite to eat and let everybody see you put it in the basket."

There was a moment's silence. Then Bill Lopez said. "Well, don't look at me. I'm one of the scaredy cats. I want that basket to be near enough *full* when it comes past me."

Zadie was trembling with fear, because she had known where Jim was going with this and she now knew what she was called upon to do. She hadn't known a moment's hesitation, let alone terror, about opening up the diner. But she knew it now. Before, she'd been a woman with her own house and a pension fund. If the diner went belly up, she could have moved to Florida or Arizona and been okay for the rest of her days in the sunshine. But now all that was going to be gone.

She could have just walked away. She could have just said to herself, *Well, that's interesting. I wonder who they're going to get,* and walked away and chalked the diner up to experience.

But because she had felt called to open the diner, and had felt called to do something about the quarry closure, she now felt called to be the disciple who put his fish in the basket. Zadie Gross had her faults, which all her fellow citizens knew well, as hers were the kind of faults that are worn on the outside. But she was not a scaredy cat.

She said, "Hector, I got quite a bit in my pension fund. You know?"

Hector's head snapped up like it was on a string somebody had pulled. A light came into his eyes that hadn't been there for a while. But with the habitual cautiousness of his profession, he said, "Mrs. Gross, you know that your retirement plan requires—"

Now that she'd done it, Zadie's steam was rising again. She cut in, saying, "Well, Hector, my retirement plan has changed. I think instead of sitting around a pool with a bunch of other old fogeys, waiting to die, I'm gonna work until I collapse." She smiled. "And attend quarry ownership meetings, of course, assuming everybody else antes up."

Pattie Walker cleared her throat. She said, "You know, Lottie and me have this little bit of money—it's only about eight thousand—that we got when Daddy left us." She looked a question at Lottie, who nodded. "We thought we might have to put it into the stationery shop, but since Mark joined the business we've been doing so well . . ." She trailed off, and Mark exhibited signs of self-consciousness. "We'd like to put that in the basket."

Jim Evans said, "It's been twenty-nine years since Linda Lou passed on and we still got her college fund. Just didn't know how to wind it up. Nothing seemed important enough. I know Mary will want me to put it in the basket."

Oscar said, "This is beautiful. And it reminds me of something."

Bill Lopez groaned. "Is this gonna be one of those long stories?" he asked. "Only I gotta get home and water the beans."

Hector was scribbling on a napkin, and Oscar turned to him. "Put us down for four thousand," he said, and then, "I forgot all about it. One night I was over to Lottie's and was looking out at the garden. I'd been thinking about . . . well, what we all been thinking about. And it just hit me, bam! This isn't about brown people against the white bosses. It's about everybody in this town, and we gotta work together if we're going to stop it. I had this vision of a rototiller, digging up Lottie's veg-etable patch—"

"A rototiller?" Bill said. "You had a vision and it was about a rototiller?"

"Yeah," Oscar said, "ripping up the plants even though they was growing."

This was a powerful image to Eudorans, who are, as has been mentioned previously in this chronicle, fanatic and competitive gardeners. For a moment, all those present imagined their own little patches of growing vegetables going down under the mechanical, impersonal blades.

Bill Lopez shook his head. "I know what you mean," he said. "But I only got about two or three thousand left in the bank. And that's where it's staying."

"Well," Hector said, frowning at his napkin, "it's a start, anyway. But we've got a long way to go."

It was here that Becky Lane broke in with her contribution. It was not monetary (the Lane men were twice as shiftless and unhandy as the Lane women were talented, conscientious, and hard-working, and as a result, Lane women tended to remain on a lower economic plane than their drive and abilities deserved), but it was important nonetheless. She said, "But how are you going to show the basket, Hector? Jesus held it up in front of everybody to get 'em going."

"I got an idea," Hector said. "Oscar, is it okay if I use that thing about the rototiller?"

"It's yours," Oscar said.

For the first time in the last few weeks, Bill Lopez smiled a little.

Jim Evans broke the mood. Turning to Pattie and Becky, he asked, "You gals got any number eight grommets?"

The doctor's mother returned to Seattle, and the reign of Janey Lane began in the doctor's office. The doctor found his work life immeasurably enhanced, though he felt guilty about preferring Janey to both his mother and his late wife.

Janey was not intense. It was not an emotional experience to come downstairs in the morning and be greeted. She had no personal axe to grind. She also was very grateful for the position and a bundle of energy. You combine those two with the attributes common to all Lane females and you have a secretarial paragon. Janey came in a little bit early that first week just to clean. And though the doctor had thought the place clean and tidy, he noticed the difference in cleaning to Lane standards. It smelled lemony and seemed brighter.

Janey herself, her honey-blond hair pulled resolutely back, was as slim and cool as a Modigliani sculpture. She spoke warmly and personally on the telephone but was acutely aware of the delicacy needed in her position. She'd even had three years of high school Spanish and had brought with her an old textbook with the section regarding the parts of the body marked with a Post-it note. She kept the thing in her top drawer.

She mastered the temperamental espresso machine on her first day, and after her subsequent cleaning it was markedly less temperamental. She brought in banana skins and shined the plants. She pulled the files on the next day's appointments before she left in the evening and laid them out neatly on the doctor's desk in order. She downloaded a free program from the Internet that would work with the doctor's computer system and allow them to keep all records online. It worked with Outlook, so that in the future this fiddling around with paper would not have to be done. The doctor had already been instructed to type his notes in the little boxes of the record software and no longer had to print them out or scrawl them by hand, saving a good four or five minutes per patient.

And it was only Thursday.

The doctor no longer really needed to go to Margery's every morning, but it had become part of his regular routine, and besides, Ben Nichols left the newspaper for him and he went to pick it up. It was eight-thirty in the morning and he didn't have anyone to see until nine-fifteen. He also had nothing to do, thanks to Janey Lane. So he decided to make a house call and see how Jim Flory was.

He whistled as he walked along Main Street. This was more like it, he thought. This was what a general practitioner had going for him. Jim

Emery had been attracted to medicine by the money, but something had happened to him along the way. He had found that he was interested in his patients. It ruined him for surgery and made emergency work extremely painful. He liked to see how the story ended, is how he put it to his med school mentor. His med school mentor shook his head sadly and told him he was a fool and would make a hell of a GP. Jim thought about that as he walked up the street, a bag containing four maple danish (Jim Flory's favorite, according to Margery) balanced on the top of his box.

The front door was ajar, but if the bell rang when the doctor pressed the button, it did so quietly and far away. He waited for a second and then rapped on the wood with his knuckles. "Mr. Flory?" he called. "Jim?"

He stepped inside the hall. "Mr. Flory? It's Dr. Emery. Okay if I come in?"

There was no answer.

Now, there is some fine oak paneling up to about waist height in the entrance to the Flory house, and a fine glass chandelier. The floor is tiled with a black-and-white checkerboard effect. But the doctor didn't notice any of this much. He was starting to have a bad feeling.

"Jim?" he called again, this time very loudly and with urgency.

He thought he could hear something, something like a pounding noise. It was getting closer.

Just then Jim Flory burst through his own front door, making the doctor jump a good two feet and necessitating quick action to save the baked goods.

Jim was wearing gray sweat bottoms and a T-shirt that read "Pink Pride." His face was red and he was out of breath. He said, "Come in," and then gasped a little and said, "Water."

The doctor followed as Flory staggered into the kitchen and collapsed at the big pine table, hitting a button on the coffeemaker on the way. There was a small bottle of water with a sports top waiting in front of his chair. He nearly choked trying to drink it before he caught his breath.

Doc Emery noted that the kitchen was pretty clean and that the previous night's dishes (stacked neatly in the sink) showed evidence of a good solid meal. When he sat down, he ran his fingers across the table and it wasn't sticky or crumby.

Jim Flory himself was, as he returned to his normal color, looking marginally better than the last time the doctor had seen him. His hair was nicely cut and his face, though unshaven, had clearly been shaven the day before and would probably be again after its owner's recovery from exertion.

"How long have you been running?" the doctor asked.

"Today?" Jim wanted clarification. "Or forever?"

Doc Emery shrugged. "I meant forever, but how long today, too?"

Jim took another shuddering pull on the water bottle. "Oh," he panted, "I did cross country in high school. Today I did about three miles and it nearly killed me."

The doctor said, "I came to see how you were getting on with the medication. I brought you some maple danish, but if you don't want it—"

"I want it." The coffee had dripped a good two cups' worth into the pot. Flory got down three cups out of what looked to the doctor like a nice shiny stack of crockery in the cupboard and put two cups on the counter and one under where the coffee still dripped as he pulled out the pot to pour. He then replaced the pot, pouring the coffee that had accumulated in the third cup into it before settling it into the center of the heated ring. "I'm not doing it to lose weight, exactly. Black, half and half, or milk?"

"Milk," the doctor said. "Why are you doing it, then?"

"Oh, to look better and to try and feel a little better. I've got more energy now, but I still feel pretty terrible."

"How terrible? I mean, what do you feel like?"

Flory sighed and ran a hand across his eyes. "I feel sad," he said. "I feel so damn sad sometimes, I think I might die from it. And then sometimes I just don't feel much of anything. It makes me almost look forward to the sadness."

After a brief discussion of symptoms and an

inquiry (entirely satisfactory) about Jim's ability to remain one of life's teetotalers, the doctor sat and sucked pecans out of the spaces between his teeth. Finally he said, "I want you to make an appointment and come in. We need to change your medication."

Town meetings are called infrequently. The last one had been about flash flooding and had been imperfectly attended. Clement McAllister was heard to say that he could have got more opinion just sitting out in front of Margery Lupin's bakery and calling folks over to his car.

They were held in the high school gym, where, since Barney Lane had not gotten around to removing the graduation seating, there was ample space for the entire population and then some.

This was a good thing.

Clement McAllister and Hector Rodriguez had announced a meeting about the quarry closure and the bank's position. Hector and Lottie Dougal had, the previous week, been spending a great deal of time in the back room of the stationery store, writing a press release. Mark Ramirez was not entirely sure that this would be needed. Though he had not previously graced town meetings with his person, he knew that members of the media did not ordinarily attend. He confided to Maria Lopez that it seemed a waste of time getting something like that ready just in case.

Maria said she didn't know. She wasn't really listening. Ever since the Three o'Clock Meeting, Bill hadn't been sleeping at all. She thought of him up there, with those explosives and everything and not having gotten enough sleep and . . . well, she just prayed to God he would be okay because none of them up there was sleeping all that well and you know what men get like when they're tired, they make mistakes.

For the third time in as many weeks, the quarry was securely locked and left to its own devices. Chuck ushered his two out-of-town patrons out the door and did the same to the Beer and Bowl. Food Barn was operating with a skeleton staff, and Lane Nichols had posted his cell number on the door of the gas station in case of emergencies and locked it up tight, too. Mayan Memories was also shut, though they would be serving a special one-plate-one-price buffet after the meeting and it included all you could get in one of their foil-lined to-go boxes. Mark, as he walked to the door of the gymnasium, like many other citizens, was contemplating whether to lay one burrito lengthways and leave room for extras or to squash it up sideways and maybe get in two and miss out on beans or salad or rice.

Mark opened the door.

The first thing he got was an overwhelming impression of brightness. Then the noise hit. People were shouting. The meeting hadn't yet started and the shouting was not coming from any of the citizens of Eudora, who, on the whole, inclined toward the soft-spoken in any case. The shouting was coming from people wearing headsets and carrying coils of cabling. The lights were theirs. There were four or five microphones on the lectern up at the gymnasium stage, where the bunting in the high school colors of blue and gold still remained, though the "Go Cyclones" banner had been removed.

Lottie Dougal was standing in a corner smiling and laughing and talking with ease to a bunch of people with notebooks and ill-fitting jackets. Over by the edge of the stage, in front of the first row of people, and—Mark peered—in front of the sycamore tree out in back of the gym, where all the cable snaked away to large, noisy vans, were a total of three people, two women and one man, all wearing dressy clothes and makeup. They were talking to cameras with urgent but smiling expressions.

The residents of Eudora sat stunned and quiet on the rows of floor seating. Betty Requena, who, like all the Requenas, had not been speaking to Mark after his breakup with Kylie (which was not, we feel we should stress, entirely Mark's fault, as Kylie had a flirtatious nature and enjoyed making Mark feel jealous and upset, though she did not of course deserve the things Mark said about her in the heat of the moment and loud enough for her mother and father to hear), pulled Mark down by his shirtsleeve to sit next to her and said, "Boy, this is something else, isn't it?"

Mark's mouth had been hanging open, and he shut it and shook his head in wonder, still not trusting his capacity for speech.

Again, his attention wandered to where his employer was holding court. She had a stack of their best blue window report covers clutched to her chest and suddenly seemed serious. The rumpled people were writing down what she said. Mark felt a surge of pride in Lottie that she had the ability to do something like that, that she was so pretty and so nice. He had felt grateful for quite some time for his position at Dougal's, but now he felt grateful just to be associated with Lottie at all. He thought about the Three o'Clock Meeting and looked around for the other participants. Jim and Mary Evans had driven in. Maria and Bill were sitting with Oscar and Hector's family. They all looked nervous. Pattie and Phil had the boys with them. The older ones seemed terribly excited by the film crews and lights. The youngest was asleep across his mama.

Zadie Gross was sitting with the Lanes. Mark didn't know of any other Grosses in town and it seemed like the Lanes had kind of adopted Zadie. Zadie appeared to be almost as excited as the Walker boys. As Mark watched, she leaned over and said something to Janey Lane. And Mark suddenly saw Janey, whom he had known since he was five years old, as if for the very first time.

Later, he thought it was probably because she'd had just gotten her job at the doctor's and radiated the confidence that (he knew well himself) comes when you have found your calling in life. Or maybe it was, as Janey said later, the nice clothes she'd found in the city and the highlights she'd had put in her hair. But all Mark knew then was that Janey Lane was suddenly completely entrancing, her slim hand brushing her hair back over her tanned shoulder, her white teeth as she smiled, the cute way her slightly off-kilter nose (broken in a softball game in which Janey, though wounded by the ball, still managed to steal third) wrinkled up as she said something that made Zadie laugh.

Betty couldn't get a word of sense out of him and started talking to her husband again instead. Mark just stared at Janey Lane until the tapping of a pen on the microphone brought his attention to a less important aspect of his future.

Clement McAllister's address was brief and factual. Though it lacked any emotional appeal, he still managed to chill his audience to the bone. Those few people who had entered the gymnasium unaware of just how serious the quarry closure would be for the town were no longer unaware. Those people who'd had a pretty good idea how serious it would be now understood it was worse than they had thought. Clement had a few charts and graphs. The one marked "Debts and Liabilities" had a red line that started low on the left and climbed up considerably on the right. The one marked "Projected Area Income" had a red line that started high on the left and plunged rapidly on the right.

There were a few questions from members of the press after Clement's speech, but the townspeople were, on the whole, too shocked and stunned to respond.

Then it was Hector's turn. Boy, did Hector look good that night. He is always a natty man, but that night his shirt nearly blinded people, it was so white. His suit looked good. He had it all buttoned up and you could see how well it fit him. His shoes shone so much they glowed in the television lights, and his tie, a rich red foulard, gave his serious and handsome face that all-important dash and verve.

For Hector was dynamic that night. When he had spoken at the quarry, he had been confident, but he had not been dynamic. He had not been convincing. He had not made you feel like he'd thought things through. But in the gymnasium that night, he sure did.

He started right at the beginning and talked about the history of the quarry. He didn't pull any punches, either, about health and safety issues and benefits. He laid it all out on the line. And he had charts, too. He showed, from year to year, how much money the companies that had owned the quarry took out of the operation and how much they put back in, in terms of investment. Both of these lines were on a chart, the profit in blue and the investment in green. The profit line was always much higher than the investment line until it got to the last owner, who had been required to come up to OSHA standards. Then it dipped down below the investment line, but everyone could now see that was just a blip.

He put numbers up that showed how much money had left Eudora over the years from the profits of the quarry. These made townspeople gasp and reporters scribble furiously.

He spoke about the quarry workers and their race and nationality. He used terms like *exploitation* and *economic migration.*

And then he talked about community. He talked about how for a long time there were two Eudoras, that even though they had shared the same schools, shops, bank, and churches, the two communities had not, until recently, shared friendship and fellowship. But then he talked about how that had changed.

He made all those of less recent immigration in the audience feel good about being so open and unprejudiced. He made all those of more recent immigration feel good about themselves because of all they had given to the community.

He said that Eudora was like a garden in July, bearing beans and tomatoes and zucchini and peppers and corn. It was fruitful and it was growing and healthy. And he said that the closure of the quarry was like a big rototiller coming to plow it all under.

He took a drink of water and let that sink in.

And then he said, "But we aren't going to let them do that. And we aren't going to let the profits from this good business go out of town anymore. What we make here stays here, from now on out."

Next he outlined again his plan for buying the quarry. He even used the same boards he'd had in the quarry meeting. But they looked different. They looked less intimidating and more possible.

And then Hector spoke directly to the quarry workers. He said they did not have to do this alone. He said that they had always felt themselves to be alone, but they were not. He said in their moment of need, they had withdrawn from the very people who both wanted and needed to help them. He said, "We assumed nobody would care and so we assumed a mantle of shame." He said this mantle must be cast off and that they must let their neighbors see their need, because, as Clement had so clearly demonstrated, it was the neighbors' need as well.

When he got to this point in his speech, Clement, who had been sitting behind him on one of those folding chairs, got up and went to a table over by the steps leading up to the stage. He had paper and pens on there and a little box.

Hector then put up another board. On the board was a drawing of a big basket. There were numbers along the side. A green infill came up just under halfway. He talked about how the bank and some business owners and ordinary people had put money into the basket to save the quarry and the jobs and the town. He spoke about how, in the future, quarry management meetings would be held not in a room on the twenty-fourth floor of some building in New York City but right here in the school gym, and that unless he did not know Eudora at all, they might as well call them town meetings because everybody in town was going to put something in that basket.

At this point, Hector had to stop because of the thunderous applause. Mark wished his parents were still alive to see this moment. He looked around and saw that many of the quarry workers, huge men, hard as the rock they worked, had tears running down their faces.

Hector then said that anyone who wanted to pledge a contribution right now was welcome to come and talk to Clement. There was a stampede and then another stampede as the film crews interviewed just about everybody they could get their hands on who was standing in line. The whole thing took quite a while and nobody really wanted to leave. Hector had a green highlighter and, at signals from Clement regarding total investment, would color in more and more of the basket.

Mark himself had five hundred dollars he had saved up to buy a better car. He had been one of the first ones to get to Clement, since he had been at the Three o'Clock Meeting and so had been provided with time to think it over.

He then stopped to talk to Hector and make sure he had enough ink in his highlighter and a backup.

He sat back down in his chair. Most people around him either were in line or had left. Mark saw across the way that some folks had gone to the buffet at Mayan Memories and brought it back into the gym to eat it. His tummy rumbled.

And then it was like somebody else took over his body, somebody smooth and confident and certain. He got up, thinking he was going to walk out the door and down the street. Instead, he walked up to where Janey Lane was sitting with her sister and said he was going to go get a bite to eat to bring back and would she like to come with him? Janey took the orders of all her family and Zadie and gathered together a sum of money, and she and Mark walked down the sidewalk together. The dim streetlights allowed the stars to the right and the left of them to be clearly visible, as was the waxing moon above. Trees and flowers exhaled as they passed, and the night was soft and faintly warm.

It was only ten or eleven blocks. But by the time they had arrived at the restaurant, they had also arrived at an understanding.

Bedtime may mean other things in other places, but in Eudora, it means ten-thirty. By nine forty-five all the film crews had gone and Lottie, Hector, and Clement were alone on the gymnasium stage. Three empty cartons and three half-full beers on Clement's table attested to their repast and refreshment. Clement yawned, saying, "I'm just not up for these late nights anymore."

Lottie said, "Oh, I hardly ever finish my consultations until about now."

Clement said, "If your daddy'd had your get-up-and-go, he would have beat me in that election. He'd have ended up a senator."

Lottie said, "Well, Daddy had other things besides get-up-and-go."

Clement said, "Yes, ma'am. He was a fine man. We all miss him."

They both looked at Hector, who had stopped using the calculator at long last. Hector shook his head. "We're still short," he said.

"By how much?" Clement asked. "I still got a little held back."

"Nearly a quarter of a million."

"Hellfire," Clement said. "I ain't got that much held back."

Hector took the pile of papers and started to go through it again, but Clement took it and the calculator away from him and put them in his briefcase, which had been hidden behind the curtain. He said, "Now listen to me, you two. You did fine work tonight, both of you. And we got the whole town on our side now. I want you both to go home and get some sleep."

"But," Hector protested, "it's not enough."

Clement sighed. He said, "I ain't learned much in my lifetime, but one thing I have learned is that you can't do good work if you don't look after yourself." Lottie nodded agreement. "Now, I don't know what the answer is going to be. But I know damn sure we aren't going to find it tonight."

Just then Barney Lane appeared in the doorway, leaning on his broom. He said, "I gotta clean up in here."

So they left. It was cooler than it had been when Mark and Janey walked to the restaurant, and Lottie shivered in her blouse. Yet she stood, as they all did, for a moment on the sidewalk.

Hector said, "In the movies, everything goes all right once people get together."

Clement gave a sad smile. "In real life, sometimes the bad guys win."

Lottie sighed.

Clement said, "Look here. We're all three supposed to be Christians. We need to turn this over to the Lord, just for one night at least. Go home and get some sleep. You done good, Hector. You done your best."

And on that note, they separated, Lottie and Hector to walk their divergent paths homeward and Clement to get in his Cadillac and drive to where Lucy waited with another dinner and more badly needed beer.

Lottie Dougal walked swiftly. This was because she was both cold and angry.

She stomped into her house, muttering to herself about how it wasn't fair, and yanked the curtains closed. She flicked on the television with one hand while she unbuttoned her blouse with the other. She was tapping her foot the way she often did when she was annoyed.

And then she stopped.

She looked at the remote control in her hand and punched the button again. Yes, it was the national news. Hector's face, which looked far more handsome on-screen than it did in real life, looked back at her.

For a moment she couldn't hear.

Then it was Oscar Burgos saying, "We just didn't think they'd care," and then the camera cut to the line of people, including Pattie, carrying Ben, who was asleep with his head on her shoulder. One of the highly polished people was saying, "This is one rural community that will not go quietly into that good night."

Back in the studio, the anchorpeople smiled at each other. One said, "That's a nice story."

The other said, "I'm going to send them a check."

They had a little laugh about it and went to the sports.

Lottie still had one hand on her blouse buttons and one hand on the remote control. She stared at the television as if she'd never seen it before.

And then the phone rang.

Lottie knew it was Pattie because she had caller ID and also because she'd heard Pattie scream before. It was an intense sound, so high-pitched that Lottie thought parts of it could only be heard by dogs. Here and there you could pick out words: "television," "national," and "Ben."

Lottie said in a calm, soothing tone, "I saw it, I saw it, Pattie. I saw it," until Pattie could calm down enough to catch her breath.

"Oh," Pattie finally said, "it's so exciting."

"I just can't believe it," Lottie said. "I knew the local news was supposed to have it on tomorrow and there was the cable news and that guy from Reuters, but . . ."

Pattie exclaimed, "I was just sitting down after cleaning up the kitchen and Phil put on the news and I *just couldn't* . . ." Here she degenerated into a long scream again.

During this one, Lottie clicked off the television and sat down on her sofa. She looked at her hand, which was shaking.

Once again, Pattie recovered. In the background, Lottie could hear Phil saying something about going deaf.

There was a moment while the two sisters listened to each other breathe. Then they both said, at the same time, "Didn't Hector look handsome?"

As soon as Lottie put the phone down, it rang again: Mark. And again: Clement. And again: Oscar, who had seen it out on duty at the quarry and was dying to talk to somebody about it. They talked about various aspects of the coverage, but they all seemed to come back to how handsome Hector had appeared on-screen.

In fact, the only person who didn't seem to know how good he had looked on national television was Hector. He had come home to a quiet house, the excitement and pride having been too much for his parents, who had gone to bed with palpitating hearts. He had brushed his teeth without looking at himself in the mirror, depressed and angry. It was he, he felt, who had failed everybody. He had made them believe in something that wasn't true. His calculations had been way off, way, way off. When they found out how wrong, how *stupid* he was . . . Hector Rodriguez threw his good suit over a hanger and himself in the middle of his bed and went to sleep with tears in his eyes.

Jim Flory had been at the meeting and had given some money he could ill afford. Dr. Emery had been there, too, as had Terry Walker, Phil and Artie's cousin, who sold insurance with a fervor that made him the most avoided man in Eudora. In fact, when Doc Emery saw Terry bearing down on him with his big smiling face and his hand outstretched, he wished he could turn and run away. But he was cornered, just as he'd been a few months back when he walked into Terry's spiderweb of an office as a man needing car insurance so he could get state tags and had come out as a fly insured for various unlikely events up to his eyeballs.

But for once, Terry grew on somebody. Because as he relentlessly pumped the doctor's hand, he also reminded him that he'd taken out a $100,000 life insurance policy on his wife and that Terry had filled out the claim forms on the doctor's behalf and just needed a signature.

So when time came for all to contribute their bit, the doctor contributed $50,000. Clement like to have died.

Doc sat back down by Jim Flory for a second while he watched Hector fill in a substantial part of the basket with Angela's legacy. Jim's hands were shaking badly. He said, in response to the doctor's inquiry, "The shaking comes and goes. I haven't felt real sure about opening up the cinema, though, because I'm worried about the Cokes."

"When am I seeing you?" the doctor asked.

"Day after tomorrow."

"Good."

T he next person who called Lottie Dougal on the telephone that night was Dr. James Emery. She decided not to answer it, but somehow her treacherous hand pushed the button and she had to say hello.

The doctor hadn't seen the national news. He'd been too busy down in his office, looking at books and on Internet sites about various antidepressants. What he'd read nearly depressed *him.*

"Lottie," he said, "I'm calling you on a professional matter."

"Okay," she said guardedly.

"I'd like to call you in for a consultation regarding a patient suffering from depression. The patient has reactions to all the main agents in antidepressants and I'm wondering if there might be a natural alternative that would better suit his needs."

"There's three or four," Lottie said. "Who is it?"

"I don't want to do this over the phone," the doctor said. "Do you want to come to me, or should I come to you?"

"Well," Lottie said, "let me get my date book."

She swallowed hard as she went to her bag. Just hearing his voice made tears run down the back of her throat.

When she picked the phone up again he said, "We have to do it tomorrow. I've got eleven-thirty."

But Lottie had a farm machinery calendar to organize. She could do twelve-thirty.

At last they decided on three. Lottie would come to his office.

Afterward she sat and stared at the silent phone. So was it going to be like this? Was he going to stay in town and she was going to just be the stationer and the herbal practioner to him? She would see him here and there, they would sometimes consult. He'd marry Janey, Lottie thought, unaware that Janey's affections had already been given away elsewhere. And she herself would slowly wither and die of a break, not just in her heart but in her very soul.

Lottie was a practical woman. All the publicity in the world did not make up a $250,000 deficit. And the man she loved no longer even knew she was a woman. She lay in the dark of her bedroom on her back, her arms out of her grandmother's quilt, and stared up into the blackness of the night.

Becky Lane was in a delicate position. She hadn't yet given Pattie her notice, and Zadie hadn't quite decided when the diner should open. She had tried to broach the subject with Zadie at the town meeting, but Zadie had been too full of emotion to pay much attention to anything besides Hector and the chicken enchilada with fixings that Janey had brought back from Mayan Memories.

She and Pattie were due to look at Halloween

craft items and materials that day in late June with an idea of getting their orders in to the suppliers fairly soon. You had to think ahead in the fabric business. They were already doing a brisk trade in Fourth of July projects—the stitch-your-own-flag kit was particularly successful, as Becky had told Pattie it would be, because it was a low-skill-level item that mothers could buy for daughters to do. This was particularly attractive because it (a) had a deadline by which the work must be accomplished and so would not drag on neglected for years, and (b) came in handy just when the first flush of summer vacation had faded and cries of "I'm so bored—I got nothing to do" were beginning to surface.

In fact, Pattie had complimented Becky on her vision and prescience just yesterday afternoon, and this was one thing that had made Becky feel uncomfortable about her position.

So she went over to Zadie's in the morning. Zadie had already been out to Food Barn for all the newspapers and had managed to find quite a few mentions of Eudora. The *Douglas County Gazette* had pretty much filled half the paper with last night's goings-on and interviews. It concentrated on why Eudora had survived until now in the first place, going back into when the interstate decided not to build an exit leading to the town and when the railway had closed its station. The *Star,* from the city, also had considerable coverage, but from the angle of big business and money going out of the state, which always seemed to get the paper's editorial panties in a bunch. These articles could be read later. What was avidly pursued around Zadie's kitchen table were two mentions in the national newspapers. One was in the *New York Times* itself, talking about how the pressures of globalization are killing rural communities all over the world and what we lose when we lose rural communities. There was Eudora, along with a place in Malaysia and one in Bosnia and Herzegovina. Along with the faces of villagers in the hills and jungles were faces from last night's town meeting: Oscar talking to Pattie with Ben asleep over her shoulder, Hector gesticulating passionately from the gymnasium lectern.

Ordinarily, folks would get all worked up about Eudora getting a paragraph under "State News" in *USA Today.* But after all that, Zadie and Becky barely glanced at it, only reading it three times.

Zadie said, "This is all Lottie Dougal's doing, you know. She wrote this press release thing and faxed it all over the place. Clement said there weren't any whoppers in it but that it came close in parts."

Becky said, "She's a talented woman." And then, trying to lead Zadie's mind to her own agenda, said, "Seems like everybody took a picture of Pattie with Ben."

Zadie said, "Did you see the cable news?"

Becky, a single mother of four girls, two still in school, had not seen fit to squander money on more or better television when sitting down and watching television seemed to her way of thinking a waste of time anyway. She said, "No, you know I don't have it."

"Well," Zadie said, "it showed us listening to Hector with our mouths open."

Becky said, "How did we look?"

Zadie said, "Pretty good. Of course they picked us because of your girls. Janey's really blossomed, hasn't she?"

At this point in the conversation, both Becky and Zadie were led away from what they were trying to say by a discussion about Mark Ramirez, his tragic family circumstances, the steadiness of his employment, and his looks and taste in clothes. When Becky Lane glanced at her watch, she knew she was going to have to come right out with it. She drew breath to do so, but then Zadie said, "I know it's still not completely safe, but I'm ordering food tomorrow. How much notice you gotta give Pattie?"

Becky said, "Well, I'm supposed to give her two weeks."

"You do that, then," Zadie told her. "I got to drive in and see my lawyer today. I'll get a real employment contract drawn up at the money we talked about. You'll get tips, too, probably."

Becky smiled, and so did her friend. Zadie said, "It's going to be so nice working with you. I think we can really build something out of this."

Becky, who was overwhelmed with emotion, said, "You know, we better order them shoes. It takes forever for them to ship."

But Zadie knew exactly what she meant.

Pattie went over to the stationery store about three o'clock, but her sister wasn't there. Mark said she'd gone out to a meeting but he didn't know where—it wasn't in the desk calendar. This was deeply suspicious, but Pattie was too worked up to think about it then, though she did later. She went over to Mayan Memories and poured out her employee woes into Maria's willing ear. Maria poured her coffee in return and sat down for a moment in one of the booths, just letting Pattie talk it out.

Finally, Pattie wound down, saying, "Well, I suppose it was inevitable. She wanted more responsibility, and really, it's just not that kind of a job." She sighed. "But I don't know where I'm going to find anybody else. Everybody who knows anything about fabric around here has already either got a job or is about a hundred years old."

Linda, who had been filling salt shakers on the adjoining tables, broke into the conversation. She said to Maria, "What about Carla?"

And Maria said, "Yeah! Do you think she'd do it?"

Linda nodded her handsome head. "I think so. She's always complaining about how she wants a steady paycheck." Linda then talked directly to Pattie. "It's my cousin, Carla Bustamonte. Her mother is Betty Requena's sister."

Now it was Pattie's turn to nod, indicating that she was familiar with both the speaker and Betty Requena and understood the kind of employee assets thus indicated. In Eudora it is common to give a bit of genetic background when describing people for the first time. It saves a lot of trouble.

Maria scooted over and Linda sat down. "Carla went and did a degree in clothes designing," Linda said. "And she even got a job and everything, but she didn't like it and she hated New York. So she came back here. She does a lot of wedding dresses and things like that, and she does okay. I mean, you won't get her cheap or anything. A lot of people come from town, and she goes up there . . ." Linda trailed off.

"Do you really think she'd be interested?"

Linda nodded. "She wants a steady paycheck. You know how hard it is to get an apartment around here. Well, she can't get no mortgage, either, and living with her folks is about to drive her crazy."

Pattie said, "There's an apartment right above the shop. We store fabrics in one of the rooms, but there's quite a bit of space up there. Nobody's lived up there for a long time. It needs work, but . . ."

And that is how Carla Bustamonte first came to A Stitch in Time to such incredible effect. Of course, Carla's subsequent career and Pattie's involvement in the same cannot be discussed within the confines of this particular chronicle. But anyone who knows Eudora would be interested to know the seed from which this peculiar tree eventually grew.

And anyone who knows Eudora will also know that it was not long before Pattie's curiosity about Lottie's whereabouts was satisfied.

Lottie Dougal had not been in a doctor's office since her last vaccination at the age of eight. It is a tribute to Janey Lane's composure that she didn't allow the astonishment in her mind to register on her face as she took her through. Still, she quickly rang her mother to let her know the incredible news, which was waiting for Pattie when she returned to the fabric store in a much better frame of mind and gave Becky her blessing on the new enterprise.

The doctor stood up when Lottie entered his consultation room, and leaned over his desk with his hand out, saying, "Thank you so much for coming."

Lottie took his hand and shook it. There was a moment, Janey said, a definite moment, when they touched. She thought she might have seen Lottie blush a little, and the doctor had to clear his throat before offering Lottie a seat. Janey asked Lottie and the doctor if they'd like some coffee and Lottie said she'd love a cappuccino, as she didn't get one as good as they made very often, and the doctor asked for his usual.

These things take time, and the milk-steaming nozzle of the doctor's fancy coffee machine is very noisy, so we know nothing of what went on in the beginning of the meeting. But when Janey went in with the tray and served the cups out, she said the atmosphere was different. It was comfortable. Lottie was sitting right up at the desk and leaning over her side of it. She'd taken a big book out of her briefcase and the doctor was looking at it with her. The doctor thanked Janey, as did Lottie, but before Janey closed the door again, she heard the doctor ask, "What's the chemical makeup of the root?"

Lottie said, "Now, Jim, you know that's not the way I look at things. I've got no idea."

And the doctor said, "Well, let's look it up on Google. I don't want to get his hopes up only to discover it's got some of the same stuff in it."

A few minutes later, the doctor buzzed through and asked Janey to get Park Davis of Maple Leaf Pharmacy on the line. You could hear Lottie arguing in the background, saying something about "unnecessary."

The phone call with Park was brief. Still, discussion was occurring in the doctor's office, and voices were starting to be raised. As the waiting room was filling up with interested parties, Janey thought it might be a good idea to go in and get the cups and let the doctor know his three-thirty had arrived.

She knocked, but they didn't pay a blind bit of notice. The doctor had run his hands through his hair, and it was standing up. He'd also jerked his tie down. Lottie was leaning over the desk now and pointing at him.

Janey closed the door behind her and cleared her throat.

She said, "Doctor, I thought you ought to know—"

But Lottie said, "Just tell me what the difference is between getting it in a bottle and getting it out of a sack in my garage?"

And the doctor said, "I'm concerned about potency, storage—"

Lottie said, "I've been helping to gather and store this stuff for twenty-five years. We haven't lost a man yet."

The doctor sighed.

Janey said, "I'm sorry to interrupt, but—"

"I have a problem," the doctor said, "with entrusting the mental health of my patient to something that was dug out of the woods at the state park."

"Is it that?" Lottie asked. "Or is it that you have trouble entrusting his mental health to *me*?"

There was a brief moment of silence during which Janey watched both of their chests heave with emotion. Later, she thought she should have tried to break in again, but right then, she just wanted to find out what the doctor would say.

He said, "God help me, Lottie, I don't know."

Lottie started to shove things back into her briefcase. Janey said it looked like she was trying to do it with her eyes closed. She grabbed her jacket and pushed past Janey to get through the door, saying, "Thanks for the cappuccino, Janey, it was lovely."

The doctor sat back in his chair. His eyes were closed, too. Janey gathered the cups and put them on her tray. Then she tidied his desk and pushed the folder containing the records of his three-thirty appointment across to him.

When he opened his eyes, he looked five years older.

He said, "Show her in, Janey." And blew his nose.

Lottie walked back to her shop and straight into the bathroom, where she washed her face. But even before she made it back to the counter, her sister had heard all about it.

Meanwhile, down at the bank, people were coming in with checks. All over town, folks were cashing in policies and certificates of deposit, winding up trusts and pulling out of investments. Hector's stomachache became a permanent thing. Because though he could smile and shake hands just as well as Clement could, he could not be as sanguine as Clement was about the futility of these exercises.

Clement kept saying it would be all right, that something would happen to make up the missing $250,000. But Hector found this hard to believe. So while he was smiling and shaking hands and filling in the more permanent version of the basket illustration for the lobby of the bank, internally he was adding up all the lost interest and penalties of early withdrawal and adding that to the sum total of the town's economic losses due to the quarry closure.

It didn't help when he got a phone call from Representative Dale Winslow. Winslow wanted Hector to know he was mighty proud of him, mighty proud, and that Eudora was a fine community, fine, and that he was looking forward to visiting for the Maple Leaf Festival, really looking forward to it, and wanted to shake Hector's hand. He told him he'd had the *New York Times* article blown up and it was hanging in his office on Capitol Hill, yes sir, right in his office, because he was so dang proud of Hector and Clement and the whole town, but mostly because he was so proud of Hector, dang proud, yes sir.

And Hector, while making all the right noises of appreciation, was cringing internally because he knew that as soon as his failure was made public, Dale Winslow would be doing some hasty office redecoration and cooking up some spurious reason why it would be impossible for him to travel in the second week of October. As soon as he got off the phone, he reached for another tablet of a well-known antacid preparation and chewed it vigorously.

Just then, Clement came into the little cubby-hole that served Hector for an office. As he shut the door, he looked at Hector carefully. He said, "I don't know if your nerves are good enough for politics, son. You got to learn to let things go."

"I will," Hector said. "I will let it go, when it's over."

"Well, it ain't over yet. Royle Deacon's coming in to see about the quarry fund's position and to talk about management transition strategies."

This was not good news, and Hector allowed it to show on his face.

"I tried putting him off," Clement said, "but if I'd a tried any harder, he would have smelled a rat. I reckon we just got to level with him."

Hector did something he'd never done before. He sat down while Clement was standing, just sank into his chair. He said, "If he knows we can't do it, he'll quit." He covered up his eyes with his hand. "And if he quits, it's all over. Everybody will know why before sundown. All those people, cashing in securities—I've been taking them with a smile, and all along I've known . . . and they'll *know* that, Clement. I'll be done in this town. In this state! I'll just be done."

Clement sat down in the uncomfortable little visitor's chair with a sigh. "Yeah," he said, "I've been thinking that, too." He sighed again. "We got to keep our nerve, Hector. We got to go into this meeting confident."

"Confident?" Hector looked at his employer with disbelief. "How am I supposed to be confident?"

Now, this chronicle does not cover a wide expanse of geography and so will not take a stance upon the frequency of what happened next happening in the state or the region or the country at large. It might be uncommon or it might be common that two bankers would reach for each other's hands across a desktop and pray. But this is exactly what Hector and Clement did, Catholic and Lutheran, brown and white, clinging as if one of them was over the side of a cliff.

They said the Lord's Prayer together, and Clement put particular emphasis on "thy will be done."

When they finished, Clement reached for Hector's roll of antacid tablets and popped one into his mouth.

● ● ●

Mark Ramirez sometimes wondered if he spent too much time thinking about his employer. He found her fascinating and could observe her and discuss her with Maria for hours. Before his parents' tragic accident, he could remember sitting around the house while his mother did various tasks and chores, but he could not remember ever noticing her moods and expressions the way he noticed Lottie Dougal's. Even now that he was completely and irrevocably in love with Janey Lane, he still found the personal energy to devote to his self-imposed task of observing and commenting on his employer.

He had spoken to Maria about this once. She had said that it was a small town, and in a small town, people notice one another a lot. She also said you notice some folks more than others and that Lottie was interesting. She also said that fourteen is no kind of age for a young man to be noticing anything about his mother and that if she had lived he'd be noticing more now, which greatly comforted Mark, who had worried about this at times in the long stretches of the night.

And so it was with very little self-consciousness that he watched Lottie ripping up cardboard boxes for recycling. There were a few interesting things about this work. First of all, it was one of Mark's own tasks, as the cardboard fibers got all over you and it was rough on your hands. Second, when he did this task, he used a Stanley knife, not his bare hands. And third, he did not argue with the boxes or growl and mumble at them as he destroyed them, as Lottie was doing.

He had already heard from Maria, who had been the recipient of Pattie's confidences, that the consultation with Doc Emery had not gone particularly well, but he had never seen his employer quite so angry. Usually, with her red hair and everything, Mark reasoned—he not being the kind of man who can tell a highlight from a headlight— she blew up kind of fast but calmed down even faster. But this was a kind of slow burn. She'd been getting more and more angry all afternoon, all the way through getting the back-to-school area organized, until she volunteered to do the boxes.

"Uh," Mark said, "Miz Dougal? Would you like a cup of coffee?"

Lottie stopped and pushed her hair back from over her eyes. "What?" she snapped.

"Would you like some coffee?"

Lottie sighed. She said, "I don't think caffeine is a good idea for me right now, Mark."

Mark was standing in front of their refreshment shelf in the back room. He said, "What about this chamomilly tea? You had that before when you didn't want caffeine."

Lottie smiled. "Good prescription, Mark. I think I could use some chamomile tea. Do you want me to make it?"

"I can do it."

Lottie let the half-torn box she was working on fall from her hands, and sat down in the back doorway. The small and irregular remains of cardboard boxes surrounded her feet.

Mark came over while he waited for the water to drip down. He said, "You know, you only have to tear up the big ones. The little ones they'll take just broke down."

Lottie said, "I know. I got a bit carried away."

Mark poured the water into a cup and put the tea bag in. Then he figured what the heck, and poured the water back into the pitcher and added a couple more tea bags to the whole of it. He said, "Do you put honey in with this?"

And Lottie said, "A spoonful in the cup makes it nice. But you have to stir it like the dickens."

Betty Requena came in for some paper doilies, but after that the tea was ready to pour. Mark joined his employer and handed her a cup. He said, "Hey, you want to talk about it?"

Lottie said, "Mark, look at you. You're all grown up."

Mark blushed and looked out at the alley fence. He said, "I don't think that's why you made cardboard confetti."

Lottie sighed again. She said, "You know, I think it's easier sometimes if things are going completely wrong. You know, if there's a tornado or a flood or something like that. If the person you love isn't speaking to you. If you've got no money and no credit."

Mark made a little sound that meant he was listening, though it wasn't assent. He couldn't imagine a situation where any of those things would be easier.

Lottie said, "Because when things are almost good, it hurts more than when they're completely bad."

And now Mark related this abstract concept to his own concrete experience. In this case, he related it to the resilient chastity of Janey Lane and how his ache for her was worse after she allowed him to do the little she allowed him to do than when they were in a situation where he could do nothing at all.

He said, "That's true, Miz Dougal."

She said, "Don't you think it's about time you started using my first name, Mark? Or am I going to have to call you Mr. Ramirez?"

He said, "So is that why you got so mad, Miz . . . Lottie? Because things were almost good?"

The alley in summer is a pretty place. The pocked road surface, in the afternoon, when it's in shadow, seems more romantic than treacherous; the Dumpster is hidden behind an effusion of vines that also engulf the telephone pole; the weeds and escaped garden cultivars flourish as plants do only when completely neglected. In one way, and for Mark especially, the alleys of downtown Eudora *were* downtown Eudora. As they sat, a few people, mainly older brown people who could not get used to the front door of local businesses, passed, nodding to them politely.

"Oh," Lottie said, now thinking less about Jim Emery and more about the $250,000 deficit, "things *were* good, Mark. They just didn't last."

Later, Zadie Gross realized she phoned in her dry goods order at the very same moment Royle Deacon was walking into Clement McAllister's office.

They had decided upon the office, rather than the boardroom, because Clement said this was going to be all about trust, and the best way to make somebody trust you is to have nothing to hide. The bank had a plethora of old wooden deed boxes, and all of Hector's quarry things were in one of them. He brought it right into Clement's office and took the lid off.

Royle Deacon was a long, brown, clean-limbed man. He had a natural talent for being still, cultivated to near perfection by his many years of bird watching. Hector had done most of the talking, telling it like it was a story, taking Royle through the whole shebang step by step, as Clement had advised. Now the story was done, and Royle had said, "Hmmm," once quietly and shielded his eyes with his hand. Since then, he had just sat still, thinking.

Clement and Hector looked at each other kind of through him. At this point, Hector's nerve was just about ready to break. It was only his employer's eyes that held him steady. Clement told him later that when he was a boy and horses were more plentiful and he was more interested in them because he hadn't yet discovered beer or women, he'd trained a raw colt. He used that same trick a couple of times with that horse, just looking right at it and trying to radiate calm and goodwill. And it had worked.

It worked now. Hector did not break down into tears or go running down the street in his shirtsleeves, screaming. But it was a close thing. He thought he was going to go loco, waiting for Royle Deacon to think.

Finally, Royle's hand shot out to the phone. He didn't even ask permission; he just dialed nine and the number of the head office of the corporation that owned the quarry. Hector knew this because the number began with the New York City area code and also because Royle asked for the man in Assets who had done the previous negotiating.

"This is Royle Deacon from the Eudora Limestone Quarry," Royle said, then, "No, no, it's nothing like that. Everything is going along fine, business as usual."

He listened for a moment.

"Well, yeah, it is. We've been doing some fund-raising and . . . Oh, you heard about it? You saw

Hector on TV? Yeah, he's here right now. I'll let him know."

Royle briefly dropped the phone down onto his shoulder and whispered, "He thinks you looked really good on television."

He listened some more, then said, "Well, we're not exactly ready to write you a check, no." He cleared his throat. "We find we have a deficit."

He listened. "Well, I'm not sure it *is* a significant deficit. It's a big number to us, but I'm not sure it will be to you." And then he said it: he said, "Two hundred and fifty thousand."

He listened a long time, shielding his eyes again, and kind of curling himself over the phone. He said, "Uh-huh . . . yeah . . . yeah," at intervals. Once he said, "Oh!" as if he was surprised, but neither Hector nor Clement could tell if it was a good surprise or a bad surprise. Hector absent-mindedly reached for Clement's personal water bottle at that point and downed nearly half a quart of Evian in one gulp. When he realized what he'd done, he looked a mute apology at Clement, who only smiled tightly.

Finally, finally, finally, Royle Deacon said, "Well, thanks so much," and hung up the phone. But he didn't uncoil. He just sat there some more.

Clement couldn't take it. He said, "What did he say, Deacon?"

And Royle said, "He said that they've shaved this one down to the bone anyway, that we've caused them a bit of negative publicity, that one guy on the board wanted to withdraw their offer for sale, and that there is no way in God's green earth he can take even one penny short of the price they quoted."

Hector slumped into a chair. Clement said, "Well, it was a good idea, Deacon, thanks for asking."

Royle nodded, still hunched around the telephone. Hector yawned. Suddenly he was tired. It was over. It was going to be horrible, but it was over, and he could sleep again. Clement had been right. He didn't have the kind of nerve it takes to make it in politics. There was a reason he'd been such a successful banker, and that reason was a love of routine, detail, and safety. All of those things had been disrupted by the events of the past forty-seven days, and Hector, for one, just couldn't take any more.

He wanted to go someplace far away, maybe by the ocean. Someplace that never got real hot. Someplace gray and foggy. Maine. San Francisco. Seattle, even—he could look up Mrs. Emery. He'd get a job in a bank, a large corporate bank, where you never even saw your clients. He'd do well. He'd buy a nice apartment and have pale beige carpet. He'd drive something just a little sporty. He'd play a lot of tennis. He'd never come home again. Well, there wouldn't be a home to come to, would there?

Royle's head snapped up again and he said, "I held something back. At the town meeting. I put in ten thousand when I could have put in twelve. If everybody else did the same thing . . ."

Hector, or the ghost of Hector that still sat in the chair, shook his head. He said, "I don't think we should ask people for any more. We don't want to win the quarry only to lose with foreclosures because people have overextended."

Clement nodded. He said, "If we was to get another flood come through here, or a tornado, or even some of those grasshoppers they got back east, folks would be hard pushed to pay their deductible."

Royle Deacon, the cool brown man whom nobody knew, nodded. His chin wobbled and collapsed and a tear rolled down his cheek. He said, "Sorry," in a brusque tone. Hector would have cried, too, but it was only the ghost of Hector sitting in the chair, and it couldn't feel anything. The real Hector was already living his new life, missing his mother more than he had thought was previously possible and wondering if he should swap his apartment for a house in the suburbs his parents could share.

Clement reached down into his bottom drawer and came up with a bottle of bourbon and three glasses, which last he polished on a Kleenex. He poured generous amounts and nobody complained. Nobody talked, either. They just sat there, taking their medicine and contemplating their future.

• • •

No, it's not Saint-John's-wort," Dr. Emery was saying to Jim Flory. "It's something I can't pronounce. The Latin name is bad enough, but the common name is in Pawnee." He wrote it down and passed it over. He said, "Evidently the Branch family has been harvesting it for quite some time and has used it successfully on several patients."

He sighed. "I'm not so sure about this, Jim. I didn't intend to talk to you about it at all. But if your side effects are getting that bad . . . I mean, you could *try* Saint-John's-wort, but Miss Dougal feels it's better for women. She also says there's such a slow uptake that you might feel the need for . . ." He didn't finish the sentence.

Jim Flory drew his mouth into a thin line. Through it, he said, "She thinks I'll fall off the wagon."

"Well," the doctor said, "well, yes, Jim, she does. And I'm afraid I'm worried about it, too. You've made such progress."

"I feel more like myself," Jim said. "I just feel sick. I couldn't run this morning." He looked at the bit of paper. "What do you do with this stuff?"

The doctor sighed. "Evidently you peel it, mash it up, and make a tea with it."

"Huh. Well, that's different."

Jim Flory thought about the shiny pills he now took. Dr. Emery thought about clinical trials, then said, "I don't even know why I told you about it. It was just an idea. Why don't we try to find something to relieve the nausea? And then I think there's an antispasmodic that was developed for multiple sclerosis sufferers that might help with your shaking." He started tapping on his computer keyboard.

"I'm gonna try the root," Flory said, surprising himself as much as the doctor, who stopped tapping.

"You are?"

"Yeah, I'll give it a shot."

The doctor said, "Let me see if I can get her on the phone—"

But Flory cut in. "Naw," he said. "I can go over tonight and sit on her porch with everybody else."

They thought about it for a moment. No one of European heritage had ever gone to Lottie's back door before.

Flory said, "When I get over these shakes, I've got big plans for the cinema. What do you think about an Almodóvar season? Do you think Father Gaskin would condemn it?"

And the rest of the appointment passed agreeably discussing various directors of Spanish descent.

Jim Evans was driving his old, beloved International Harvester tractor back to the barn. Lottie and Mark were still sitting in the alley doorway. Zadie was calling in her dry goods order. Doc and Jim Flory were talking movies while Janey Lane was practicing signing her name Mrs. Jane Ramirez. Becky was on the chair behind the fabric counter, reading a book about successful restaurant management. Pattie Walker was picking up her two older boys from school; they'd get Ben from Candy Cane on their way home. Artie Walker and Clarissa Engel were meeting to discuss building a collection of modern poetry. Ben Nichols and Odie Marsh were investigating shotgun holes in a nearby deer crossing sign. Margery Lupin had just closed the bakery and was totaling up the day's sales while Betty Requena mopped the floor. Maria Lopez and Linda Bustamonte were eating their afternoon meal before the rush hit. Bill Lopez was cutting rock and thinking about Maria and wondering if she'd remembered to put her feet up during her break (she hadn't). Oscar Burgos's alarm was going off. Phil Walker was stuck in traffic on a baking road in the capital and thinking about Pattie and the kids walking home down the shady brick sidewalks of his hometown.

Hector Rodriguez, Clement McAllister, and Royle Deacon were drinking their medicinal bourbon and trying to talk about it. None of them was getting very far, and in any case, all three felt there was absolutely nothing to say.

Linda Lane tapped on the door. "Come," Clement said, out of habit, and she did.

She stopped short when she saw the meeting, the glasses on Clement's desk half full, the bottle sitting open, the papers everywhere, and Royle Deacon hunched up with his head in his hands. She nearly backed out again, saying, "Oh, I'm sorry, it can wait."

Clement sighed. "No, come in, Linda. What can I do for you?"

She had a sheaf of papers in her hand. She said, "Well, it's just these checks that keep coming in for the quarry fund. Do we actually have an account yet to post them to? I've just been keeping them in my cash drawer and it's starting to get crowded."

For a moment, complete silence descended on Clement McAllister's office. Neither he, Hector, nor Royle Deacon either inhaled or exhaled. They didn't even blink.

It was weird, Linda said later. It was like they'd all died just sitting there. She didn't know what to do. She shifted from one foot to the other and said, "Only, if you want me to put them in the safe or something, you should tell me so they don't get lost. You know what it's like in there."

Clement coughed. He said weakly, "Could you just repeat that, Linda?"

"If you want me to put them in the safe, you should—"

"No, what you said before that."

And she said, clearly and slowly, as if she was talking to a kid or to Old Lady Bumgartner, "I don't *know* where to put all *these*"—at this point she waved the sheaf once again—"checks."

Now Hector exhaled. He said in a trembling voice, "Could I just see those for a minute, Linda?"

"Sure," she said. "Some of them had little letters with them; I paper-clipped all those to the slips."

"Good job," Hector said absently.

Royle Deacon said, "Are those what I think they are?"

Hector nodded and reached for the calculator Clement slid across the desk, then changed his mind and first reached for his glass of bourbon, which he shot down his throat. A few years later he said that right after he had done this, he felt a little click, as if he had actually come back into his body. The color in the room had been fading throughout the meeting to a washy watercolor. When he heard the click, he looked up and the room was bright and glowing. He pushed the calculator back to Clement, because his hands were shaking. Clement turned it on.

He said, "Ten dollars from someone in Kentucky," and turned over a check. Clement punched it in. "Twenty from . . ." He turned over a small note with a teddy bear on the front. "Somebody who had lunch here once on a cross-country trip forty years ago."

"The big ones are at the back," Linda said. "I put them in amount order."

Hector's hands shook as he turned to the big ones. "Eighty thousand dollars," he said, and now even Royle Deacon remembered how to breathe. Hector looked at the embossed dark blue heading on the handwritten note and said, "Senator Brown Gilly. Oh, sorry, he wanted to be anonymous.

"Fifty thousand from . . ."

All told, $348,920.50 had come in during the first few days. Later, as everyone knows, the total was three times that amount. The quarry's economic foundation was as solid as the rock it dug.

Linda Lane didn't really understand why Clement McAllister picked her up and did the polka with her around the room or why Hector Rodriguez started crying. It was weeks before the annual chili cook-off when Clement had a bit too much beer trying to put out the flames in his throat, and told the whole story of the town's near demise to an interested party of Rotarians, and nearly two further weeks until the news permeated the entire community and Linda was finally able to explain her superiors' strange behavior.

Zadie Gross nearly had a fit that she'd been calling in an order for $2,448 right when the future of the town, her diner, and her own personal finances hung so precariously in the balance. She said later that it was a good thing we didn't know everything all the time, and she wondered how God could stand it.

A few minutes after the downtown polka, Lottie Dougal had heard the shop phone ring. She got up and walked to it, motioning Mark to stay and finish his chamomile tea (which, to his surprise, he was actually enjoying).

After she said, "Dougal's Stationery Supplies, Lottie Dougal speaking," it was Clement's voice she heard.

"We got it, Lottie. We got the two fifty. And then some."

Lottie sat down on the high stool behind the glass counter and wept into the phone.

He said, "I know, honey, I know."

She said, "Thanks so much for letting me know."

Then they both hung up.

There was nothing more to be said.

Jim Flory hesitated when he got to Lottie Dougal's back porch. He didn't know what time to come, really, but figured she'd need time to walk home, have a shower, change her clothes, and have something to eat, so she must start consulting about seven. And then he figured she'd want time to wash and brush and watch the news before heading for bed, so she must stop about nine-thirty, ten.

He walked over at eight.

He saw two burly men at work in the garden, harvesting beans and looking over tomatoes in the twilight. There was evidence of watering and weeding. On the porch itself, an impossibly old woman was sitting on the swing wrapped in a shawl, while two young girls giggled together on a wicker love seat in the corner.

Jim hesitated.

Just then Maria Lopez came down the path, taking her apron off as she walked. She said, "You waiting?"

And Jim made his decision. He said, "Yes, ma'am. But I'm not in a hurry. You go first."

He was swept up in the wake of Maria's energy and took one of the two basket chairs.

Lottie came to the door, drying her hands, and said, "Right, who's next?"

The impossibly old woman emerged from her cocoon and toddled through the back door. Maria Lopez sighed and stretched out her legs. "God," she said. "I never been sick a day in my life before this."

Jim made a small noise. She said, "Look at them ankles."

Jim looked. They appeared rather thick. "Nice," he said, not knowing what else to say.

"They're all swollen! They don't look like that normal."

"I thought they looked a little on the thick side but I didn't want to say."

Maria smiled tiredly.

Lottie appeared at the door, drying her hands. She said, "Next, please," and the two giggling teenagers went in.

Maria thought Kylie Requena was probably after some love spell to get Mark Ramirez back, but she did not know Jim well enough to mention it or mention how absolutely useless this effort would be, seeing as Mark and Janey Lane were already planning their engagement announcement.

The two burly men came and got the nest of shawls, leaving a peck basket of harvest in its place. Jim had a vague idea that this was payment of some sort for services rendered but thought it was a little on the skimpy side to give produce out of the service provider's own garden.

"You come early, you gotta garden," Maria said. "Otherwise Lottie would get behind."

Jim revised his opinion. He said, "How much *are* consultations?"

"Oh," Maria said, "it varies as to how much hard work you are and what you can afford. You can usually come to a good agreement."

"I don't think my insurance will cover this," he said with a laugh.

Maria did not laugh with him. She said, "I never had no medical coverage, so I wouldn't know."

Jim was shocked but tried to hide it. Maria liked

him for trying, even though he failed. She said, "And now I'm an employer and I still don't provide it. When the quarry gets its HMO plan, I'll be covered there, though. So will Linda."

They fell silent. There was a low voice talking inside the house, talking seriously and at some length. Maria guessed that she'd been right about Kylie's mission and that Lottie was giving her a little lesson.

Jim shuffled his feet. He looked nervous.

Maria said, "Sure was something, what Hector did, wasn't it?"

Jim made a sound of assent and nodded.

"Did you see him on TV? He looked so handsome."

Jim felt more qualified to comment on this aspect. "Yes, he did," he said. "Better than in real life, even."

Maria gave him a sideways glance, now knowing something about Jim Flory she had not known previously, having missed the house parties of ten years before and not having discussed Jim with anyone who had not missed them on account of Jim being largely, politely, invisible during the majority of the period when Maria herself had become visible.

Jim said, "I'm thinking about having a Latin American film season. Would you like to go see a film in Spanish?"

Maria smiled. She said, "I'd like it okay, but the

old folks would love it. And the young ones, too, especially if it's got English written on the bottom."

"What kind of movies do you like?"

"Anything with Mel Gibson."

Lottie came to the door, drying her hands and said, "Next!"

"Go on," Jim said.

Maria said, "You sure?"

And Jim nodded.

He sat alone and looked out to where Lottie's pumpkins were just starting to swell.

Inside, Lottie was asking a lot of questions.

Maria was answering some of them but was largely complaining. Her back hurt, she was tired all the time, she was bloated and retaining water, especially in her ankles.

Lottie asked one of the questions again, more urgently, and the truth suddenly dawned on Maria.

She was going to have a baby.

Five minutes later, Lottie appeared at the back door, drying her hands.

Jim stood up. "I'm next," he said. And, as they went down the hall, "I hope you aren't going to make me scream, like you did Maria."

"I doubt it would be for the same reason," Lottie said. "Don't worry, it was good news." She paused, then said, "You've been waiting a long time. Would you like a glass of water?"

"I don't think I could drink it," Jim confessed,

holding out his shaking hands. "Not without spilling it all over myself."

"I'll give you a bottle."

When Jim left, with a burlap sack full of roots over his shoulder, he reflected on the unusual experience. It wasn't just Lottie's asking quite intrusive questions about his personal life, or the odd way she took his pulse several times and stared at his tongue until he thought it was going to fall right out. No, it was the whole thing, the sitting on the back porch and talking to Maria. It had felt warmer, more human than any other medical experience in Jim's life, and he wasn't sure he liked that.

He'd had some of the tea in Lottie's kitchen as she coached him on how to prepare it. Before he got all the way home, the tremors had left. He had some hot milk, as directed, which didn't taste as bad as you might think, especially if you added the nutmeg Lottie had recommended. And he slept for ten straight hours, something he hadn't done since he was seventeen.

The next morning he woke up with evidence of vigor he'd not experienced for quite some time. And then he overdid it, running five miles on a hot day, and came home shaking, fearful, and uncertain. But he managed to make the tea, even though he had to drink it with a straw, and after sitting down for a while, he got up, showered and dressed, and went down to the movie house just to look around.

・ ・ ・

The printing press in which Dougal's Stationery Supplies owned a half interest was located in the county seat. That morning, Lottie left Mark in charge of the shop and went in to look at the delivery van, which Max Breyer had said was on its last legs and would have to be replaced.

Now, Max was not untrustworthy, nor would he lie. But he was a nervous man, thin, hunched, and bespectacled. He frequently announced the demise of equipment or other infrastructure that only needed repair. He also foretold disaster with new personnel until he got used to them. On the other hand, he was a heck of a printer and mastered new technology quickly and with surprising enthusiasm. There were four of them in the press now, but not so much as a postcard left the shop without Max's personal inspection.

Lottie found it hard to get used to the quiet. In her youth, when coming to this press, the noise had hit you in the parking lot and, when you opened the metal door, nearly knocked you down. Now, the great press with its jangling type was gone and instead big printers hummed and vibrated. Lottie also kept forgetting to knock, since it had been a useless exercise before. And so now, as she did every time, she went back out and knocked.

Danny Burch let her in. She said, "How's it going?" in a whisper.

He smiled and nodded. "It's okay. I like it. And he's . . . he's not bad once you get to know—"

"Dannnnnneeeeeee! Didn't I tell you to keep an eye on that magenta? If you don't watch it, that poor woman will be orange like a pumpkin!"

Max came around the corner. "Oh," he said, "it's you."

"Hello, Max." Lottie embraced his unwilling body and planted a kiss on his stiffening cheek.

"You might as well come in, now that you're here," he said. "I've got some of that tea you like."

"I'm here to look at the van."

"Bill's loading it now, so we'd better go see it before he goes. There's no telling if he'll make it back, poor soul. I worry, Lottie, I really worry. He's a good boy and I don't like to send him out with it."

The good boy was fifty-five years old and, though still stocky and strong, was now completely bald. He had his back to them when they walked to the bay. When he saw Lottie he smiled. "Hello, little partner," he said. "How's you?"

She said, "I'm fine, Bill, but I hear the van's in a bad way."

Max said, "It thumps. And it shivers."

Bill put in, "Well, I think the back end is getting a little tired. It's not the suspension. I stiffened the shocks. And the frame . . . well, it's done a few miles, Lottie. She's starting to get a little loose, and you notice it on the highway."

"Honest to God," Max said, "it shivers like it's about to fall apart. I had to hold on to the handle."

Lottie inspected the van. The panels on the side were faded and the bumpers and fenders showed evidence of Bill's unique parking style. She said, "It's not much of an advertisement for us, is it?"

"We get a new van," Max said. "I'll do you a four-color screen. *And* put 'Dougal's Stationery Supplies' on the back."

Bill said, "I been down to Eudora to the Ford dealership. They got a good deal, but it runs out end of next month."

Lottie said, "We get a new van and I *will* want a favor. But that's not the favor. You make me some of that tea, Max, and I'll tell you what the favor is." And then she told Bill that if she ever caught him in her hometown again without letting her buy him lunch, he was in big trouble.

Afterward she discussed her printing requirements with Max. It took a while for them to find the perfect color to go with the red and white. She didn't want blue and she didn't want green, but something in between, and nothing as girly as aqua.

Bill delivered it three days later, when he came in for the deposit on the new van. He did just what Lottie asked and put it on her back porch under a tarp, instead of bringing it into the shop. And, since he was not a Eudoran in any sense of the word, he then forgot about it entirely, as it was not his business. He enjoyed his lunch at Mayan Memories without referring to it again.

At times, Lottie found this odd behavior, so common in the outside world, restful.

She waited until after midnight to bring the boxes into the house and secrete them under her bed, but Oscar Burgos was having a nice long walk home in the summer moonlight. Oscar was a true Eudoran.

He wondered about the boxes for days.

Life in Eudora went back to normal with a vengeance, as if such municipal excitement they had recently experienced had been so unpleasant that the only cure was routine and boredom. The Fourth of July celebrations and the Rotary Club's chili cook-off came and went with little incident.

The cook-off used to be held in February, when the heat of the spices in the savory concoctions were more welcome. However, the ladies of Eudora had objected to having their precious jars of tomatoes raided in such a cause, and so it was moved to summer, when the town was, so to speak, swimming in tomatoes and nobody minded.

Hector Rodriguez used his grandmother's recipe and made an interesting pot of cubed pork and chiles without any tomato in it at all, but a kind of thin, oniony gravy substance. Everybody had to try it, just as they did Park Davis's vegetarian option, but both failed to win a prize. The prize once again went to Ed Marling of Marling's Maple Hill Funeral Home for his toothsome entry. Every year it just kept getting better and better. But this was not news.

Though events proceeded, of news there was little.

Zadie opened her diner and people began eating breakfast again. This cut somewhat into the profits of both Margery Lupin and Maria Lopez in the first week, but then, providentially, there was some construction work started on the interstate and people began using the old state highway again to avoid it. Traffic in town increased exponentially, which pleased everyone except the children, who had a whole new set of rules to deal with about what you could and couldn't do near Main Street.

Now, because of Zadie's previous employment as the town GP's receptionist, she was well known, as was her name. So when she unveiled the sign above her door, nobody thought much about it. It took the out-of-towners, getting out of their cars to laugh and, later, stopping with their cameras, for Eudorans to see anything funny about Gross Home Cooking.

When Zadie herself finally realized her faux pas, she understood why the matchbooks imprinted with the restaurant's name were disappearing so quickly. She asked Lottie, who put her on to somebody else, and she had T-shirts for sale before you could say Jack Robinson. The out-of-town business made lunchtime crowded, and so locals tended to go to Mayan Memories for lunch, and Maria Lopez's cash register showed it.

Margery Lupin's, however, did not.

Margery had been at the bakery (for it had no other name) for some fifty years. She had thought, now and then, about retiring but knew that she would, to the end of her days, wake up at four in the morning ready to go, and as long as she was awake, she thought she might as well be doing something. Now, though, as her profits dipped and the weather began to turn scorching hot, she thought about retiring again.

She would need to sell the bakery. Margery knew that though she was tired of running it, she wasn't completely tired of working, and what she wanted to do required relocation. The Lupins are a scattered bunch. Janine and Dot stayed in the county as farmers' wives, but Lonnie and the younger girls were all over the place: Phoenix, Orlando, and Chickasaw, Missouri. It was to the last Margery thought about moving.

Margery's daughter, Margaret Lupin, had been one of Eudora's odder birds. Even before she left town, her reliance upon kohl for her personal appearance had caused remark, and she returned to visit once with green hair and another time with it blue. She dressed in black. Jim Evans once remarked that she always looked like she was going to a funeral and half the time looked as if it was her own. Well into her thirties, she had not married, and nobody ever wondered why.

She had been a great reader (spending so much time on her own) and had even made the acquaintance of the town's Famous Author. There is too little space remaining in this chronicle to explain why Eudora had a Famous Author in its environs and why so few Eudorans took notice of his status, but the Famous Author was little visited and did not generally mix. He was also known to be quite choosy about his companions. The news that he deigned to notice Margaret Lupin had baffled most of the town.

After long sojourns in New York and some time spent, if we can believe Margery, in Paris and Milan, Margaret Lupin had come back to the Midwest of America and written herself a book. Artie Walker liked it but Clarissa Engel said it was too hard to read and that parts of it were nasty. It was thus kept behind the counter at the library and available only on request. Because everyone in Eudora knew that everyone in Eudora would think they just wanted to read the nasty bits if they asked for it, the volume languished there.

Other books followed. There were rumors to be money in the writing business.

Margaret herself had come to town two years

before, still in black, but very glossy and upmarket with it. Her hair was a shining waterfall of chestnut. She was on the arm of a large, powerful-looking man, who was, we later learned, something in engineering. He went all over, fixing things with hydraulics in dams. Saudi Arabia, Ukraine, Los Angeles. They had settled in Chickasaw because they liked the lakes and the plateaus and it was close enough to an airport.

They spent lots of time together and lots of time apart. When they were apart, she wrote books. When they were together, she made babies. Four of them in four years, boom, boom, boom, boom.

Margaret Lupin was forty years old with four children under school age and a variety of publisher's deadlines. She wanted her mommy.

It was unfortunate, in a way, that Margery Lupin felt galvanized to at last do something about the bakery situation the second week of July, because the second week of August was the mayoral election. If she had waited until, say, September, the ugliness that subsequently reared its head might not have appeared at all.

As it was, however, Margery and Betty Requena had a talk about numbers. Then Betty and Don went down to Clement McAllister's office and talked about numbers with Clement. Then they all got together at a lawyer's office in the county seat and Margery handed over the keys. The whole thing took three days.

Betty had been keen to make innovations in the bakery, and she did so without delay. The old back-door serving hatch was closed and a hallway was installed leading from the back door to the front counter and the restrooms. Old brown ladies began to be seen in the bakery line, taking a number from the new roller machine and waiting their turn like anybody else. The pastries suddenly multiplied. There were also these amazing ham and cheese things. The picnic table disappeared and was replaced by bench seating and small round tables. There was a rack for newspapers.

It looked tidier. It looked smarter. It looked cleaner and brighter.

But to Barney Lane, it only looked browner.

Barney was not one of life's happy campers. He had enjoyed ten years of marriage to Becky (which he always described as happy but were, according to the more detailed reports available from Becky, hell on earth), but these were over. He was pleased to brag about the achievements of his children but complained that they never came to see him (without mentioning that he never went to see them, either, and that he had not contributed, except intermittently by force of judicial order, dime one to their upbringing or had, in fact, attended any ceremony or sporting event linked to the achievements of which he so glibly bragged).

For Barney, and for anyone unlucky enough to get the stool next to him at the bar of Chuck's Beer and Bowl, life was a misery.

He was also unhappy in his work. Now, being the school janitor is a thankless job, but the previous holder of the post used to whistle. The previous holder of the post used to keep an eye out for the loners and report bullying to the principal. The previous holder of the post used to warn smokers of approaching faculty, interrupt makeout sessions that went a bit far for the girl's liking, and assist with both the putting up and the taking down of decorations. The previous holder of the post (who is actually Jim Evans's brother-in-law Luke Cash) did, in fact, have a collection of little notes and gifts accumulated from students and faculty over his time of service and still, some twelve years after retirement, found it difficult to buy himself a beer or a cup of coffee with his own money.

In fact, Luke is probably the best person to listen to when it comes to the shortcomings of Barney Lane, as Luke is well placed to understand the work Barney does and has no personal axe to grind (as does anyone remotely connected to Becky). At about this period he and Jim were discussing this very topic in a corner booth at Gross Home Cooking.

This corner booth had become a favorite with the old codgers, as Zadie called them. Some of them, especially those, like Jim, who were still farming, ate a hearty breakfast now and again, but most of them just drank their bottomless cups of coffee and nattered to each other. Zadie was not opposed to this activity in the least. You could not have a diner where the old men did not gather to denigrate their neighbors. It would not be anything like a diner without them, nodding together in their feed caps and cackling like hens.

When the out-of-towners came in (and boy, did they start coming—young people from the city driving out for breakfast, their parents and grandparents taking a nice little drive for country air and to have lunch—Zadie and Becky were hopping), they looked for just such a gathering. Nor were they ever disappointed, for as the Carhartt jackets and overalls disappeared toward the luncheon hour, the polished shoes and shirtsleeves of local businessmen took their place, Clement with his personal bottle of Tabasco in front of him and Park Davis, Ed Marling, and various other local luminaries holding court with dignity and gravitas over the blue-plate special.

Barney's name had come up in relation to a chance reference made to the momentous town meeting of which we have heard so much. Luke Cash was remote during the discussion under way (the subject of which no one recalls), and this was not like him, so Jim asked him what was the matter.

Luke sighed and said he was thinking about the

gymnasium and how dirty it had been. He said it was lucky in a way that the chairs hadn't been cleared and the bleachers hadn't been folded, but in a way it was a crying shame. He said that the bunting had been bought fifteen years ago and was already looking tacky, and that was because it wasn't taken down sharp and put away. It was getting dusty and faded with overuse. He said things like that made him sick inside because the school was going to have to buy more soon, and if you took care of bunting, it lasted upward of thirty years.

One of the other men at the table, who was distantly related to the Branch family and farmed over on the east side of town, interjected that it was Barney Lane all over again and that everyone knew he was no-account.

Jim Evans said, "If he ever had any get-up-and-go, it got up and went."

There was increased cackling, and Becky came over with the coffeepot. She said, "What are you all laughing about now?"

And this same Branch cousin said, "Becky, I'm afraid it was your ex."

To which Becky replied by rolling her eyes and saying, "Don't get me started."

Such was Barney Lane and his standing in the town.

Eudora is an enlightened community and the words *white trash* do not pass any citizen's lips. Still, there are pockets of housing and farming that do not prosper. Residents may put this down to bad luck, but Eudorans rather feel that a lack of effort is the main problem. They point to Becky Lane as an example of what people unafraid of hard work can do for themselves.

Becky Lane started life as a farm girl near McLouth. Her father, denied by advances in surveillance and telecommunications of his inheritance as a moonshiner, took up sullen staring as his major occupation. Animals were left to breed and feed on his acreage with little aid or disturbance until his quarter-yearly intervention, which hauled the more promising to market. The quality of the livestock thus slowly declined. Her mother, who died when Becky was twelve, was conversant with the food stamp system.

Becky, inheriting the housework and the raising of two younger siblings, became equally conversant. Three or four days out of five, she still managed to catch the school bus and attend classes at Eudora High, where, at sixteen, Barney Lane seemed like her way out.

And so he was, for the first few years. The small ranch house on the tract slab seemed extremely pleasant to Becky when she first moved in. There were no leaks in the roof, and the central heating system worked. Revived by warmth and regular trips to the grocery store, Becky had the energy to find a distant cousin to take her siblings and more or less cut her ties with her father, having reasons, she later said darkly, that she didn't want to go into.

She cleaned that little house until it shone and put food on the table every night. She studied for her GED. Barney, who was working shifts at the gas station, spent his leisure time at home and was glad to do it, because it was such a nice place.

But then she changed. She started to notice things. She noticed that her clothes needed replacing and asked for money. She noticed that Barney didn't wash as well as he could after his shift and asked that he take a shower before coming to the table. She noticed he tracked dirt all over the nice clean floor and asked him to take off his shoes. She got ambitious.

On that tract, within three years, theirs was the only house with flowers in the yard and a green lawn.

When the babies came along, she wanted to move. It was Becky who got Barney's application together for the janitor job. It was Becky who coached him about what to say during the interview.

Barney began to spend time away from home. Becky didn't really notice. By then, she had hit her stride. She had worked out a schedule for the house and lawn work, and all the little girls had their own little tasks to help. When Barney did come home, he felt he was in the middle of a beehive. Everybody else had their place, but his was missing. He was stationary in the middle of activity. Becky told him she loved him, but by now he knew this was not really true. Eventually, so did she.

Barney stopped going home except to eat and sleep. If anything disturbed either of those functions, he hit it. The girls soon learned to stay out of his way, and Becky learned to hit back.

When all the girls were old enough to go to school, Becky got her job with Pattie. Her father died two months later, leaving an unexpectedly large insurance payout in her name. She used it as a deposit on a house and did not discuss the move with her husband. He knew he was not coming along.

It took three years for the flowers to die completely, but the small house eventually looked exactly like its neighbors. And Barney liked it better that way.

In the middle of this neighborhood, Barney Lane was not despised. In fact, people listened to him. In the small gatherings around a bottle in lawn chairs when it was too hot to sleep without efficient air-conditioning, when Barney held forth, his words were noted. He mixed with the world, did Barney Lane. He went down to Chuck's and had himself a beer and didn't dress up to do it. He was on the town and he knew things.

And one of the things he knew was that Hector Rodriguez should not be mayor.

His interlocutors agreed with him. "Them damn Mex'cans are takin' over" was the way someone put it, and it was frequently repeated through the coming weeks.

At this point, we should admit that this chronicle is aware of the names of these interlocutors. This chronicle also has a very good idea of who first said the above phrase. But though visibility has come to both the Latino community and Jim Flory, it does not mean that Eudora feels visibility to be an inherent right. Much of Eudora has kin represented in the aforementioned pockets of poverty, and none of the visible citizenry is interested in shining any sort of light under this particular bushel basket. They feel, perhaps wrongly, that these are sleeping dogs that should be left to lie in the calm darkness of ignorance.

And yet they, too, have a vote.

It was astonishing how many, and how many of the more visible citizenry who had previously been willing and able to make an X on their ballot by Hector Rodriguez's name now wondered if this part of the community might also have a point.

Jim Flory had chosen this week to run his Almodóvar season. It could not have been more badly timed if he'd done it on purpose.

Well, there was muttering. There were even walkouts and demands for money back. In fact,

Jim said later, if both his doctors had not been in attendance for every one of the showings and if the cinema had not been so completely and joyously full to the rafters, he might have reached for the vodka once again.

Gross Home Cooking enjoyed more custom from the underclass than Mayan Memories ever had. There was the $2 chili bowl. There was the rice and beans vegetarian option at $2.65. There was the bottomless cup of coffee. And though they did not rise to the blue-plate special, at midmorning Zadie was granted the company of quite a large and variable customer base, some of which might remain, on a rainy day, clear to closing. Zadie was of two minds about this before the political question of the day.

After it, she was livid.

Zadie did the cooking and worked the grill. She also served the counter. And it was the counter where these people tended to sit, spinning quarters and talking trash. The conversational level was always tedious. But when she daily heard references to "beaners" and "wetbacks" and how they "stole good people's jobs" and should be "sent back across the Rio Grande," she found it more than tedious. She found it infuriating.

Zadie had a word with Ben and Odie when they came in for lunch. But Odie said if someone came in, sat down, and talked bullshit all day, it did not constitute a legal infraction. Odie said that Zadie was free to refuse service to anyone but that he'd think about it long and hard if he was her. As this was a reference to the family ties many of the loafers had with many of Zadie's valued customers, Zadie did as he suggested and thought.

She was still thinking when the political agenda came to the fore and these comments accordingly increased. She had already established a rule of no profanity. This had been hard won but in the end successful. You could not cuss at Gross Home Cooking, and soon everyone was aware of this.

Now she made a rule of "no racism."

Zadie was well intentioned in this, but unfortunately it was exactly the wrong approach, as her rule gave the Barney Lane party their first lesson in political guile. As they spoke around the counter about the Almodóvar season and the changes in the bakery, they had to find new and creative ways of saying what they didn't like about these things. These strategies formed a great deal of the discursive style in the upcoming election and debate.

Clement and Hector were, at this time, largely unaware of the undercurrent of unpleasantness in the Eudoran underclass. Clement, in particular, felt his work as mayor was done. He had completed his term of office and had appointed a successor. The successor had been proved politically astute and at one with the hopes and dreams of the constituency. The July 31 ballot was a mere formality, as Hector was running unopposed.

Then Barney Lane, urged by his fellow underachievers, made the trip to the county courthouse and registered his name as a candidate, writing the first good check he had presented in quite some time. The same day, he called Clement on the telephone and proposed a debate.

Clement thought it was a joke. At the annual Baptist ice cream social (which everyone supported, less out of ecumenical motivations than because Mary Evans used her family recipe and annually cranked out forty gallons of the nicest, freshest, lightest ice cream you could find anywhere), he found he was wrong. He then found Hector.

"Hec," he said, using the hand not supporting his triple-dip cone of strawberry, raspberry, and blueberry to draw his junior partner to one side, "we got ourselves a problem."

Clement said later that Hector had looked almost relieved. He had time to notice this because Hector was eating chocolate with caramel nuggets out of a sugar cone and had his back teeth stuck together and so was not immediately able to answer. Hector later admitted things had been running too smoothly and he'd been worried. Nothing in his experience of the political life ever ran that smoothly, and so it had meant there was something he didn't know. Now he was about to find out what it was.

He was less relieved once he'd heard, however.

"I'm sorry," Clement said. "But I still find it hard to take this seriously. I mean, Barney Lane for mayor? He'd leave the Christmas lights up all year to save the trouble."

This was too good to waste just on Hector, and so Clement repeated it the next day at the corner booth over his blue-plate special (fried chicken, mashed potatoes with gravy, and green beans, no substitutions).

"Well," Park Davis said, "I don't know. He's kind of got a point."

Clement was dumbstruck for a moment, which doesn't happen often. But he recovered, saying, "What on earth do you mean, Park?"

Ed Marling leaned back and probed his molars with a toothpick, ostentatiously taking no part in a discussion so likely to turn nasty.

"Well," Park Davis said, "I don't know. It just seems like the town has gone a certain way in one direction and maybe we ought to think about whether or not that's the direction we really want it to take."

"You mean we got two new restaurants bringing lots of new business into the town and the town's major employer is on a sound financial footing? You talking about that direction?" Clement said in a very loud, hissing whisper, leaning forward aggressively over the table.

Park put his hands up and gave a little deprecating laugh. "Now, Clement," he said, "you know what I mean."

"Yes, I do," Clement said. "But I'll be damned if I'm going to sit here with you meaning it." And then Clement McAllister got up and *left half his lunch on the table* to storm out of the diner. Zadie was out on the floor helping Becky clean tables and ran right after him, even though she had a burger that was going to need turning soon.

When she caught him by the arm he was making pretty good time. He swung around, ready for a fight, until he saw it was Zadie. She asked him what was wrong, fearing there was something bad about the food or that he'd gotten bad news on his cell phone.

Clement told her it was nothing like that. And then he told her about the conversation.

Zadie told him about the loafers at her counter every day, talking trash and spending nickels.

He said, "Lord have mercy, what is this town coming to?"

And Zadie said, "I don't know. I just don't know."

After some to-ing and fro-ing, the debate was set to be held in the Eudora High School gymnasium. The form of this event was simple.

302

Each candidate would speak twice, and then both would give their answers to questions from the floor.

Luckily, Barney Lane had still not managed to remove the chairs and slide back the bleachers, so there was plenty of seating, for once again the place was packed.

There's no need, really, to detail the speeches word for word. Hector lost the toss and went first. He took a moment to tell everyone the exact financial state of the quarry, which was a subtle reminder of how much they all owed to his efforts, and then concentrated on policy matters. He said that the parking meters were not a significant form of income but that they were a significant form of hassle and that he thought they should be removed. This got a cheer. He said that he thought it might be time for whoever was elected mayor to revisit the idea of incorporation and levying municipal taxes, and outlined briefly the kinds of responsibilities we might have to take on if such a thing was done.

It was not a sexy speech. It was an exact speech. He looked great giving it, but it wasn't (except for the parking meters bit) all that attractive or dynamic. In fact, some of it was a little on the dull side, to do with facts and figures.

Barney's didn't bother with facts and figures. And Barney Lane was dramatic, practically foaming at the mouth. Hector's oratorical style was kind of like a teacher's. Barney's was like a preacher's.

Barney looked good in his navy blue suit. He hadn't worn it much for the past thirty years, but it still fit good. Much of his audience had a suit just like it, taken out for weddings and funerals and cleaned every five years or so. With Barney's hair brushed and his face shaved closely and a collar and tie on, people who had never before been able to understand what Becky Lane had seen in him suddenly had more understanding for the ill-fated attraction.

He talked a lot about "roots" and "community." He talked a very great deal about "heritage" and "continuity." And then he kept asking, "What kind of inheritance do we want to leave to our children? What kind of town will this be?"

He spoke about the beauty of the English language. He spoke about food, yes, food, reminiscing about the cinnamon crispies that had recently disappeared from the bakery's shelves (nobody ever bought but maybe one or two of them a week, and so Betty delisted them). He even spoke about diversity—diversity of hair color and eye color and how nice it was to walk down the street and see all kinds of them. And at the end of every little bit of chatting, he'd ask, "What kind of inheritance do we want to leave to our children? What kind of town will this be?"

Then came Hector's turn to rebut. He had been sitting down, regarding Barney Lane with shock and disgust. The cable news people, who were representing the media in this matter, got his reaction on tape.

Hector sighed when it was his turn and shuffled his notes. He said, "I'd like to speak to the issues just raised by my opponent, Mr. Lane." He put a heavy emphasis on the word *issues*. He said, about the language, that when Eudora was founded, in 1843, people tended to speak English when in groups but other languages at home. He said that there had been Scottish, Swedish, German, and French settlers and that they all managed to get along and build our beautiful little town.

He said it was a shame when old foods got less popular but that's the way it was. He himself used to like those little candies that looked like pillows and tasted like peanut butter, but he couldn't find them anymore.

He said that he didn't think Eudora was the kind of place where people thought a lot about hair color, eye color, or skin color. He said this last one in a low voice that shook a bit.

It was good stuff, but it still wasn't dynamic.

Then it was Barney Lane's turn again. He shook his head and smiled at the audience. He praised his opponent and said that he was a fine man but that if he thought Eudorans didn't care about any of these things, he was wrong. He asked what kind of schools they wanted for their children. He asked if they were happy spending their own money to give jobs to people they didn't even know. (This was effective, many people just now starting to feel the pinch of their generosity during the quarry closure threat.) And then he said, "Now, what kind of town do you want to live in? Our town? Or theirs?"

Artie Walker had been considered a disinterested party and, since he was used to speaking to crowds, had volunteered to chair the debate. As a surprisingly large proportion of the audience began to clap and cheer for Barney Lane, he made haste to tap his microphone with a pen, causing a loud booming kind of noise that shut everybody up. He then asked for questions.

An individual Artie did not recognize put up his hand with such rapidity and intent that Artie had to call upon him. The individual read from a pink index card. "Uh," he said, "uh, Mr. Rodriguez, now that the quarry's got all this extra money, what is it going to do for the town?"

Hector took a drink of water. He said, "The best thing the quarry can do for the town is to remain economically solvent and provide a secure income to its employees. As a banker, I would not advise operating with less cash reserves than are absolutely necessary—anything to do with raw materials can always require sudden unforeseen technical investment."

The individual had listened with his mouth open. "Uh-huh," he said.

Artie said, "Would you also like to answer this question, Mr. Lane?"

"What can the quarry do with that money?" Barney leaned over the lectern, banging the side with his hand. "Give"—*bang*—"it"—*bang*—"back"—*bang*. Portions of the crowd cheered. The individual who'd asked the question looked around with a visibly great sense of pride and then sat back down.

A girl displaying a vast expanse of unattractive midriff was next, waving at Artie so aggressively, he was helpless not to recognize her. "Hiya," she said, and then peered at a pink index card. "Mr. Lane," she said, and then smiled rather sickeningly at Barney, who leered at her with a wink to the crowd. She simpered, but then managed to carry on. "What is your chief priority for the town?"

Barney looked serious. "That's an easy one," he said solemnly. "Law and order." Again, part of the crowd cheered wildly.

Artie cleared his throat. "And you, Mr. Rodriguez?" he asked.

"I don't think I have a chief priority," Hector said. "I don't think it works like that. I think whoever does this job has to let go of their own agenda and really listen to what the people say. His"—he stopped himself—"or her," he added, "priorities need to be whatever their priorities are."

This got a polite smattering of hand claps.

Lottie Dougal jumped to her feet and waved at Artie with all of her characteristic energy, which was a lot. She was nearly doing jumping jacks.

Artie pointed to her, even though the room suddenly seemed to him to be full of people with grooming problems clutching pink index cards.

Lottie said with disarming sweetness. "I've got kind of a two-part question for Mr. Lane, if you don't mind, Mr. Chairman." Artie was mopping his brow with a handkerchief and nodded for her to carry on.

Lottie beamed her full thousand-watt smile at Barney Lane, and he rocked back a little on his feet. She said, "Mr. Lane, would you also get rid of the parking meters?"

Barney Lane pointed his finger and thumb like a gun and said, "You betcha, little lady."

Lottie once again became sweet. Pattie Walker dug her nails into Phil's arm, but even without this rather painful communication he was sufficiently knowledgeable about his sister-in-law to sense she was about to make trouble, so he shrugged Pattie off, patting her knee for reassurance.

"I was just wondering," Lottie said, "how you thought you would manage to make up the revenue."

Barney Lane struck his looking-serious pose again. "Get it back from the quarry," he said solemnly. Again the crowd went wild.

As Artie gave Hector the cue to respond, Lottie bored her eyes into Hector's, willing him to give the right answer, which he did. He said, "Any disposal of quarry assets would have to be agreed to by the quarry board, Mr. Lane. I'm afraid mayoral responsibility does not stretch to seizing personal assets!"

It wasn't much of a joke, but still quite a few people laughed at it.

Next on his feet was Luke Cash, with a question for Barney. "I got me a two-parter, too, if that's okay. Do you think you'd do a good job as mayor?"

Again, Barney struck his pose. He said in a low, controlled voice, "Yes, Luke, I think I would."

Luke held up three graduation programs and a to-go box from Mayan Memories and said, "I found these just under the seats I could reach. Do you think you're doing a good job now?"

This time the laughter was long and pronounced. Barney Lane's mean little mouth drew into a line, and for a moment he looked like what he was. Then he somehow remembered where he was and what he was doing and forced himself to laugh. He said, "Well, Luke, I haven't prioritized cleaning this gymnasium, and I've been caught out at it twice now. I guess nobody here's ever been caught getting behind on their work but me, huh?" and grinned.

It worked. Much of the audience grinned back.

By now Artie looked like he wanted to be sick. He said, "Mr. Rodriguez, could you tell us if you think you would do a good job and if you are doing a good job now?"

Hector spoke for nearly two minutes about his achievements and his employee record, just mentioning awards and promotions and giving the dates, not really bragging. He said at the end, "I don't think any of us can judge whether or not we are doing a good job. That's for other people to decide. But all of these things were awarded by other people, and when I'm worried whether or not I've bitten off more than I can chew, their opinion of my abilities gives me great comfort. I hope it does to you as well."

The smattering of clapping became louder and more persistent, if not any more widespread.

Ten people with pink index cards jumped up, but Artie said, "I'm afraid that's all we've got time for. Let's give the candidates a big round of applause."

Lottie and Mark were outside, unpacking boxes on a table borrowed from the cafeteria, when Doc Emery came up. He said, "How'd we do?"

Mark said, "We got creamed. Hector was like a stiff or something."

Lottie said, "Nonsense. It's harder to talk sense than to talk nonsense. Nonsense always sounds better."

The doctor said, "I'm sorry to have missed it."

He took one of the buttons, a bumper sticker, and a sign from the table.

Lottie smiled up at him. She said, "You be careful. Half your patients are in there cheering for Barney Lane."

He said, "Yeah, maybe. But if both of us are working for Hector, where else are they going to go?"

Then the stream of bodies erupted from the big double doors on the east side of the gym and carried the doctor away. Mark said, around the pleading smile he was using to offer buttons to a largely uninterested populace, "He still likes you."

"Now who's talking nonsense?" Lottie asked.

Lottie Dougal had a busy morning. By the end of it, nearly the whole of Main Street was decked with Hector Rodriguez posters and nearly all the people who owned businesses wore Hector Rodriguez buttons. It looked as if the election was already won, but Clement, Hector, and Lottie, in a meeting held in Clement's office later in the day, knew differently.

"It's them damn crackers," Clement said. "They don't do diddly for this town except suck it dry, but that *useless* Barney Lane's got them all riled up."

Lottie said, "I don't think you should call them 'crackers,' Clement." You could hear the quotation marks clearly.

"Why the hell not? That's what they are!"

Hector and Lottie exchanged glances. She said, "We should be above that sort of thing—racial slurs, name-calling . . . we're the party for people with brains."

"And that's another thing," Clement said. "That bastard's running as a *Republican*. I voted Republican since I was twenty-one years old. It's gonna kill me to put my mark by Independent instead." He fumed for a minute. "I already called up Cliff Hamilton and asked him what in the Sam Hill those boys thought they were doing taking scum like Lane into the party, and he said if I couldn't manage to get my candidate to take party leadership, I had effectively *resigned*."

Hector said, "I'm sorry about that, Clement."

"Hell, it ain't your fault. There ain't a Mexican in town can bring themselves to vote Republican, let alone run under the banner."

For a moment, they all chewed over this basic truth and another, related one, which did not need to be mentioned to be manifest in their thoughts. The fact was, farming people are notably conservative, as are oil people. Because of this, the state in which Eudora was located has gone Republican in every election since Abraham Lincoln and will continue to go Republican until the star our planet revolves around burns out and allows our descendants to shiver to death or relocate. Even then, if the survivors of the state gather into a cooperative community on some distant planet to take up the challenges of space exile, it will be a Republican cooperative community.

Now, there are pockets of rebellion in this conformity, the county that houses the state university being one, often represented on local election news as a small blue dot in an otherwise red sea, but these are so outnumbered that they seldom cause even a minute waver in state policy and do not so much as ripple the calm waters of the state electoral college.

"I got me to thinking," Clement said, "about just what old Cliff was up to, and had a word with a few buddies here and there." Again, significant looks were exchanged, both Lottie and Hector being well aware that though Clement liked a drink or five, he could hold his liquor pretty well and was thus in a good position to notice things about his fellow mayors and gubernatorial staff members at the annual conference, things that they might prefer not to be generally known. "I think," Clement continued, "them sons of bitches are getting ready to help us incorporate again, on them old terms I told them to shove up their backsides ten years ago. They know the quarry's solid and they're itching for a big slice of tax pie. Poor old Barney will be their puppet without ever even figuring out he's sold us all down the river, sorry possum-eating crack—uh . . . crackpot that he is."

"Well," Lottie said, with a smile acknowledging

Clement's adjustment, "they'll have to go to the city for their printing needs. I made sure Max Breyer is too busy to do anything extra this month."

Clement said, "You saw this coming."

Lottie shrugged. "My own sister won't wear a button because she's just hired Carla Bustamonte. She's making Carla work in the back until this is all over. I tell you, we're fighting for hearts and minds right now."

Hector said, "Maybe the best thing is for me to let somebody else—"

"No!" Lottie and Clement said together.

Clement said, "I've been running things in this town since disco. This is a nice place, a heck of a nice place, but it needs steering, it needs leadership. Take poor Pattie Walker. She just wants it to be all over. Well, it won't ever be all over if you don't win."

Lottie said, "We need you."

There was a moment and then Hector said, "I got this in the mail yesterday."

He took a small envelope out of the manila folder he'd carried into the meeting. It had a stamp, but the stamp wasn't canceled. They all knew that the stamp was there to try to make it look as if the letter could have been mailed from anywhere, but they all also knew the reason the stamp wasn't canceled was because if anyone, even someone who lived next door to Hector, tried

314

to mail him a letter, it would in all probability not reach him before the election. It would have to be collected, taken to the city and then to the sorting hub, back to the city for more sorting, and then to the county seat, where it would be loaded onto the area post office truck for dispersal. Eudorans who felt called upon to use the mail for their Christmas cards generally did so straight after Halloween just to be sure.

The stationery was something Lottie did not carry, a rather sickening strawberry-scented sheet in a virulent pink with a large-eyed kitten peeping myopically out of an orange-toned representation of a basket in the bottom right corner. The handwriting, in contrast, was in no-nonsense black ink. The message was short and to the point: *Go back to Mexico, you fucking beaner. We don't want you here.*

Lottie wiped her hands on her skirt automatically, even though she hadn't touched the letter.

"Oh, that's just great," Clement said. "You see the kind of people we're dealing with here, Hector? Now, you let me and Lottie deal with the election side of things. You just keep thinking about policy and walk around looking good. Eat out a lot. Go for a beer at Chuck's. Smile a little more, and pat dogs and babies. We'll do the rest."

Hector smiled now, as if he was practicing. He said, "Well, you're the boss."

And Clement said, "Damn right."

315

After Hector let himself out of the office, Lottie turned to Clement. "So," she said, "just what is it you think we can do?"

Clement was quick to reply. "Damned if I know," he said.

"Yeah," Lottie responded. "I was kind of afraid of that."

Much of Eudora had not known when their fate hung in the balance over the quarry closure. By the time they knew of the danger, it was all over. It was rather like hearing about something your child did that day, walking across the train trestle or diving off the high board, when the child was safely tucked up in bed. Alarming, but not terrifying.

The election was not like that. The election was like standing right by the deep end while your child was falling. It was terrifying.

The worst bit was not knowing what everyone thought. You could not greet your neighbor with news or insight because you did not know where your neighbor stood on the election issues. And, after some ideological conflict and associated bad feeling following your initial inquiries, you soon learned that you did not *want* to know where your neighbor stood.

This left individuals isolated with their own thoughts and judgments. There were no pithy sayings from Jim Evans or confident pronouncements from Clement McAllister circulating in the rounds of tittle and tattle. When posters went up or buttons went on, no remarks were passed. Eudora was divided three ways—the supporters of Lane, those behind Rodriguez, and the uncertain—and it did not like the division and the self-consciousness it engendered. A new, shifty walk became the norm in town as residents learned to avoid one another.

In this climate of unaccustomed reticence, Eudorans suffered. The annual sidewalk sale was sedate and noticeably somber. The county fair was attended, and Eudora's pies, jams, and jellies were awarded blue ribbons, but there was no general jubilation. In fact, some people only read in the newspaper of Lucy McAllister's final triumph, after years of competition, over her lemon-meringue rival, who lived west of Tonganoxie. Some never found out what Lucy had done to her recipe to at last lift it into pie preeminence, and those who did find out didn't think to ask until nearly Christmas.

As you can imagine, Pattie Walker was not alone in wanting the elections over.

The Famous Author was heard to say that he had only once felt such municipal tension, and that was in Jerusalem during the Six-Day War.

Clement and Park Davis ate their blue-plate specials in noticeable gloom at different booths alone. Nobody wanted to commit to sit with either of them for fear of suffering a similar quarantine. The rest of the local businessmen kept to the round booth and talked about baseball with a determined, if simulated, interest.

Hector's mother, though so proud of her son, told him that there was a reason why her generation had remained invisible and that this was it. Everyone of Mexican descent in town was trying to fade back into a shadow that was no longer there, feeling the eyes of every person they saw of non-Mexican descent on the backs of their necks, as hot as irons. Every person of non-Mexican descent found it hard to look anyone of Mexican descent in the eye, lest the latter should think the former was a Lane follower, or because, regrettably, they were.

During this time, Jim Flory showed some classic musicals, which were well attended and seemed to break the mood. For a few hours, there was chatter and ease. But then the doors opened into the street-lit night and repression fell upon the audiences once again.

It fell hardest on those who were uncertain.

Park Davis, who had been grinning and whistling the reprise of "Singing in the Rain," heard his whistle falter and then cease and was aware that once again his soul had taken up its heavy burden of trouble. Stacey Harper (for she and Park were one of those newer types of couples who had not bothered with a marriage ceremony until the children came along, by which time Stacey was so well established in the business world of the city she did not wish to take Park's name in case it led to confusion) looked sideways at her husband and wondered if, once again, he would end up tossing and turning in the spare room that night. She had enlisted her aunt (Lucy McAllister, who was born a Harper) to have Frieda and little Damien (Stacey dealt in modern art) as overnight guests, and she had glossed her hair and lips, taken a black silk dress with spaghetti straps out of storage, and used her best perfume. Now she suspected it was all in vain.

Her suspicion was correct. Park had a glass of milk at the fridge when they got home, rubbing his stomach. He then belched and excused himself. He said, "Honey, you look great, but I . . ." and just left it hanging there.

Stacey was a good wife and had known Park since kindergarten. She gave him a big hug. She said, "It's okay, babe." And then she said, "It's all going to be all right."

"Well, I think that's the problem," he answered. "I don't know what's right."

Upon which she stiffened slightly and they moved apart. She said, "You know what I think."

And he said, "Yes, I do."

Silence fell upon the slate floor of the Davis-Harper kitchen in great, angry lumps. Park waded through it and up the stairs to bed, but Stacey stood there, soaking in it, for quite some time.

The bed in the spare room was comfortable. More comfortable, in fact, than the king-sized one he shared with Stacey, as the latter needed a new mattress. Every day they kept on forgetting to do anything about it, and then every night they were reminded, as it felt just that bit too lumpy and saggy. They tended to end up together in the middle, leaving a large expanse of unused bed on either side, but that could not be put down to the mattress, for they did that wherever they slept. In fact, though the spare bedroom's bed was comfortable, the comfort did not motivate Park (as he later confessed at the upcoming Maple Leaf Festival to an auditor who shall not here be named) to choose to sleep there. No, the motivating factor was that he could not bear to wake another morning and find he and Stacey had slept the entire night on their own sides of the bed.

It was his own thoughts that kept Park Davis awake. He had at his disposal any number of remedies for insomnia, both conventional and alternative. But he did not avail himself of them. Instead, he lay there and tried to think through the whole knotty question.

Park did not think himself to be a prejudiced man. He had not been overly surprised or alarmed at the incorporation into visibility of the various members of the Mexican American community, and had, being the only supplier of tampons and other necessities within walking distance, already acknowledged to himself the economic importance of the quarry, and had donated accordingly. He and Stacey were thrilled about the opening of Mayan Memories and had entertained any number of Stacey's odd associates over there, all of whom, no matter what their bizarre tastes in clothing and eyeglasses, had loved Maria's food. Park also had a weakness for cherry danish and was grateful for the plumpness and toothsomeness of Betty Requena's new recipe, which had improved immeasurably the secret life he protected from his beloved spouse.

And yet.

And yet, there was beginning to come a feeling of being slightly pushed out. One week it had been two customers who had run into each other by the first-aid section, two men who'd started speaking Spanish and then had got a little loud and laughed. If they'd been talking English, Park would have listened and maybe learned something or had a little laugh himself. But because they were speaking Spanish, he felt excluded, an intruder in his own store. And something inside him started to burn, just a little.

It happened more and more. Once on the corner of Main Street, someone called to someone else in Spanish and then they both laughed. What was that all about? What was so funny? Park, like his uncle Hal and all the Davises, dressed sharply and conservatively and had his hair cut regularly. He was also blessed with the Davis temperament, which was even. There were no tendencies toward paranoia in Park Davis. And yet he wondered if they were laughing *at him.*

Now, Park was an intelligent man. Heck, you had to be to become a pharmacist these days. And he was a self-aware man. He looked at this wondering and he cast it aside as unworthy and small-minded. He and Stacey were not regular attendees of Lutheran services, but he knew right from wrong when he saw it, and he saw wrong in this kind of wondering.

And yet he wondered again.

It kept happening. While furtively in line for his danish. While waiting to get his dry cleaning out at Food Barn. While filling up his car at Lane Nichols's place. And once at his own son's school.

So when Barney Lane came along and said what he said, something in Park Davis said yes to that. This was, after all, his town. The Davises had been here since the founding. When Stacey was younger and hankered after life in big cities and he'd had to choose between keeping Stacey and losing Eudora, he had chosen Eudora and let Stacey go. All right, she had pretty speedily come back, but he was not to know that at the time. He had made the ultimate sacrifice for his home. And so it was important that it remain *his* home. People did not say things you did not understand in your own home. People did not have parties and not invite you. People did not just *ignore* you in your own home, like you were part of the dispensing equipment.

No, Park thought for the 347th time, Hector Rodriguez should not become Eudora's mayor.

The bed seemed suddenly hot, even though they'd had a nice cool spell and the windows were open, the curtains billowing softly as the cool breeze filled the room. Park shifted, turning over on his other side and throwing the covers back. But Barney Lane should not become Eudora's mayor, either.

Park Davis had no illusions about Barney Lane. They had been only one year apart at Eudora High. Barney was a cheat, a sneak, a liar, and lazy to the bone. That he had managed to ensnare and imprison Becky Lane for an entire decade never ceased to make Park wonder.

And yet Barney was . . . Here Park turned again, made uncomfortable, not by the temperature of the evening or the Sealy Posturpedic mattress or the soft gray-blue suede-effect wallpaper but by his own thoughts. And yet Barney Lane was . . .

Park buried his head beneath his pillow, as if that would shut it out, but still it came. Barney Lane was . . .

White.

Pattie Walker was not a stranger to controversy. She was Lottie's sister, for one thing, and her mother's daughter, for another. And then there was the whole strange relationship of her father and mother, how they had lived separately for some thirty years while still remaining married in every sense of the word. Her reluctance to allow Carla Bustamonte to serve at the counter was due not to a fear of what people would say but to a gut instinct for trouble that had served her well since fourth grade and which she had learned not to ignore.

Taking an afternoon coffee break with Maria Lopez and Betty Requena, she found this instinct validated. When Pattie arrived, the first thing she said was, "I can't stay long. I left Carla at the counter and I really don't want her to have to be there for any longer than I can help."

Betty gave Pattie a measured look, which Pattie correctly interpreted as an inquiry about her motivations. She explained. "I don't know. I just feel like I'm asking for trouble. Something weird's going on in this town."

Gabe Burgos, who had been hired now full time, had come over to the table with something for his aunt to taste. She tasted it and said, "Mmm-hmmm. Now what do you think?"

"I dunno. It seems a little flat," he said.

Maria said to him, "Did you remember the

lemon juice?" which made him scurry away. To Pattie and Betty she said, "I got another one of those letters. It said it hoped I lost the baby because there's too many Mexicans already."

"Oh, my God!" Pattie exclaimed. "Did you call the sheriff's department?"

"Ben and Odie come by every day and pick them up," Betty said. "I got four last week. And some stupid kids keep coming in and asking for cinnamon crispies."

Maria said, "Make some. Make them big. Charge five dollars apiece. Shut them up."

The three ladies laughed and the conversation turned to how the doctor and Lottie had sat together at the last three movies and what Kylie Requena had worn to church. But, as Pattie told Phil later, it was all getting to be too much, and something had to give.

Pattie remembered that coffee break a great deal over the coming months—what Betty wore, how she spoke, how she laughed, letting her chin come up and her strong neck show. She thought about Betty's fingers on the coffee cup, so clean—the nails bare and trimmed short, the plain gold band of her wedding ring. How she'd pointed out that Lottie and Doc hadn't shared popcorn, as if that was the defining element of intimacy. The story she told about dating Don.

Had she said anything about driving into the county seat to get new tags for their cars? Pattie didn't think so. It was the kind of thing it was sometimes easier for Pattie to do, too. If Phil was on a contract on the city side, she would just leave the shop for a couple of hours. And it must have been the same with Don and Betty. It was easier for Betty to get away. She always did that kind of stuff.

Lottie Dougal had also been in the county seat that day, dealing with an insurance company headquarters and trying to figure out how to incorporate their new logo onto their extensive range of branded stationery supplies. She had dropped by to see Max, to get his thoughts, on the way home, and so was a little later than she'd planned. Subsequently, that seemed important.

The interstate highway, which had so rudely spurned Eudora, had simply blasted through the few hills in its way, but the railway was constructed at an earlier, gentler time and had put in a few bridges here and there. The old highway, which Lottie was taking back to town, had avoided both courses of action by following the Santa Fe Trail and the curve of the landscape. At one point, close to town, there was a trestle railway bridge between two hills, and under it, the old highway curved the long way around through the valley.

The interstate maintenance had come to an end,

and the stream of traffic that had brought such prosperity to Gross Home Cooking had died down to its usual thin trickle. When Lottie first saw the car slewed across the road, she thought tires. And then she thought Betty Requena, because by then she'd identified it. And then she saw the blood and largely stopped thinking.

She pulled up right behind it and put on her emergency flashers. Somehow she got her cell phone out of her purse and was using it while she ran, asking for an ambulance, paramedics, and the sherrif's patrol before she even wrenched open the door. It was obvious what had happened. Someone had thrown a large chunk of concrete off the bridge and through Betty's windshield. When Lottie opened the door, the full horror of the damage hit her just as the emergency dispatch operator signed off.

Lottie ran back to her car and wrestled the hatchback open to get out the first-aid kit. She said later that even as she carried it back, she felt hopeless and the kit felt completely inadequate.

Head wounds always bleed a lot. Inside the first-aid kit were some clean dressings. Lottie tore the paper off three or four and made a kind of pad. And then she looked for where the bleeding was coming from, turned aside to vomit, and, wiping her mouth on the sleeve of her jacket, reached for her phone again.

Janey Lane took the call. "Get me Jim," Lottie said. "It's an emergency."

Janey didn't even hesitate.

"Dr. Emery," was all he said into the phone, and then he just listened.

Lottie was crying. "I'm dealing with a head wound," she said. "Paramedics are on their way, but there's so much blood, there's too much blood, and it's coming from . . . her face is all smashed and I can see bone sticking out of . . . I think it's her brain, Jim. And I don't know where to put the pressure, or if I should . . . but she's bleeding so fast, Jim."

She was shouting. Jim Flory could hear the whole thing clearly from across the desk.

The doctor said, "Think about the circulation patterns. Try to find a place to put the pressure where the organ isn't exposed."

"It's her eye, too, Jim. She's all smashed up."

The doctor was standing up and throwing things in his bag. "Who is it and where are you?"

"God, God, God."

"Where are you, Lottie?"

"I'm inside the car. Her legs, too, Jim. It hit her legs."

"Where is the car?"

"Three miles north of town on Highway 10."

And then the doctor was gone, leaving Jim Flory shaken. He went and told Janey Lane in front of a roomful of patients, who all suddenly wanted to call home.

$\bullet \quad \bullet \quad \bullet$

The worst part of it was, Lottie said later, that Betty kept kind of coming to. In the end, when Jim got there, most of what Lottie did was just talk to her, try to talk to her as if this pulpy mess was the same as the person she knew. The paramedics had taken forever. When they arrived, Jim kept working with them, the three of them together, while she was off on one side, with a blanket Odie Marsh threw around her and a cup of coffee from Ben Nichols's thermos. Those two were up on the bridge, looking for evidence. There were some chunks of wood further down the track, a badly made barricade that probably wouldn't do any damage to one of the infrequent trains, though you could never tell. They cleared it away and then called in what they'd done only to be told that they'd messed up a crime scene and not to touch another thing, forensics were on their way.

Had Lottie seen anyone on the bridge? they asked. It seemed she might have seen two fair heads peering over, but she couldn't remember when she'd looked. It would have been when she was heading back to the car for the first-aid kit. No, she didn't think she could swear to it in court. No, she didn't think she could identify them in a lineup, though maybe she could, later, once she'd had some sleep. For Lottie was tired, weary clear to her bones.

When the helicopter landed on the highway,

329

blinding them with light and deafening them with sound, the paramedics and Jim shouting to the copter crew as they, impossibly swiftly, loaded Betty in and left, the wind from the blades flew into Lottie's open hatchback and made a miniature tornado of paperwork inside her car, and all Lottie wanted to do was lie down on top of it all, lie down and sleep forever.

Jim talked to Odie right in front of her, about shock and driving her car, and, in some kind of a dream, she saw Ben get in and drive her car away and then the doctor was strapping her into his and reclining her seat and that's all she remembered until she woke up in her own bed with Pattie anxiously bending over her.

"Betty?" was the first thing she said.

"She's in ICU. She's had some surgery already. She's still critical."

"Jim?"

"He's been calling all morning. He's going to come see you right after office hours."

Lottie got up and went to the bathroom. She came back with her face washed and her teeth brushed. Pattie said, "I made you some oatmeal."

But Lottie's eyes were dipping closed. "Thank you," she said politely, and went directly back to sleep.

Father Gaskin knew that there were times when religion and politics met, but he personally preferred that they remain in their own separate arenas as often as was practicably possible. A little discreet nudge here or there in the homily or a little pointed intercessional request was about as far as he chose to go. But this horror had now come upon them, and Tim Gaskin knew that he was called to take some sort of stand.

There is a lot of talk around these days about evil. There is a lot of bandying about of Satan's name. But in Father Gaskin's opinion, these terms were nearly always misused. Humans were fallible and could be cruel, especially in the pursuit of their own agenda. They tended to put such things as their own families and their own ways of life up on a pedestal as universally good things while not allowing other people's families and ways of life equal importance. This was bad, and led to much of the unhappiness suffered in the world, but it was not evil. It did not intentionally set out to harm or destroy. Harm and destruction just happened along the way.

And so it had been with this.

No one knew exactly which two towheaded rug rats Lottie Dougal had almost seen on the railway trestle, but everyone knew where they'd come from and why they'd done what they'd done. And while broken fingernails and strands of dishwater blond hair were being examined on a molecular basis, and everyone else was roundly condemning them, Father Gaskin was praying for their souls.

Satan was not those children.

Father Gaskin knew Satan.

Satan was a quiet voice that urged the setting up of pedestals, which closed your eyes to the needs and desires of your fellow men and women. Satan was the one who told you how wonderful, how truly great you were, better than anyone else in town. If Satan was anywhere Father Gaskin could see, he was in the ear of Barney Lane. And so the priest went to see Barney.

Now, as you can imagine, the television crews were back.

If it had been a lovely and heartwarming story to see a community brought together across divisions of religions and race, it was not really news. The only reason Eudora and Hector had got any airtime for the quarry salvation was because nothing much else was happening at the time. Brotherhood and cooperation did not boost ratings. Injury and turmoil boosted ratings. Right now, Eudora had plenty of both.

And so, just as Father Gaskin arrived at the small tract house where Barney Lane laid his head, so did two other interested parties. One was a television crew.

But one was not.

Don Requena hadn't thought, at first, of the cause of his wife's terrible injuries. He had been busy crying and praying, sitting and

332

squeezing her hand, urging Betty to fight, to come out of the anesthetic, to come out of the short but worrying coma. He had been busy becoming, in a very short amount of time, an expert on the right frontal lobe of the brain and well versed in orthopedics. On the fourth day, when the danger of death had largely passed, Betty was moved into an ordinary room with an ordinary bed. Then Don had suddenly noticed how dirty he was and became able to listen to his family telling him to go home and get some sleep. By then he was able to read his wife's chart and understand the implications of any changes in body function or medication.

In fact, it wasn't until the drive home, sitting in the front passenger seat of a young nephew's car, that he began to think of what had happened to make this new, horrible way of life necessary. And so he turned to the cousin, who was Kylie's brother, Bruce, and asked him.

Bruce Requena was seventeen years old and full of the solemnity and responsibility of the occasion. He had been very flattered to have his offer of a drive accepted by all the Requenas gathered in the family waiting room. It seemed to him to indicate he had reached a man's estate and that his 1977 Ford LTD, which he had lovingly restored to perfection, had become a reliable conveyance and therefore a testament to his judgment and skills.

An older and less eager to please Requena would have tempered the account of the cause of Betty's injuries. But Bruce did not have the wisdom with which to make such alterations. He told the truth as he knew it, and unfortunately, he knew quite a bit.

He said, "I think it was the Coleman kids. They got a big chunk of concrete and pushed it off the trestle."

And Don said, "Why . . . ," unable to finish his sentence, which, he said later, could have had so many endings. Why did it hit the windshield? It's not an easy shot—did they practice? Why Betty? Why did they have a chunk of concrete? Why wasn't there anybody watching them kids?

And Bruce, correctly guessing the many endings the inquiry could have, launched into an explanation of the Colemans (with whom he had gone to school, though they were younger), their racial outlook, the cinnamon crispie campaign, the rubble and spare parts that constituted the Colemans' landscape gardening, and the way they had gotten in trouble before for messing with the train tracks.

Don listened in silence.

It was going on five o'clock when they arrived in Eudora and Bruce dropped his uncle off at the house. The men were coming home from the quarry. Bruce asked his uncle if he wanted him to stay, but Don waved him away vaguely. Still,

334

Bruce sat in the driveway for a moment to watch his uncle into the house.

But his uncle did not go into the house. His uncle went next door to the Sanchezes and talked to Juan and Ricky, who were just getting out of their truck. And then Juan and Ricky and Don went to intercept Bill Lopez and then they didn't have to intercept anyone else, because all the men coming back from the quarry went to where they were all standing in the middle of the road to find out what was going on.

A few minutes later, many of them returned to their trucks or went into their houses or sheds and then came back. Now they had things in their hands, baseball bats, shovels, picks. And then they began to walk.

Bruce, still sitting in his uncle's driveway, suddenly understood the meaning and use of the word *discretion*. His mother was forty-five minutes away and had her cell phone turned off in the hospital. So he did not know what to do.

Barney Lane had been practicing looking noble in front of the mirror. He had a new suit and a new haircut, both provided by the county Republican committee, as would be a variety of campaign materials (buttons, leaflets, and banners) just as soon as the printers got over their unaccountable delay. His house was dirty and there were dishes in the sink, but looking noble in a suit had far more appeal than dealing with these trivial issues. Also, he fully expected a certain young lady and her exposed midriff to come calling soon, and planned to have her do the cleaning if she wanted to stay.

He looked at himself in the mirror again. Oh, she would definitely want to stay. It was a pity she couldn't do the school as well. It had become such a nuisance to go there each day, and he was uncomfortably aware that the summer cleaning schedule and his achievements in this area were not identical. In fact, as the campaign wore on, the one ceased altogether to resemble the other. And the gym was still dirty.

When the knock came, he changed his noble look for his sexy look and undid the top button of his shirt, loosening his tie. Having thoroughly practiced, he opened the door, leaned on the door jamb, and, with a leisurely smirk he thought was the essence of James Bond, slowly raised his hooded eyes to . . . Father Tim.

He straightened up and switched off sexy in a flash.

"Oh, sorry, Father, I was expecting . . . oh, never mind. What can I do you for?"

Father Tim never had a chance to answer. There was a noise behind them, and they both swiveled to see the tide of quarry workers sweeping down the street.

Now, these are men well known to this narrative. They are largely good family men, sober and industrious, who treat women and children with gentleness and work their overtime when it comes. But they didn't look that way that day.

None of them was little. If any of them had started out employment at the quarry somewhat skinny and undersized, the job had soon caused them to fill out. Don Requena himself had shoulders like hams and thighs like turkeys.

Then there was the fact that they were, all of them, dirty. There is something about a dirty man that is much more threatening than anything about a clean one.

Also, they were, all of them, angry. Brows were lowered and veins stood out on necks. A little green makeup and any one of them could have played the Incredible Hulk. The massed effect was impressive.

Barney Lane nearly wet the trousers of his new suit. But though they shouted and gestured at him, they marched right by his house, and he sank against the door jamb with relief, showing his sense of civic responsibility by saying to Father Tim, "I wonder what all that was about."

But Father Tim, like the news crew, had left Barney's house and was running after the mob of angry men. Now, Father Tim might be a little tubby these days, but he was a sprinter and a hurdler in high school and college (before he transferred to the seminary), and he still had a surprising turn of speed. He caught up to and passed the men in the twinkle of an eye.

He stood in the middle of the road and folded his arms. "Now, Don," he said, but he didn't say anything else because the mob simply opened up like the Red Sea and flowed around him, leaving him standing there like a fool. The news crew caught it all on tape.

Father Tim was no quitter. He made another little end run. This time he took his crucifix out of his shirt and held it up. He said, "In the name of our Lord Jesus Christ, stop!"

The mob was only twenty feet away from the Coleman house, the last place on this sorry edge of town. Curtains had been hastily drawn and blinds had been pulled down. Not only the screen door but the front door was closed tight.

Don stopped, and everyone else stopped, too. Don stared at the house as though he could burn it down just by looking at it.

Father Tim had to shake his arm to get Don's attention. He said, "This is not the way to settle this, Don."

But Don's eyes were glazed. He swayed from foot to foot. He looked at Father Tim and blinked at him, but he didn't seem to focus.

Trembling, Father Tim reached up and put his hand on Don's sweating forehead. He prayed a short blessing. When he took his hand away, Don's face crumpled, as did his legs. He sank to his knees. The big man began to weep.

The other men circled him, and some bore him up. Dark looks were cast at the Coleman place over shoulders, but no one went a step farther. The Sanchezes suggested that they go back and get their truck, but Don insisted he could walk; he just needed a minute.

The shot went over everyone's heads. No one ever found where the bullet landed.

"Git away!" Wayne Coleman screeched, the deer rifle barrel poking out of a hole in his bathroom window screen. The blind had been retracted, but no one had noticed in the unfolding drama. "I got plenty of ammo. I'll shoot every one of you beaners."

Our faults can sometimes aid us as much as our virtues. It was Barney Lane's cowardice that made him call 911 immediately upon seeing the mob. It was Ben Nichols's indolence that kept him sitting at Gross Home Cooking, having just one more cup of coffee, and it was Odie Marsh's vanity that let Ben do it, because it allowed Odie to tell his side of the story of the accident to various interested parties. All of these combined to have Odie Marsh's voice ring out on the black-and-white's bullhorn at this precise moment, no earlier and no later.

"Now, everybody just stay calm, and Wayne, put that rifle down right now and get out here."

Odie looked around and took in the situation in a single glance. "Why don't you boys get Don in the back of the cruiser and Ben and me will take him home? You want to sit with him, Father Tim? Then you'd all better get home or you'll miss your suppers."

The men shifted uneasily.

Odie said, "Or we could do this the hard way. I could notice that you've all got weapons in your hands."

There was a little muttering. The Sanchezes broke first, getting Don over to the car and opening the door. Everyone else milled around uncertainly.

Ben wasn't having much more luck at the time with Wayne Coleman. "I ain't coming out while *they're* here," Wayne said.

Odie was working on that. "Right now," he said, "I'm figuring you all went to work a little on the high school baseball diamond. It needs shoveling and picking after last season. It probably needs some grass seed, too, though I'm thinking you're planning on leaving that until the next rain. And I'm guessing you all got to chatting about your work there and took the wrong turn home. And if you turn around and go home right now, that's what I'm always going to think."

The Rodriguezes took the arms of the other men and turned them around. The Sanchezes left Don Requena in the care of Father Tim and joined them. Much more slowly than they came, they all walked home.

Wayne Coleman emerged and was told to be more careful when cleaning his gun.

Odie and Ben went back on patrol, conscious of a good job well done.

But they had forgotten the film crew.

One week from the election, Jim Flory held an "election festival" featuring such classics as *All the President's Men* and *Mr. Smith Goes to Washington*. Lottie Dougal had not been around very much in the intervening week. Though by Wednesday she had begun to take her place in the stationery store and in her consulting room, she had done so without her usual bounce or energy, just getting through every day in a way that made you tired to observe.

The doctor had come by one night to check on her and was astonished to see she was already working evenings, seeing her patients. He stomped around on the back porch and stormed in the back door when Lottie called "next," completely ignoring those patiently waiting. Maria Lopez, who was there for her checkup and who was the actual "next" he displaced, heard the argument quite clearly, since the doctor's half of it was conducted mainly in a shout. He said a lot about "rest" and "energy levels" and told her she was a "damn fool." Maria could not hear Lottie's soft replies, but the murmur of them continued long after the doctor had stopped yelling.

When Lottie called Maria in, Maria fully expected to find the doctor gone and Lottie in tears. But the doctor was still there, sitting on a kitchen chair in the corner, and Lottie was smiling really big. Lottie asked Maria if she'd mind if the doctor sat in on their consultation. Maria was not a shy woman and agreed. It was an odd experience. She'd never had two doctors looking at her before. They were chatting back and forth over her enlarging belly as if she wasn't even there. The doctor acted like that was perfectly okay, but Lottie kept apologizing for leaving Maria out of the process and tried to explain what they were talking about.

In the end, Maria sat down on the sofa and Lottie said, "I think we're both really impressed with how well you're dealing with the pregnancy, Maria, especially considering it's your first and your age."

Maria said she felt hot, like she was blushing. She said something about exercise, and the doctor said, "That's just what I was telling Practitioner Dougal here. Your occupation has actually kept you moving in all kinds of ways beneficial to the process. I think you'll also find it helpful during labor."

"Well," Lottie said, "nobody can tell how that will go. It's not all up to the woman, you know. But you've given yourself the best chance by how you're treating yourself. As time goes on, get your feet up more and more. It should be a gradual thing. Every week, you should be resting a little more than last week. It'll help get Linda and Gabe used to doing without you."

The doctor said, "Is this going to be a home delivery?"

Maria said she got frightened then, because of the look on his face.

Lottie said, "Yes, of course. What else, with a healthy mother like this?"

The doctor said something with a Latin word that sounded like a kind of pasta. Lottie snapped at him, "That's got nothing to do with it. Maria wants to be at home in her own bed with all her things and her friends and family around. We'll let the hospital know what's happening if there're any problems we can't deal with. But I don't expect any."

The doctor looked at her. She said, "I did a midwifery course when I was in London, part time. I thought it might come in handy one day."

He said, "This is during your time at the LSE?" like he couldn't believe it. Maria found out later this was a big-shot business college that Lottie was at for three years.

But Lottie said, "Yeah," like doing both was no big deal, and added, "Most of my classmates spent a lot of time socializing. I put my energy into that instead."

"And still went to the Oxford Ball. And the boat race. And Ascot."

Lottie giggled. Actually giggled. She said, "I didn't say I was a hermit. I said I didn't spend much time on my social life."

She turned to Maria with a smile still lingering on her lips. "Now, have you got any questions?" she asked.

It wasn't easy for Maria to say no and just get up and leave, but the pregnancy was going so well she couldn't think of anything to say. She got up and was almost at the front door before she remembered something she really did want to know. She said, "Doc? Is it true Betty's memory is all gone?"

Lottie's smile dropped away. The doctor said, "Parts of it are a little shaky. She can still remember recipes, but she's not sure who Don is."

Maria felt sick inside. She said, "I want to go and see her, but . . ."

The doctor said, "Not yet. She's only seeing a few family members right now. She gets confused easily."

"I can't do it, anyway," Maria confessed. "I don't want to even think about her that way."

Lottie said, "You can't see any of it anymore. It's all bandaged up. They're starting skin grafts on Tuesday."

"You seen her?"

Lottie nodded.

Maria said, "I'm a bad friend."

"No," Lottie said, "you're a good mother. You know you can't get upset like that right now and so you're doing what you have to do to stay calm."

"She remembers recipes?"

"Yeah." The doctor smiled. "When she first came out of her coma and they took the tube out, she sat there for an hour, telling Don and the nurses how to make cream cheese danish before she finally fell asleep."

Maria went away holding on to that story like a hot water bottle.

The next day, the bakery reopened.

It was Zadie Gross who had called Margery Lupin and told her what had happened to Betty. Now Zadie was putting Margery up in her guest room, even though the two women had never been friends, and dealing with Margery's untidy gray hairs all over the bathroom and in her dark rose shag pile.

Every morning, Margery left the house at four forty-five, just as Zadie was waking up. Every evening, they spent an hour or so together before Margery's bedtime and then Zadie had an hour or two to herself before hers. It wasn't so bad.

Margery Lupin was working the bakery for nothing, on Betty's behalf. She said that Betty had worked for her, done quite a bit extra, for a long time and it was the least she could do.

345

Evidently she already had Margaret's life back in Chickasaw running on rails. She'd hired a Swedish au pair, a lovely girl, and mapped out a series of play group visits and other activities to keep the kids occupied. She'd stocked Margaret's freezer with homemade meals and contracted with a local grocery store to deliver what could not be frozen ahead. She'd moved Margaret's working space from the lovely rosewood-paneled library up to a rickety area in the attic, which had doubled Margaret's productivity, as she couldn't hear diddly up there and never got distracted. She'd hired a local handyman to put up an impregnable wooden fence around an area outside the kitchen door and had invested considerably in outdoor play equipment. She'd found a college girl, home for the summer, who was a big fan of Margaret's, to come and do her filing and other assorted administrative tasks for free, just so the girl could add it to her resume.

Of course, Margery knew it would all fall apart in time and need restructuring. But for the moment, she was not desperately needed in Chickasaw.

When the bakery opened, two things were noticeable. One was that Margery had faithfully followed Betty Requena's recipes, going against the habits of many years to do so. The other was that Ben and Odie were not there.

T he mob had looked even more frightening on television. This was because the cameraman, who had put in a lot of time covering the NFL, held the camera down about knee level and shot up. They didn't show how the men had stopped for the crucifix or how Don had collapsed in tears. They only showed when the men walked around Father Tim, the shot that was fired, the gun poking out of the bathroom screen. They also showed Don getting into the back of the squad car and made it look like he was being arrested.

But Ben and Odie were on suspension because they hadn't arrested anyone.

Ben and Odie had a new superior. This was not uncommon. The office of sheriff is an elected one, but it is largely decorative and managerial. It is the role of assistant sheriff where you get your bright sparks with criminology degrees itching to show what they can do. They come, change things so that in some numerical way benefit can be proved, and move on to more lucrative employment in a major urban center or one of America's central agencies of investigation.

The current assistant sheriff was new, terribly keen on procedure, had a small bristly mustache, and ran ten miles a day. He had spoken to Ben and Odie before, in a small seminar of their peers, about avoiding the anecdotal in their reporting. Odie had tried to argue then about the importance of context in human interaction but did not have the vocabulary to put his point across and had no success in the argument. Indeed, he had only succeeded in calling his failings to the notice of the assistant sheriff, who took him aside later and told him that his ideas were old-fashioned and that he himself was going to drag the department into the twenty-first century, kicking and screaming if need be. His bristly mustache had twitched as he said it and his eyes had narrowed.

On that occasion, as Ben and Odie went to their squad car, Ben remarked, "He's going places, that one."

Odie answered, "He can go right now, as far as I'm concerned."

And they both enjoyed a hearty laugh.

They weren't laughing now.

What they had done evidently put the entire Eudoran citizenry at risk. If anyone, the assistant sheriff said, in a quiet, controlled voice that was somehow worse than shouting, in the town was hurt or killed in any subsequent clashes between the Mexican American community and the Coleman family, the liability rested entirely on Ben and Odie's shoulders. The department had no choice but to suspend them immediately in order to limit its own exposure to liability.

He then said, "You are not cowboys. You are police officers. Your job is to observe and investigate crime and then to take direct action against the perpetrators. Did you do that?"

Odie said, "There weren't any perpetrators to take direct action against. It was just a bunch of guys a little worked up."

"Attempted murder," the assistant sheriff suggested.

"Oh, naw!" Odie protested. "Everybody knows Wayne Coleman's a crack shot. If he'd wanted to kill anybody, they'd be dead."

"Well, then, discharging a firearm within town limits."

Odie sighed. Ben said, "Yeah, but old Wayne was scared."

"Yes, and what about that mob? Assembling with intent to cause harm."

"What, you would have tried to arrest them *all*?" Odie asked.

"I would have arrested the shooter and taken everyone else's names down and visited them with an official caution."

Odie sighed again and rubbed his nose. Ben said, "Yeah, but that's only going to get everyone more riled up. Both sides will blame the other for being in trouble. This way they're all ashamed of themselves. It will last longer."

The assistant sheriff had a set speech about where the role of the policeman ends and the role of the judicial system begins. It lasted about four and half minutes and he delivered it in a tight, tense undertone, his voice vibrating with rage.

At the end of this speech, Ben and Odie were well aware of where they had gone wrong. They were sent home to await the election next week and the imminent arrest of the Coleman twins, whose DNA was all over the crime scene and who *were* to be charged with attempted murder. If after these events no violence had occurred and the department felt its exposure to liability from their foolhardy assumption of higher responsibility was now past, then they would be given an official reprimand and allowed back to work.

They slunk home to tell their wives the news and stayed inside, taking few visitors. The heat wave had just hit, anyway.

It was a comfort to Bruce Requena to know he had been right. His mother and his aunties had been assiduous in letting him know all about where he had been wrong in his dealings with his uncle Don, and it was some balm to his wounded dignity to know that though he had spoken foolishly, he had spoken truly. The Coleman twins were to stand trial for wounding his aunt Betty.

Bruce had not been able to become as angry as he had expected when his suspicions were confirmed. If he was a little younger, or smaller, he might have suffered under the Colemans' implacable persecution, but as it was, he had only registered them as something unswervingly unpleasant. It was not nice to have a girl, badly dressed but not unattractive, spit at your feet as you walked down the hall, but it didn't actually hurt you. It had been an additional irritation when, in the early days of his ownership, the LTD refused to start just as everyone was leaving the parking lot and the boy jeered, but it had not actually prevented him from inspecting and repairing the solenoid.

Attempted murder could get you a long time. And the trial was months away. All that time, they'd both be in jail. But though he had not developed any anger, he could not feel sympathy. Where else would they have ever ended up but jail? Prison was, to Bruce, the Coleman natural habitat. They had intentionally desired to cause harm all their lives. Inevitably, one day they would succeed. Inevitably, one day their malevolence would be punished.

It was just a shame that his aunt Betty had been involved.

He had seen her twice. The skin grafts were raw and red. The broken teeth had been replaced with a temporary denture and she was learning to eat again. As soon as she could eat, she would get to come home.

Two broken legs, three broken ribs, a messed-up face, and a head injury. And not any of it, really, he thought, on purpose. It was just like they teach in church or *Star Wars*. Two forces on this earth.

One good. One bad. The Colemans went to the dark side, and this is the kind of stuff that happens when you do that. You gotta be careful and stay on the light side of the force, Bruce thought. And when Kylie and his cousins started talking about what they'd like to do to the twins, he gave them that counsel: stay on the side of the light.

It was roundly rejected at the time. After all, nobody cared what Bruce Requena thought.

Quite a lot of people, however, cared about what Park Davis thought. Including Park Davis. And nobody really knew what he *was* thinking, also including Park Davis.

There were two main bodies of thought about the events for which Odie and Ben were taking their enforced vacations. One body of thought was concerned with the overwhelming anger and sorrow Don Requena must be feeling, and was inclined to be understanding. Another body of thought was concerned with law and order and the unpredictability of the Latin American temperament, and was inclined to be censorious.

Park was both. In the scraping silence that had become the Davis-Harper family's dinnertime, he looked at the "Hector" button on his wife's chest and, perhaps because it was much closer to said chest than Park himself had been in the past few weeks, he inclined toward the law and order body of thought. But in the dark reaches of the night, tossing and turning in the spare room, he let himself imagine, just for a moment, Stacey's face smashed to pieces and Stacey unable to recognize him or their children. Then he veered not just to understanding but to admiration for Don Requena's restraint.

Now, the reticence that had unaccustomedly enveloped the environs we chronicle had been briefly broken to relay news. This news was truncated compared to normal news, however, by the elimination of the thoughts and feelings of the teller and the listener regarding the events relayed, which was, again, abnormal behavior in Eudora. Indeed, a new conversational style had developed whereby the speaker and the interlocutor stood at a forty-five-degree angle to each other and stared off into the distance, not looking each other in the face, to avoid any sight of emotional reaction.

So when Lottie came into the Maple Leaf Pharmacy to canvass, she went cautiously.

She said, "I imagine you've heard about the Coleman twins being tried in the state capital."

"Yeah," Park said. "Seems like they got a pretty good lawyer."

"Well, they'll need her," Lottie said.

She had been bent over, examining nursing pads on the bottom row. Now she stood up and looked him in the eye.

"Now, Lottie," Park said. "Don't even start."

She raised her eyebrows inquiringly. "Start what, Park?"

"If Stacey can't get me to commit, why do you think you've got a chance?"

"I don't know what you're talking about," Lottie said, but her eyes twinkled.

They looked at each other for a moment.

Park said, "I just want what's best for the town."

Lottie said, "Well, me too, Park."

There was a silence. Then Lottie asked, "What do you think *is* best for the town?"

"Hell, I don't know!" Park said. "But I want to make up my own mind."

Lottie nodded thoughtfully. She said, "I imagine there's quite a few folks with you on that."

Park nodded. "I don't think I'm the only one having a hard time with it all," he said. "By the way, they're discontinuing that valerian root powder. I'm gonna have to source it through the California outfit."

Lottie said, "Looks like you could use it yourself, Park. You getting any sleep at all?"

He shrugged and looked down at his counter. "Not much," he said. "I keep going over everything in my mind. And now this violence . . ."

"It hasn't helped you make up your mind?"

"No," Park said. "Because you got what the twins did, but then you got that mob . . . and it's not like either Hector or Barney was involved either way, you know. What I think is—"

But the bell tinkled and he fell silent as Kylie Requena came in with a list of things she needed for her cousin Betty's reception at home. As he pointed out where the dressings were and got the catalogue down for the mobility aids, Park's eyes met Lottie's one more time.

She said, "I understand, Park. Really, I do."

Two people passed her on the way back to the stationery store and one greeted her, but she didn't notice.

Pattie looked out of the fabric store window as Lottie walked by. "Uh-oh," she said to nobody in particular.

She could tell her sister was thinking.

Now, as on the day in question, as Ben and Odie and Margery are all in the bakery together watching Clement open the bank with Hector by his side, any fool could figure that Ben and Odie got reinstated and that Hector did not get run out of town. A wise person would also realize that Betty Requena's recovery was protracted and that the doctor and Lottie Dougal's return to romance was ditto.

What even an astute person wouldn't know is *how* it all happened. And how has a lot to do with Lottie Dougal.

Mark Ramirez, who was in on the whole thing, said that it showed depth of mind and plotting abilities that did, in fact, verge on the occult. He only knew what he needed to know at the time, but by the end, he had figured out the rest and told the whole to Maria Lopez the following day, which indeed had made Maria laugh so hard she nearly had a maternity incontinence episode, and Mark's face hurt from laughing along with her.

Four parties were involved: Mark, Ben and Odie, Barney Lane, and Lottie herself. The cover stories were as involved as the participants. Mark was to act as if he was out of the loop when it came to town gossip and just pretend to be sincere. He was also to "prepare for a walloping," which he did as best he could, keeping his eyes on the prize. Ben and Odie, their watches synchronized with the stationery store clock, had "decided to work on their resumes together and had come in for some nice paper." And Barney Lane was told, by Lottie, that she had been thinking about her support for Hector's campaign and could really use a heart-to-heart, so could he drop by? She had a window about four o'clock.

At 3:45, Mark went into the storeroom to lie concealed, but with the door open. At 4:05 (a little late, but Lottie had allowed for this), Barney Lane swaggered in the front door and began to extol his own virtues to Lottie. At 4:10, Mark came out of the storeroom and was introduced to Barney, who, one eye on Lottie, shook Mark's hand. At 4:11, Mark told Barney that he was destined to become his son-in-law, though he was in no hurry, as he was fully enjoying the favors of Janey Lane anyway and they might as well wait until she got pregnant. At 4:13, Ben and Odie arrived to save Mark and arrest Barney Lane for assault. Ben just happened to have his handcuffs in his jacket, and Odie just happened to have a card with the county dispatcher's number in his.

By 5:00, Mark had pressed charges and Ben and Odie were reinstated. Lottie had also called in the incident to her insurance company and was in a fair way to recoup the damage caused to stock and display units. Mark then proceeded to the hospital, where he was met by several photojournalists. He had swelled up beautifully.

At dinner in the Davis-Harper household that evening, Park Davis admitted he had been a fool and begged Stacey's forgiveness, which she freely gave.

Three days later, Hector Rodriguez won by a margin of 96 percent.

Eudora collectively exhaled. That had been a close one. For a moment there, no one had known *what* to think. Now they did and it was a great relief. Park Davis said, "You know, for a minute I was almost taken in. He sure was smooth. But he showed his true colors in the end."

He said it over and over, with glee, to anyone who came in the pharmacy. It was such a great relief to be able to talk about it, to have the customers say what *they* had thought about the whole campaign and to react to *that*. With his Mexican American customers, he said, "I was almost taken in, I'm sorry to say." But he was not really sorry to say, he was delighted to be able to say.

Lottie Dougal, when questioned by her sister the following Sunday about the incident in the stationery store, was wide-eyed innocence. She said, "It wasn't a wise thing for Mark to have said. I don't know what got into him. Pass the green beans, please."

To which Pattie replied, "Have some corn, too, I got a good crop this year." And "You do too know what got into him, Lottie. That whole thing has you written all over it."

In reply, Lottie only praised the corn and asked about Pattie's watering techniques, which, as Pattie confided to Phil later as she washed and he dried and Lottie played baseball in the yard with her nephews, drove her right up the wall.

Phil said, "The whole town knows she did it, Pattie."

And Pattie said, "Yeah, but she'll never admit it. Not even to her own sister."

They went through all the bread-and-butter plates before Phil replied, "Well, that's just the way she is, honey. She doesn't want to shut you out in particular."

And Pattie said, "She's been that way since

Mom died. Something inside of her just closed up."

Phil had occasion to remember this conversation later.

The Eudora Empire Cinema had been well attended during the entire election, and Jim Flory had been making money. It was a phenomenon with which he was unfamiliar.

He had so much in his checking account that Linda Lane had drawn him aside and taken him to see Clement about various saving and investment options, and Jim had been on the Internet looking through what all of them meant and what all of them were. It was like snorkeling, he said later—there was this whole world all around you that you hadn't been aware of.

He had replaced the foyer carpet and had the front wall painted. The worst of the seats had been sent out to the county seat for reupholstering and had come back no longer liable to poke holes in ladies' panty hose. The inside could use painting, too, but it wasn't yet real bad and he had heard he might be able to get a grant for that.

He had joined an Internet bulletin board for independent movie theater owners and had found out all kinds of things. He went to a midweek conference in Cincinnati and picked up tons of hints and tips. He began surveying cars during the feature to see how far his catchment area had spread, conducing exit polls, and using portion controls on his new offering of nachos. Acting on advice given by fellow members, he began to be well versed in release dates of Hollywood block-busters. He did not show them himself, as they were too pricey, but he did show retrospectives. If the movie was, say, the fifth in a series, he would show one through four the week before the release. If a movie star was about to be featured in a new film, the week before it came out the Eudora Empire Cinema would show four of the star's best previous films.

It was a successful move. More money began to come in, and the catchment area, judging by the cars outside, spread all the way to the city.

Eudora had become a rather popular destination for a day or night out for your city dweller. Whole carloads of rapidly sobering young people came into town for breakfast at Gross Home Cooking and bought T-shirts to testify to their feat. Their parents and grandparents would often follow days later, to take their own pictures under the sign and talk about what a pretty drive it had been. Word had gotten out about Maria's recipes, and over at Mayan Memories they'd started to reserve two tables for locals on Saturday night just so no one would get upset if the restaurant was full of city folks and they couldn't eat. And now, with Jim Flory's canny marketing, there was another reason to make the drive and breathe the country air.

Lottie and Mark, never slow to pick up on trends, produced a series of postcards showing the frontages of each of these three buildings, as well as one of the whole Main Street, several shots taken at the Maple Leaf Festival, and three exceptionally pretty spots Lottie had noticed on her drive to and from the city every week. For the back, Max had found a template from a 1950s attempt to sell Eudora as a tourist destination—a rather stylish frame effect with the words "Eudora—Delightful!" in script across one corner, which added the perfect touch of irony. They sold like Zadie's hotcakes.

The Maple Leaf Festival Committee, which had been Clement and two old ladies for as long as anyone could remember, was injected with new blood, and Hector had several meetings with Lottie about publicity. In the end, he bought four quarter-page ads in the city paper, which in gratitude wrote a big two-page article about the festival, due to be printed a week before the event started. It was going to be huge.

And Jim Flory was going to miss it. He was going away for a little while, to do a short training course called "The Independent Movie House—Maximizing The Potential." It was one month long and wasn't cheap, but it promised so much that he had decided to go. He had one last examination with the doctor, who had brought Lottie in to consult, and they had both agreed that

361

he was doing well and that, should things continue as they were, they need not see him for six months.

He had reduced his use of the root but would still put some in his suitcase just in case. He embraced them both upon leaving the doctor's office, something that Lottie was used to but which rather threw Doc Emery.

It was a quiet time, after the election and before the Maple Leaf Festival. And the residents of Eudora were content that it be so. The heat wave had come and stuck, as it did every year, and conversation tended to revolve around reservoir levels and the use of bathwater in gardening. Ailments were few. The doctor had plenty of time to luxuriate in the excellent air-conditioning of his apartment on Main Street, viewing and selecting movies for his sale table while eating his microwaved dinners. Lottie Dougal would often sit on her own back porch in her pajamas, while the ceiling fans inside the little house did their work of making the bedroom cool enough for its purpose.

News from the Requena household was good. Betty had learned to use a spoon and had remembered her wedding day. If this good news caused some people's hearts to drop with grief and sorrow, they hid this and, in front of the Requenas at least, rejoiced and were positive.

Hector went away to the mayors' conference. Canning and preserving hit their apogee and then went into retrogression. The quilt frames arrived at the arts center and this year's offerings were solicited. The Coleman twins were arraigned. The other kids went back to school.

As Jim Evans said, "Nothing stops life from going on."

It was nearly time for the Maple Leaf Festival.

In the early, heady days of the township, the railway had briefly succumbed to the wiles of a local booster and had unwisely put a station and a stop at Eudora. This was somewhat south of town and has long since been abandoned and dismantled, but there are photographs of the opening ceremony hung up in the library for any doubting Thomas to see. During this brief flourishing of connection to the iron road, a consignment of trees was unloaded onto the platform by persons unknown and left.

There were no labels.

While the stationmaster made his fruitless inquiries as to the ownership of these trees, he and the porter took it in turns to water them twice a day. They had good root balls inside their burlap sacks, and plenty of earth packed around them. While they still hoped to discover who had ordered 319 maple trees, the care was assiduous, Eudorans even then having a natural dedication to gardening and a healthy respect for other people's property.

By the time new leaves were sprouting on the bare branches and watering had begun to take up nearly half the available work time at the station, the stationmaster made an executive decision. They were never going to find the owners. The trees might as well live as die. He offered the trees to the native population.

Trees were important to people newly arrived from more wooded spots on the prairie. Somebody from the state agricultural college did a survey in conjunction with a historian from the state university. They reckoned every single householder in early Eudora planted at least one maple tree, and one planted five.

The effect, the second week of October, is electric. The whole town blazes scarlet and orange. It is something to look forward to, and Eudorans do. The festival has grown up from the simple delights of neighbors playing music and sharing their handicrafts together to the dramatic, artistic, and culinary extravaganza it is today by small, organic steps. It is now felt to be just about perfect. It takes all the work and gives all the excitement Eudora can stand.

The last week of September, a couple of things happened.

The first thing was that Barney Lane got fired.

The general feeling in town, at least according to how it could be measured the next morning at Gross Home Cooking, was not surprise.

Zadie Gross, now that she had mastered the art of running a successful diner, had time to comment and receive comment on current events, which pastime had indeed been her avocation for all the days of her life and which now suited her occupational interests as well. At the counter in the morning, before the erstwhile Lane supporters awoke, she held forth with the coffeepot in one hand and the spatula in the other. Conversation was general and occasionally heated, with interjections from the old fellas' round booth.

"I ain't surprised," she said. "He done nothing but run around in that suit all summer."

Clement, who had taken to coming in for his breakfast right after opening the bank, as part of the gradual slowing down he had undertaken in this, his retirement year, said, "That suit was bought for him out of party funds," and shook his head in open disgust and secret satisfaction. Cliff Hamilton, the chairman of the county Republican party, had resigned over the whole Lane incident, and Clement had been reinstated into the party with full apologies.

"I heard tell there was a squirrel's nest in one of the girls' bathrooms and a whole mess of cockroaches in the gym," a junior undertaker volunteered.

The men who drove the trash truck were in as well, having thoughtfully removed their overalls and gloves. One said, "You talking about the janitor over at Eudora High? He put out eighty-five sacks of garbage the week before school opened. Damn near filled us up. Worse than Christmas."

Zadie rattled the swear tin. "Sorry," she said. "That *damn* will cost you a dime."

"What's he gonna do now?" someone wanted to know. "Ain't nobody in town will hire his sorry cracker butt."

Again Zadie bristled. She said, "Now, Frank, we do not use racial language. The only crackers in this place come with chili or soup. That'll be a quarter."

And then, having received this, she said, "Of course, you got a point."

Becky Lane, just joining the conversation from the far corner, where she had been ferrying a selection of Denver omelets and large stacks of pancakes with assorted accoutrements to a big table of young people in last night's partywear, said, "He told the girls he was leaving town. He wants to go to Hollywood and take some acting classes."

The laughter made the glassware ring on its shelf.

The second thing that happened the last week of September was that Lottie Dougal called the doctor in for a consultation. He had been availing himself of Lottie's expertise more and more over the summer, having found that most of the medical plans on which his clients' health care rested would allow for consultation with alternative medical practitioners, though not referral. But this was the first time she had called him.

Maria Lopez was in her seventh month of pregnancy and her blood pressure was rising. Not dramatically, not yet, but steadily and worryingly. When the doctor arrived in Lottie's living room, Maria was expected.

"When?" the doctor asked. Lottie had just said goodbye to one patient and was washing her hands, preparing to call in the next.

"Soon," Lottie said. "I told her to come tonight and she said she would, after seven-thirty—she wanted to get everyone seated." She went to the back door and called, "Next!"

"Do you expect me just to wait around?" the doctor asked.

Lottie looked surprised. "Well, yeah," she said, "I do."

Kylie Requena had an ingrown toenail. The doctor sat and fumed on the sofa while Lottie fussed around over it. He would have had it out in about ten seconds, but Lottie was looking all over the foot and even (at this point the doctor started chewing his fingernails) asking her to take off her sock so that she could examine the other one.

At last, Lottie said, "Well, Kylie, you're going to have to either cut this out or have it cut out by the doctor here. But I'm a little concerned about the health of your feet in general. Why don't you tell me about your new shoes? And have you been going dancing in them?"

Kylie responded to this by enumerating a number of bargains in shoe shopping at the summer sale. Lottie listened carefully and then recommended she not wear one of the pairs for more than an hour or two and that she wear another of the pairs only with hose. Just the third pair was any good for dancing. She said that feet got more and more important as you got older and you could really end up hurting yourself if you didn't start paying attention now, and she praised Kylie for coming straight to her when the first thing went wrong. She said she should wear nothing but sneakers and her cheerleading shoes for a few weeks until the toe healed and the red bumps on her little toes went away and then to always check the height of the toe box of every other shoe she ever bought.

The doctor said he'd be glad to take care of the toenail after school the next day, and Lottie put a poultice on to hold it from infection until then.

Lottie went to wash her hands while Kylie put on her socks and shoes. The doctor followed her.

"I'm sorry," Lottie said, "if you feel like I'm wasting your time."

"No, I'm sorry," he said. "You work your own way. It's interesting." He thought for a moment. "I would have never thought about footwear choices. I would probably have just kept treating the symptoms."

Kylie saw Lottie look up at him and smile, and the doctor leaned over as if he was about to kiss her. Kylie had one hand on the front door, ready to leave, but was just standing there, watching. It seemed to take forever, she said; they were looking into each other's eyes, and then . . .

"Next!" Lottie shouted, and turned away.

Kylie sighed and limped home, where she told of the incident to various interested parties.

Maria Lopez was not surprised to see the doctor when her turn finally came. He was sitting on the sofa drinking iced tea when she came in, but he stood up fairly quickly when he saw it was her, and went to wash his hands at Lottie's sink.

Lottie told him what Maria's blood pressure had registered over the past few weeks and about the chamomile infusion she had recommended. She then asked Maria if she was worried about anything.

"No, not really," Maria answered. "I mean, I got some little bits of trouble, like anybody, but there's nothing really big . . . except for Betty."

Lottie said, "I'm going to put the cuff back on your arm, and then I want you to talk about Betty."

Maria shrugged. "I don't know," she said.

"There's nothing really to talk about. I mean, I told Pattie, there's no real use in me keeping going there—she don't remember me at all. But still I try and go over and take some food, you know, stuff I know she likes. I'm really doing it for Don and her sisters. He's back at work now, and somebody's got to be with her all the time. Even Bruce takes a turn and she don't know him from Adam."

"Stop there," Lottie said, letting the air down. She looked at the doctor.

He said, "Do you feel in some way responsible for what happened to Betty?"

"I don't know," Maria said. "It just seems like ever since I opened the restaurant things have got real complicated."

"That's silly, Maria," Lottie said. "If it hadn't been Mayan Memories, it would have been something else. The Latino community makes up nearly half of the town's population. You couldn't keep going through back doors forever."

"That's like saying every time there's racial violence at a sporting event, it's Jackie Robinson's fault," the doctor put in.

"I guess." Maria didn't seem convinced.

"Right," the doctor said. "First things first. I want to put you on bed rest."

"What?" Maria said. "I got a business to run!"

"Which can run just as well without you," Lottie said. "They're going to have to do it sometime,

Maria, and it might as well be now." She looked at the doctor again. "I think we need to shift our care roles," she said. "I want the doctor to take over as your primary caregiver and I want to be your consultant. I think we can put your birth plans on the shelf, too, Maria."

Now Maria looked frightened. She said, "What's happening?"

"Nothing right now," Lottie said. "But there's this condition called preeclampsia. If you get that, you'll get real sick. And one of the warning signs is high blood pressure. It's just not good for the baby, either. It's bad for its air."

Maria started to cry.

Lottie put her arms around her. "I'm going to call Bill," she said, "to come and pick you up in the truck." She picked the phone up and dialed with one hand. "Now, there's nothing to worry about right now. The heartbeat is strong and everything looks real good. But I'll bet the doctor will want you to go for a scan and to be monitored for a few hours"—Doc Emery nodded—"and he'll probably want to take some blood samples, too."

"I don't want none of that stuff," Maria whimpered. "I just want to have a baby natural."

Lottie's voice turned from placatory to stern. "You want to have a healthy baby, Maria. And you don't want to die. So the best thing for you to do is to do what the doctor tells you."

Bill picked up and Lottie made her request, stressing that there was nothing wrong and that Bill should drive slowly and carefully.

Doc Emery, who had been standing with his arms folded, now came and took one of Maria's hands. He said, "Don't worry, Maria. I'll do everything I can to make sure you and the baby stay happy and comfortable."

She looked up from Lottie's shoulder. She said, "I just don't want . . ."

He said, "I know. Nobody wants to go to the hospital. But there's a reason why we have hospitals. I want what's best for you and your baby. Don't worry. I'm going to listen to you, just like Lottie does. And Lottie will still be there."

And Maria said, "Okay. Okay, Doc."

He said, "Now, no cooking breakfast tomorrow morning. You'll have to make some phone calls, so take the phone to bed. I want you to have a shower and go right back to bed, feet up, loose clothing, lots of liquids. I'll come and see you during lunch."

"Lunch!" Maria said. "I gave Gabe the morning off."

Lottie said, "Now repeat after me, Maria: Linda will figure something out."

"Linda will figure something out."

All three smiled, and then the pickup horn tootled.

"I'll see you tomorrow," the doctor said. "And I

expect the house to be dirty and there to be dishes in the sink. If not, I'm gonna be really pissed."

Maria smiled again. She said, "Okay."

Lottie had three more patients that night. The doctor stayed for all of them.

Hector Rodriguez had never been a ladies' man. It was not that he did not date when younger, he did, but his attention had always been firmly fixed to his career and girls had tended to simply slip away. Later, when he was a prime matrimonial catch, he seemed to have lost the knack of asking someone out, and was too traditional to be asked out himself. He went to a few matchmaking dinners in the city, but nothing really set him alight and it was not in his nature to dally. It had always been all or nothing with Hector, and so for quite a few years now it had been nothing.

Discreet overtures by Jim Flory, at a time very much previous to this narrative, had proved that Hector's interests did not lie in that direction; he was just . . . busy. Of course he had stayed busy, and was even busier now with his mayoral responsibilities.

Hector was an intense, private fellow as well, who knew nothing about the art of small talk. Eudora had often wondered just what it would take for him to find the right girl. And at this year's Maple Leaf Festival, they found out.

Now, what with the downright trendiness of

Eudora as a destination for a day out and the national television coverage, the Maple Leaf committee had fielded a number of subtle mentions of availability for personal appearances from state celebrities. Senator Pyle, for example, who had been "too busy" for the last fifteen parades, suddenly found a window for this one. A well-known cookbook author who had previously made her living as a soap opera actress let it be known she would love to come. And the state beauty queen also invited herself.

The elder majority of the Maple Leaf committee was star-struck and said yes to everybody, without consulting Lane Nichols on the availability of vintage convertibles. And so it was that the gorgeous six-foot blond girl who was just about to appear in the Miss America pageant found herself, just yards down Main Street, stranded on foot as her erstwhile chariot (a mechanically faulty pink Cadillac borrowed from someone unknown to Lane personally) was pushed aside. Hector, who had led the parade in the first car, tapped on his driver's shoulder and motioned for the lady to join him. She flashed him a stunning smile of blinding, brilliant white, and Hector himself got down, opened the door, and helped her in, her long white glove in his brown hand, her shining sheath of royal blue satin brilliant against his suit. She tossed her hair and adjusted her crown, in which latter operation

Hector also assisted, and they chatted merrily the length of the parade route.

She stayed.

She changed into a smart pantsuit and was escorted by Hector to the quilting exhibition, the Battle of Black Jack reenactment, and the pig roast, where she got a spot off Hector's tie. She tapped her foot at the preliminary round of the Gospel Fiddling Contest. By the time she rejoined her chaperone (who had been ably looked after by Clement and Lucy McAllister), the sun was nearly down and her arms were full of souvenirs. She had a full-color quilt-of-the-week diary from Dougal's Stationery, a bag of Margery's brownies, a DVD of *Notting Hill* from the doctor's stall, and a large plush maple leaf pillow (one of a plethora run up by Carla Bustamonte of A Stitch in Time), which she kept squeezing while looking at the handsome young mayor as he enjoyed the fellowship of his citizens.

Henceforth, Hector spent his weekends in various places around the state and began to appear in the city paper under the sobriquet "Hector Rodriguez, mayor of Eudora and frequent escort of Kelly Burke." He had to order a second tuxedo because the first one was so often at the dry cleaners out at Food Barn. His mother started a scrapbook.

If it seems impossible that such a woman as Kelly Burke would spend her rare free evenings in

Eudora, you only have to check the reservation book at Mayan Memories to see that this is indeed the case. Eudora as a whole is hopeful about where this might lead.

With such a communal distraction, and added to the commotion attendant upon this most well-attended ever occasion, you might think it would go unnoticed that the doctor, in the middle of the day, would cross the street and give Lottie Dougal one single red rose. But of course you'd be wrong.

What had she done with the rose?

Mark was asked, but he didn't know. She had looked at it, said, "Thank you," without a smile and then . . . where had it gone? If it got tucked next to her heart, that was one thing, but if it ended up in the trash can, that was another. The next day, Pattie came by with some fresh lemonade (it had been unseasonably hot) and while there she did a great deal of snooping under cover of using the bathroom and borrowing a scarf, but she didn't see it displayed in a vase any-where, or even notice any good flower-pressing books had been moved or weighted.

The doctor had smiled sadly and turned away. Of all the people wondering about the rose's fate, he must have been wondering the most. But he didn't know, either.

On Tuesday night, the doctor's luxurious apart-ment on Main Street seemed to suddenly be con-fining. He left it about eight o'clock and aimlessly wandered downtown. He wasn't hungry, but he looked in the window at Mayan Memories. Gabe and Linda seemed to be coping all right. Ordinarily, in a mood like this, he might go see Jim Flory, but Jim was still out of town. The Eudora Empire Cinema was dark, the coming attractions only reading "I'll Be Back." The doctor scuffed at a few dandelions growing out of the cracks of the sidewalk.

For a moment, he stood and considered Chuck's Beer and Bowl. And then he turned and walked rapidly, as people do when they're afraid that they might change their minds, down to the Walker house.

At that hour, downstairs, the Walker house is serene. Upstairs is pure pandemonium as three boys are convinced, through threats, bribery, and brute strength, to bathe, brush their teeth, and have their hair combed, but downstairs it is the moment when Phil Walker finishes the dishes and cracks open a beer, either on the front porch, if the weather is good, or inside in front of the tube, if it's inclement or there's a game on.

Just as Doc put his foot on the bottom step, Phil opened the screen door with two beers in his hands. They looked at each other for a moment, and then Phil laughed. He said, "I guess this one is for you," and handed Doc a can.

Phil had a big round papasan chair with a faded green cushion. He sank into this and motioned toward the rocker for Doc, who took the beer and the seat in one smooth movement, as if he'd been coming there all his life.

They popped open the cans, drank, and said, "Ah," together, as men will do. Phil uttered a discreet belch, which was neither apologized for or resented. Doc sighed. He said, "Nice night."

Phil said, "Indian summer. Sure was good for the Maple Leaf."

Now, Doc had been in Eudora fifteen months. He knew the right thing to say and said it. He said, "Pattie do okay at A Stitch in Time?"

Phil said, "Shoo," and shook his head. "You know how much they sold them big orange pillows for?"

Doc shrugged.

"Twenty-eight dollars. Each! And fifteen for the little ones. Sold clean out."

"Shoo!" Doc agreed. "My cousin bought one," he added.

They both shook their heads. City folk were all crazy, and city women were the worst of the lot.

"How'd you do?" Phil asked.

"Not bad. Sold out."

They nodded again.

It was that point of the conversation when the doctor was called upon to explain his presence. It was either talk about it right then or not talk about it at all. If he chose the latter, it was going to get awkward and embarrassing, but something seemed to have him by his throat when he tried to choose the former. He said, "I . . . uh . . . I came by . . . ," and trailed off, drinking more beer.

Phil drank some more, too, just to keep him company. He said, "I'm gonna go get two more. Now, don't you run off."

The doctor looked uncomfortable while he waited. Lance Baumgartner, walking Virgo the black labrador, came by and smiled and nodded. Doc nodded back and said, "Nice night."

Lance said, "Sure was good for the festival."

Doc nodded again.

Lance said, "See you."

Three young teenage boys came tearing down the road on their bicycles and suddenly rode more circumspectly when they saw him. He could hear them saying, "It's the doctor, slow down, it's the doctor," as if he was the recognized authority over bike speed limits.

It seemed to take Phil forever to come back with the beers. That was because he'd also brought some tortilla chips and salsa.

"Now," Phil said, "what were you saying?"

"Uh . . . ," the doctor continued, "it's just that . . . I . . ."

"Oh, yeah," Phil said. "I remember now." He grinned. "Just spit it out, Doc, we got no secrets here."

"It's . . ." The doctor looked like he was about to explode. He scrunched up his face and finally

379

managed to get the word past his lips. "Lottie," he said. "It's Lottie. I . . . I really . . . I mean, I know it sounds crazy after all we've been through this year, all *I've* been through . . . but I never really stopped . . ." He stopped at this point and, coming close to crushing a full can of beer between his palms, looked dumbly and pleadingly at Phil Walker. "You know?" he finished, opening the beer and taking an almighty slug.

Phil said, "Yeah, I kind of thought it might be." After a pause he added, "I heard about the rose."

"What?" the doctor said, looking suddenly hopeful. "Did Lottie tell Pattie about it?"

"You gotta be joking." Pattie Walker, hot and disheveled, opened the screen door with a tall glass of lemonade in her hand and lowered herself into a wicker armchair. She helped herself to a chip and a large dip of salsa and talked around it. "She never tells me anything. I heard about it from Maria, who heard about it from Mark, who saw you give it to her but not what she did with it. I know it's not in her house, that's for sure," she continued with narrowed eyes, "but I don't know where it might be."

"Oh," the doctor said, and slumped back into the rocker.

"Try some of this salsa," Phil said. "I got a recipe off Maria. It'll blow your socks off."

Unenthusiastically, the doctor obligingly dipped.

"Could you ask her?" he said. "Could you ask her what she did with the rose?" And to Phil, "That's great stuff. Is there a little oregano in there?"

Phil beamed. "I knew you'd figure it out."

"You gotta be kidding," Pattie said. "I can't ask her nothing. She just clams up."

"She's like that with everybody," Phil said. "You know that, Pattie. We talked about it just the other night." He shifted a little in his cushioned nest. "One thing you gotta know about, Doc," he said, "is that Mrs. Dougal died when Lottie was just fourteen. Just at the time when girls really need their mommies, you know? Lottie didn't have any real good friends at school or anything, and her and Pattie . . ."

"We were always fighting. Right up until then, we were always fighting. I was nearly seventeen. I tried to get her to open up about it. I tried to be a real big sister to her." Pattie's eyes filled with tears. "But you know, before that, whenever I'd been nice to her it had just been a trick. She didn't fall for it anymore. And she never let her guard down for me again. It's been over twenty years now, and she's still kind of waiting to find out if all my caring for her has just been a nasty joke I've been playing."

The doctor leaned forward. He said, "We get on really well on a professional level. And when I meet her at social events, she's warm and chatty, you know, just like Lottie. But when I try and talk to her seriously about everything that's happened this year, she just . . . well . . ." The doctor made some wild hand gestures that caused the tortilla chip he was holding to shed its load on his trousers, and Pattie handed him the paper towel that had been around the bottom of her lemonade tumbler. As he mopped the salsa off his left leg he said, "She just pretends like she didn't hear me or pretends like she didn't understand what I said . . . or she just stares off into the distance and then changes the subject!"

"Or excuses herself to go do something else and leaves you standing there like a fool," Pattie said. "Once when she was in London I called her and tried to talk to her about Daddy drinking too much, and she excused herself for a second and just put the phone down on the table and went away! I stayed on and listened and I heard her agree to go to some pub with her friends! I even heard her put her coat on and ask if anyone had seen her hat and heard the front door getting locked! I just . . ." Pattie blew upward until her bangs flopped. "It drives me right up the wall."

"Look," Phil said, obviously feeling the need for some intervention, "we promised ourselves that we wouldn't get involved in how you and Lottie manage things . . . or don't."

"Oh," the doctor said. He said, "I'm sorry," and made to stand up.

"Not you," Phil said, "*her,*" jerking his thumb at his lady wife. "You gotta stay out of this."

Pattie opened her eyes in innocence. "What do you mean?" she said. "I'm not interfering. I'm just agreeing."

"You did the right thing coming here," Phil said to the doctor. "It feels real natural. You just sit still. You gotta come around more often."

"Well," the doctor said, "I might do that. But next time I'll bring something."

The next thing that happened was a phone call. The doctor had called to update Lottie on the results of Maria Lopez's fetal monitoring. He said, "I'm sending Clement back to you. His bursitis. I gave him an anti-snoring preparation."

"Which he wouldn't need if only he'd stop drinking," Lottie said tartly.

"Well . . . ," the doctor said tolerantly.

"Speaking of drinking," Lottie continued. "I hear you've been spending time with my sister and brother-in-law."

"I like Phil," the doctor said. "He's good company."

"I can't imagine what you all find to talk about." If her comment about Clement had been tart, this insinuation was fully acidic.

"Now, Lottie, not all of us have two jobs. Some of us like to socialize."

Sounding stung, Lottie said, "*I* like to socialize."

And the doctor said, "Yes, and how is your cat?"

There was a pause. Lottie said, "Caspar ran off. I kept putting off getting him fixed and he's been all over town. I tried to catch him a few times but he's pretty much gone feral now. I only hope he makes it through the winter."

It took all the fun out of it, as the doctor confided to Pattie later that week over a bottle of chardonnay and some filo pockets stuffed with quince jelly and goat's milk brie. He hadn't known what to say.

He said, "I'm sorry to hear that."

And she said, "Thank you," in that same glacial tone with which she'd received the rose.

After a preseason checkup with the basketball team, the doctor recommended they ask Lottie to come and teach them some yoga to strengthen and lengthen their ligaments. Lottie obligingly attended three practices a week in her sweat clothes, leading the team through a series of movements that looked almost laughably easy but were all terribly demanding for participants. The coach, doing without Stevie Wiseman's services this year, was pleasantly surprised when jump heights soared, and he became a huge and lifelong fan of yoga in general and Lottie in particular.

The doctor often managed to clear his own schedule to attend these sessions, and agreed heartily with Coach.

He sent her two more pregnancies. He sent her another case of depression. Where other wooers would send flowers, he sent patients. Lottie began to feel the strain of her two jobs, even though Mark was taking on more and more at the stationer's. At one Sunday lunch, as Pattie washed and she dried, she confessed that she was soon going to have to make a choice between her two occupations, and asked how Pattie would feel about Mark becoming manager. It would mean a pay hike and a cut out of profits.

Pattie, to her surprise, didn't seem at all shocked by Lottie's confession. She said she'd been expecting it and that, really, if they were to take Lottie's own salary down to, say, half time for cover and consultancy, the business would actually be saving money.

When Lottie said, polishing an already bone-dry dinner plate, that Pattie seemed to be taking it all very calmly, Pattie said, "Well, you know, the doctor said how busy you were getting and that it was only a matter of time. . . ."

Upon which Lottie very carefully and calmly placed the plate in the cupboard and excused herself, not returning until the following week.

Now, it's important to get on record that the doctor had done none of what he had done solely to provoke Lottie Dougal. At the same time, it is also vital to note that at no point was he unaware that this provoking was probably occurring. And so he was not terribly surprised when Lottie was sitting on his stoop waiting for him upon his arrival back from visiting his cousins in the city and that she pounced upon him before he even got a chance to open his car door.

"Get upstairs," she said. "We're going to have a little talk."

He hid his smile, which was wise, considering that if Lottie had seen it she would have probably wiped it off his face by physical means. She was not, as we know, a girl who lost control easily. But as we also know, when she did lose control, the results were likely to be spectacular.

As soon as the door shut, she started. "If you think you can manage me from afar by insinuating yourself into my family life—" and then she broke off. "You've had some work done up here. It looks terrific."

"Yeah, Don and Albert did it when they were fixing the roof," the doctor said. "I couldn't get it all done, but they made a start. This blue area is going to be another waiting room. I think I'm going to have a curved wall here, so it will get the skylight. Then all this lilac bit is going to be partitioned off into two consultation rooms and a little treatment room with a massage table and running water. I thought I'd leave the bathroom pretty much as it is now, but put a wall in here, so that if someone's using the Jacuzzi, other people can still use the toilet. Now, when this door is removed, the patients can walk right upstairs from Janey, so we won't have to hire another receptionist. Anyone who can't manage the stairs can stay on the ground floor."

"But where's your kitchen?"

"Oh, I've been living on microwaved stuff anyway. And fruit. Mom always asks me if I'm eating fruit." The doctor smiled. "I'm kind of camped out in my bedroom for the interim. It reminds me of student life."

As Lottie looked around, her anger, which she had nursed so successfully throughout the afternoon, faded away in wonder. "It's going to be lovely," she said.

"Oh, I'm glad you think so. I really should have consulted you about the colors, and I didn't want you to see it just yet, but I thought it—"

"Consulted *me* about the colors?"

"Well, yeah," Doc said. "You'll be working up here most of the time."

"What are you talking about?" Lottie's famous composure had now entirely deserted her.

"Well, you know I said we should consider a merger, and you were all in favor, so—"

"Wait, wait, wait." Lottie sat down on what was going to become the waiting room sofa. "I don't remember that."

"Yeah, I did," the doctor said. "When we talked to Dr. Langley about Maria."

Lottie closed her eyes and put her hands over her head. "I thought that was a joke!" she said.

"Well, you can't keep on seeing patients in your own house," he said. "I thought when we move out of here we could turn the bedroom area into a resource room for you—get your stuff out of your garage and your books out of your kitchen and store them in a more controlled environment."

"This is like a bad dream," Lottie said. "I'm going to wake up and you'll be gone." She stood up and turned to him. "And why *aren't* you gone?" she asked. "Why didn't you just leave town? After everything that's happened, do you think you can make a life for yourself here?"

When Pattie later described this conversation to Maria Lopez, after listening carefully to the doctor's own version, Maria Lopez cried at the following speech. But it is important to remember that Maria Lopez was then eight months pregnant and could be moved to tears by cookie commercials.

"No," the doctor said. "I'm not going to make a life for myself. I'm going to make a life with you."

"It's impossible!" Lottie shouted. "There is no way we can . . . what? Get married?"

Doc sat down on the sofa and pulled her down, too. "Father Tim thinks we can," he said.

"You talked to my priest? My priest, my sister! What about me, Jim? What about talking to me?"

Her big eyes filled with water and her lower lip trembled.

"Don't give me that, Lottie," the doctor said, suddenly stern. "You know how many times I've tried."

"Okay," she said, sniffling. "Okay. I'm going to listen to you now. Just what do you think is going to happen between us?"

"Well," the doctor said, "we'll merge our practices and buy a house. Mark will become manager of Dougal's, and Janey will need a raise because of additional responsibilities. With more money coming in, they'll probably want to get married and set up a home together. I thought your little place would suit them down to the ground until they start a family."

"Oh," said Lottie, recovering from her tearful state dangerously quickly. "So you're selling my house, too? That's interesting."

"Then I thought we could camp out here while we're doing up the old Spencer place."

Lottie started to speak, but the doctor held up his hand. "I know it's just a burned-out shell but the stonework is still good and I think it would make a really nice family house if it was rebuilt."

"It's not that, you fool. Delilah Spencer won't sell it. She said that she'd never sell it, even though she never leaves Chicago. She said the only way it would ever be sold was over her—"

"Dead body," the doctor completed. "Yeah, I know, but she passed on last week and I've already agreed on a price with her nephew. Did you know Charlie?"

"I went to school with him."

"He seems like a jerk."

Lottie nodded. "Oh, yeah, blue-ribbon jerk," she agreed. "But Jim, as interesting as all this is—"

"Yeah, so if we eat breakfast at Gross Home Cooking—I laughed my ass off when I saw the sign, did you?—and lunch at Maria's, then I don't think we'll need much in the way of dinner, and Albert and Don know somebody who says he can do all the work in six months if he starts in March. I've got some plans. . . ." The doctor went to stand up, but then the look on Lottie's face made him sit back down again. "But I can show you those later. And we can talk about kids and dogs and cats and stuff later, too."

"That's nice," Lottie said. "It's good to know I'll have some input."

At last the doctor had run down. He said, "Well . . . I was going to come and ask you to . . . you know, see the place and tell me what you thought . . . but . . ."

"Which place was that?" Lottie asked. "My work or my home?"

"Uh," the doctor said, at last sensing danger, "uh . . . both? Either one?"

Lottie got up and paced the length of the big, and for now still open-plan, room. She was muttering to herself.

She said, "Look, Jim, it's . . . well, it's not all bad, you know. You've got some really good ideas, and some of them I'm kind of interested in."

"Which ones?" the doctor asked eagerly, but she ignored him.

"But I just think it should all start a little slower."

"Oh, obviously," Doc Emery said. "I wasn't going to show you this for weeks, until the walls were up."

"That's not really what I meant," Lottie said. She sighed with frustration and squeezed her temples with her hands.

"I know what you meant," the doctor said. "I was going to ask you out to a movie. Once I'd captured Caspar."

"You've been trying to trap Caspar?"

In answer, he peeled up his shirtsleeve and displayed five long scratches crusted in blood. "Yeah."

"You idiot. He'll eat you." Lottie started to laugh. She laughed and laughed, until she had to sit down on the sofa. "You were going to bring me Caspar and then I'd be so grateful I'd go out to the movies with you?"

"Well . . . ," the doctor said, "well . . . yeah."

"Look," Lottie said, "why don't you just ask me?"

The doctor got down on one knee. "Lottie

Dougal, would you grant me the favor of your hand—"

"No, you idiot," Lottie said, laughing again, this time even harder. "To the movies."

"Oh." The doctor stood up. "Would you like to go to the movies with me?"

"When?" she said.

"When Jim gets back next week. I think he's ordered something in."

A naughty smile played on Lottie's lips. "You mean you don't know what's playing?"

"No," the doctor said. "Nobody does yet."

"And you don't know what day it will be?"

"He gets back Sunday. I reckon it won't be any later than Thursday."

"So you're asking me out on Thursday?"

"Or Wednesday. Or maybe even Tuesday."

"Oh, Jim, you're right." Lottie stood and walked to the door, the heels of her boots clicking on the wooden flooring. "You've been totally assimilated. You'll never leave Eudora."

The doctor's heart walked down the stairs with Lottie Dougal. "You haven't said yes or no," he reminded her, calling down after her.

"Yes," she said, "I'll go with you to the movies. Whatever it is and whenever it's showing. I'll close shop for the night and meet you there."

She looked up the stairs for a moment. He saw her heart-shaped face upside down. Her eyes were dancing.

It was nothing like how he'd hoped it would go. He had been clumsy and crude. He'd have to just hang back now, let her set the pace.

Still, the doctor felt happy. And Pattie and Phil felt happy, too, when he told them all about it on Tuesday night.

A nd now we are back to where we started. It is Wednesday, and Ben and Odie are sitting in the bakery, Odie somewhat uncomfortable behind one of the new little tables. Odie is having a Bavarian-cream-filled maple log and house-blend decaf. Ben is having a pain au chocolat and a cappuccino. He approves of the changes Betty made before the accident, and plans to ask after her progress before they leave.

He observes Lottie's dancing promenade with no little sense of foreboding and makes eye contact with Margery and Odie, who he can tell are feeling the same. He attempts to reinterest himself in the article about prehistoric reindeer droppings and the light they shed on global warming, but is unable to concentrate. Again he looks up. Lottie has gone inside the store, visible as a flitting figure but not as an observable human being.

Odie says, "Well, well. Wonder if the movie's gonna be any good."

Margery says, "I know for sure it ain't gonna be *that* good."

Ben says, "I heard tell Lottie Dougal was sitting

two hours Sunday afternoon on the doctor's back stoop, just waiting for him to get home."

This news, in conjunction with Miss Dougal's observed high spirits, hits everyone hard. There are unanimous sighs accompanied by three rueful shakes of heads.

"Oh, my Lord," Margery Lupin says, "whatever next?"

Ben and Odie chew silently.

There is nothing more to say.

ACKNOWLEDGMENTS

When you start writing a book, it seems personal, but by the time you finish it, you are aware it has been a team effort.

On my team has been (as always) my wonderful London agent, David Riding, and my new New York agent, Kathy Anderson. I've also had two superb editors on this book, Gillian Dickens and Anika Streitfeld. In fact, I need to thank everyone at Ballantine Reader's Circle for their help, and the best copy-edit I've ever seen.

"Eudora" is a made-up place, but I've been lucky enough to live and work in some amazing communities. I'd like to thank everyone in Lawrence, Kansas, all the seasonal staff in Yellowstone and Grand Teton National Parks, all the boaties on the Kennet and Avon, everyone from Dorchester Court Apartments in Streatham, the parishioners at St. Dunstan's and the citizens of my new home, Keynsham, for helping me imagine Eudora. As always, I also need to thank my incredible community of colleagues at Bath Spa University's Creative Writing Department, particularly my mentor, Richard Kerridge, as well as Nicola Davies and Carrie Etter, who have so kindly supported Eudora.

Lastly, I thank Andy and Libby Jo Wadsworth, for supporting my writing and my life, and all my friends and family, who remain patient and forgiving in the face of my continued neglect and abstraction.

READING GROUP QUESTIONS AND TOPICS FOR DISCUSSION

1. People are often invisible in Eudora. What causes this state for various characters? Are there invisible people in your town? Have you ever felt invisible?

2. How does Mimi Thebo create Eudora as a character? Did you find it effective? Could you easily imagine the town as you were reading?

3. Were Lottie and Doc Emery fated to be together? Do you believe in fate and love at first sight?

4. The novel has many general themes, including small-town life, corporate versus personal interests, community and the individual, family, and race. Which ones resonated the most strongly for you?

5. At one point, Angela says that love is not necessary for a good marriage. Do you agree? What makes a strong marriage?

6. One of the things we see in the novel is the effect that one small decision by an individual can have on an entire community. Did you ever make

a decision that felt insignificant at the time, but which you later saw to be one of the most important decisions of your life? Did the effects of that decision remain with you, or did they ripple out to friends, family, and community?

7. Was Zadie crazy to invest so much in the diner? Would you have done the same thing, or something entirely different?

8. Mimi Thebo often talks about "models of redemption and recovery" in relation to her fiction. Who is redeemed in this novel? And who does the redeeming? If you are a person of faith, do you feel that these models are consistent with what you believe of redemption?

9. Although bad things happen in the novel, are there bad characters? Do they, too, have a chance at redemption in the novel?

10. Would you want to live in Eudora? Why or why not?